*Praise for* COLIN HARVEY

"*Damage Time* is for science fiction readers who love *Homicide* or *The Wire*, a gritty cop drama set in a future New York on the verge of collapse. Peter Shah is a memorable hero and the memory rip technology will make your skin crawl."

   C.C. Finlay, *author of* The Patriot Witch *and*
   The Demon Redcoat

"If Charles Dickens had written a futuristic SF thriller, this would be it. Colin Harvey has outdone himself with creating memorable characters, a page-turning plot, and a world that is far from and somehow like our own."

   *Christopher Barzak, author of* One for Sorrow
   *and* The Love We Share Without Knowing

"Harsh, sometimes grotesque, strongly compelling – a classical journey told in a new, uncompromising voice."

   *John Meaney*

"Harvey paints a grimly convincing portrait of a subsistence existence on the inhospitable world. Harvey's novel depicts a fascinating universe of want and plenitude, to which he will hopefully return in future novels"

   *Eric Brown, The Guardian*

# COLIN HARVEY

# *Damage Time*

ANGRY
ROBOT

ANGRY ROBOT
A member of the Osprey Group

Lace Market House,
54-56 High Pavement,
Nottingham
NG1 1HW, UK

www.angryrobotbooks.com
I read you

Originally published in the UK by Angry Robot 2010
First American paperback printing 2010

ISBN 978-0-85766-064-0

Printed in the United States of America

9 8 7 6 5 4 3 2 1

*For Steph*

# I

Less than ten hours before the dead woman's body was pulled from the icy clutches of the East River, Detective Pete Shah sat watching hockey. Each time the New York Rangers surged forward in search of the goal that would take them into the Stanley Cup final, Shah stood up, his feet on the cross-struts of his stool's legs, making him six inches taller. "Come on," he growled, deep in his throat, ignoring his drink. "Come oooooon!" As the attack fizzled out, Shah slammed his palm down onto the antique stainless steel bar in time with several hundred other fans. "Dammit!"

The bar reeked of unwashed bodies and stale sweat. Its walls were lined with flock wallpaper and faux-mahogany smart surfacing that ate gum or any other material that didn't move for more than sixty seconds. "That guy oughtta watch out," the drinker queuing behind Shah's stool nodded at a man resting his palm on the wallpaper. "People lean on it too long, it absorbs them."

"Urban myth," Shah muttered. No one ever knew anyone it had happened to. In any event, the wallpaper was almost hidden by rows and columns of sports pictures,

from antique black and white prints from the early
twen-cen of men in ludicrously cut hockey uniforms,
through color to the latest 3D of Kuntsler smacking a
Red Sox pitcher almost out of the stadium. Most of the
bar's largely blue-collar clientele had, like Shah, come
straight from the office, shop or worksite.

Leaning on the bar, Shah sipped at a carbonated
water and, sighing, shredded a toasted bagel while trying to ignore the grumbling of his stomach. It was dry,
of course, and had no more flavor than the cardboard
packaging that it had been served in that bore Matty's
logo. He'd spent most of his daily pittance, so to buy the
coffee and meatballs whose aroma drifted by would eat
into tomorrow's pay. Unlike most of the kids who were
raising a rumpus around him, he had neither the time
nor the energy to supplement his calories by taking second and third jobs, so had to get by on the twenty-two
hundred a day he earned. That the kids burned off all
the calories they earned wouldn't occur to them, but it
turned up one corner of his lips.

To take his mind off his hunger and the cardboardy
bagel, he wiggled his butt to stop the stool's central
ridge from giving him hemorrhoids and dreamed of
punching out the windbag on the next stool.

Shah had wanted to watch without constant interruptions from social networkers and work calls, so he'd
switched his eyepiece off. The guy next to him also
stared at the screen, but kept talking – so his piece was
switched on. He'd kept up a steady stream of snide
comments about "East Coast putzers" all evening, until
Shah wanted to slap his fat face and smash his – no
doubt – fifty kilocalorie eyepiece. It looked like half a
pair of antique spectacles from his left ear to the bridge
of his nose, with a bud spiraling into his eardrum.

The game resumed, and in the last seconds of normal time, the Rangers' attack foundered, and the Islanders countered. Shah saw the Rangers' defense-men look up at the clock as they entered damage time, the limbo between normal and overtime, and a hundred-twenty 3D screens and several hundred eyepieces showed the momentary lapse, and Jari Kaarinen jamming the puck into the net.

Kaarinen's arms went up in sync with the other players', and as Shah closed his eyes in despair, the klaxon sounded, counterpointing groans from the other Rangers fans. Mixed with the groans were cheers from the few Islanders in the corner, who were watching the game in the enemy territory of Manhattan.

Karl behind the bar shook his head sadly so that the beads in his hair danced. "Bad enough to lose," he sympathized. "But to lose to the second best team in New York?" Shah had heard that Karl lived in Queens, and was sure that the barman made equally scathing comments about the Rangers to the Islanders fans.

"Third," Shah corrected him. "Rangers, Rangers Reserves, then the Islanders." It was a feeble joke that couldn't conceal his disappointment. The Rangers were out for another year.

"Shee-it," someone snarled behind him. "If they hadna chalked off Page's goal, it wouldna gone to overtime anyways. We was robbed by the bastards that decided referees could add a little," he lapsed into a soprano whine, "*damage time.*"

Damage time, allowing the referees to add a few last seconds in their own judgment for any missed stop-clocks by the timekeepers, had proven a hugely controversial amendment, which had the NHL account-ants rubbing their fat little hands with glee. Controversy was good for the box office, and Allah knew the NHL needed good box office.

"Don't matter anyway." The windbag half-turned on his stool. His little exec carry-case leaned up against its base. "The Senators'll kick the Islanders' asses in the final."

Tension made the sudden silence almost crackle.

Shah surreptitiously clicked his eyepiece online. YOU HAVE FIVE NEW MESSAGES, his eyepiece said via the insert into his ear. They would only be ads. "Delete all," Shah whispered and flipped out his badge.

NYPD hadn't used badges for a generation – Shah had bought his online from a Chinese vendor. He'd bid the calorie equivalent of seven hundred new yuan, almost a year's salary, but it bore the name of an Officer P Shah from the 1970s, so Shah thought it worth it, even though it was so heavy it sometimes felt as if he was carrying a brick in his pocket.

The other men's eyepieces would have identified Shah – his eyepiece was sending out the identifier of an off-duty cop, but the movement of flipping open the shield stopped the drunken local from lowering his forehead into the windbag's face and he glowered at Shah.

Shah stared at the windbag: Jean Drake. Shah's eyepiece ran Drake's data. *Canadian*, Shah read. *No priors, a typical ten kilocalorie a day exec who thinks that 'cause he pays Supertax, the sun shines out his ass.*

Shah knew the other man. Owais Klass was a tattooed construction worker who, unlike Drake, had plenty of priors, most involving alcohol and violence. His tool-belt carried laser bradawl and sonic hammer, and more traditional tools like a monkey-wrench and screwdriver. Shah didn't want to think what any one of those could do to Windbag's skull. Nor the paper-work accruing from it.

Klass was smeared with dry sweat and dust, and his eyes were glazed with too much drink while his nose-ring swayed in time with his body. "Why don't you…" he slurred, "rack off back to where you belong, scum-bag?"

Drake blanched. He would be no match for Klass, so Shah interrupted, "Hey, Owais, easy."

At one-eighty-three Shah was nowhere near as big as Klass, but his badge might make him a mite taller in the construction worker's mind. Or it might make him a better target. Only one way to find out.

"Come on, bud," Shah said. "Bad enough to lose to them," he jerked his thumb at the cavorting Islanders fans in the corner, "without a night in the cells for as-sault. Mr Otta-wah here will buy you a drink as an apology for mouthing off."

Otta-wah opened his mouth to protest and Shah, who had nudged his way between them, thrust his face into the other man's rippling jowls. "Don't even think about it," he growled. "I've just had my retirement age raised today. A month away from getting my clock, and now I got another five years to do. Third time the bas-tards have screwed me. So right now I don't give a shit if Owais rips your frigging arm off and beats you to death with it. Get me?" Otta-wah nodded. "Good." Shah chuckled mirthlessly and pointed at Otta-wah's maroon sleeve. "At least the blood wouldn't show on your suit." He added, "Now, just buy him the drink and frack off. Yeah?"

"In this weather?" Otta-wah pointed at the window. The threatened tropical storm had passed Baltimore, and was headed their way. The rain that had been a drizzle thirty minutes earlier was bouncing ten centimeters off the pavement, and taxi-pods threaded their way between lake-sized puddles. The inevitable steam surged out from beneath a manhole cover, although it was nothing like the plumes Shah remembered from childhood.

"Cab or hearse, Otta-wah. Your choice. You got five minutes. Mouth shut 'cept for ordering. Got it?"

Otta-wah nodded again. "What'll it be?" He croaked.

"JD and coke. Large," Owais said. Shah stifled a snigger. The calorie count on that would be high enough to tip Otta-wah into a purchase surcharge. Then again, the guy was fat enough that he probably ate five thousand calories a day, on top of what he bought his friends and family, so he could obviously afford it.

At Otta-wah's questioning eyebrow, Shah said, "Pepsi. Thanks."

"Least I can do." Otta-wah looked away, avoiding eye contact.

"You don't wanna proper drink, bud – ah, officer?" Owais said.

Shah shook his head. "Pepsi's fine. It's sweet enough to rot your teeth, so I couldn't never normally afford it." He didn't mention that he was a Muslim, even halfway to being a lapsed one. In theory all Americans were brothers, but some New Yorkers had long memories and drunks like Owais were volatile.

Owais took his glass and melted away like the ice would in the tumbler of Pepsi that Karl dumped onto the bar. "Thanks." Shah lifted his glass to Otta-wah. "Now. The nearest subway's a block away. Yeah?"

Otta-wah took his card back from Karl, picked up his carry-case, and left with his chin as high as he could manage. Shah plonked himself back down on "his" stool, drained his glass of water, and munched on some bagel. He stared at his Pepsi, watching the bubbles rise, and sipped it, holding the sweet liquid on his tongue.

"That was neat." Karl took the empty water glass. "I thought it was all going to face-off back then." Shah grunted. Karl added, "Bad day?"

Shah nodded a fraction but said nothing. He glimpsed a flash of maroon slide back onto the stool that Otta-wah had just vacated. He stared at his glass. If the jerk really couldn't take the hint, Shah wasn't going to pro-tect him. Even if it meant a ton of paperwork.

Karl had retreated to the washer, empty glasses in hand. "Same again?" he called.

But instead of Otta-wah, a woman answered, "Water. Still. And whatever Officer Shah's drinking."

Shah looked up, half-smiled. "Hi." On the stool next to him, the maroon chador unfolded and a pair of very long legs stepped out of it; Shah had been fooled by the color into not looking. *Assumptions that if you caught a rookie making at work, you'd rip 'em a new windpipe.*

The chador's wearer stood up and smiled down at Shah. While she shook her blonde curls loose, a ripple of silence spread outwards as the men around them noted her presence. "Get you a drink, Officer? A proper one?" She folded the chador in half, allowing the fab-ric's electrostatic coating to shiver off the last droplets, then folded it again and again as delicately and precisely as a master of origami with a paper sculpture, until it was smaller than a handkerchief.

Its color faded when she put it into a transparent holder. A mood suit, Shah realized. Normally they took their cues from their wearer's emotions; if she could control it – and he couldn't believe that its maroon tint, identical to Otta-wah's, was coincidence – then she must be very good at channeling her emotions.

Shah shook his head. "No thanks, Aurora."

"Come on," she urged. "I've still got the remains of that cee-note burning a hole in my pocket." She leaned close and whispered, "I told that doorman standing behind us like a graven idol that I was your guest. Don't make me look even more a fool than I looked earlier on today."

"A graven idol, huh?" Shah raised an eyebrow. "I'd never have pegged Stevie as idle, graven or not."

"You wouldn't?" Aurora grinned. "I think he looks very graven, especially when he folds those big arms like that."

Shah swiveled, beckoned the doorman. "Put her entrance fee on my tab, Stevie."

"Sure." Stevie bowed to Aurora, who tilted her head almost imperceptibly in return, then returned to the door.

Shah ran his eyes over the almost non-existent dress. "You got pockets in that?"

She was half a head taller than him even without the seven centimeter stilettos she teetered on, and the body-belt that barely covered her from breast to crotch only accentuated her skinniness. Aurora locked eyes with his, then looked down. He followed her gaze to where she ostentatiously took several bills from her cleavage. "Harcourt says I'll get my new ID card in the mail tomorrow morning. So I thought I'd celebrate by getting rid of this." She looked around. "I thought it'd be busier. Isn't there a game tonight?"

"Was. We lost in damage time."

Her lips formed an "oh." "Why don't they go straight to extra time? Why damage time as well?"

Shah shrugged. "Someone said it comes from brownouts knocking the official clocks off-kilter, so they added a little on. Or that some official toured Europe, got the idea from some other sports. Thought a little unpredictability would spice things up."

Karl approached and seeing the notes Aurora proffered, his face darkened. "This isn't a laundry," Karl grated. "ID-supported cards only."

For the first time since they had met, Aurora's composure deserted her. Her mouth opened and worked, but no words came out. She shook her head in bewilderment." My card was stolen," she implored. "I'm not trying to launder anything."

"Better drink somewhere else, then," Karl closed his mouth so firmly his lips almost disappeared between sentences. "We aren't running that kinda place. Card or nothing."

Shah proffered his card. "Allow me. Get the lady what she wants, Karl."

"Water," Aurora said.

Shah knew she'd been planning something more expensive than the cheapest drink on the house. "Make it carbonated, at least," he pleaded. Karl's eyebrows lifted, but he went to fetch it. Shah stage-whispered, "He's OK, generally, but if he takes against someone, he really takes against 'em. Comprendez-vous?"

"Oh, yes." Aurora's voice was barely a gasp. "Je comprend very, very much. The French for his kind of guy is 'jackass', I think." She shut her eyes, bit her bottom lip. She looked down at the water pooling around her shoes, where the electrostatic coating had shivered it off. Finally she said, "Sorry. Your pay can't run to subsidizing clueless companions."

"Hey, it's OK. Don't worry about it."

"No. I hate owing people anything. I thought I'd pay you back the loan. Instead you end up bailing me out for the second time." She shook her head. "Bastard of a day."

"Tell me about it." Shah waggled his now empty glass at Karl.

# II

The sun beats down. When you spit, it sizzles on the rocks. The sole time you were caught out in it, it fried your skull until you were sure that you could feel the waves of ultraviolet beating down on you in time to the throbbing of your brain. Never again.

The landscape across to the horizon is sere with occasional dots of green where the saguaros stand as mute sentries to the deep desert. The solitary blight on the beauty is the disused CAP pipeline that used to vampire the water from the Colorado River to fuel the nuclear power plant, both now abandoned since Mexico effectively bought back the south-west. You're surprised at how much you remember; you thought that you'd slept through Lancaster's history lessons, but clearly that wasn't the case.

A breeze lighter than a spirit's kiss carries the scent of rosemary, fighting for dominance with a spicy waft of thyme. A lizard skittering across the road away from the half-buried cistern breaks the silence. The lizard is tiny, whereas the cistern that your family uses to catch the rain is an old five thousand gallon gas tanker relined and resealed, now painted with Hopi Indian designs.

Two of its four compartments are filled with gray water in various stages of leaching for use on the garden. Another holds the rainwater for drinking.

Some of that rainwater is run-off from raised patios and paths that separate sunken planting areas filled with dragon fruit and immigrant fruits – tomatoes, eggplants, and squash. Out the back from where you hear a couple of hens squabble are the bigger plants, *nopal* cactus and mesquite, as well as oranges, figs and pomegranates,. The hens alone – with you – have decided not to siesta today.

For as you shelter beneath the vase-like branches of a Chinese Pistache, picking a sliver of its peeling bark away and gaze around the undulating series of Indian terraces and basins that form the family's yard with a melancholic surge of pride, you know the truth.

Though your parents and grandparents have spent the last forty years perfecting the system – selecting, breeding and refining the plants, covering much of the garden with black gauze cloth to reduce evapotranspiration by a third, optimizing the pipes running from the roof to the tank, even reshaping the road – it's not enough. There is only so much water that can be wrung from the land, and the family has one thirst too many. The twins aren't old enough to go, so you must.

Tomorrow.

At first light you'll take your cycle and scoot over to Gran Tamales, and catch the daily bus from there to Tucson.

# III

Six hours before the almost-fight with Owais and the windbag, Shah sighed and closed the feed.

"Anything?" Marietetski said. The light glistened off his shaven scalp, which was so black it looked blue.

"Maybe," Shah tried to suppress an ache at leaving those searing blue skies behind for the sooty rain of New York. "The memory's from Arizona, and it's a boy, which fits our amnesiac. It's fresh too, no softening of the images like you'd expect with old memories – no imprinting what we'd have liked to have happened, over what did."

"Arizona would fit the soil type taken from the vic's fingernails," Marietetski said. "He's got Hopi tattoos on his forearm. Did you say that there was a cistern with Hopi style designs?"

"Yep," Shah said, running thumb and forefinger down an invisible beard on either side of his mouth. "I think we've got enough to farm it out to Nuevo Mexico. 'Bout time they started running decent ID files on their new citizens, isn't it? They wanna buy the state, they should take responsibility for their new citizens."

Marietetski's laugh was more of a grunt. "Too busy

building their new border," he said. "Besides, most people want to go the other way nowadays. Maybe their Missing Persons people can turn up some long lost relatives here? Had to be a reason he ended up in New York."

"I think they aren't too bothered about talking to any of the Displaced about whether any of their relatives are missing," Shah said. "Besides, if that memory was him, and his family couldn't support the kid while he was fit – that was why he left – what chance will there be of their taking back a vegetable? The bastards that did this – ripping almost all his memories and posting them, for what, for a few calories?"

"Easy, easy," Marietetski said, patting his shoulder before walking away.

Shah hunched over his desk, surrounded by meter-high mountains of clear plastic folders, each bulging with paper. Around him, the ten by ten meter square room was packed with desks at which uniformed and plain-clothed men and women sat and worked quietly.

"Doodling?' Captain van Doorn's quiet voice cut through what noise there was.

"The psych analysts like to call them thought representation graphics," Shah said without looking up. The thoughts they represented were primeval – anger, sadness, fear – but his voice was level.

"I've heard you say you grew up calling them doodles. You going to clear some of these?" Van Doorn slapped his hand on one of the miniature mountain ranges on the desk.

Shah stared up at the seamed face. "Better we don't have 'em at all. Heaven knows, we shouldn't save the last of our trees if it means we can't find a file for two seconds."

"That's right," van Doorn said, ignoring Shah's sarcasm.

Shah continued as if van Doorn hadn't spoken, "My old man used to talk 'bout how a hundred years ago the futurologists claimed there'd be paperless offices. Hah. Turn of the Millennium they gengineered parasites, auditors, who made everyone afraid about everything. They scared our bosses 'bout seventeen different types of backups all crashing at once and how if we couldn't find a tiny piece of paper, that it'd send us all to hell; that they reckon it's better we spend our time shuffling papers than catching perps."

"You finished ranting, dinosaur?" Van Doorn added, "Paper isn't made from trees anymore. Everyone knows that."

He didn't wait for an answer, so Shah had to settle for glaring at his broad back and muttering, "Yeah, pseudo-yeast. I know that's where it comes from, helmet-head." He tore a corner off and chewed it, then spat it out. "Don't taste any better than it ever did, though." He stood up, and placing one hand on the top of the nearest pile to hold it in place, pushed the bottom six inches of the pile off his desk and into the garbage can.

Shah returned to his doodles. His stylo gouged deep holes in the scrap "paper" that he used up faster than anyone else in the office.

"Got you a coffee." Marietetski placed the cardboard cup with its steaming inky contents beside his pad. "NoCal OK?"

"Thanks," Shah said without looking up. Then he straightened, for even the thirty-seven calories of the murky sewage would go onto Marietetski's account, and count toward his young partner's government approved fifteen-hundred-calorie basic allowance. "NoCal's just fine. Thanks for remembering it." Kids of Marietetski's age had long ago had any kind of sweet tooth ripped from them by a world of shortages.

Marietetski shrugged. He had as many cases as Shah, but far fewer folders, and they were anorexic by comparison. He picked up a particularly thin folder and replaced one piece of paper with another. "Couldn't have you spitting coffee all over me." When Shah didn't rise to his provocation, he added, "Bitch, huh?"

"I got nine-hundred-ninety-seven ongoing cases." Shah poked the stylo savagely through the "paper." "You know, I know most of them lead back to a single source. Arson, burglary, petty theft, prostitution, memory-ripping; their common denominator's called Kotian. And can we prove it?"

He glared at the windows, which for all their self-cleaning implants, seemed to accumulate grime in the way New York's windows had always picked it up. Then he turned that glare on Marietetski. He said three words: "Five more weeks."

Marietetski made a *what-can-I-say* gesture.

"Five more fricking weeks and I could have, should have, been sleeping late, strolling down to *Manny's* for breakfast, then working out how I was going to spend all of that free time that retirees earn." The words spilled from him now, a white-hot lava flow of accumulated resentment and frustration. "Van Doorn just comes out with 'SuperAnn Fund Deficit' like it's a traffic report. No frickin' 'sorry, we're raising the retirement age by another five years, and you've got to work till you drop'."

He stopped abruptly. Took deep breaths, and visualized a beach, waves breaking on tropical golden sands.

Gradually, his heart-rate slowed, and he opened his eyes. Marietetski's patrician features were carefully blank, composed into their usual impassive mask. Only his eyes gave him away. But instead of their usual distant contempt, Shah had caught a flicker of sympathy.

Then Marietetski grinned. "Walk down to *Manny's*? You'd die of boredom in a month with no Kotian to bitch about!"

"I'm a dino, all right," Shah said. "I arrest perps, not make up shit about why our cleanup rate for hour-old crimes has dropped from seventeen-point-three per cent, to seventeen-point-two."

"Huh, Triceratops, it's up to seventeen-point-five. Climbed point-three of a base point over that bust of Jeffrey's yesterday. The perp owned up to eight more dockets."

"Well, hallelujah," Shah raised his cup in a mock-salute. "It might even get us off the bottom of the league, but hijo, I got to tell you, while you're yoked to me, you aren't going to get that Cop of the Month award."

Marietetski shrugged. "Who wants to go to the Micronesian Enclave anyways? I went there on my honeymoon. And Beijing? Big deal. No, I'm just happy being a dino-sitter."

The sheer outlandishness of the claim made Shah burst out laughing, and his partner grinned.

Both men sipped at their coffee, staring into space. Then Shah strolled across to the recycler, and stared out of the window at Ellis Island and the radioactive stump that was all that was left of the Statute of Liberty, bathed in the watery sunshine that separated several bands of showers.

A woman's voice called from the partition separating the front of desk from the office. "Excuse me... sir? Sir, you there with the dark gray suit? Could you help me... please?"

Shah looked over. It had been on the tip of his tongue to tell her to talk to Hampson, who was staffing the front desk. Then he saw the line of people, and let out a low whistle, before double taking on the woman herself. Shah turned to see Marietetski's raised eyebrows, and caught his partner's nod toward the desk. He noticed that almost all of the men had stopped working to stare, and that Marietetski was grinning. "Your treat," the young man mouthed.

"What's the problem, ma'am?" Shah said. Hampson hadn't even looked over, but was trying to calm a couple of irate Chinese down.

"I've lost my ID – or it's been lifted," the woman said in an accent that smacked of money. She was jaw-droppingly beautiful. Probably – Shah guessed – cosmetically enhanced, and any of her clothes probably cost more than what he made in a month. She glanced round at the people around her as if she had awoken in the midst of a pack of hungry feral dogs. She looked close to tears. "I've been waiting for almost an hour and this, ah, gentleman," she nodded at Hampson, "well, he's clearly very busy, but I don't even have enough credit for a glass of water. Please?" Her voice rose on the last word, but she subsided at Shah's outstretched hand, palm down in a *stay calm* gesture.

"It's OK, ma'am" Shah said. "I'll get you a glass of water. You just have a seat, and take a few deep breaths, and I'll be back in a few seconds." On the way to the cooler, Shah passed Hampson and hissed in the duty officer's ear, "What the hell's going on? She's been waiting an hour."

"No she hasn't," Hampson said without taking his eyes off the Chinese tourist, nor allowing his fixed smile to waver as he answered the Mandarin tirade in a loud, slow voice. "I understand your frustration, sir, but until we can get an interpreter – and we can't get one for another hour – we're just going to have to try one another."

Shah reached the water cooler. "Fine looking woman," Detective Stickel said. The vertical line between her eyebrows deepened. "Course you'd help just as much if it were a guy, wouldn't you?"

Shah filled two cups. "Course I would. Good Samaritan and all."

"A what?" Stickel's head retreated an inch, as it often did when she was surprised.

"Read your Bible," Shah said.

This time Stickel's head recoiled a full three inches, and her eyebrows shot up. "You? Telling me to read that old book-thing? Ha, that's a good one!"

*Does she know I'm a Mussulman-boy?* Shah wondered. *Is that what she means by the "you?"* He kept his face deadpan though, letting none of his thoughts show. "Oh, I'll quote any old bit of religion." Shah raised one cup. "L'chaim!" He tossed it down and refilled it, slowly, all to irritate the waiting Stickel who was a royal pain in the ass. "See, Hebrew too! I'm covering all the bases, just in case God turns out be real, and he's affiliated."

"Yeah," Stickel said to his retreating back, then removing any doubt. "Salaam."

As Shah passed again, cups of water in hand, Hampson turned from the Chinese tirade for a moment. "Can ya take care of her? Please?"

Shah almost said, "Loss of ID – while it's serious – only needs the counter-sig of one of the duty officers." But it had already been a long day, and he had five more years of long days. "Ah, fuck it," he muttered, and kicked open the partition door. "Ma'am?" he said. "Follow me to one of the interview rooms. We'll sort this out now."

"Thank you," she said, her voice wavering momentarily.

Shah waited, then walked alongside her, listening to the clack of her heels on the floor tiles, breathing in her faint perfume and studying her out of the corner of his eye. Tumbling blonde hair, tip-tilted nose almost too perfect, and he'd already noticed the wide but rosebud mouth and cornflower-blue eyes. That she was half a head taller than him in her heels was all that marred her perfection – and oddly enough, that made her human.

"That a mark on your temple?" He said when he sensed that she was about to make a smartass comment about him looking her over.

"This?" She pointed at the faint pink scarring on her skin, but didn't touch it, which impressed him more. "Where they caught me when they lifted my eyepiece." She grimaced. "I am *such* an idiot. You hear stories about the street gangs mugging people for their pieces, but you never think it'll happen to you. They left my purse, which only makes it more galling."

Shah held the door to the interview suite open for her. "Thank you." She shot him a dazzling smile, and he stood in the doorway collecting his thoughts and enjoying watching the play of her ass beneath her expensive skirt.

He strode in and waved to the visitor's chair." Take a

seat, Miz..." and wondered idly whether everyone knew and shared Marietetski's pity over his bad news; anything to stop staring.

"Debonis." She sat and crossed an elegant leg. He guessed that just her pointed-toed stilettos cost a few thousand bucks, or duty-free rupees, as seemed more likely. "Aurora Debonis. The little bastards skinned me while I was out shopping."

She held up a tiny paper tote bag, no doubt containing her equally tiny but expensive purchases. "My friends all work the dayshift, so there was no one I could call. I thought that I might as well report it straight away. And see if I could beg the cab fare to a friend's place. Please don't suggest the subway."

Shah bridled, but then laughed silently at himself. *Of course she wouldn't want to ride the subway; you might be OK, but her clothes would scream target louder than a damn siren.*

"I'll just call up some details," Shah said. "Social security number?"

She rattled off a string of digits which Shah repeated, the tiny sensors in the eyepiece picking up the movements in his jaw, although, as often happened, the numbers that appeared in front of his vision included an incorrect "five" instead of the correct nine. He repeated the number, mentally cursing, and this time the number came up true. While his eyepiece responded, he took a retinal scan. Within seconds, her face stared back at him from his lens. No criminal record, he noted. "You're a–" he almost said hooker, but suspecting that it would be inappropriate, changed it to, "companion?"

"I am." The crispness of her answer endorsed his guess. "All licenses and taxes paid up. Does my profession change anything? Perhaps you'd have left me waiting where I was?"

Shah tried to keep his face straight, and gave up, allowing a small smile to creep across it. "Not a darn thing, ma'am. As long as you're legal, I've got no issues at all." Many of his colleagues were still old-fashioned enough that they would have left her in the line, but the thought of ducking his outstandings to help a hooker made him feel as if he'd really flipped the Mayor the bird. He checked his eyepiece and checked the whistle that he almost made. "You live in Llewellyn? Business must be good – think I should change careers?"

She took in his rumpled suit, the faded coffee stain on his tie that wouldn't come out, and his mournful face and grinned back. "You'd clean up in no time, officer. I think the house next door's for sale."

Shah grunted. "How many millions?"

Aurora made a moue. "You know the old saying – if you have to ask…?"

"You can't afford it. Yep."

"Do you foresee a problem with issuing a replacement card?"

"No more than you would expect from the FBI," he said with a smile that she didn't return this time. "I'll call the attorney you have listed as your contact." He rattled the number off to the meeting-phone that sat on the desk. Moments later an androgynous voice echoed round the room: "Harcourt and Robinson; how may we help you?"

"I'd like to speak to Stephen Harcourt, please," Shah said. "I'm Officer Pervez Shah of the NYPD, calling about Ms Aurora Debonis."

Faster than any human could have managed, a

fractionally more masculine voice said, "Officer Shah? This is Stephen Harcourt. What's this about Ms Debonis?"

"I have a lady with me who's been mugged and lost her ID," Shah said. "If I turn the cam on her, and she says a few words, can you provisionally confirm her ID pending DNA verification? It'll only cut a day or two off her waiting time for a replacement ID, but every little bit helps." Shah swiveled the cam.

"Of course," Harcourt said. "Hello, Aurora."

"Hello Stephen, yes, it's me. That'll teach me to be casual in NYC, won't it?"

"I'll need you to answer some security questions. You have a memory copied to me for identification. What is it?"

"A tennis tournament I played in when I was fifteen. I won when my opponent back-handed into the net."

"Great. Please provide the police officer with a DNA swab."

Shah took a tiny scraping from the inside of her cheek and inserted it into the analyzer. After a few second's delay Harcourt said, "I provisionally confirm the voiceprint as Ms Aurora Debonis," and repeated her social security number. "Thank you, officer."

The line went dead, saving Shah the job of wondering about the etiquette of how to say goodbye to an AI on the Micronesian fleet. He called the DHS number, recited the coded instructions, and hung up. "They're not good with routine requests – too many emergencies – and making you sweat a couple of days gives them time to nose through your trash. But you should have it in a few days."

"Oh." She sat blinking through the implications. "That means no travel, no–"

"Shopping. Yeah," he said sympathetically, standing up. "I can loan you cash to buy food, maybe at a corner Mashriq. I'll call you a cab, and put it on my card."

"Thank you," she said. "I"ve been worried sick," she explained with a little laugh, her eyes glinting." I walked all the way here." She showed him blistered heels, and echoed his thoughts. "And in these shoes!"

He walked her down to the pickup point. Although it was six floors down; he had the native New Yorker's aversion to riding in elevators since continual brown-outs had started with power rationing and multi-sourcing of energy, and waited with her for one of the rare and hideously expensive little yellow pods. She turned, as she climbed in. "You've been a great help. Thanks."

"My pleasure."

"See you soon, I hope." She flashed him a smile. He was sure it was purely professional, but was still surprised at its warmth.

"Who knows?" He smiled back.

# IV

"When you said 'see you soon' I didn't think you meant this soon," Shah said.

Aurora smiled.

"Can I get you something else?" Karl shouted over the background noise of the bar.

At Shah's enquiring look, Aurora shook her head. "I've had enough for now." She glanced him a momentary smile he almost missed. "To drink."

"Ah." Shah kept his voice carefully neutral. He had found over the years when lost for words that "ah" was a good expression. He also found it useful sometimes to stay silent, and let the silence squeeze the next answer from the other person. If Aurora had shown any signs of wanting to leave he might have said more, but she looked as if she was settled.

The lengthening silence repaid his faith. Aurora stared at the counter and said, "You know—" and stopped. She looked up at him. "You're not making this easy." Her nervous little smile robbed the words of any rebuke.

"Making what easy?" He knew now where the conversation was going, but he wasn't sure why.

"I was going to repay you with your own cash," she said." If I can't do that, I have only one thing that I can offer. But normally, I don't have to work quite so hard to sell it."

"Well," he said, nodding slowly, gravely, to show his sympathy. "That must be very difficult for you. Having to work quite so hard at whatever it is that I'm not making easy."

Her laugh was an explosion of air that ended as abruptly as it started. "You're very funny," she said, tone belying her words. "Are you fully partnered, or just as slow as you make out?"

"Partnered? Yeah, I have one, though she's mostly on a different shift from me. We overlap slightly, occasionally."

"Ah." She tilted her head back, and her little smile suggested she was deliberately mocking his earlier non-commitment. "So… complicated, huh?"

He laughed staccato, betraying a slight attack of nerves. "If we lived out in the boonies, it wouldn't be an issue. Everyone's reverted back to working daylight time only, to save on the power bills."

"Not everywhere. We live shifts in Llewellyn." She ran her finger around the rim of her glass and studied him. "Stop changing the subject, Officer Shah. Is your name Persian, by the way?"

That she recognized its ethnicity warmed him inside. "It is. And I'm not changing it so much as trying to work out what the subject is." He looked straight into her eyes, and held her gaze until she looked away. "I'm an old man–"

"Middle-aged."

"I'm an old man," he insisted. "I'm not young enough, or ruggedly handsome enough in an old-man kind of way to be remotely attractive to a woman like you. Nor rich enough to afford your rates."

"Do you know," she snapped, "that's the first sweeping generalization you've made since we met?"

She tapped her finger on the bar, and he guessed it was to help her think of what to say next. "Why do you think my clients come to me?" she asked, flushing slightly. "Apart from the obvious."

He puffed his cheeks out. "Dunno."

"Good answer," she said sarcastically. "There's as many reasons as clients. Some come for sex, no two ways about it. Others book me for a massage. Sometimes they'd rather talk – they just need someone to unload onto, because they're lonely, or they have friends, but they think those friends aren't interested in their problems." She stared at him and tipped the dregs of her glass down her throat, but when he reached out to signal Karl, she put her hand on his arm. "And you think you know why I want to go back to your place!"

"Sorry." Shah held his hands up in surrender.

Aurora took a deep breath, then grinned. "Even whores have feelings," adding quickly, "not that I consider myself a whore." She leaned closer to him and whispered in his ear. "There's one other reason."

"Yes?"

Aurora straightened so that the gap between them was again a meter or so. She tipped the salt shaker up and sprinkled grains of sand on the counter, and licking her finger, dabbed it on the micro-mountain she'd made. Then she sucked her finger and when she'd finished said – not loudly but clear enough to carry, "I like to fuck."

Shah sat, his face burning and thought, *It's so quiet in here they must all be able to hear my heart racing.* "Oh."

"Oh," Aurora echoed, her face straight, but he could hear the not *quite* suppressed laughter in her voice. "I'm here, you're here. I like you. Do we really need to complicate it with our motives?" She sprayed perfume from a tiny atomizer and held out her wrist. "Like it?"

It wasn't strong, but the perfume seemed to poke him between the eyes. *Wow, must be some powerful pheromones in that.* "Yeah, very nice."

Aurora stood up. "Come on. Let's go back to my place."

Shah stood too. "I'm not going all the way to Llewellyn tonight. My place is three blocks away."

Aurora took his hand and led him to the doorway. Shah felt every pair of eyes in the place tracking him. One of the construction workers grinned at him, and Shah winked. He couldn't ever remember feeling so good, or so young.

Outside the rain had slackened off and was barely worthy of the name any longer. Men and women still strained between the shafts of their harnesses as they hauled their cabs along, while the clop of a few horse-drawn hansoms echoed along the street, interspersed with the beeping horns of the even rarer yellow cabs. One chugged past, bloated hydrogen bag on its roof now almost empty and drooping, spilling over the sides of the roof onto the tops of the windows.

Aurora took his arm and led Shah to the curb. "Nah, it's OK," he said, suddenly feeling very lethargic, and determined for some reason to fight it. "We'll walk to my place. Three blocks."

"Let's get a cab," Aurora said. "I've a town house a mile or two away."

Shah took a great lungful of air and with a huge effort hauled himself upright. It was the hardest thing he'd ever had to do, though not quite as hard as what he did next. Somehow it seemed important, though he couldn't quite fathom why. "No," he said. "I have to go to work tomorrow. Not until late, but I have to work. My place – or nowhere. Sorry, Aurora, but that's the deal. And I can't afford cab fares."

"Then let's compromise. If they'll take this c-note of yours, we'll see whether it'll carry us to your place. OK?"

"OK," Shah sighed.

He was acutely aware of her hip pressing into his as they sat scrunched close together in the back of the pedicab, the fragrance of her perfume tickling his nose, and the warmth of her breath on the side of his neck.

The cabbie, a muscle-bound giant who probably ate every calorie he got in fares just to stay alive, grunted with exertion.

"See." Aurora sprayed her wrist again, "I said we should get a cab."

"But that note of yours wouldn't have got us to your place, even the one in town." Instead he'd run his credit down that little bit more. He shifted slightly, hoping she wouldn't feel how much he wanted her, but she ran her hand over his erection, stopping his breath. "We could always go on to my place afterwards," she crooned. "I've got something that'll keep you going all night, my fine stallion." She nibbled his ear.

"We're here," he croaked, running his card through the cab's scanner, and hearing the clunk of the doors unlocking as it successfully validated the payment.

She held onto his arm as they ran through the rain to the lobby, stopping to wipe their feet on the mat. "We'll break our necks on the floor if we're not careful," he explained.

"It doesn't absorb the water?" Aurora sounded shocked.

He sniggered. "The landlord would put another thousand a month on the rent if it did."

Too tired to walk, they took the elevator for once. He caught her chewing her lip slightly as she straightened her hair in the mirror. He looked up at her, and touched her arm. "Leslyn and Doug will be asleep." He added, "But they have their own room."

"Leslyn switches?"

"Yeah – our shifts intersect once a month or so."

"Doug's fully hetero, then?"

"Both of us are." He smiled slightly. "Our generation weren't quite as, um, flexible as yours. It's Leslyn and me, or Leslyn and Doug." He added, "Do you know, I had only one set of parents." He laughed at her shocked look. "They called it a nuclear family."

"They were toxic?" She leaned her shoulder into his.

"Boom boom," he said, adding an equally ancient punch line.

She seemed to understand for she said, "It's the way I tell 'em," a line almost as old as her previous joke.

"Hard as it may be for a young lady like you to believe," he said straight-faced," but it worked perfectly well for thousands of years."

"Yeah," she drawled as the elevator juddered to a halt on fifty-four, "but we don't live on raw meat nowadays, or club each other unconscious as a pick-up line."

"It only broke down in the end because so many people worked all around the clock, and partnerships split up all the time. It was pressure that broke it, not inherent flaws in the idea."

She shuddered theatrically. "Imagine it – only one set of parents, and just blood-brothers and sisters."

They emerged from the elevator into the thickly carpeted corridor. "Hush now," he said. "This is a respectable building."

She snorted. "You just want the last word. No one in New York goes to bed before 3am."

Shah awoke muddled, the room swimming. An image, of him naked and her head moving down his torso, past his waist–

–the thunderous pounding that had dragged him from sleep resumed, and a male voice shouted something that Shah didn't catch. The room seemed to wobble and waver.

"Wha– Aurora?" Shah peered blank-eyed, head tilting one way then another, to offset the wobbling of the room.

The door crashed in and a man's voice shouted, "NYPD! Flat on your face! I said flat – NOW!"

# V

The Assistant Medical Examiner looked as crappy as Harper felt. Maybe he got his ass hauled out of bed at some unearthly hour as well, Harper thought sourly.

More likely the kid had spent the night sleeping on one of the slabs – he was probably only a couple of years out of college. No one with any seniority would work the early shift on a Saturday morning in this bleach-tainted icebox.

The AME had ginger hair long enough to curl slightly and a patchy attempt at a beard. He pulled out a tray on which lay a shrouded body, his breath streaming on the chill late April air. "She was pulled from the East River down by Pier 18."

Harper nodded. He knew the broad details, but there was always the chance that his earlier briefing from the 19 1/2 Pitt St. Murder Squad had omitted or distorted some vital point. The AME continued, "DNA traces match the records for a woman named Aurora Debonis, DOB October 23rd, 2023. Registered profession companion–"

"A hooker?" Bennett was instantly silent at Harper's warning frown.

The AME took a few seconds to visibly pull together the torn skeins of his thoughts. "The height of 1.89 meters, and weight of 64 kilos matches the identity, though it's hard to be sure since the face is smashed to a pulp, and the perp damaged her eyes enough to preclude a retinal match. The cuts have the pattern of something hard, and I've sent some traces of carat gold off to the crime lab." He added, "We're sure it's her. But we need formal ID though it's proving hard to find surviving family. Parents killed in a car crash when she was seventeen. No siblings."

"We'll keep looking," Bennett said.

"Cause of death?" Harper said, keen to keep the briefing on track.

"We can exclude death by drowning," the AME said. "No fine white froth or foam in the airways or exuding from the mouth. The absence of water in the stomach suggests death prior to submersion."

"So she was dead before she hit the water?" Bennett said. A rumpled, weary-looking man, he was at the opposite end of his career from his partner, and it showed. The younger cop – Harper hadn't caught his name – looked almost gleefully enthusiastic.

"That's what I said."

Bennett soothed, "Just being sure, Doc. Like to hazard a guess to the cause of death?"

The AME frowned. "Broken hyloid indicates that she was strangled. Lack of traces beneath her nails, she didn't put up a fight. If I can separate out the marks from beating against moored boats and the pier I may – just may – be able to confirm whether she was conscious when she died. But I doubt it. I think that she was strangled then dumped in the river."

Bennett shook his head. "All this for a hooker." He

didn't just mean the gathering for the prelim findings, but Harper's presence as well.

The AME snapped. "Ms Debonis had a Batchelor's Degree in Psychology, and a Masters in Asiatic studies–"

"A what?" Bennett barked.

"Asiatic Studies," the AME repeated. "It's a mix of massage, philosophy, acupuncture, eastern religions and several martial arts."

"You mean she was studying Pan-Islamist and Pan-Asian shit?" Harper could almost see Bennett's pointy little nose quivering at the thought of a political motive.

*Yeah, wouldn't you just love to palm it over onto the FBI, bud?* Harper thought. "How long has she been in the water?" Harper said. The younger cop frowned at the interruption, but Bennett looked unperturbed. Nothing perturbed Bennett, Harper guessed.

The AME said, "We think she went in sometime about five this morning, but water makes it hard to tell. Death was up to an hour earlier."

Harper motioned Bennett away with his head, and the old cop followed him, the younger one in tow. "I'll take this one on now," Harper said.

"But–" the young one said.

Bennett stopped him with a gesture. "No use complaining. The AME confirmed her ID within two hours of her being found. We traced her movements last night via a cab her doorman called for her, to *Manny's Sports Bar*. The bar-help weren't very happy being rooted out at first light, but tough. When he said that someone matching her description in the bar was with a cop, it becomes an IA affair." Bennett looked even more tired than usual. "I've known Pete Shah longer than you been breathing, and he's a good man. Do what you have to do. He may be innocent."

"Let me get this right…" Harper stopped. "Her eye-piece – where is it?"

"We can't find one," younger cop said. "When we checked on the files, she reported it missing yesterday. Shah filed the report, a replacement was on order."

Harper frowned. "Is that usual? A plain clothes filing a missing piece report?" Any little fact could be crucial, one way or the other. He hoped that Shah was inno-cent, but experience told him otherwise.

"Unusual," Bennett allowed. "But not unheard of."

"OK." Harper let out a long sigh. "You've brought him in already?"

Bennett nodded. "Soon as the barman confirmed they left together. We're questioning the cabbies who were on-shift early this morning, but you know how it is – there are thousands who might've been there, and interviewing them will take time. Shah was due on shift about now, but we thought it better not to wait. Same time we called you in, we sent in a SWAT team who rousted him out ten minutes ago."

"That was nice for him," Harper said dryly.


Walking from the Medical Center to One Police Plaza would take too long, Harper decided, so he rode the subway. Normally he would have pedaled himself a dis-count aboard one of the cycles in the carriages, but he told himself that today's token gesture in off-setting consumption was secondary to the job. He didn't want to arrive sweating, to grill a senior cop. Even if that sen-iority were age rather than rank.

He frowned. *What kind of cop is the lowest rank of plain-clothes at – what, retirement age?* He called up Shah's records on his eyepiece, and whistled silently. *Yesterday he was told his retirements been deferred? So what was this, rage?*

He counseled himself against making too many assumptions. As the last *known* person to see her alive, of course Shah was prime suspect, but he wasn't automatically guilty. The girl might have met someone else on her way home, and ended up in the river at their hands. But Harper replayed Bennett's interview with the barman, uploaded via Bennett's eyepiece, and the barman had stressed how friendly they'd seemed when they left the bar. "The old guy – Shah – he staggered once, when he stood up. You know, like old guys do sometimes when they get to their feet. She put her arm around him, and they left that way."

As Harper climbed the steps up from the station, Bennett called. "We just found an eyepiece down by the river near the ferry terminal – right where we predicted the body went in." Modeling the river currents wasn't always a completely exact science, but it seemed to have paid off on this occasion.

"Is it Shah's?"

"Serial number on the frame matches. But it's been trodden on pretty bad. It'll take the CSU a couple of hours to reconstruct it. They've already taken it over to 1PP."

"What about the spousal interviews?"

Bennett had told Harper as he left the morgue that detectives were interviewing Shah's wife and co-husband. "They share her, apparently," Bennett had said. "She ain't much to look at, but she must have something to get them both to go halves."

"Still ongoing," Bennett said. "Anything else you need from us?"

Harper thought for a few seconds. He didn't mind using Bennett to do the legwork, but it was now clearly an IA case – until Shah could be charged or excluded.

"No. Not until those interviews are filed. But thanks. I appreciate it."

"No problem." Bennett cut the line.

Harper could guess what Bennett was saying to his partner when he ended the call, but he tried to put it out of his mind. He considered himself a decent, hard-working cop. He didn't see why his manner should be held against him, nor his reluctance to mix with people who might be colleagues one day and suspects the next. The first and only time Harper complained about the regular cop's slurs, his supervisor had only shrugged and said, "You should grow a thicker skin, or get out and mix with them." But that wasn't Harper's style. He'd heard the nicknames: *The Monk* and *The Robot* were the only two he could tell his wife about.

It was a short walk to Police Plaza and the late April sunshine crept between the buildings, lifting Harper's spirits as he strolled.

One of the few pleasant side-effects of the Dieback – when the downward curve of the effects of antibiotics on viruses crossed with the upward curve of international travel –was that New York wasn't as crowded as in his youth. But even on a Saturday morning the streets were thronged with people on their way to a late start, out shopping in Chinatown, or just breakfasting. *New York*, thought Harper with a surge of local pride. *Still nowhere like it – even if the world is going to hell in a handcart*, he mentally added as he skidded on something squidgy beneath his shoe.

He sniffed at the waft of stir-fry hanging on the breeze – soy, garlic, ginger and coriander, and debated whether to stop and snatch breakfast, but decided against it. If he didn't eat, he wouldn't have to exercise, thus saving calories.

As he was fighting his hunger, he heard a drone, and the weekly UN patrol flew overhead on its way out of the city down to Washington, the copters' blades clattering, almost ultrasonic in the morning air. The pretzel man nearest him muttered, "Freakin' you-enn! They should stuff off back to Beijing and Mumbai, and take their meters and kilograms with 'em! We don't need 'em here!" He spat on the sidewalk, and Harper, his appetite suddenly gone, turned and walked on.

Too soon he was climbing the steps to the ugly monolith that housed as many of the NYPD's centralized departments as they could cram into it before protests stopped further expansion a generation before.

Harper submitted to the retinal scans, fingerprints, DNA traces, and random memory download identifications – sometimes he could reach the ninth floor with no memory of going through them – and headed for his office. As he left the elevator, the downloaded interviews arrived, and he watched them while walking to his office – using his free eye to keep him from stumbling into anything.

The interviews yielded nothing. Neither Leslyn Calea-Shah-McCoy nor Doug McCoy had seen or heard anything. They'd been asleep when the third member of their household brought home his latest friend.

Harper didn't believe a word of their wide-eyed innocence.

Powell was waiting for him there, Harper's slouching bear-like supervisor perched on the edge of his desk, foot swinging idly. "Morning," Powell said, apparently blasé about IA lodging one of NYPD's finest in an interview room along the corridor.

Harper wasn't fooled for a moment. "I'm dropping everything else. I figure complaints from Joe Public can wait while a capital crime's investigated."

Powell nodded assent and while he tried to look as unconcerned as ever, Harper noted the slight lifting of the other man's shoulders. "You need anything, you tell me," Powell said. "I'll have Wong handle the media briefing. We'll keep it vague for as long as we can, but someone's already talked to the *Times*."

"OK." Harper wondered whether to wait for the eyepiece to be reconstructed.

Powell seemed to realize his thoughts were elsewhere. "I'll leave you to get on," he said amiably, as if it were just a social visit or they'd run into one another by accident.

Both men's eyepieces chimed simultaneously. "Priority incoming call" Harper read, and frowned in puzzlement.

"Damn," Powell said. "It's the commissioner."

A grey, sour-looking woman appeared split screen with two men. Both looked Indian or Pakistani. The older one – *Abhijit Kotian*, he read, *Born*– he cut it off with a curt, muttered, "Name only" – looked like a stereotypical Bollywood Prince. Harper wondered how much his good looks were down to nature, how much to sculpting.

Kotian's son, Sunny, would have been even better looking if it weren't for the sneering frown, so severe that it really was off-putting. Harper wondered at the tensions that produced so affable a father and so petulant a son.

He realized that the commissioner was talking. "Clearly this is an internal investigation, Mr Kotian, but we appreciate that if our initial identification is correct, then you've lost a good friend, which is why we've taken the unusual step of reaching out to Captain

Powell, and copying his operative, so that they know of your concern. Captain Powell will brief you each day at midday, starting tomorrow, without breaching any confidentiality."

"I appreciate that, commissioner," Kotian continued to look bland, but there was a hardness visible now that Harper suspected he seldom revealed. "You'll appreciate our concern. The man Shah has been particularly zealous about investigating us—"

"Obsessive, more like," Sunny said.

"Sun-*il*," Kotian said and the boy shut up instantly. Though he looked furious, Harper glimpsed a flash of fear and wondered just how amiable Kotian was in private. "As I said at the start, I just want you to satisfy me that *if* it is the same officer under suspicion, as gossip suggests, and *if* it is Aurora, that it's merely an unfortunate coincidence, and not part of a vendetta."

"We'll make sure that we answer all your concerns, Mr Kotian," the commissioner said.

When the call ended Harper said, "How much does that guy pay into City Hall for that kind of ass-kissing from the commissioner?"

"Tut," Powell said. He added, "Ignore it. I'll speak to the commissioner and make sure you're not dragged into this again. Keeping goons like Kotian happy is my job. Yours is to find the truth."

*Easier said than done*, Harper thought, but said nothing.

When he'd gone Harper checked himself in the mirror, finger-combing a rogue red hair that had strayed a millimeter out of line, and repeating the process on his tight-trimmed beard. He straightened his tie and closed his eyes, visualizing the coming interview, breathing deeply. *OK. Let's get to it.* He'd already read Shah's personnel file on the way over via his eyepiece, knew his history: almost fifty years on the force, he'd volunteered straight after university, barely weeks before 9/11, and the shockwaves rippling out from the event that had changed everyone's world.

Harper walked down the corridor, thinking of Shah's rise through the ranks. Steady, rather than meteoric, until he'd found a niche. No one it seemed was quite as good as Shah at reading memories. *How does that feel?* Harper wondered. *To be so good at one particular job? Does he feel he's indispensable? Does he feel he's been sidelined by his own talent? Because he has. Too good to promote for the sake of seniority, not quite good enough to get it on merit, watching younger guys come and pass him by. Like me; he'll probably resent me. So be it.*

Harper realized that he was already building a case against Shah, looking for motivations. *Stop it; remember, innocent until proven guilty.*

He opened the door to the interview room and noted with disappointment that another man sat beside Shah. Even if Harper hadn't already known Alonso, everything about the man shouted *legal representation* – the ceiling lights gleamed off black slip-on shoes, the creases in his suit would damn-near slice a man's thumb open, and his haircut bragged "expensive".

"Officer Harper." Alonso inclined his chin a fraction in response to Harper's "Good morning" and recitation of the date and time and those present. "I must protest this heavy-handed assault on my client's home–"

"Save it for the court," Harper growled. "It's a capital crime, we already have an instance of evidence tampering, and we're taking no risks."

"What evidence?" Alonso said.

"Missing an eyepiece?" Harper asked Shah.

"You tell me. I had no time to look for anything before my door flew off its hinges."

"What happened to your hand?" Harper said, pointing to swollen knuckles and bruises. He liked to think
that he could read people, and Shah's puzzled frown
looked genuine as the cop studied his battered right
hand. "Want us to treat it?"

Shah glanced at Alonso and shook his head. "My
client exercises his right not to reply," Alonso said. "And
we'll get it treated at the nearest ER."

"Your client isn't going anywhere," Harper said. "We
have the body of a dead woman pulled from the East
River this morning, identified as Aurora Debonis, companion, last seen being companionable with Officer
Shah as they left *Manny's Sports Bar* just after midnight."

Alonso laughed. "And that's it? You have no motive,
no witnesses beyond them getting a cab home last
night, nothing to link them."

Harper nodded at Shah's right hand again. "I'd bet
you a week's wages that we'd find cross-contamination
on those knuckles."

Shah shrugged. Alonso shook his head. "Circumstantial. Show us one piece of proof."

Harper's eyepiece beeped. He'd switched it off, but
left an alarm on to alert him of urgent calls. He held up
a finger to Alonso to say "wait", and took the call.
"Yeah?"

"I've rebuilt as much as I can of his eyepiece," CSI
Moriarty said without preamble. Like many of her
peers, Moriarty's social skills were almost non-existent.
"It's been doctored to prevent full access to its memory—"

"Hold on. Doctored beyond simply being trodden on,
or whatever?"

"Exactly! It's an erasure program almost five years old. Bit of a botch job."

"Enough," Harper said. "What's on it? Anything relevant?"

"See for yourself." Moriarty's image in Harper's eyepiece was replaced by near-total darkness. Harper heard the sound of heavy breathing, whispers and giggles. *At least he took it off when he went to bed,* Harper thought. *Even if he did leave it running.* It could have been worse; often people filmed their dates in too-candid detail. Home-porn was still the biggest presence on the inter-web.

The eyepiece blanked and static scrambled the scene. Then Harper heard a man yell, and the bedside light came on to illuminate Shah and a blonde woman whom Harper guessed was Aurora. The picture kept jumping.

Shah seemed to teleport across the room, watched by a horrified Aurora. Shah wasn't teleporting; the jumps were where parts of the rebuilt eyepiece testimony were missing.

Shah swung an uppercut into Aurora's nose; blood spattered the room, a few drops part-occluding the eyepiece's tiny camera lens. The picture went, but Harper heard the soft, wet thuds of Shah's fists on Aurora's face, her cries of "No, please! Stop it!" and Shah's wordless grunts and soft sobs. The picture returned as Aurora tried to turn away, but unable to dodge the swing of Shah's roundhouse uppercut, Harper heard the crunch of bone on bone. Her head snapped back and she slumped off the edge of the bed.

"Get out!" Shah roared as he drew back his foot to kick Aurora as she lay prone and sobbed. "Get out you filthy–" and the picture cut out again.

Harper felt sick. He sent the footage to Bennett and added a voice-tag: "Re-interview Calea and McCoy, see if they want to change their testimony. There's no way that they could have slept through the noise of that beating. Remind them that they could be charged with obstruction of justice."

Alonso tutted. "Resorting to threats already, Officer?"

"Let's see how funny you think this is." Harper re-played the footage on a wall-screen, and Shah and Aurora's amplified gasps in the darkness echoed across the interview room. He watched Shah. The older cop's face turned ashen and he refused to meet Harper's gaze. But as the footage jumped, Shah's shame gave way to puzzlement, then to relief. Shah was hiding something, but damned if Harper could work out what.

"That all you got?" Shah said. "Sure, I roughed it up some, but – she was alive when she left." Alonso held up a hand, but Shah said to his counsel, "Nah, it's OK. Look, she wanted to do some kinky stuff – rimming she called it – then French kiss afterwards. No way was I going to kiss a tongue that's been up my ass. So I threw her out."

Harper didn't believe for a nanosecond that that was all there was to it. The violence of Shah's reaction had been far, far too extreme for an old guy confronted with kinky sex. *What the hell did he expect anyway, sleeping with a whore?* Judging by the closed look on Shah's face, he must have spoken aloud or allowed his feelings to show.

"Anyway." Harper tried to recover the momentum. "We'll talk to your wife and husband again. I'm inter-ested to hear what they got to say about what we seen there."

"They'll have nothing to say," Shah said. "They'll have heard nothing. We got the whole damn top floor of the apartment – we could have had a freaking party on our side of it, and they'd have heard nothing. You can bully 'em all you want, but short of making something up to get rid of you, that's all they'd have heard. And if you do bully 'em into a fake confession it'll come out."

Harper produced a small box about twenty centimeters by fifteen, by two and a half high. "I assume that you know what this is?"

"Oh come *on*," Shah replied. "What is this? You basing your interview technique on old flat-screen dramas? Of course I know what it is. I spend most of my life investigating the consequences of using a ripper." He pitched his voice into a parody, "It's a Deep Cranial Memory Copying Probe, Officer."

"Be as sarcastic as you want," Harper said. "It was found near where we calculate the body went in. It has your prints on it. How do you account for it, Officer?"

Shah shrugged. "I'd like my representative to answer all further questions."

# VI

Shah leaned his forehead against the door while he fumbled for his keys. When he found them he twisted the key in the lock with one hand and punched the code into the keypad with the other. The perennial stink of overcooked cabbage drifting up from the mad Pole's apartment three floors down gave way to the heavenly smell of a slow-cooking casserole permeating the apartment and his stomach growled. "Anyone home?"

Silence.

"Thanks be." Shah closed the door behind him. He wasn't sure he could face Leslyn's concern just yet, nor the Chocolate Fireguard's sarcasm, or – worse – his pontificating.

Hanging his jacket in the hallway, Shah wandered to the bedroom, stared at the desolation that was his bedroom after the entry and searches of the SWAT and CSU teams. He experimented with opening and closing the splintered door that hung by one hinge. Fetching a screwdriver from the utility room, he removed the door and leaned it against the wall. He looked around but couldn't see anything else that looked remotely fixable, so grabbed the antique phone. "Alonso? It's Shah. They owe me for a broken bedroom door. Can we make any-thing of the force with which they entered? I'm not a master criminal or a terrorist, am I? I'm a seventy year-old who's got to sleep in a ruined room." Shah paused, listening to Alonso. "Thanks, appreciate it."

After a minute or so, Shah sighed and taking clean sheets from the bedding box in the communal laundry room made the bed in their spare room. He spent the next half an hour slowly straightening pictures and or-naments and when he had run out of things to tidy, ventured onto the roof garden that formed a terrace all the way around the penthouse.

For want of anything better to do, he filled a watering can from rooftop rainwater barrels and topped up the water levels on the various fruits and vegetables – tomatoes, peppers, potatoes, baby carrots, apples, pears and strawberries cascaded from the Gro-bags that filled every available square centimeter.

Every few minutes he stopped, and pressed the fin-gers and thumbs of his left hand to the bridge of his nose. *Fists swinging, the thud of his knuckles against bone and flesh.* Shah shook the flashback away as a dog shakes water off its coat. He stared across the canyons of Manhattan, at the splashes of green speckling the other roofs and every window ledge visible, and sighed. Far below the LPG and electric cars that tussled with pedestrians and pedicabs for dominance weaved pat-terns in the traffic.

When another flashback – this time of hands reach-ing for him in the darkness and lips searching for his flesh – stopped him in his tracks, he went inside to the bathroom, diverting to pick up a shirt from the laundry room. He stripped to the waist and rinsed his face, star-ing at the stranger who looked back at him: Levantine skin, bags under bruised eyes, the beginnings of an old man's paunch and man-breasts, for all that he was careful what he ate and exercised as much as his aching joints would permit.

*You can only fight entropy for so long, old man.*

Voices from the mezzanine roused him. He threw the old shirt in the trash and, re-dressing with the clean one, went to the front door.

On the monitor Leslyn fumbled for her keys, "Can't find them. Damn. Do you have yours?"

"Somewhere." Doug went through his pockets.

They froze as Shah opened the door. "Yeah, I'm real." He attempted a smile.

"Nice to see you." Leslyn kissed his cheek as she passed him on the way in, followed by her other husband in his usual cheap clothes, all at least thirty years out of date. Shah resisted the urge to say *nice platform trainers*; he needed every ally he could get at the moment.

"Yeah," Doug echoed with little conviction. "They let you go, then?"

"Suspended, but not charged." Shah allowed the front door to swing shut. "Whether that changes… well, we'll see." He sighed. "That depends, I guess on whether Harper is as fair as he likes to make out. He likes to talk 'bout how he won't fit a cop up who's innocent. But we'll see, like I said."

"You've watered the plants!" Leslyn cried from the doorway to the garden. Wet patches showed where the can had dripped, or Shah had missed his target.

"It's that much of a surprise?" Shah tried not to bristle.

"Just that you haven't changed into your gardening clothes," Leslyn said quickly, and Shah wondered whether he caught a flash of fear cross her face. *Just how much is this going to damage us, Les?* There was no point in asking her now, not with McCoy present, and no look of welcome on the other man's face. "What I've been wearing today smells like I'd slept in it for a week."

"So you gonna be here all the time?" McCoy said.

"Hey Doug, don't sound so enthused," Shah joked.

It fell flat, judging by the frown it met. "We got a deal, Shah." Doug's wheeze worsened as always when he was stressed – which was most of the time. "You have the place during your time, we have it at ours. Remember?"

"No problem," Shah said. "I'll go sit in the park with a news-sheet."

"For over six hours a day?" Leslyn said. "Don't be so silly, you damn fool!" She gave him the smile Shah always though of as her terminal one, reserved for the cancer patients and other inoperable cases. "It'll be a chance to spend some time together."

"Yep." Shah grinned to show he was joking. "I think that's what's worrying Doug."

Leslyn winked and took his hand and gave it a momentary squeeze. "We've worked different shifts for so long now," she said, "That our entire lives seem to run on different zones sometimes. It'll be nice." Shah wasn't sure who she was trying to convince the most. Turning to McCoy she said, "This is no time to squabble. Come on, Doug, show some sympathy." Shah squashed a smile as she marched into the kitchen, impressed by Leslyn's show of spirit. If he let it show, he risked being accused of gloating.

Shah stood aside, allowing Doug to follow her into the kitchen, the other man stooping to clear the door

lintel. Shah sighed, wondering whether he could survive dinner with his pedantic, abrasive alligator of a
co-husband without giving into the urge to throttle
him. "Count to ten," he muttered, but kept going until
he'd reached a hundred, before following.

When he entered the kitchen, Leslyn was ladling out
the casserole. She looked up. "I made extra, so you're
welcome to join us. Mr Patel the butcher had a sale on
goat." She chuckled. "I suspect he's had to give up
whatever site he's had to graze them on, and decided
to slaughter some of them rather than move them all
on." Disputes over land gone back to the wild where
animals could graze were common, though no longer
Shah's concern now he was ten years out of uniform.
Leslyn said, "I was going to plate up a meal for you for
later, anyway." She always cooked for three.

Shah had heard McCoy complain that she was more
like Shah's housekeeper than his wife; that was Leslyn,
showing her love in practical, unfussy ways.

"Are you sure?" Shah looked at Doug. "I can take it
to my room, give you guys some privacy."

Doug looked down at his feet, stroking his unkempt
beard. "Just for tonight," he said, looking up at last.
"Let's eat together... maybe out on the patio."

At that moment Shah thought that Doug McCoy almost attained a grubby sort of nobility. "Thanks." Shah
felt a lump rising to his throat. It had felt all day as if he
was fighting the world, and the sudden relief that he
wasn't alone almost undid him. "I really appreciate it."

"Don't get all sentimental," McCoy growled. "I'm not
your brother just cause I feel sorry for you for one
evening."

"That's more like the Doug McCoy I know," Shah said.
"I was beginning to wonder what you'd done with him."

"No fighting!" Leslyn called. "Come and eat – oh, grab the bread will you, Doug? Pete, bring the pot – there's spare if you want it. I packed it out with vegetables."

Shah's mouth was already watering at the aroma of casserole. He'd been allowed ham and pastrami sandwiches – deducted from his allowance of course – at lunchtime, but as usual he was ravenous. "Been out for a stroll?" Shah said. Leslyn worked six days on, two days off, her shifts at the hospital half-overlapping with Shah's at the precinct.

"Went for a meeting with the lawyers," Doug answered for them both. "See whether we can break through this damned smokescreen that BAT's thrown up to wriggle out of paying the settlement."

Shah resisted the urge to remind his co-husband that no one had put a gun to his head and made him smoke, but now wasn't the time to re-open that old quarrel. Instead he said, "Nice day for it."

"They've invited Doug and me to a faculty reunion," Leslyn said. "Next Tuesday. To celebrate his sixtieth birthday. I'll put something in the oven before we go out. That is, if I need to…" She waved a hand in the air to complete the sentence, or hide her embarrassment, Shah wasn't sure which.

"You wearing a tux?" Shah said. He shouldn't provoke McCoy, but something about his insistence on wearing turn-of-the-century shell suits and gangsta outfits was *so* irritating. "Or whatever retired Professors of English Literature wear?"

"Bourgeois nonsense," McCoy snorted.

But before he could start on one of his rants, Leslyn put down her spoon and laid a hand on each man's arm. "Please, can't we have one meal together without you two behaving like overgrown children?"

"Of course, dear," McCoy said, and not for the first time Shah was touched by how gently the man spoke to Leslyn. It was about his only redeeming feature. For a moment he wondered what McCoy might consider his to be, then dismissed the thought.

"Anyway," Shah said. "He started it!"

"Did not!" McCoy drew himself up like an indignant skeleton, and then saw Shah's shoulders shaking with suppressed laughter. He exhaled. "I suppose that you thought that that was funny," he said with as much dignity as he could muster.

"Perveza called," Leslyn said.

"How did she sound?" Shah said.

"Not good." Leslyn paused. "I think she's been thrown off her rehab course." Leslyn was slightly more tolerant of their wayward daughter than Shah, but even she had long since reached the limit of her patience. "And after Rex worked so hard to get her on it."

Shah grunted. He suspected that their son had been more concerned with the effect on his budding career if it ever came out that he had a junkie sister than simple altruism, but he said nothing.

For once the subject of Leslyn's fascination with Post-humans and what they were supposed to be doing in Montana wasn't the only elephant in the room. *Tonight,* Shah thought, *there are two of them. Which will we bump into first?*

After several minutes of silent eating, it was McCoy who answered Shah's internal question by saying, "So what happened?"

"They interrogated me, but they haven't enough evidence to bring a charge," Shah said, deliberately misunderstanding the question.

"But what are you supposed to have done?" Leslyn said.

Shah took a few moments to answer while he chewed on some carrot and potato. Everyone with gardens used them to supplement their calorie allowance as much as they could, and the vegetables were home-grown, which meant that the quality was much more variable than the mass-produced homogenized crops that he'd grown up with. He had a horrible feeling that the mouthful he was chewing on included some sort of animal protein. "I, uh, brought someone home last night."

"We heard." McCoy fell silent at Leslyn's warning nudge.

"Something happened to her after she left here last night," Shah said, not knowing how else to put it. A blunt "she's dead" seemed an even worse alternative.

"So she did leave under her own steam, then?" McCoy said. "Only the cops that came here were suggesting otherwise. Some of–"

"Doug," Leslyn said. She was silent for a while as she ate. "After she'd gone – and it sounded more like you threw her out – I saw you in the hallway. If I didn't know better, I'd have said you were drunk. You were staggering, and I had to prop you up."

"You walked me back to my room?"

"You don't remember?"

Shah shook his head. "All I've got are vague fragments."

He tried to put the flashes of tangled bodies in the darkness out of his head. "It's– holy crap." He realized that the effects were those of the after-effects of a drug dose. It had to have been while they were in the bar, unless it was their proximity in the cab. Shah remembered the sudden horniness that had set in while they sat side by side.

Why was obvious, had been since he'd waited in the interview room for Bailey to interrogate him. Someone was setting him up. His next monthly anti-tox injection was only a few days away, so the resistance was at its lowest. *Did they get the dosage wrong? Or was I supposed to remember some of last night? Was I supposed to still be able to function after a fashion, so I could be in the frame for murder?*

And who wanted him framed?

# VII

"It's still not moving." Jeanette rubs her temple – a sure sign she's suffering a migraine. She rummages in her vast handbag, fishes out two Tylenol which she swigs down with a sip of water from a plastic pint bottle. Her orange-blonde hair, once such a vivid red, is plastered against her forehead. You had to turn the air-con off ten minutes ago to stop the engine overheating.

You unbuckle your seatbelt and half-stand in the driver's seat, feeling your shirt peel away from the leather, but you can't quite fit your head through the sun roof. *Shame we couldn't afford something a little bigger than a baby Chevrolet.*

Nonetheless you can see enough: The freeway ahead of you is gridlocked with a vast cavalcade of cars, as if every car in Delaware County is on this particular stretch of freeway. The line extends all the way down the slope and up the other side to the top of the next hill – and maybe beyond it for all you know, perhaps past Philadelphia and onwards, all the way to the Atlantic.

You switch on the radio, ignoring Jeanette's irritated tut. The news stations seem to have switched to a diet of what passes for music: country rock on one station, more of that gangsta crap or whatever it's called, then another country station, and finally a conversation. But these people seem to be living on another world, one where they can talk about bulb propagation while their country grinds to a halt.

You keep flicking through channels until you come to one where the announcer says, "We'll be going to the newsroom after this record," and launches into Don McLean's *American Pie*. Something about driving his Chevy to the levee touches a chord within you, although you can't say why. At the end of the eight minutes and something seconds of the song there is only silence, and you wonder whether the station has gone off the air.

Then the announcer intones, "It's fifty years ago today that Don McLean first performed that song. America's changed almost beyond recognition. If that was the Day the Music Died, today is the Day Freedom Died. We're going to the newsroom now."

You take the opportunity of a gap to roll forward nine inches as the announcer says, "The headlines at three o'clock: US forces in the Gulf have surrendered to the Arabic OPEC Alliance. The President will address the nation at five o'clock, including further restrictions on gasoline rationing. Shares on Wall Street have fallen faster than on any day since the Wall Street Crash ninety-two years ago." You switch the radio off.

"Thought there might be some traffic news." Your explanation comes out like a bird's croak in your own ears, so that you clear your throat.

"The only news is, that nothing's going anywhere," Jeanette whispers, still rubbing her temples. "Do you have any idea where we're going to sleep tonight, assuming that we actually get into Philadelphia?"

"Sign up ahead says it's only ten miles."

"It's taken us the best part of three hours to travel ten miles. At this rate it'll take us a lot longer to travel the next ten…"

"Then we'll sleep in the car," you say with exaggerated patience.

"We can't live in it forever," Jeanette says. "It looks as if everyone and their dog are moving back into the city." Her laugh is a bitter bark, devoid of humor. "It's the Oklahoma migrations of a hundred years ago, in reverse."

"It's been happening for some time." You think of the increasing numbers of derelict, boarded-up houses that you hadn't really noticed until about a week ago, when American forces moved into the Al-Dukkhan oil fields off the Kuwaiti coast. "The guys on the radio said we've reached a tipping point, whatever that is, in terms of keeping the country motoring." Jeanette doesn't answer, so you continue, "Hon, you know that we can't afford to live in Bethel Township any longer. Even before this it's been getting unbearable going in and out of Philly to work." You've had this conversation before. You suspect that you're going to have it again. Many more times.

Jeanette sighs. "If we could've stuck it out a year longer, Jimmy, you wouldn't have had to commute. Retirement's so close." She wipes away a tear angrily, then points across the central barriers at the empty lanes on the other side. "Look at it! The outbound side's damn well empty – no one's going out there! If only we could get across to it, we could go home!"

There's no point in arguing with her. She's so deeply in denial that nothing you can say will convince her. Only your threat to leave her alone in the empty street was enough to persuade her to come with you and now that the shock of your threat has worn off, she's reverting to her usual stubbornness.

The central lane begins to move forward faster than those on either side, and for a moment you're tempted to follow the lead set by several other cars and try to maneuver into the lane, but the line stops as soon as it starts. Car horns blare like maddened elephants.

Several drivers get out of their stationary cars, then run across the other lines of traffic. Many stop when confronted by the sheer height of the side wall, but a few clamber over it and jump down into the adjacent gardens.

Within minutes dozens of other drivers are following these pioneers' example; leaving their possessions in their cars and abandoning them both, clambering over the barriers and running across the gardens toward the city center, like lemmings hurtling toward a cliff.

# VIII

## Monday

Still haunted by images of crowds scampering across suburban Pennsylvania gardens, Marietetski removed the sensory-deprivation hood and unpeeled the scanner, rubbing sensation back into his shaven scalp. It would sting like hell when the local anesthetic wore off, but without Shah, he'd have to get used to it. And it would be many years before he could work without the safety-net of the hood, unlike Shah, who could just blank his surroundings by closing his eyes.

"What you viewing?" His partner's voice made Marietetski jump. Shah leaned across him, cheap aftershave tickling Marietetski's nostrils.

"118-395-04." Marietetski pointed at the screen with the clip he'd downloaded from the web while putting his eyepiece back on.

"Huh," Shah said. "You been studying a burn, bud. Entirely legal downloaded copy."

"Oh, crap. You sure?"

"Positive. You can tell by the very faint sense of loss that usually accompanies any rip that the criminals make, as if the memory itself is hurting. Did you get that feeling?"

Marietetski shook his head. "Nah. Just great sadness."

He described the scene to Shah who scratched an earlobe, fiddling with his new eyepiece. He clearly hadn't yet gotten used to it yet. "There are a lot of these death of suburbia clips out there, all looking for some wealthy connoisseur to give them some tender loving care. For a lot of these people, losing their cars and the scattered lifestyle their motors supported was worse than anything else. They've convinced themselves that someone will be interested. We always think that people are interested in our own little obsessions." Shah paused. "What were you looking for?"

"Just trawling." Marietetski pushed his chair back and smiled at a passing girl in a sharp suit, who returned the smile with interest.

"OK," Shah muttered. "Don't tell me."

Marietetski ignored him. "How ya doing, Kimi?"

"Oh, OK." Kimi waved her hands to illustrate her OK-ness. "I'm starting to learn where all the files are now."

Marietetski caught her glance and said, "This is my partner, Pete Shah. Pete, this is Kimi. Works in communications." *Answering the phones, they used to call it,* he thought.

"The one who–" Kimi caught herself in time. "Nice to meetcha!"

"Nice to meet you too, Kimi." Shah gave her what Marietetski recognized as his friendliest smile, although his face barely creased.

Kimi turned back to Marietetski and eyed his lean, muscular frame. "You work out down in the gym?"

"When I get the time." Physical training was mandatory – even Shah spent time in the gym – and provided a token offset to the building's power consumption, but finding time when shifts seemed to get longer and longer was proving increasingly difficult for everyone.

"There's one piece of equipment that I can't get my head around," Kimi said. "I'm a little embarrassed to ask people down there – I feel like a fool – but maybe you could spare a few minutes at lunchtime? Show me how it works?" She flashed him what Marietetski thought of as a sixty-watt smile, shy and slightly hesitant.

"Sure." Marietetski tried to ignore Shah's muffled snort of laughter. "Twelve-thirty?"

"Yeah, that'd be great." Kimi's smile increased to a hundred watts, then to a hundred and fifty. "Thanks." She walked away, hips swaying.

"Oh, John, you are such a bad, *bad* boy." He mimicked Kimi's hand-waving falsetto, "Maybe you could spare a few minutes to show me how your equipment works?"

"Hey, old man," Marietetski said. "I can't help it if the girl has taste." He flexed his arm. "This is lean, mean muscle, almost perfectly built." He grinned and to forestall the inevitable comeback headed for the coffee machine, calling, "Time for some sewage. My treat." It usually was; Marietetski knew that Shah wasn't rich, and with both wives and a co-husband pulling what were comparatively good wages Marietetski could afford the coffees, although Shah made a point of buying periodically.

Marietetski slotted his card into the machine and punched up the codes for their coffees when a deep male voice behind him said, "What's the old guy doing back in here?"

Marietetski swung around and gazed at Peruzzi with a distaste that he couldn't have explained, if asked to.

The uniformed patrolman was thinning on top but his hair curled over his collar at the back, while his shirt was a size too small for his muscular upper body. None of that was really justification for Marietetski's hackles to rise.

More likely it was the too-knowing way that Peruzzi talked. While Marietetski might have sometimes doubted Shah's competence, he was the only one allowed to do so. "He's back at work. Got a problem with that?"

"No, no," Peruzzi said. "Just ah, wondering…"

"Yeah?" Marietetski took first one cup from the dispenser, then the other.

"Whether it's wise to let a guy who's under investigation into the building."

Marietetski stared. *How'd you like to wear this coffee, asshole?* Instead he said, keeping his voice even with great effort, "In case you hadn't noticed, Officer Peruzzi, there's a chronic shortage of resources."

"Well, sure…" Peruzzi said, as he inserted his own card into the dispenser.

Marietetski said, "Shah's been reinstated as far as he'll be working under really close supervision, and with restricted access to files. Only what's directly connected to the cases, and each file will be signed out by van Doorn or me." He added in a low voice, "And the simple truth is that he has a talent for identifying and linking apparently unrelated memories that's almost unequalled in the whole freaking NYPD. Shah is *the* expert on memory rips."

"I guess," Peruzzi said, walking away with his cup of coffee.

"Believe it!" Marietetski called to his back. He turned and found Shah leaning against a wall, clearly trying to stifle a slight smile. "What?" Marietetski said, rubbing the toe of his right shoe against his left instep. "What's so funny?"

"Ah, John," Shah said. "You sweet talker, you." He sighed theatrically and leaned his head back, resting it against the wall. "A talent almost unequalled in the whole NYPD..."

"Well, I can hardly say you're a boneheaded waster, can I?"

"That's more like the typical picky Virgo I usually have to put up with! I wondered where you'd stashed him."

"Picky Virgo? Put up with me? Put up? With me?" Marietetski raised one eyebrow.

"Weeeell," Shah said. "I do like the slightly pompous tone you get sometimes. His voice deepened: 'Each file will be signed out by van Doorn or me'." Shah tried to raise an eyebrow, but succeeded only in raising both – and Marietetski burst out laughing.

"I guess I have certain, ah, standards," Marietetski said, when he'd stopped laughing.

"Standards." Shah nodded. Then he too started to guffaw.

"Yeah," Marietetski said. "So how are Leslyn and Doug? Did they have a nicer than usual day?" Marietetski suspected that the day before had been the first Sunday Shah hadn't worked in about thirty years.

"Oh, they're a little shell-shocked. But Leslyn's getting used to having me underfoot. And Doug's as big a jackass as he ever was." He grew serious. "I know that you're not allowed to talk about the woman, but..."

"No, I'm not. There are no other perps in the frame, Pete. That's all I can say. If they get one piece of evidence beyond circumstantial that points to you..."

"Leaving me in limbo." Shah sipped his coffee and winced. He stared into space for a while. "Listen, John. I appreciate that this is difficult for you. You're ambitious – I get that."

"Don't make it sound like a crime, Pete."

"I'm not," Shah said. "Ambition's almost extinct nowadays, but I'm not criticizing it. What I meant was if you want reassigning, or if you want me to ask, I'll do it. I may joke about you making commissioner by the time you're forty, but I won't do anything that'll blight that career in the Justice Department or wherever it is that you've lined up."

"Thanks," Marietetski said. "But don't worry about it." Both Linda and Dolores had suggested the same thing, and Paul was wavering, but Marietetski knew how his co-workers thought better than his partners did. If anything else turned up then he would seriously consider it, but at the moment Marietetski was getting office points for loyalty to a partner who wasn't a formal suspect and who might yet be cleared. The time to jump ship would be when something else broke that nailed Shah. *At the moment you're only a damned fool for sleeping with a hooker, Pete. But lack of professionalism doesn't make you a killer.*

They returned to their desks. Shah said, "What files you going to sign out for me?"

Marietetski lowered his voice. "The clip I was looking at?"

"The death of suburbia thing?"

"That's the one." Marietetski stroked his chin. "There's an old man ricocheting around HHS amongst other places. Someone ripped his memory, left him halfway to a vegetable. But because he's physically fit HHS say he's not their problem – they're as short of case workers as any other agency. Victim Support's as stretched and can't help."

"In some ways it's worse than if they're dead. But what's that got to do with the clip you were looking at?"

"The old guy's originally from Philadelphia. I know now that it isn't him, but I was trying to find something to lock me in on relatives, maybe get him shipped back there."

Shah shook his head. "Probably no more than ten thousand people living in Philly now. They got hit harder than most by the Dieback. They'll no more have the infrastructure to support him than anywhere else." He thought for a minute. "Was there any sense of a residual signature to the rip left in this guy's brain? Sometimes you can pick up clues – like is there any residual fear? If so, chances are the vic knew what was coming. If not, you may still get a lingering sense of shock spreading throughout the nervous system. We can chemically scrape the brain, but not the nervous system, where some of the emotional impact is stored."

"They only picked him up Friday afternoon," Marietetski said, and it sounded lame even to him. He simply hadn't thought of it. *Damn.* It was only now, that he had to work alone that he realized how much he relied on Shah. What Marietetski had dismissed as plodding was now starting to look like attention to detail, allowing Marietetski to do the theorizing that he was good at or to process the simpler cases, the invasion of privacy or other spin-offs where someone else in the memory objected to their presence at a scene being publicized.

"So come on," Shah said. "Let's go see your vic, put that Masters in Forensic Criminology to some use."

• • • •

The sheets of rain outside meant that every pedicab and other type of transport was fought for by pedestrians determined to stay dry. Instead they took a subway ride to the compound that was the victim's latest version of limbo.

"I think this Harlan Buffett is related to the guy whose clip I was looking at," Marietetski said as they left the station to venture back out into the downpour. "I guess that old guy – Jim Powell – sold his memory to finance life in Philly."

"He wouldn't have got much for it," Shah said. "They're dime a dozen, memories like that. It's the rarer stuff that makes the money."

"Which of course includes the illegals."

"Yep."

The compound was only a block from the station, but they had to duck from awning to doorway to canopy to stay even half-dry. Marietetski wrinkled his nose at the smell of horses at the stand – sweat and dung. As they scampered from cover to cover he finally plucked up the nerve to ask, "So what actually happened?" If his eyepiece were studied it would reveal that he'd broken orders to not broach the subject, but it seemed unreasonable of van Doorn and IA to demand that he stay off the topic.

"I took her home. I guess she dosed me with something in her perfume and took my eyepiece. I woke up with a SWAT team standing over my bed and about a million guns pointed at me."

"I wondered what had happened to it." Marietetski pointed at Shah's new piece. "I guessed it'd been impounded. Tough getting used to a new one?"

"Not as much as maybe going to prison," Shah said. "But tough enough."

"You don't remember anything? Nothing at all?" Marietetski said. "That sounds more like a rip than a dose."

"I get flashbacks." Shah looked decidedly uncomfortable, "nothing coherent, though."

Marietetski wondered what Shah was holding back. Because he looked so ill at ease that Marietetski wanted to laugh. *If doctors make the worst patients, I guess cops would make the worst liars.* "Seems ironic you get your piece stolen the day after hers was taken. Makes you wonder if it's the new crime of choice."

"Just coincidence."

"Teach you to hang around with funny women."

"What the hell does that mean?"

"Nothing, nothing." Marietetski held his hands up in surrender. "Hey, sorry. OK?"

"Sure. Look, I'm sorry too. I shouldn't have snapped."

"Anyway, we're here," Marietetski said.

'Here' was a shelter, a cold, damp warren through which the dispossessed wandered like ghosts or sat and stared into space.

Harlan Buffett was in his mid-fifties, Marietetski guessed, but he could have been a decade younger or older.

"Harlan?" Shah said, voice gentle as a moth's landing. "I'm Officer Pete Shah of the NYPD."

Buffett stared at them and swallowed.

"He doesn't respond to anything," the accompanying orderly said. "They took so many of his core memories, both episodic and procedural, that he's basically a vegetable."

"Catatonic, I assume you mean," Shah said, glaring. Marietetski could almost read his mind: *Show some respect, asswipe.*

"Not in the strictest medical sense, no." The orderly flushed at Shah's tone. "He isn't rigid, nor does he show any purposeless activity. He simply sits, staring into space."

"I'm going to show you some pictures, Harlan." Marietetski took out a reader that was no bigger than an old style cellphone, before eyepieces supplanted them. "See if you recognize anyone." Marietetski held the reader in front of Buffett's eyes, but elicited no other reaction. Shah held a portable encephalograph close to Buffett's head and peered through the viewfinder, watching to see whether any of the pictures Marietetski flashed up drew a response.

"Nothing," Shah said when Marietetski had finished.

"Not to Sunny Kotian?" Marietetski said.

"Nor Kotian senior, not Junior, nor to any of the other half-dozen less likely candidates to Ripper-dom," Shah said. "You showed him the pictures of the Powells?"

"Everything that I could find." Marietetski put away the reader with a sigh. "Come on, let's head back. We're getting nowhere here; just another wall to bang our heads against."

# IX

"How was your equipment?" Shah leered as Marietetski eased himself into his chair with a sigh. "Was Kimi suitably impressed?"

"Very funny." Marietetski settled himself down, then looked across. "What ya doing?"

"Trawling the web." Shah looked up, refocusing on the here-and-now. "Public postings, nothing classified. I haven't hacked your password."

"Never thought you did."

"Either I murdered Aurora, or I didn't. Since I didn't, someone wants me implicated. Why else take my eyepiece and leave it where the body was tossed in?"

"It's a working hypothesis. I'll check the intraweb, see if anything's been posted today." They were silent a while. Marietetski said, "Pete?"

"Uh-hmm?" Shah's eyes never looked away from the screen.

"Take a deep breath when I ask this…"

"Deep breathing now," Shah said, still not looking up.

"But you seem a little on edge when we talk about the night before. I'm sure it isn't 'cause you killed the girl, so what is it? I'm not trying to interrogate you or anything…"

"So what are you doing?"

"If I take a beautiful girl home when I'm your age, I'll want to talk about it."

"When you're my age, hey?"

"Don't divert. We're not talking 'bout your age, we talking 'bout the fact that you aren't talking about *her*. Why?"

Shah looked up at last, rubbed his eyes. "If I admit that my memory about the journey home is a little hazy, what conclusions are you going to draw?"

"You was drunk?"

"Exactly," Shah said. "And I don't drink."

"So what *are* you saying?"

"If I don't drink but I was showing symptoms, what does that leave? A brain seizure? I'm fine now. A fast-dissolving drug?"

"If you were doped, that implies access to drugs powerful enough to override the regular anti-tox injections." Marietetski frowned. "I don't know anything that would dissolve fast enough to be undetectable in only a few – what, eight or nine – hours."

"Depends," Shah said. "My monthly booster's on Friday. You know your resistance dips slightly the last few days of the month. If they could afford to, they'd boost us more often, but I guess they've had to trade off protection against us getting spiked to save money."

"But that would mean either they took a chance…"

"Or they knew when my booster is."

"You saying you're the victim of a conspiracy?"

"Conspiracy's a big word," Shah said. "All I'm saying is slip a cop or a civ a few giga-calories or some foreign currency to copy a few internal files. Don't mean that they paid 'em specifically to get at me. Maybe that was coincidence–"

"You don't believe in coincidence."

"–or I was collateral damage."

"Hmm, don't buy it, Pete."

"I'll admit I was flattered by Aurora's attention," Shah said. "Maybe thinking 'bout it, she was a little too interested in work. At the time I just thought she had a ghoulish streak. My… eye for the ladies is hardly a secret, is it? But what if she was a plant?"

"Double 'hmmm'."

"I guess I wouldn't believe it either, if I was you," Shah said. "But you asked why I didn't want to talk about it. I'm thinking some fucker's out to frame me."

"Let's assume that's so, Pete. *But you're still an idiot for taking a hooker home. Too many chances of things getting out of hand like this has.* "Why? Who?"

"You tell me."

Marietetski thought, then took Shah to one side and taking off his piece, murmured, "I shouldn't tell you this, but van Doorn doesn't think you're guilty, or if he does, he isn't admitting it to anyone. He's got everyone pulling double time. No one minds, cause for all you're a miserable old bastard, people seem to like you for some reason."

"My natural charm." Shah almost allowed a smile to seep through. Almost.

"They're going through any cases past or present where you've crossed paths with a perp. And after fifty years that's a lot of people." He sighed. "I've done what I can, pulling out the stuff that I can offload onto you, and taking up the slack, and I've gone through as many as I can. Which leaves…"

They put their eyepieces back on and Shah shuffled through the mountain of files. "My caseload's primarily made up of two major investigations, and truckloads of smaller ones like Buffett."

"I can see where this is going."

"Unless one of those smaller ones has sparked this off, the odds are that it's one of the two major cases," Shah said.

"Yep."

"Of the two major cases, unless we've stumbled across the Ripper who's leaving these people the mental capacity of a cheeseburger – in which case we're screwed because we've no idea what we've stumbled across – it's the other investigation."

"Kotian."

"Kotian," Shah agreed.

"It's a little paranoid, isn't it Pete, to put *everything* down to Kotian?"

"Maybe," Shah agreed. "Or you could look at it like I have, that very little happens in this boro without his involvement, even if it's just getting commission for working his patch. Look at the odds. If you look past me, then it's more likely to do with a major than a minor case. And of the two major cases, which one is more likely? The investigation where we know who the suspect is, or the one where we don't?"

"Let's assume your idea will fly. We still can't do anything about it. IA's leading the investigation, not us."

"It's absolutely right that they should lead the investigation into the murder of Aurora Debonis," Shah said for the benefit of their eyepieces. "We just carry on working on Kotian."

"Uh-uh," Marietetski said. "Van Doorn was very specific. You're working the small cases. It's hands-off checking out Kotian for the time being."

"Of course, *sir*."

"Hey, man, I'm only doing as I'm told."

"I understand," Shah said. "I wouldn't dream of approaching anyone connected with our local Mr Big…"

"At least in my capacity as a cop," Shah said a half hour after his shift had ended. "Nothing to stop me paying a visit to a friend of my co-husband, is there?" He held the glass door of the Bellwether Institute open. "Who has a new sponsor. Who just happens to be…"

"You are so out of order." Marietetski grinned. "Van Doorn's going to seriously fry my ass if anyone complains."

"Why should Erokij complain?" They strode across a cavernous lobby, which with its paintings and discreetly placed view-screens was more like a vast upmarket art gallery than a research center. "We were passing on our way to the bar, and thought we'd stop by."

"Given where I live," Marietetski said with a chuckle, "that'd be the longest detour ever." He sniffed. "Something in here smells nice."

"It's called potpourri, or something." Shah pretended bewilderment. "You don't like eau-de-chemical, like at the station?"

"Bleach makes my eyes water. Though I suppose it's better than the piss and puke it covers up." Marietetski touched Shah's arm. "What's this professor's connection to Kotian?"

"As far as we can see, none. Kotian may be laundering his money through Tosada's research, or it might be his legit money he's spending on it." Shah chuckled. "Yeah, I believe that Kotian's gone legit as much as you do."

"Might be a first step."

"Nah, there's an angle, somewhere."

They finally reached a marble-effect reception desk. Shah flashed his badge, eliciting the usual smirk from Marietetski. "Officers Shah and Marietetski for Professor Tosada."

The receptionist, a burly man in his mid-forties who Shah thought he recognized as an ex-cop, nodded. He dialed a number, announced them, and passed them temporary badges. "Professor Tosada said someone will be down in a few minutes, officers. If you'd like to take a seat until then…" He waved at some low chairs clustered around an equally low table.

"Thanks," Marietetski said. "We'll stand. Been sat on our asses all day."

The receptionist flashed them an I'm-not-interested smile.

Several minutes later a man appeared from behind a painting-dotted partition. Shah watched Marietetski study the newcomer. His colleague would know Tosada from the news channels, of course, but in the flesh he appeared less like a photographic negative; in person the pockmarks marring his jet-black skin were more pronounced, while his mane of fashionably cut hair was less blinding white than dishwash-gray. But his epicanthic-folded eyes were so dark that they looked black as well. "Pervez!" He cried in those accent-free tones familiar to anyone who was interested in popular science. "How are you?"

"Hey Erokij. We was on a visit. Thought we'd see if you wanted a coffee."

"Alas." Tosada looked regretful.

Before he could continue Shah said, as if only just realizing, "Oh, let me introduce John Marietetski, a fan of yours. Ever since he found out I knew you, he's driven me nuts to introduce you to him."

Marietetski caught Shah's wink and looked suitably overawed. "It's an honor, Professor." He stretched out a hand. "I hope that we're not calling at an inconvenient time."

Tosada made a resigned gesture as they shook hands; it was clear that their visit was ill-timed, but the researcher didn't feel able to say so.

Shah had said on the way over, "He is *such* a sucker for flattery. He knows it himself, even laughs about it – but you get more from buttering the guy up than quizzing him."

Shah said, "Are we going to live forever, Erokij? Come on man, I'm running outta time here!"

Tosada laughed. "I've almost as much incentive as you in making the breakthrough."

Marietetski said, "I guess we've intruded, Professor. We should let you get on."

"Nonsense," Tosada snorted, falling for the reverse psychology. "I can spare a few minutes for my favorite ignorant flatfoot." He added quickly, "That's him, by the way," head nudging toward Shah.

Shah roared with laughter. "You've changed your tune since we first met! John, this guy wouldn't give me the time of day when we first met – till he found out who my co-husband was!"

"But that's the whole point, Pervez." Tosada leaned forward, the pedagogue unable to resist lecturing even now, adjusting his trademark gold cufflinks, smoothing with his finger the pinstripes of his suit, checking his reflection in a handily-placed mirror. "A man should be judged by the company he keeps. That's what social networking is!"

"That's how he knows Kotian," Shah had explained on the way over. "So I've been cultivating him, and I guess Kotian's been encouraging him to do the same."

As Shah and Tosada continued bantering along the reception space, Marietetski checked his eyepiece; *Erokij Tosada. Born Brooklyn April 9th 1985, educated Harvard, Research Professor of Biomedical Gerontology at CCNY. Height 1.75 meters. Father Japanese, Mother Nigerian* – he cut the link when he realized he'd missed something.

"–population bell-curve isn't slowing down as predicated, so they fear we can't afford so many more mouths – hence these latest regrettable maneuvers."

"Well, let's hope it works out for you," Shah said. "Though till the treatments deliver, it looks a high-risk investment, whatever the long-term profit."

"Maybe." Tosada glanced toward Marietetski. "But there are intermediate benefits – every decade that we can extend longevity at peak physical and mental condition generates spin-offs for everyone from athletes to – maybe, who knows – interstellar voyagers."

Marietetski almost groaned aloud. "Haven't we got enough challenges on Earth, Professor? Without squandering resources we don't have–"

"John," Shah warned.

But Tosada smiled beatifically at the thought of an audience. "I'm amazed a man born in a country whose embracing of Manifest Destiny is almost religious should take such a blinkered view. Think of all those resources!" Tosada pointed skywards, but before he could continue his eyepiece chimed an incoming call. "Hello? One moment please, I have visitors." He paused almost imperceptibly. "Excuse me, gentlemen, but I'm afraid I must take this call. Perhaps we could continue our conversation another time?" He shook hands two-handed with Shah, then, "John, I look forward to locking intellectual antlers with you again, soon."

Tosada turned, only speaking when he was about a dozen paces away.

Shah couldn't make out the conversation. "I'll bet you a dollar to a new yuan that that's Kotian. Washington's getting twitchy about the fallout from paying to extend lifespans at such a sensitive time. Tosada hinted a couple of weeks ago that the next Federal Budget will see cutbacks."

"To him?"

"And our wages."

"Hardly surprising. The interest on our National Debt's bigger than our entire national budget."

"Yeah, but we'll slip back into the Dark Ages if we don't keep Government functioning. That can't be in Peking's interest, however much the Meccans might cheer."

"Yeah, I'm sure Sacramento will write another aid check," Marietetski scoffed. The USA was effectively subsisting on the charity of foreigners, especially since California's secession and Washington's subsequent abortive attempt to retake the world's newest republic. Only Asian pressure had stopped the invasion before it got too bloody.

"Whether or not they do, Tosada needs funds to continue, John. I dunno what Kotian's angle is, but there's one somewhere. If our friendly ganglord is going to pick up Tosada's funding shortfall, then judging by all the 'rents' those shops in Midtown pay for Kotian's help, he'll want a big, big payback." As they exited the Institute, Shah added. "We need to find out what that angle is, whether it's one of Kotian's legit fronts, or part of his real business."

# X

## Tuesday

The next morning Marietetski was a few minutes early, arriving in an office as near empty as it ever got. Still a thin figure sat at his desk, staring at his screen. "Jeez, Pete," Marietetski said, "You shit in the bed or something?"

"Couldn't sleep." Shah looked up. Dark rings circled his eyes. "No cracks about guilty consciences, heh?"

"Never dreamed of it." Marietetski held his hands up in a gesture of innocence. The twitching corner of his mouth told a different story. "How's life with Doug and Leslyn?" Marietetski could guess why Shah was in work so early.

Shah shrugged. "Doug's as big pain in the ass as ever. He'll never change. If I'd known how big a pain in the ass he'd be, I'd have objected when Leslyn asked to bring him into the marriage. But at the time it didn't seem such a big deal. He made her happy, I wanted to still have access to the kids and we couldn't afford a divorce – legal fees alone woulda killed us."

"You could always stay with us–" as soon as he said it, Marietetski knew it was a mistake.

Shah seemed to realize it too. "Nah, you need to keep your space – that's really where we gone wrong. We'd never have been able to afford our place before the Dieback, but we still need somewhere bigger. But we can't afford it. If Doug and I didn't have to spend so much time and effort not getting in each other's hair, maybe we wouldn't resent each other so much, but I *certainly* can't afford to move out." Shah pushed his chair back, signaling that the subject was closed. "I'll get the sludge. You been buying for days now."

As Shah walked to the coffee machine, Marietetski called. "What ya bin doing?"

"Watching Tosada play the morning news. 'Essential we extend human lifespan. Valuable resources being wasted,' blah, blah. All the stuff he rehearsed on us last night."

Marietetski stood looking at the screen. "Guy looks better in the news conferences. Must've airbrushed him. His looks can't have hurt his media career – distinctive, isn't he?"

"Yeah. But looks aren't everything. He knows his stuff and he can talk about it." Shah returned, bearing cups in each hand. "I don't get why a businessman officially specializing in importing luxury spices and taxi-pods from India and renovating and restoring classic second-millennium cars wants to get involved in Tosada's research. Unless he's laundering."

"Maybe we're looking at this wrong." Marietetski chewed his lip. "What if it's not profit behind this? What if it's just personal – he's doing it cause he wants to live forever?"

"Nah," Shah said, ticking off his fingers: "Drugs, prostitution, protection. Guy does nothing but it turns a profit. Don't go sentimentalizing him. He might wear the sharp suits, but he's still lowlife. There's a link somewhere."

"I'm not sentimentalizing anyone, Pete. If Kotian wants to live forever, that's just another form of greed." Marietetski sipped his coffee. "Let's not let Kotian and Tosada distract us. The cap will be chasing us up about the case-solve rate if we're not careful."

"Cleared three this morning: Reunited 'stolen' eyepiece with its owner after it was handed in – left in a cab. Tied fingerprints on a burglary to a juvie released last week. And found Harlan Buffett's uncle in rural Ohio. We'll ship him over there later today. Buffett's uncle isn't happy, but we should get him off our books as soon as possible."

"You finally learning to play the numbers game?"

Shah's refusal to concentrate on easy solves to increase his solve rates was legendary. He shrugged. "Without clearance I can only work the low-priority cases." He wasn't happy, but before the conversation could degenerate into an argument, his new eyepiece chimed. "Hey!" He began a conversation which Marietetski didn't try to follow. Instead the younger man focused on his own work, only looking up at Shah's triumphant "Hah!"

"Good news?" Marietetski said.

"Couple of guys I know moved across to the FBI – or what's left of it. They've agreed to cross-check their databanks on the girl as a favor."

Marietetski stared. "You. Are. Kidding. Me." His voice rose: "Are you *crazy*?"

"Easy, easy, John."

"Easy, nothing!" Marietetski yelled. Heads turned, and he lowered his voice; "You want to get suspended, fine, but you will *not* take me down with you 'cause you haven't got the sense to stay away from a case under IA's control. How many damned alarms you think going off as soon as your buddies look at her files?"

"You seem to have got this the wrong way around, John. They got their own files – they don't need ours."

"Yeah, well." Marietetski calmed slightly. "They can pull our eyepieces any time."

"Only if they got probable cause. Did you know she studied psychology at CCNY too?" He shoved a printout at Marietetski, who ignored it for at least twenty seconds.

When he glanced at it, Marietetski grunted. "My degree's in Criminal Psychology, which at least has practical value. Her degree's in General Psychology. Dilettantism."

"Snob."

"Let's focus on the memory-ripper, Pete."

"OK. What we got?"

"The seven subscriber conglomerates in the Pacific net-havens have – as one – refused to release lists of either their subscribers or their customers. The Swiss have come through, though. I'll give you their list. You can go through them, and match them against purchases – see if there are any downloads that match the various victims that we have on file."

The rest of the morning was spent poring over a customer list. Marietetski pulled up the client's details, while Shah scrutinized each of their purchases, looking to see if any of the clips bore the hallmarks of a rip, or could be tied to their amnesiacs.

It was close to a sweltering noon after hours of pointless, frustrating work when Shah's new eyepiece chimed again. At the same moment Captain van Doorn appeared by their desks. "In my office, Shah – now. You too, Marietetski."

Shah said, "Call you back." He followed the Captain into his office. Van Doorn said, "Close the door behind you," and Shah pushed it shut with his foot.

Van Doorn said without preamble, "You're reinstated."

"Great!" Marietetski punched the air. "What's changed?"

"Seems our friends the Feds were doing a *random audit*," van Doorn said. "Yeah, right, I believe in coincidences like that like I believe in the friggin' Tooth Fairy. They turned up a file on Aurora Debonis, buried beneath the public one. Seems our lady weren't quite such a lady, isn't that right, Shah?"

"Huh?" Marietetski said.

Shah felt his stomach plummet and his face burn. *Jesus, here it comes. Now they know. I can just hear the comments; "Shah so dumb he can't tell a freak from a real woman. Or he so horny he don't care no more."* He stared down at his shoes. "Dunno what you're talking about, sir. Far as I can remember – and it's all a bit hazy – we never got as far as getting her panties off. She made a disgusting suggestion–"

"Yeah, you've had *such* a sheltered upbringing, Shah."

Shah repeated, "She made a suggestion I thought disgusting, *sir*, and it went downhill from there. Shouldn't be surprised though: kinky in one way, kinky in another." He looked up at Marietetski. *You dare make a joke, John, I'll freaking kill ya.*

Marietetski seemed to get the silent message. "So this uh, Aurora was transsexual?" he said. "And the corpse in the morgue is a real girl?"

"Seems so," van Doorn said. "The real Aurora Debonis was – maybe is – *inter*sexual, born with both male and female sexual organs. They used to cut one or other of the extra off, but then 'bout forty, fifty years ago they eased back on that. Decided to let the children choose for themselves. Most go one way or the other, but a few like the best of both worlds." Van Doorn added, "So the attachment said. Feds thought maybe we needed a bit of explanation. Dumb flatfeet like us. Still, it was lucky they was doing a random audit, heh?"

"Sure was, Cap," Shah said levelly, mentally breathing a sigh of relief. *If it weren't for her balls I'd be so damned pleased it weren't her on the slab. Shame, too. She weren't just a looker, she was nice.* Shah couldn't remember the last time a woman with that combination had been interested in him. *Course she was interested, dumbo, she was doing a number on ya.* But he said only, "What now?"

"Get out of my sight is what now. If I find out you had anything to do with this, or you been holding out on me, you'll swing from the nearest lamp post." They turned to go, Shah leading. As Marietetski was following out through the door, van Doorn added, "Course, while it rules out the victim being who we thought, it opens up a whole new set of questions."

Marietetski turned. "Who was the girl?"

"Exactly." Van Doorn added, "No wonder her counsel demanded proof of death, and refused to divulge any information until we confirmed her identity – which we couldn't do 'cause we couldn't raise any next of kin." Van Doorn frowned. "Bigger question is how was someone able to hack into NYPD databanks and change her identity? And why?"

Shah wandered back, filling the doorway, his presence easing Marietetski further into the office, "Maybe my idea it was to fix me up wasn't quite so paranoid. Maybe they hacked into some of the Federal files as well. Did they do a match?"

"That's what set off the klaxons," van Doorn said. "Then they checked deeper. What's this about a fix-up?"

Shah explained his conspiracy theory. Van Doorn frowned. "I'll ignore you talking about it to Marietetski. It's a stupid and unworkable rule. Only some moron in Human Remains could come up with something so half-assed." He thought for a moment. "Not only do we have the case that IA took off us tossed back into our lap, we got an extra one. But you stay the hell away from this. It's a clear conflict of interest to have you investigating a case you're involved with. It's going across to Beckett and Hughes. They'll quarry through every case you've been involved with." The captain took a deep breath. "I'll have them swear out a warrant for Aurora Debonis' arrest for ID fraud."

# XI

The torches and burning crosses flicker and flare in the hot, humid night, casting malevolent shadows that caper on the white walls of your house.

You had thought that the people of the United States had left such practices behind; you've taught for years in your college classes that racism is on the decline – but now you see the stark truth. Civilization is just a wafer-thin veneer over savagery. You've done the best you can, but now you see with despair that it's not enough.

Your hands are tied behind your back by one of the white-cowled mob. "Damn nigra," comes a growl from one of the nearby men, and you know that voice. You don't know the man's name, but you've seen him hanging around on street corners in nearby Charleston, glaring at you as you drive your old hybrid Prius off to the CSU campus, heard him spewing racist filth. Yesterday you waved when he flipped you the bird, and you wonder whether that single act of defiance called their wrath down upon you.

There's been too much talk of End Times lately, too often words like "apocalypse" and "rapture" have been bandied about, but you thought that words were all they were. Armageddon couldn't come to Kiawah Island.

Until the rock through your kitchen window tonight. You raced out with your shotgun in hand, for even a good Baptist has the right to defend himself. But chasing the intruder around to the front of the house, you realized with a stomach-plunging jolt that all of President Obama's good words mean nothing now, when times are hard.

"You kin take a few of us down with you, Perfessor!" one of them shouted. "Or you kin lay that gun down, in which case we might spare your bitch and pups!"

You recognized the technique of dehumanizing the victim, to objectify them by using animal imagery, but didn't know how to talk your way out of it. From the moment when you heard Millie and the children screaming in the house you knew this was no ordinary burglary. You turned, but before you could move white-cowled men moved to cut off your return.

"Put the gun down, Perfessor!" another voice shouted. "We ain't gon' ask nicely a third time!"

You guessed that they want you alive for a purpose. Dead you can't help Millie or the kids, so you tossed the weapon on the ground. Six bullets wouldn't dent the mob's numbers.

As they bind your hands, you see Millie dragged out of the house, while a couple of burly men each carry your struggling, squirming children. "Why?" you shriek, the word sandpapering your throat. "We've been good neighbours, we've done none of you any harm!"

"You speak when you're spoken to, nigra!" A fist slams into your nose.

"These are the end times!" someone bawls. "We should cast them out, the sinners!"

You recognize words like "sinners" and "cast out." Just as Satanism inverts the Christian lexicon, so these people have taken the Lord's words and twisted them to their own ends.

But the phrase implies exile, and for a few moments as they drag you down the street, you hope that you're simply being run out of town. You can cope with that. *Lord, give me the strength to come through this,* you think. *I shouldn't look to horse-trade, but I'll even take a tar and feathering if you let Millie and the children come out of this alive.*

Too late, you realize as they march you around the corner and you see the crosses, two of which already have bodies dangling from them. The men's mouths twist in screams drowned out by the rumbling of the mob.

"Damn nigras, setting' yore-selves up as Gawd Almighty!" The man you belatedly recognize as their leader yells. "Yew and yore Bar-ack Hossein Obama, doing his deals with them OPEC devils to make our country weak!"

"For God's—" A fist punching your mouth ends your protests.

"Yew and yore kind wanna set yorselves up in place of the Almighty with your soft, twisting words, well, you kin suffer what the Lord suffered. He gave his son, yew kin give yores, Perfesser!"

They drag little Barack to the central cross, and you wonder how it could have come to this so quickly. You squirm and struggle, but the hands won't let you look away, for all that you writhe.

As they lift your struggling, yelling son into place, you would give anything to be able to forget what follows.

# XII

## Wednesday

"Wow." Shah took a deep, juddering breath as he unclipped the scanner.

"What was that?" Marietetski said. He hadn't seen the clip, only its effect on Shah.

"That's maybe the oldest clip I've ever seen," Shah said. "It's listed as a burn, but the documentation looked a bit off, so I thought I'd better check it out, especially as some of the properties had the same qualities as a rip. But extreme trauma can do that as well as the actual ripping process. Turns out this guy was one of the earliest victims of the God Wars down in South Carolina."

"Ew." Even now, mention of the Deep South made many New Yorkers – secularists and faith worshippers alike – deeply uneasy.

"Yeah." Shah rubbed his eyes as if that would clean the memory from his head. "Guy was the head of a nice, middle class, well educated, decent black family – who didn't know their place, according to the bigots. So when times got really hard down there and people needed scapegoats, guess what old-time prejudices crawled out of the shadows?"

"Who?"

"Some bastard offspring of the Klan mixed with back-woods evangelists talking up the End Times. Poor bastard saw his son crucified, so when memory rips became available, he went for it. Course, rippings are illegal, so they had to doctor it."

"Anything tying it to other open cases?"

"Nothing obvious. I guess all we can do is slap a sub-poena on the provider to take it down, and red-flag the memory itself so no more sickos can twist off on how it feels to see your family attacked." He looked up. "Hey, Cap." *Amazing how such a big man can move so silent.*

"Got a call from Organized Crime Unit last night," van Doorn said.

"What did they want?"

"There was a little, uh… friction… between some Ko-reans and some Italian kids. Not big enough to interest them, except they've heard whispers that a couple of the Koreans are friends with Sunny Kotian. And that one of the kids had a ripper slapped to his head. Luckily it didn't take properly. Keep your eyes and ears open for whispers of a fragment, will ya?"

"Sure, Boss," Marietetski said.

When van Doorn went Shah said, "You taking it?"

"And get my unsolved pushed up by another one? I thought you were the rebel who doesn't play the num-bers game?"

"I might be a rebel, but I'm not that stupid. I'm not volunteering to take on one that we've got no chance of ever solving."

"I guess we flip for it." Marietetski took a ten yuan piece from his top drawer. "Heads or tails?"

"Let me look at that." Shah's beckoning fingers spi-dered at Marietetski. He caught the coin and looked it over, squinting at both sides. "I'll toss. Heads or tails?"

Marietetski grinned. "You do this most every time. Makes no difference. Heads."

Shah flipped the coin, caught it and stared at it. "Damn!"

They had barely got into the rhythm of checking downloads flagged as 'of interest' by the subroutines when Shah and Marietetski's eyepieces chimed together.

"Gentlemen," said an avatar in each man's screen. Shah recognized the voice, but not the image of a prosperous man of indeterminate race in his mid-thirties. "I'm Stephen Harcourt, counsel for Ms Aurora Debonis."

Shah grinned, then wondered whether his own avatar looked unprofessionally smug, and finally gave up worrying.

"We're not–" Marietetski started to say.

Shah interrupted before he could say *the people you need to talk to:* "Good morning, Mr Harcourt. How can we help?"

"I understand that an arrest warrant's been issued for my client."

Shah thought, *why'd it take so long?* He had a suspicion that something wasn't right about this case. Normally it should have taken only an hour or so.

Harcourt continued, "I'm petitioning the State Legislature to quash the warrant and to slap a confidentiality seal on any potential discussions about her."

"Her?" Shah said, "Don't you mean him, or it?"

Harcourt simply bulldozed on, "My client has not only done nothing wrong–"

"Hang on! Marietetski shouted, "She has false information on her ID data!"

"–but as the victim of a mistake by the NYPD, she is probably due for compensation. As to the supposed offence of providing false information, the Supreme Court agreed in 2042 that in the event of someone put at risk due to their beliefs or their background is entitled to issue a public ID, and a private one." Harcourt paused. "What difference does keeping her gender out of the public eye make? None whatsoever. Your investigation is to catch a killer of a young woman incorrectly identified as my client, not fish for juicy details about her before chatting about them on the web."

"That's offensive," Marietetski said.

"That's happened in the past, Officer. Forgive me wanting to prevent a repeat of it." Harcourt paused. "Any public investigation would be a de facto punishment, taking the very steps that Aurora has sought to avoid – public exposure. Just listen to Officer Shah's Neanderthal comment – 'it', Officer! I'm more an 'it' than she is. You *will* cease this witch hunt immediately." The line went dead.

Their eyepieces chimed again. "In my office," van Doorn said.

When they entered van Doorn was sitting, eyes closed, eyepiece off, pinching the bridge of his nose. Eyes still closed he said, "Judge's chambers called to say the warrant's been quashed. No reasons given. Proceedings took place in camera."

"Crap," Marietetski said.

Shah privately thought, *Just as well we didn't spend too much time on it.* They were already in danger of being blizzarded by cases only tenuously linked to their specialty. But he said instead, "Is she still a material witness? I mean, you don't usually get used as an alias for a murder victim unless you have some connection to the killer or the real victim."

"You prove a link," van Doorn said, opening his eyes and replacing his eyepiece, "you can make a case for subpoenaing her, but it's chicken and egg. How you going to prove it? Get back to your core cases, and forget this one."

The rest of the morning was as enjoyable as quarrying rock; none of the overnight proliferation of new clips seemed to jigsaw into any existing cases, but instead simply created new dockets.

At lunchtime Marietetski said, "Been announced that Federal funding's been withdrawn for Tosada's longevity project. The newsrooms are quoting the government line that the last thing the Earth needs is an immortal population mushrooming exponentially."

Shah grunted, and kept studying the clip he was looking at.

He left early, unable to say why he felt so tired and disillusioned, but on returning home, he found no solace there.

Leslyn and Doug were on the terrace tending the plants, as they often did in the afternoon; below them the commuters' bickerings were far enough away that they blended into one homogenous hum, a mere ghost of the chaos of Shah's younger days.

"Hey," Shah said. "How was today?" The greeting was a formula, abandoned temporarily at the weekend. That alone was an indication of how much Shah's arrest had rocked the equilibrium of the marriage.

"Same as always," Doug said. That too was formula.

"I've got to go," Leslyn said. Shah stared. That *wasn't* formula. Before he could ask what was wrong, Leslyn said, "Your girlfriend was on the newsfeeds today. I assume she was your girlfriend. Unknown blonde fished from harbor still unnamed. No mention of you, and I didn't get a very good look at her when you smuggled her in, in the small hours of Saturday."

"I'll bring her into the bedroom next time and introduce her." As soon as he said it, Shah knew he should just have let it ride. "Sorry."

"I wouldn't have thought she was your type at all," Leslyn said, the acid in her voice shriveling Shah's testicles.

"I'll try to be quieter in future."

"Actually, although you were being sarcastic, introducing us wouldn't have been such a bad idea." Leslyn stalked inside.

It was one of their nights together tonight, but somehow Shah didn't think Leslyn would be in the mood. *She rarely is nowadays.* They had always had an open relationship, and as the years passed, open had become a yawning chasm.

"I'll be back after midnight," Leslyn said in something nearer to her normal tone, giving them both a peck on the forehead as she passed each in turn. "Don't wait up."

"OK," Doug said.

"See you later," Shah added, and flashed her a wan smile.

Leslyn gave him an equally washed-out one in return. "I changed the beds today," she said. It was a peace offering, by her standards.

"Thank you." Shah had given up saying, "You didn't need to do that," or "I was going to do that tonight." Leslyn worked to her own timetable.

When she had left, the men sat in silence for several minutes.

Doug said, "Bad day?"

"They're all bad days at the moment Doug. I get these sideways looks from people at the precinct. They're obviously wondering how true the allegations were. Not everyone, but enough of them to make me wonder what I'm doing there."

"You want a beer? Alcohol free…"

"Yeah, go on, then." Shah sighed. "I dunno, Doug. Things'll get better tomorrow. It has to get better tomorrow, doesn't it?"

Doug returned with two bottles, Shah's non-alcoholic, Doug's whatever locally brewed muck he was currently drinking.

"What the hell was that all about?" Shah wondered aloud, then took a swig. "Leslyn's never been jealous before. She knows they're strictly temp."

"Ever bring home a six-foot supermodel less than half her age before?"

Shah barked a laugh. "Haven't heard that word in years. That's all it's about?" It was unusual for Doug and him to talk about Leslyn. Usually it was him and Les discussing Doug, and he guessed Doug and Les did the same – she acted as messenger for them, bringing them to some sort of consensus when their aging pride wouldn't allow them to talk to each other. Shah had heard that some trinaries and quads had all the partners in bed together, but he and Doug were too old, too hetero and too zipped-up for that.

"Is that all it is?" Shah said, belatedly realizing that he'd interrupted Doug in full flow. *Oops.* "Is it just that Aurora's so much better looking than any of the previous ones?"

"All?" Doug spluttered. "Is that *all*?"

"Les has never been the jealous type before, and she was the one who opened that Pandora's Box."

"What? So you're getting her back for wanting more than just you? Shah, you are such a jackass. You left her on her own for days, weeks at a time, and instead of dumping you, she tries to compromise by opening out the relationship. So you decide to punish her?"

"That wasn't what I meant! Dammit, Doug, stop twisting everything! She never discussed opening it out beforehand!"

Doug didn't answer but went inside for another beer, and in disgust, Shah stomped out.

Shah had always found that walking eased his frustrations, like opening a safety valve on a pressure cooker. His walk downtown took him past the mosque near the Meatpacking District. On an impulse he stepped inside, into coolness and shade, and away from the stink of ruptured sewers tainting the air outside. Dozens of male heads were bowed in the *Asr*, pre-dusk prayer and the Imam's voice called out the *Azan*, the call to prayer for the sluggards.

Afterwards Shah hung around, still troubled by his need to talk about Aurora to someone who might understand what was bothering him.

The Imam who approached Shah with a "Good evening" was younger than Shah's son Rex, but had the dignity of a man fully aware of his responsibility. Shah was surprised to see that he was almost clean-shaven. "Beards out of fashion this season?"

The Imam smiled slightly. "I find it uncomfortable – itching constantly. You are a stranger, but your accent is local."

"I– I guess, I'm sort of lapsed."

"We are of course pleased to see you. Have you come for a reason?"

"I guess, I'm–" Shah stopped. "I'll try again," he said. "I need to talk to someone who'll understand me." Slowly, hesitantly, then with greater fluency as he got into his story, Shah told the Imam about the events of Friday night and Saturday morning.

"So why have you come?" The Imam said. "For *Tawbah*?"

"Repentance?" Shah guessed, dredging his memories of the Qur'an.

"Not exactly. It refers to the act of leaving what God has prohibited and returning to what He has commanded. In this case, a return to rightful sex – within marriage, perhaps – from this sort of experience?"

"This sort of experience? So she's what… an abomination?"

"Not at all," the Imam said with a chuckle. "I meant casual sex, rather than her gender. Hard to believe perhaps, but there are Islamic laws for intersexuals."

Shah lifted an eyebrow.

The Imam continued, "Intersexuals are called *khuntsa* in Islam, and have their own rituals and rules which are completely different from those applying to women and the *ikhwan* applying to men."

"Hang on," Shah said. "You're saying that there are three genders in Islam?"

"Effectively," the Imam said with a smile. "*Khuntsa*, akhwat, and ikhwan – Intersexual, female, and male. *Khuntsa* are allowed to marry either men or women. They're allowed to live as women or men, but we suggest that they wear clothes that are 'in-between'. During prayers, a *khuntsa* prays between the males and the females. A *khuntsa* has most of the obligations of males and most of the obligations of women – and all of the rights of both."

"Holy crap," Shah breathed. He added hurriedly, "Sorry, sorry."

The Imam raised a *don't worry* hand. "The Prophet Muhammad created the *khuntsa* concept because in his life an intersexual – perhaps even a true hermaphrodite – lived in a nearby village. Shee-hee wished to join Islam, but was confused over the rules. The Prophet then told hir all the rules Shee-hee needed to be a good Muslim intersexual."

Shah exhaled.

The Imam nodded a few times. "There were many transsexuals in Malaysia at one time," he said. "We have had to learn to address the question without alienating our people." He caught Shah's look of surprise and smiled. "Food for thought?"

"Absolutely," Shah said. "I still couldn't ever... you know, with hir or whatever the term is... but I feel bad for treating her so rough. I thought I'd get fire and rage from you over the whole situation."

"Only for the disrespectful way you treated your partner," the Imam said. Now Shah looked at him, he did look Malaysian or from some other part of South East Asia. *Probably a refugee from the Pan-Islamic purges, or the Asian Wars or something.* Shah made himself concentrate. "Islam wasn't always such a repressive, patriarchal religion," the Imam said. "It's been hijacked, as have so many things, by intellectual thugs."

"Unfortunate choice of phrase," Shah said. "But thank you... *Pedar.*" It still seemed odd calling a man younger than Rex, "Father", but Shah guessed he was out of practice at dealing with clerics.

"May the peace of Allah be with you at all times," the Imam said with a smile, as if reading Shah's mind.

# XIII

**Thursday**

"Come on." Shah pushed back his chair. "Let's go kick some doors in, roust some perps, shake down the bad guys."

Marietetski stared at him. "You been drinking too much coffee? Or just stir crazy?"

"Cabin fever. Two more pointless days of looking at downloads, and I have had enough. My ass is spreading like lava down a mountainside."

"Before we go," Marietetski held up a hand. "Look at this."

Shah ambled around the desk, narrowly missing dislodging a small hill of prints.

Marietetski said, "I've found this on a random trawl. It's a rip."

"It" featured fists pounding into a young woman's face on Marietetski's screen. Shah felt his stomach lurch. For a moment he'd thought that the woman was her, but though the face was bruised – and even more bruised as by the time the fist thudded into her face for the tenth, twentieth, thirtieth time – it wasn't Aurora.

"Cap," Marietetski said into his piece, "I'm sending you a clip. I reckon it's the dead girl. You can see that the hand clearly isn't Shah's. It looks… I hesitate to say Indian, but it sure isn't Caucasian – say Asian or mulatto. Yeah, Shah's going to be watching this a *lot* today." He grinned as he cut the connection. "Cap says to take the damn thing apart."

Shah did:

It was dark in the clip, but Shah got a sense of space. A *warehouse*? he thought. The woman had done something wrong, but either she wasn't thinking about it, or she genuinely didn't know, or most likely that part had been cut out. Now someone was on top of her, in her, hurting her. As she always did when she was working, she blanked her mind – *think of nothing, or* – then the clipped memory jumped to the fist smashing into her mouth, the sudden taste of blood, the adrenaline spike of fear, but she couldn't move, although she tried to wriggle out from underneath him. The memory jumped again, and she was crying and begging for mercy from lips already swelling with bruising. Her sobbing almost – but not quite – drowned out her assailant's ragged breathing. *Jump.* "–w," another voice said, higher pitched than the first, before everything went dark for the last time.

Shah frowned. He played it again, reaching the point at which Marietetski had shown him the clip; one hand holding her head in place while the other fist landed blow after slow metronomic blow, gradually speeding up into what ended as a frenzy of fists, the whiff of cologne or something on them. Ragged breathing almost matching hers as it degenerated into sobs. Fists slowing then stopping, and as the sense of the world faded with oncoming unconsciousness, the sting of someone clipping a probe to the victim's scalp, and simultaneously hands wrapping around her windpipe. The girl was too beaten down to struggle for more than a moment – even as her fingers dug into her killer's gloved hands, the world slipped away...

Shah broke the connection. "I can't get into the sense of this like I could with an un-chopped memory. The discontinuity keeps throwing me out."

"What *did* you get?"

"There were two of them at least. Normally memories from immediately pre-death involve a fractional gap as the killer pauses to fit the probe before delivering the kill. This time they were simultaneous."

"Not even an almost imperceptible gap? Some of these guys are very practiced. The gap can be tiny."

"No, nor was anything chopped to reduce the gap. The two happened together. I'm going back under." Shah ran it again, this time concentrating on smells; the cologne, or whatever it was. Stale dust. A metallic smell. Water. Shah stopped it, and thought. He restarted it. *River water, that's the smell – mud.* A heavy tang, of metal. *Storage drums? Or something industrial?*

Shah ran and reran the memory, each time concentrating on a different sense; any taste was all but obliterated by blood, and the fear that blotted out almost everything else. It was hard to get past the forebrain and the terror, knowing that she was in trouble, and that she was going to die. But below the limits of conscious thought and what the killers had obliterated, there were a few sensory clues. Occasional faint voices, of people passing nearby. The feel of rough clothing against her skin. The bulk of the man, pressing down on her, his cock inside her, the taste of his salt sweat where her lips inadvertently brushed his skin.

"They've cut it about pretty badly," Shah said when he finally conceded he could wring no more meaning from the clip. "But we got a few pointers." He blinked widely, trying to refocus on the here-and-now, the taste of water suddenly unfamiliar in his mouth. Deep probing always made the real world strange on re-emergence. He outlined what little he'd gleaned from the memory, allowing a pause between each point to allow Marietetski to recite it loudly and clearly into the vocal function of his eyepiece and from there into an official note to be circulated to all precincts.

"While you were under," Marietetski said when they had finished, "a call for you was routed through to me: the FBI. An unrelated investigation has turned up something. An NYPD data code tester who admitted to falsifying information. She had access to all the files, including those concerning the dead girl."

"Yes!" Shah hissed, feeling the exultation of the hunt for the first time in a long while.

"She was working the morning that body was found, and while she's erased a lot of her traces there's enough to show a correlation." Marietetski paused. "Trouble is, she was killed in a prison riot before she could be turned."

Shah groaned. "Coincidence?"

"Maybe – maybe not. It's a start, anyway. More to the point, it's looking like it may be more appropriate to pass it over to Organized Crime Division."

*That's supposed to make me feel better?* Shah thought. Marietetski was always doing this, taking the aloof, disinterested view, what was right for the good of the whole NYPD and the Justice system, rather than thinking about actually solving the case that they'd spent days or weeks on. Shah knew his colleague's game.

Marietetski was more interested in furthering his damn career by being viewed as a 'team' player, one who could suborn his personal ambition to the lofty ideals of the whole system, whereas what he was really doing was using those ideals in an apparently disinterested way.

"That's good," Shah said, but Marietetski seemed to miss the sarcasm.

It took the shine off of what could have been a very good day, so Shah finished early. He strolled across to the Bellwether Institute and gave his name to the same receptionist who had been on before. "The last day of my shift pattern," the man said in response to Shah's pleasantries. "I get a couple of days off then I go on onto a block of nights." He pulled a face to show what he thought of nights. His eyepiece chimed. "He'll be down in five minutes."

It was more like ten, and when Tosada did appear, he had company.

"Officer Shah," Kotian said. "What a surprise!"

"We have some surprising mutual acquaintances, Abhijit." Tosada's explanation to Kotian sounded more than a little defensive.

Shah bared his teeth in what he hoped looked like a friendly grin.

"You can never have too many acquaintances, Ero," Kotian replied. The slight lilt only enhanced the rich creaminess of his voice with its hint of upper-class Britishness – or so it seemed to Shah, who had never actually met a Brit.

"Except when bad things happen to them," Shah said, provoked despite himself.

"Officer Shah," Kotian waved a beringed finger, and as they stepped closer, Shah caught a waft of expensive aftershave, and he thought a hint of spices, cloves, cinnamon and garlic. "My lawyer is continuously having this conversation with you: I have a huge network of people, and these people don't just work for me – I am only one of many businessmen who subcontract. The days of tycoons behaving like European medieval lords have long passed us by. This is the Third Millennium, after all. Please do not make me call my lawyer again to protest harassment against your insinuations."

"Apologies, Mr Kotian. I actually came to see Professor Tosada. I can wait, though."

"I am just going anyway," Kotian said. "Perhaps one day we can have a talk without us being some sort of adversaries. We have a common background, both coming from Asia. Isfahan and Bangalore are closer than New York and Seattle, after all." He was a few centimeters taller than Shah, but seemed to look down from a greater height than that. Shah had the impression his princely opponent had got through life on looks and charm, especially as he grew older.

"Maybe." Shah stepped away as Tosada and Kotian said their goodbyes.

When Kotian had gone Tosada waggled a finger in reproach. "Please don't embarrass me like that again, Pervez."

"Apologies, Erokij," Shah said. "I came to ask you a few questions, but if you feel that it's not possible…"

"Absolutely not!" Tosada looked a little sheepish. "He admits that he sailed close to the wind, especially when he was younger, but now he wants to repay his debt to society for making him wealthy." Tosada hesitated. "He's one of several wealthy people I've approached to keep funding going, ever since our government indicated they intended to prioritize other works. He's agreed to underwrite the research, in return for receiving any benefits."

*In other words, he wants to go legit,* Shah thought but said nothing.

"But I am in no way beholden to him," Tosada continued. "Ask your questions."

Shah transmitted a picture of Aurora from his eyepiece to Tosada's. "You ever seen this woman before?"

Tosada squinted in concentration. "I've think that I've seen her with Abhijit. One of his many female... acquaintances."

"You know her name?" Shah fought not to appear too eager. He didn't want to be accused of leading a witness.

"I think that it's something like... Aurora. Yes, that's it."

First thing next morning Shah told Marietetski and van Doorn about the conversation, replaying it to their eyepieces.

Van Doorn nodded approval. "You did well."

Shah said. "Do we call Kotian's lawyer for a little chat?"

"Not yet," van Doorn said. "He'll just admit that he knows her, but they were just friends, yadda yadda. Let's keep this ace up our sleeve for the moment." He turned and picked up a print. "Meanwhile, here's something else for you."

Shah and Marietetski stepped out onto the rooftop and stared across the rows and rows of algae growing in water-filled trays, covering the whole roof.

Shah took a deep breath. "That climb was one floor too many."

"You just out of breath, old man," Marietetski said with a grin. He was breathing hard as well. "Though it's a shame that when they picked a disused building, they couldn't have picked one with a few less floors to climb up." He wrinkled his nose. "Jeez, it stinks up here. Like sewage crossed with... I dunno. Whatever it is, it reeks man."

"Don't knock it – without this stuff, we'd have no bulking out of protein burgers."

"That's supposed to make me feel better about it?" Marietetski hadn't had a protein burger since he was eight. No matter how poor he ever got, he'd find the money for real food, somehow.

"Can I help you, officers?" called an overalled worker who walked toward them.

"Mr Singh, isn't it?" Shah said, recognizing the algae-farm's owner, a small dark-skinned man from Goa. "How ya doing, sir? Been years since I seen you."

"I'm well, officers, but aren't you a long way from home out here in the wilds?" Singh said with a smile that didn't reach his eyes.

"Queens is hardly Outer Mongolia," Marietetski muttered.

"Your farm suffered several attacks of vandalism earlier in the year." Shah transmitted a picture of a young man. "Ever seen this guy?"

Singh shook his head.

"Let me remind you," Marietetski said. "He was seen around here, picked up on surveillance cameras. Then the attacks mysteriously stop, and this guy shows up as a walking vegetable. Who did you pay off?"

"No one."

*Singh looks scared.* "Was it this man?" Shah sent a picture of Sunny Kotian

Singh's eyes widened. "I've… I've never seen him before," he gasped.

Shah sent a picture of Kotian senior, and Singh shook his head again. "They're your countrymen, at least compared to black half-Polacks like my partner here," Shah said. "You going to tell me you don't recognize important people in your community?"

"Oh… yes," said Singh weakly. "I know them distantly, now I think of it."

"Mr Singh, we're going to keep digging," Marietetski said. "If we find you're paying protection money to these guys, you're going to need another sort of protection… from us. But if you were to recall anything, let's put it this way, he's never going to be in a position to threaten you again. We'll protect you, Mr Singh."

Singh shook his head. "I don't remember anything."

# XIV

"Take it," Myleene says, a beatific smile lighting up her drab features. A cold sore has split and a spot of blood slowly distends, creeping down her face. Four of the five other people in the suburban lounge have similarly blissful smiles, as they lie back in the raggedy chairs cluttering the room.

You envy her such happiness, even if most of it is from the weed she's smoking that – despite the home-made joss sticks burned to mask its odor – is stinking the room out. Even after she comes down, Myleene will no longer be the semi-suicidal fourteen year-old of last year. She's achieved a measure of peace that you can only dream about.

If you could only pluck up the courage…

Jamie is the only person in the room without that stoner smile, but he's dispensing the happiness, not receiving it. He takes the probe, a clunky foot-long square box that's almost antique compared to the latest ones, and places it on one side of Myleene's shaven head, just below the waxed coxcomb that's all that's left of her once-beautiful hair. "Sorry, babe." His Brooklyn accent is strange to hear so far out here on the far end of Long

Island. "This is going to hurt; there's no analgesic left in the tank." Later models have bigger tanks and use smaller doses, but even they run out and bootleg refills are all but impossible to get since the Dieback. "What do you want to lose?"

"Just pick a memory at random." Myleene closes her eyes.

When Jamie's done she opens them again and stares at you. "Hey, beautiful." You never guessed your oldest friend had sapphic tendencies before, but at least it's a connection now she doesn't know you, so you don't mind too much.

Loving her, being loved by her, would be a way of forgetting Bradley.

The door bangs open, and a black guy enters. He's shaven-headed, his skull scarred with the repeated nicks and cuts of the regular user. He doesn't meet your eyes.

"Hey, Bradley, you got it?" Jamie says.

The black guy nods. "What she doin' here?"

His disapproval pierces even your misery. "*She* has a name, Bradley." Your voice wavers. You shut your eyes. He's already told you that crying women turn him off, so he mustn't see your tears, or whatever faint chance you have would be gone.

When you open them the man you love has gone again, his mystery delivery complete.

"You sure you want to join us?" Jamie says. "Ripping away parts of your memory is illegal. You – deep down you – knows it's fundamentally wrong so it has your nerve endings send out pain signals throughout your body."

"You do it, don't you?" You don't mean to sound so sullen, but the words are said now.

"I retain more of my memories than the others," Jamie says, "That's the price of being the priest. It's a sacrifice, rather than a short cut to Nirvana. But I couldn't tell you anything about me. Even my name may not be my name." He shrugs. "That's not what I'm asking you, Roxanne. Are you sure about this? We can't replace your memories once they're ripped."

This new, intense Jamie with the serious face and the intent eyes is so unlike the happy, laid-back tripper you've grown to like over the last few weeks that you wonder whether someone's taken him over. Or maybe this is the real Jamie, and the other a mask.

Perhaps this is a test. You think of Bradley, the smiling hooded-eyed guy you used to see from time to time, clearly checking you out, making small talk; but then you think of after you'd made it with him, his sudden disinterest, even contempt. Do you really want to carry this around forever? Would a lifetime of misery and remembrance be better than joining the Sisters of Lethe?

"I'm sure," you say.

And happy, laid-back Jamie is back. He smiles and gives you a wink. "Then I'll do you after I've taken care of Myleene."

# XV

Shah stood at the coffee machine, staring into space.

"You OK?" A young man asked.

Shah dragged himself back to the present. A uniformed officer, five o'clock stubble already casting a shadow over youthful features, watched him intently.

"I'm OK," Shah said. "Just daydreaming." He searched his memory – more and more new faces, it seemed. "Nikolides, isn't it?"

"That's it. Just transferred in from the 73rd."

"Nice to meet you." Shah waved him forward. "Sorry to hold you up."

"De nada. Finish what you're doing. I got ten gazillion reports to write up back at my desk, so a couple minutes away isn't going to hurt."

"I know the feeling." Shah took Marietetski's coffee and punched the code for his own.

"Hope you don't mind me saying this, but just then you looked like you wanted to tear someone's throat out." Nikolides laughed nervously, but he seemed genuinely concerned.

"Sometimes the job gets to you." Shah took his own cup.

Back at his desk he passed Marietetski his cup.

"That last clip really got to you, didn't it?" Frown lines creased Marietetski's forehead. "Sure you're not overdoing it? Regs say you can take longer breaks if you need to."

"Nah, it's OK." Shah sighed. "For all that I live through kilo-hours of other people's lives – good stuff, but mostly the garbage – occasionally there's a clip that gets to me. A fifteen year old taking the chemical equivalent of a parmesan-scraper to her brain and cutting out bits of her life because she's depressed." He sighed. "Did Perveza feel like that?"

"Your daughter's a grown woman, Pete," Marietetski said. "Don't beat yourself up about things you can't do anything about."

"Thanks, Confucius."

"That's more like the grouchy old bastard I have to put up with every day. Anything useful on the clip?"

"Bradley!" Shah slipped his eyepiece on. After he'd ripped the scanner from his head and thrown it onto the desk, he'd forgotten it while fetching coffees. "There was a kid called Bradley. He looks familiar." He groaned. "This means having to go through thousands of mugshots."

Marietetski reached across, hooked his fingertips around the scanner's frame. "Why don't I look at the clip? I may not have your analytical talent, but I can remember a face well enough to look through half the rogue's gallery – we'll split the work."

"Good idea."

"I have them occasionally."

"Yeah." Shah desperately tried to think of a comeback.

"I love it when your face says you want to put me

down, and you can't come up with something. " Marietetski laughed. "Who needs neuro-kits when your face is an open book?"

"Swing on this." Shah gave Marietetski the finger, but his partner was already under the hood.

They walked from the subway to Kotian's garage on West 59th Street. Marietetski said, "You heard the Islanders lost last night to Ottawa? No Stanley Cup for them after all."

"Good," Shah said absently, his thoughts elsewhere. "Only thing worse than an Islanders fan is a smug Islanders fan. Better the Senators win it than those bastards." He was silent for a moment. "Do you know," he voiced what he'd been thinking about before Marietetski's interruption, "that when I started in the NYPD, my whole working life revolved around a few blocks?"

"Yeah, but they had steam engines and sailing ships then."

"Oh, ver-ee fun-nee, junior. Gimme a second while I hold my aching sides."

They jay-walked between pedicabs.

Shah said, "I suppose the good thing is that crime's got just as disorganized as everything else."

"That's supposed to make me feel better?"

"You saw the stuff I did as a rookie it would. Not everything was better in the Good Old Days. Weird thing is, sometimes the tougher life gets, the fewer crimes get committed."

"More likely the fewer get reported," Marietetski said. "People just take care of it themselves."

Shah didn't seem to hear Marietetski. "Kotian's the first sign that criminals are getting organized again."

They walked in silence for a minute or two. Shah said, "Do you think that we obsess about Kotian?"

"No more than we have to," Marietetski said. "Every precinct has a key case, from which loads of smaller stuff radiates out. In ours Kotian's a key case on his own, because he mostly falls into our geography, and we're familiar with him. Used to be called Project Management, according to the Organizational Theory course." He shook his fist at a pedicab that cut across and nearly mowed him down, and shouted "Asshole!" before turning back to Shah: "NYPD finally got wise to the crims using geographical and organizational boundaries to their advantage, and restructured."

"But…" Shah's hands articulated his frustration. "We waste hours wading through crap. I know, we've always wasted time on pointless exercises. But it's getting worse, not better."

"That's just you nostalgia-cizing the past." Marietetski stiffened. "You see that?"

"What?" Shah pulled a face. "I didn't see anything."

"A flash of something in the sun – I could've sworn I saw one of the Enhanced, walking through – nah, couldn't be. Not in Manhattan."

"Where's the Californian Consulate?"

Marietetski thought. "It's out in the boonies, somewhere. They only come in for the occasional UN meeting, stuff like that."

Shah laughed mirthlessly. "That pretty much sums the UN up. You been working too hard John, if you think that one of Homo Superior Californius is going to pitch up here."

"If they even exist."

"Oh, they exist. Just not the supermen of pop-fiction. Leslyn toyed with upgrading a few years ago."

Marietetski's eyes threatened to pop out. "You are kidding."

Shah shook his head. "About the only time we've had a major row. She needed me to help pay for it, and I refused flat out. It was just after she washed her hands of Perveza. Rex had already moved out on his climb of the corporate ladder. She was at home with time on her hands... anyway, she parked the idea when she saw how opposed I was to it. Brought Doug into the marriage instead.

"Like we'd better park this discussion for now." They turned a corner onto an open lot. "Here we are – Kotian's Klassic Kars. Oh, how I hate that spelling."

"You're a snob," Marietetski said. "Would you look at those stinkpots?"

"American engineering at its finest." Shah didn't see the point in telling his partner that the stinkpot in the showroom was a 1965 Ford Mustang. *It'd be wasted on him.*

"American gluttony, more like. Things like that poisoned the planet. Surely they must have seen that, even a century ago? How could they not?"

"It's never that clear, John. We been in denial about what we was doing, even though people been prophecisizing doom since – what – a hunnerd years ago?" He exhaled. "When I was your age, scientists was busy telling us that when the gas ran out society'd fall off a cliff. We didn't, though prices went into orbit."

"Some folks can still afford what there is, Pete. Like this piece of work."

"And we found other ways to run cars, not as efficient, maybe, but still... Before that some guy called Malthus said we'd all starve to death. We're hungry but still here, though–"

A heavily built young man in a well-tailored suit stepped out of the back office, *awkward and shambling for all the flash suit, with none of his father's grace,* Shah thought. The young man stumbled over a box and cursed. "Rupa, get this box cleared out of the way," he bellowed into the office. "Before someone breaks their neck."

"Here's Kotian's brat," Marietetski muttered.

"Gentlemen!" Sunny called. Then the smile slipped. "Oh, it's you. What do you want?"

"Just passing by, Sunny," Marietetski said.

"It's *Mr* Kotian to you," Sunny said. "I pay your wages, remember?" His eyes narrowed still further. "Why don't you piss off, instead of harassing respectable businessmen like Singh and me?"

"So Singh's been whining?" Marietetski grinned. "Interesting."

Shah imagined he could almost hear the thud of Sunny's palm mentally slapping his forehead. "Bradley still working here, Mr Kotian?"

"Who?"

"Bradley Schwartz, Mr Kotian. Mechanic of yours. I've seen him working here."

"I'm supposed to remember every grease monkey that works for me?" Sunny turned and bellowed, "Rupa!"

An Asian woman appeared in the doorway. "Yes, Mr Kotian?" She would have been pretty if she hadn't looked so tired. *I guess working for Sunny has that effect.*

"Bradley Schwartz. Does he work for us?"

Rupa vanished.

"You don't want to know why we want to talk to him?" Marietetski said.

"It'll be one of your memory-ripper conspiracies,"

Sunny said. "It usually is."

"A man who robs his victims of their memories, and sells them through the Pacific net-havens to subscribers interested in living vicariously. That's a real conspiracy, huh?"

"So you say," Sunny snapped.

"The conspiracy is that the trail keeps leading us back to your circle," Marietetski said. "Victims or witnesses all seem to have passed through your network. We see them on the memory rips, in the background."

"So you claim."

"Probability doesn't lie," Shah said.

"I've had enough of this." Sunny pressed a switch and, as the showroom doors slid open, he strode across to the Thunderbird.

"So much for energy conservation," Marietetski said.

Sunny snorted. "Such words are the bleating of sheep. I might have guessed *you'd* be one of them." He gunned the engine and drove off.

Marietetski said, "There goes a man who earns his income from his father's empire of drugs, prostitution and money-laundering. Yet I find that more forgivable than that *damned* heap of junk."

Rupa reappeared a couple of minutes later. "Mr Kotian let him go four weeks ago," she said. "We have an address, if that helps." She read it out.

Marietetski checked that it was the same as they already had. He nodded. "Thanks," he said as she strode across to the switch and closed the doors.

"Come on, John. Let's go shake Papa's tree. See if anything falls out."

"You don't think they're going to be that dumb?"

Shah grinned. "No, but it'll make me feel better."

• • • •

"Mr Kotian," Shah said. "You know this lady?" He sent a picture to Kotian's eyepiece.

A few feet away Marietetski wrinkled his nose at the overpowering aroma of spices.

"Aurora," Kotian said. "She's kept me company sometimes. Is she in trouble?"

"She's missing," Shah said.

"Really?"

"Really," Shah said.

Kotian's eyes narrowed. "You're suggesting that I've done... what?" When no one answered, Kotian said, "If you have some evidence, charge me. If you don't, get off my property and stop wasting my time."

"We'll leave, Mr Kotian," Shah said. "But we'll return. Be sure of that."

# XVI

The Pacific fog is finally clearing the tops of the pines, firs and cedars, and the sun is breaking through. A chill westerly from Asia puckers the flesh on your thighs. It's been three days since you slept indoors – this part of rural Oregon is sparsely populated. You probably stink, but there's no one around to smell it.

You've been walking since first light and the blisters on your feet have split already, but you've almost reached the top of the hill and if you keep going, you might actually see your destination.

You allow your mind to go blank, lifting one foot, then the other. Trudge. Trudge. Ignore the squelch of blood and pus. Feel the sun on your face. Into the vacuum of your thoughts comes the memory of Old Man Button's voice, from one of his endless history lectures: "*We always try to reduce the world to simplicity. Think of those old films where the people of the future wore shiny silver suits. As if the whole world could ever be reduced to homogeneity. A time-traveler from the twen-cen to one part of our world would think, 'Wow! All these people and their clever devices!' If they visited another part, they might think the locals were savages.*" He sighs. "*But given that one*

*function of history is to over-simplify the past so we can
understand it, think this of your parent's generation; as the
oil began to run out, humanity was at its technological apex.
Think how things might be different had they managed to eke
out five more years' progress before we had to ration what oil
was left. Think how it would be if we could spend our time
advancing our civilization instead of – as we so often must –
merely keeping things working. To a large extent we haven't
stopped inventing, just stopped making new things, especially
those that rely on petrochemicals."*

Finally, the brow of the hill is in sight. You see a
rusting green sign that says "Siskiyou Mountain
Summit" and beneath it, "Elev. 4310 ft."

The answer to his rhetorical question is on the other
side of the summit, a mile to south – the California
Wall. Rumor has it that it's impassable, but there are
other rumors, that there are gaps in the wall.

You have to take the chance. North of Jefferson it's
over four hundred miles to Seattle, and the tales of
gold-paved streets in San Francisco and Los Angeles
make it no contest. You were always headed for
California the minute your mom's new friend Vern put
a meaty hand on your leg. It just took a few years for it
to become clear.

Trudge. Step. Trudge. Step.

Finally, there it is. The ground starts to slope
downwards. It's a mile to the state line.

There's the Wall, looming out of the fog.

It has to be at least a half a kilometer high, concave,
a beige concrete line scarring the entire width of the
valley ahead of you, running from the Pacific around
California's state line, implacable in its purpose.

You make out what looks like a township at its base.
Hitching your bag strap higher on your shoulder, you

start walking with renewed purpose and the faintest of hopes. Maybe you can work your way to an upgrade, become a cyborg – if they exist – serving the Upload Nation as an interface with the world of the flesh.

Your hopes fade as you approach, slowly, your speed decreasing with every weary step. The township is simply a ragged band of canvas tents leaning against the base of the wall, most of them with the fabric rotting away.

You sit down on the tarmac, and give way to despair.

# XVII

## Saturday

"Snow?" Shah muttered as they emerged from the betting shop. "What the hell is this? Snow in late May – what happened to the climate getting warmer?"

"That was last week's prediction," Marietetski said. "This week's is the Gulf Stream'll switch off, like they thought years ago." He snorted. "It'll be something else next week."

Shah might as well have not heard him. "Where did this come from? It weren't snowing when we set out."

"Climate change," Marietetski turned up the collar on his coat, but making no more effort than Shah to leave the comparative shelter of the awning. "Don't you just love it?"

"Especially when – as far as you're concerned – you just been in California in the summer, earlier this morning." Shah glanced at Marietetski. "Did ya study that clip?"

Until now, Marietetski had tended to concentrate on phone work and liaising with other departments – one of the reasons his solve rate was so much better than Shah's. He didn't solve cases, but moved them on. But ever since Shah's arrest Marietetski seemed to have a new perspective on clips, as if having to study them had made him realize how difficult a job Shah's was, and he carefully studied each download after Shah had been over it.

"Yeah, I had a look. No dates, no times, no signs of building work to give it a date–" Marietetski just caught Shah's triumphant grin and added hastily, "except that the building of the California wall wasn't until…" he checked his piece. "2034."

"Good man. You're improving. Sherlock Holmes used to say about Watson, 'You see but you do not observe,' and that's what a lot of download work is. Observation." Shah added, "Interesting memory of her teacher."

"The one that said that our grandfathers were at the technologial apex?" Marietetski said. "Pfui."

"Pfui yourself. You've seen the clips of thirty, forty years ago. How many more people there were, how everyone had foreign holidays, drove cars. Christ, we got to sign a car out the pool for any long distances, and walk or subway everywhere else."

"That's just conspicuous consumption, that's not clever," Marietetski said. "Did they have memory burns? Eyepieces? Look at the prosthetics available to those who want 'em; plus whatever's happening in California."

"Yeah, exactly – whatever in California's case. Eyepieces? Just a fancier version of an eyepod or whatever it was came before it. Memory downloads was the last great advance, and that's only a side effect."

"Of what?" Marietetski said. "We got twenty times the access to information that my grandpa had."

"But he had fifty, a hundred times what his grandpa had. If Homeland Security hadn't been looking for a better way to get info, we'd never have had 'pieces at all. It isn't the first time The Man's developed something that the rest of us found a better use for."

"Nah, Pete, we was always going to end up with something hands-free. And if it weren't for the Dieback and then the oil crash, we'd have much more stuff–"

"That's my point, John! We got so far, and then ran out of materials – not intelligence – to develop new technology. Most of our research now is to work out how we can stretch the lifetimes of stuff that's already built, or making things work without reliance on petrochem, not inventing new things."

"Come on, man! You can't say we're sliding back to barbarism? That's bull!"

"Not yet. We're cleverer than ever at stretching our resources, but we got less of 'em, and what we have are owned by fewer and fewer people. But unless something changes, unless California takes down the walls, or the Pan-Asians or Pan-Islamists make a *real* go of space exploration, unless *something* changes, we could be about a generation away from falling back to maybe something like a Pre-Industrial Age."

Marietetski snorted, clearly unconvinced.

Meanwhile, Shah peered up at the leaden sky. He sighed. "Not the tiniest bit of blue. This isn't going to pass over anytime soon." He shivered in the bitter wind. "Why don't we randomly audit a deli?"

Marietetski's shoulders shook as he blew on his hands. "Van Doorn will chew us a new windpipe."

"If he finds out."

"He could find out anytime he wants, just by downloading your eyepiece."

"OK, we'll compromise," Shah said. "We won't walk back yet." Earlier that morning a crash on the line had gridlocked the subway system, and the streets were mysteriously empty of pedicabs, while neither man could afford a mechanized cab. "But we'll remember some questions we forgot to ask Forry earlier." He jerked his thumb at the betting shop.

Marietetski shook his head. "Just bite down on it." He set off, followed by Shah.

The snow was just heavy enough to stick, which suited Shah. He hated it when the stuff turned to slush, which it doubtless would as soon as the flurry passed over – he could now glimpse the first tiny patches of blue in the cloud's wake.

Marietetski was waiting for him at the corner, but the younger man swiveled from side to side, impatiently looking to see if the street was clear. "Was there anything else on that California clip?"

"Nothing useful," Shah said as he caught up, and they crossed gingerly. "Sturgeon's Law applies."

"Who?"

Shah said, "This guy decided that ninety per cent of everything was crap." He laughed. "He must have worked for NYPD. This clip was one of the ninety per cent. It isn't that old, but there must be something else washing around, 'cause there's nothing there to indicate where the ripping happened, or who did it."

"So another dead end?"

"Sturgeon's Law certainly applies to our caseload."

They walked in companionable silence for several minutes, until they neared the end of the next block and the next crossing. Marietetski checked his watch. "You realize we aren't going to be back for shift end?"

"You go straight home, John. I'll finish up some things."

"Pete, you aren't going to go treading on anyone's toes, are you?"

"What do you mean?"

Marietetski looked troubled. "Showing Aurora's picture to Kotian, when it's Hughes and Beckett's case."

"Oh, I was just cranking him up, John. No, I'm going back to the office. Paperwork seems strangely appealing compared to going home."

"That good?" Marietetski said.

Shah shrugged. "Leslyn and I had a row last night. Something I should have done, and hadn't. I was getting to it, but she never believes it's next on my to-do list. Said I treat her like a housekeeper, which is crap. Just that if I don't do it when she wants it done, it's proof positive I was never going to do it."

"Oh," Marietetski mouthed.

"Needless to say The Chocolate Fireguard backed her up."

Marietetski grinned. "Some day I got to meet this guy, see if he's as big a penis-head as you make out."

"Oh, trust me. I talk him up – he's worse than I make out. Less he knows about something, the longer he can lecture you 'bout it."

They crossed another intersection. Marietetski said, "Why don't y'all come round for dinner? There'll only be three of us, 'cause Neil's working tonight. But that's good, evens the numbers up."

"What, bring McCoy? You really are a sucker for punishment."

"Go on," Marietetski said. "Be brave. Bring him round."

Shah made the call, and the others' avatars popped up split screen in his eyepiece. "Hey, we got a dinner invite, if you have no previous plans."

Shah guessed the pause was while they looked at each other. "OK," they said together.

"I'll get back to you when John's confirmed the time."

"Are you coming home first?" Leslyn said, voice still cool.

"Be home in about an hour. We're just walking back from a call uptown. And yeah, I'll be doing the laundry. Later."

"I left messages with the others," Marietetski said. "Asking them to confirm the time." He looked up at the sky. "Looks like the snow's passing over."

"Good," said Shah, promptly skidding, and slowing down even more. "I hate snow."

They walked in silence for another block, until Marietetski said, "You know, you haven't mentioned this Aurora once since the news broke that you were off the hook."

"Funny that, isn't it?" Shah said. "You think that I'd be talking about it non-stop."

"I guess that as a Muslim, you disapprove," Marietetski said. "Is that right? Does the Qur'an have opinions on intersex people?"

"I think that for most people the word 'abomination' covers it, though a few liberals think otherwise," Shah said, thinking of the Imam. He added, "Can we change the subject?"

"Because you were fooled? Or does the whole subject disgust you?" Marietetski said. "You know I'm bi? Neil and me, it's not like you and McCoy sharing a partner rotationally."

Shah opened his mouth and closed it again. *Rotationally?* He thought, trying to banish the images the word conjured. "Yeah, I know. I got no problem with that." If he were honest, one of the reasons he'd never visited Marietetski's place before was that he wasn't quite sure how he felt about the possibility of Marietetski and his male partner being openly affectionate. "So, you and the girls?"

"Oh, we got a rota for that, too. Just like your laundry."

"Yeah, funny."

"I wasn't when I asked you about your, uh, girl," Marietetski said. "I got no problem with gender, but you obviously have."

Shah exhaled. "I guess I'm mostly pissed because he – she, it, whatever – fooled me. But also, I really liked her. I let my guard down, and look what happened."

"What you going to do if we ever see her again?"

"Nothing. We had to drop the identity fraud charges. We've got nothing to say to each other."

"Haw," Marietetski said. "You're so deep in denial, you're up your own ass."

They had reached a corner, and while Shah stopped for an oncoming pedicab, Marietetski dashed across the road, drawing a barrage of abuse from the cabbie. Shah waited and crossed to where a sheepish-looking Marietetski waited. "Thought you was with me," the younger cop said.

Shah wagged a finger at him. "You are so damned impatient."

"Part of my charm."

"Maybe," Shah said with a grin. "But while I find opinion, impatience and ambition constantly amusing, not everyone finds a rookie with that combination so endearing."

"Uh-oh. I sense a wise sage lecture coming on."

"I'm not going to waste my time, John. I know you

think you already know it all."

"I know I don't. That's why they teamed me with you."

Shah continued as if Marietetski hadn't spoken, "You've already irritated a lot of people within the Department, and made enemies out on the streets – that isn't a promising combination for someone who wants promotion." He laughed. "And *you're* lecturing me on compromise? That's quite something."

"Well, maybe seeing you beat yourself up is the reason I'm suddenly embracing the concept."

"It's a bit late for epiphany."

They had been so deep in conversation that Shah hadn't paid attention to their surroundings; he belatedly realized that they were passing through a block haunted by dealers, hookers and other crims. Some sixth sense had just triggered.

It was too late. A blow sent him sprawling, and as he landed, a flare of pain shooting up his wrist, a boot caught him in the ribs, knocking the last of the wind out of him. The blow of the impact jerked his head around, scraping his eyepiece away. Moments later he heard the crunch of it being trodden on and ground to minute fragments. "Help!" Shah shouted, but the sound of blows and grunts told him that Marietetski was occupied.

Shah caught a glimpse of a masked assailant, before someone grabbed his ankles and dragged him backwards into an alleyway. Marietetski shouted, "Officer down! Track our eyepieces, we need help at eighty-sixth and–" a heavy thud cut him off as if he'd been shot.

Shah wriggled and kicked out, his foot connecting with something. "Bastard!" someone grunted, but Shah had no time to do more than clamber to his feet before a punch crashed into his ribs with the impact of a brick, driving the wind from his lungs.

A pair of clasped fists banged into his shoulder blades, driving him too his knees, and a hand gripped his hair, yanking his head back. As if from a long way away he heard a scraping sound and glimpsed two hooded man hauling Marietetski into the alleyway.

Hands pushed his wrists together behind his back and handcuffed him. He felt the sting of analgesic on his temple and jerked his head away, but the hand holding his hair yanked it back.

Someone said, "Leave him functional. I want him to be a walking, talking reminder of what happens to people who ask awkward questions."

*That's Sunny Kotian*, Shah thought. But then just as sensation faded from his temple, he felt the kiss of a probe making contact.

Then there was the sensation of something drilling into his mind, and blackness swallowed him.

# XVIII

As you leave the hotel, Denver's August heat smacks you in the face. At the moment it's still just about bearable enough to walk to the conference hall, but only barely.

Walking means you can eat your Danish in the shade of the giant carving of the bear.

More importantly, you can stop at the breakfast bar opposite the center, and buy your Danish and coffee from the cute young girl behind the counter. She's been too busy to talk the last two days, but you've caught the smile and the speculative look, and you're pretty sure that she's as interested in you as you are in her, for all that she's obviously a college student and probably fifteen years younger than you. *Maybe she likes older men.*

It's been eighteen months since you and Karen separated, and you've done the rebound thing, the promiscuity thing and the celibacy thing. Perhaps it's time now.

You heart plummets; she's not there. There's a swarthy guy with hairy arms staffing the counter in an otherwise empty bar. "Coffee and cherry Danish," you say.

As you pay for it a soft voice behind you says, "Morning, officer."

You spin round.

She's leaning on the mop with which she's cleaned the floor around the other side of the pillar.

"Morning." You feel a dopey grin stretch your facial muscles. It might as well be a big neon sign. You wave vaguely at your civilian clothes. "It's *that* obvious that I'm a cop?"

Her knowing look says *yes*. "There's only one conference this week, so I don't need to be a master of deduction." She's laughing at you, but it feels good. She rests her chin on her hands, which are folded across the top of the mop handle. "How you liking Denver?"

"It's good." *Come on Dufus, say something funny!* "But a bit, uh, quiet at night."

"That's 'cause you're not going to the right places."

"Maybe I need a local guide," you manage to say.

She lifts her head slightly. "How long till you leave?"

"Conference finishes tomorrow, but I'm taking a week's leave to look round Denver." You were going to fly back, but maybe you can change flights without paying the earth.

"You were, huh?" Her voice is getting quieter and quieter, even as her smile gets broader and broader. "It's nicer out of town, if you can afford to hire a car."

Suddenly driving around Colorado seems immensely appealing. "I'm sure I can. Maybe I could let you know tonight, after we finish for the day?"

Her eyes are hazel and very wide set, as is her mouth. You can barely take your eyes off her chewing her lower lip. "Maybe," she allows. "But Mama always used to say I shouldn't talk to strangers."

"So if I tell you my name, will you let me buy you dinner?"

She lifts her head so that she is standing up to her full roughly one-meter-fifty and her smile gets broader as she bobs her head. "I guess that would be OK."

You extend your hand. "Pete Shah, from New York."

Her hand feels tiny in yours, but she has a firm grip. This girl knows what she wants. "Leslyn Calea," she says with a smile that will burn in your head all day. "Most definitely *not* from New York."

# XIX

The commissioner always seemed to van Doorn as if she were ready to explode. *This time she might be justified.*

"Six days? This is all you have?" She said, finger to the ornate retro frame of her eyepiece, juggling input as they talked. "Two cops barely fifty brain cells from being vegetables, and this is it? This bastard's laughing at us – last night he raped a girl who was also a civilian worker for us. The media are big on the idea he's going after cops."

Van Doorn refused to meet her anger head-on. She was working herself into a state of indignation for the coming media briefing. "It could have been worse," he said. "Shah and Marietetski's telltales saved them; as soon as their adrenaline skyrocketed, their blood pressure peaked then dropped and endorphins kicked in, alarms were going off like crazy in the call center. That operator getting help so quickly saved their lives."

"And then their attackers would be facing a murder charge, instead of one of assault. That wasn't luck, van Doorn, that was cold calculation on the part of the killers, because that's what they are, killers by any other name."

"But we can't prove that. No witnesses. My squad have saturation-canvassed the whole area, two blocks in every direction. Late Saturday afternoon in early May, with streets full of people. No one saw anything. We've run facial-recognition software through every working camera in the vicinity – which isn't many." He added bitterly, "Strange how the perps knew how to stay out of view of what few working cameras there are round that block."

"Meanwhile your investigation's running out of steam." The commissioner shook her head. "Unless this next appeal turns up something, you'll have to shelve it."

*Funny how it's gone from being 'my' investigation,* van Doorn thought, remembering the media scrum last Saturday night, *to our investigation when it didn't yield immediate results, to 'your' investigation.* "We know who the perpetrators are, but can't prove anything." Van Doorn wanted to say more, but the Kotians were players at City Hall, and while he'd used Shah and Marietetski as horseflies to sting the family, he had to be more circumspect now.

He tried not to think of his men lying in hospital beds with tubes in them because he'd allowed them to act as his proxies without considering what happened to biting insects if they didn't move fast enough. "Commissioner?"

"I *said*, I'm giving you two replacements. One's a skilled memory analyst."

"And the other?"

The commissioner looked like she'd swallowed one of the horseflies he'd just thought about. "Bailey scored highly on all her tests at the Academy. She has a bright future."

"We need experience, Commissioner, not potential." *Take a deep breath – don't lose your cool.* "Shah's loss is devastating. His talent and his persistence are probably why he was attacked. Shah ploughed through as many downloads as any three ordinary men."

"But we have to replace him, and that's why we have computers – to do the legwork." At van Doorn's exasperated sigh the commissioner said, "Don't do that. If you've something to say, say it."

*And screw any hope of promotion when my name next comes up: "van Doorn? The one who lectures me?"* van Doorn gulped. "I shouldn't need to tell you that while computers recognize visual cues, human analysis is multi-sensory…"

"We can write algorithms for that too, van Doorn."

"But they don't have intuition! Until someone like the Republic of California develops AI–" he caught her scornful smile and said, "Exactly – how unlikely's that? But until then, our analysis programs can't reach conclusions. There's never been a subroutine that proposed Shah's inference of 'bruising' round the edges of a ripped memory. He's one of the very best. I don't know anyone else who can calculate memories' age and gender, even when there are no sensory cues, and when we've found the owner, to have been right so often."

"Hmm. I get the message, Orlando." The commissioner smiled as Van Doorn squirmed at the use of his hated first name. "But Marietetski's loss is even harder to take. He was future commissioner material."

"Then give me more people, even on a temporary basis. We know *someone* will post a relevant memory. It may already be out there–"

"It isn't. The subroutines will holler the minute a Person of Interest posts something."

"But it may already be out there from a witness, a newly-hired hand. You know how it works. They hire lowlifes, sometimes ripping their memories afterwards – or get someone newer still to rip 'em, on a revolving door basis. No one ever sees the whole picture."

He stopped to allow the commissioner time to think. She wouldn't take long. She believed in doing something, anything at all, no matter how asinine, so that she didn't look as if she was dithering. How she was perceived was more important to her than what she did.

"I can give you two more people for twenty-four hours, van Doorn, specifically for memory-analysis."

"Give me until Monday."

"I can't strip the other precincts for that long. You think that the crims will stop as a mark of respect to our boys? No chance!" She fiddled with her frame again. "Wait a minute." She turned her attention back to van Doorn. "Forty-eight hours. Use those programs and subroutines. They're not Shah, but use them smarter! And plan for life without him!"

As soon as she had gone van Doorn switched on his eyepiece. Unsurprisingly, calls had avalanched while he was offline. He speed-listened to as many as he could, deleting many, skipping over others that needed greater thought, archiving routine reports.

Only once did he pause, and when he had caught up on all other outstanding messages, he returned the call. "Doctor Bacon," he said without preamble. "What news?"

"No change on Marietetski. He remains in a deep coma, which he may never come out of. How much damage he sustained is hard to tell. Whether the assailants did it on purpose, or by accident, they went deeper than I've seen any attack go."

As he went into detail, van Doorn found himself paying far too much attention to the man's avatar. Like
most adults, the doctor used his head shot. But unlike
most, the doctor's image was fixed. Most avatars moved
in response to subroutines recognizing the tiny facial
movements in the muscles around the eyes caused by
the wearer's expression. Either the man hadn't bothered to upload the appropriate software, or he suffered
from some kind of 'frozen' face syndrome. Either way,
it was disconcerting.

On an impulse, van Doorn called records on a second
channel, and mentally raised an eyebrow at the result:
*Doctor Paul Bacon survived an interrupted memory rip that
left him with damage similar to a stroke victim: can't move his
facial muscles.* Sometimes it could be worse for the victim
if an attack was interrupted. He caught "Shah", and focused. "Sorry, say that again."

"I said Shah only survived at all because of training
in memory retention and his basic resilience."

*Resilience? More like natural bloody mindedness.* But
maybe we should make Shah's training mandatory for
all cops, improve the chances of a copycat attack. Yeah,
and the commissioner will love that request for addi-
tional budget. "Is the long-term prognosis better or
worse for Shah, Doctor Bacon?"

"Impossible to tell. From the initial damage and his
age, I'd have said his outlook was even worse than his
partner's. But Shah's fighting spirit is such that he may
make almost a full recovery." Bacon added, "But his
memory will be impaired and his personality scarred.
Any further rip would probably kill him."

"Better put a big warning sign over his head when
he returns to duty." *New York State doesn't recognize ripping as murder if the victim physically lives, so a murder*

*charge might put a few of the bastards off. I must check the stats later, see how many victims were ever attacked a second time.*

"*If* he ever returns to duty," Doctor Bacon said. "At the moment that seems very unlikely."

# XX

Even now you hate Monday mornings, but back then you loathed them with a passion made worse by some pissant Irish band making money out of that shooting in California. Only the paycheck kept you going.

*Maybe baiting the new guy would pass the time*, you thought. "What sorta name's freaking Rasheed, anyway?" you said on his first day. "That like rasher, like in bacon, or something?" You saw Shumaki wince. "What?" you asked your partner. "What's with you?

"Jeez man," Shumaki whispered. "There's no worse insult to a Muslim than calling him a pig!"

"So? He's coming here to live, he's got to learn our ways. Isn't that right, Shah?" The old man nodded, eyes downcast. Hard to believe this was supposed to be one of the Shah's top secret policemen, reduced to traffic duty in his new home. You squash any trace of pity. "Hey, Bacon," You called to a backdrop of sniggers. "What kinda people violate international laws, and attack an embassy?"

Shah leaned on the locker door. When he looked up, the anger in his eyes filled your bowels with ice. Not so much the emotion as what they said he would do to

146

you if he ever gave way to it. For the first time you can believe the stories that he tortured people. He said, "People who want to make a statement. That civilized agreements like the Geneva Convention mean *this*," he snapped his fingers, "much to them. That they play by different rules."

"You agree with those savages?" Damned if you were going to let some punk scare you with a look. "You think it's civilized? The pictures on the news last night?" The swirling surging mob, the burning flags and effigies. *Dammit, if we had a real president instead of a peanut farmer, we'd be kicking their asses.* You might not have that wuss Carter here, but Shah's the next best thing. *How do you know he isn't a spy?*

Shah sighed. "Officer O'Riordan... may I call you Pete? Your people have taken my wife and newborn son in, and given us a roof over our heads. I'm sincerely grateful. But what should I do? Return to Iran to fight them on my own?" Shah shook his head sadly. "That mob is not my people. Iran's new rulers are exiles, aliens who have somehow taken over the minds of ordinary people, and turned them into a mob of madmen."

Unsure what to say, you grunt.

"Life under Reza Shah Pahlavi wasn't paradise for those who disagreed with him." Shah sighed. "Actually, for those who attracted the attention of his CIA-trained SAVAK thugs, it's no better than a banana republic. But we tried to modernize the country; to return to civilization after interminable civil wars between squabbling tribes. For a time we dared to dream of joining the West, but that dream's gone, blown away like grains in a sandstorm." Shah repeated, "These are not my people." He wiped his eye, and you looked away, ashamed.

You wonder now whether it was one of his people who came with a pistol to take the guy's life. You wish you could have told him of your cousin in that compound. You wish you could just say "sorry", but it's too late for that.

You stare at the photo in *The Times*, the article on "Exiled Iranian Now Serving with NYPD Murdered", and wish you could take it all back.

Too late.

# XXI

"Aaaargh!" Shah flung the puzzle across the room at the ice hockey players battling it out on the flat screen. They could have been Martians for all he understood of them. Neither Leslyn's nor Doug's explanations had eased his bafflement, but they admitted they'd never been fans.

He held his right hand out in front of him, willing it to stop shaking. When that didn't work, he clenched it into a fist and opened it again, stretching it until fingers and thumb were as far apart as they would go – then further, so that it hurt a little. He repeated the action, over and over again: Clench. Open. Stretch. Clench.

When he had done it twenty times, he stopped, took a deep breath. Sighing, he tottered from the chair to the other side of the room and turned off the set. Crouching, he laboriously gathered the pieces with his right hand, dropping them into his left, which he made into a cup. When he had dropped almost all the pieces into the cup, his hand shook and they fell out.

Shah clenched his eyes shut almost as fiercely as he had his fist, and covered his brow with his free right hand, occasionally removing it to sweep away the seeping moisture, his shoulders shaking with a rhythmic intensity that only ceased when a hand touched his arm.

"It'll take time, Pete," Leslyn said. "The doctors said it may be months before you're recovered. It's only been three weeks. Don't push yourself so hard."

"Meanwhile the Department have given me another six weeks to decide whether I'm fit to return to work." *And I have no idea what else I can do – at least there I stand a chance of regaining what I've lost.* "Have you been waiting outside all the time?" He regretted the bitter question as soon as he said it.

"Just passing." Her voice gave no hint of any resentment.

"What do I do in the meantime?" His voice was still thick. "My body won't do as I tell it to." He resisted the urge to add, *I'm an old man.* While true, it would sound too self-pitying.

"The doctors say that it's not uncommon for more… mature… survivors of attacks to suffer stroke-like symptoms. The important thing was that they stabilized it quickly. You need to give yourself time to heal." She rubbed his shoulder, keeping her voice close to a croon, "Where do you want to sleep tonight? Alone, or with me?"

"Isn't it your night with Doug?"

"We'll swap over." She had slept with him the week before, and it had calmed him in the night, when the dreams otherwise fractured his sleep – and theirs as he yelled his awakening – into hour or two-hour long shards.

"Let's decide later." He squeezed her hand with his free one and stood unsteadily.

"Why won't you take up the Department's offer of counseling?" Leslyn said.

"Because," Shah said. He couldn't actually articulate why. *It would feel like giving in* sounded so lame. "I'd rather use how it feels right now as fuel, and run on that."

"How does it feel?" Leslyn whispered. Her eyes were still the hazel of her youth, but now the soft skin had given way to crow's feet, and her mouth was turned down in an expression of perpetual disappointment.

"Like my head is a vast warehouse. I swear I can hear the echo of my thoughts where there should be memories." He picked up a leather-bound book. "I found this yesterday." He opened the clasp, allowing it to fall open at a random page. "It's my father's journal from when he arrived, full of profound insights like 'Went to buy new stroller for Junior.' That's how he always refers to me. Three letters: J-n-r. That's what I was, a junior version of him."

Leslyn stared at it. "It's a Filofax." Then her training reasserted itself. "Sorry, daydreaming. Well, Pervez, by all means sail on a voyage of self-discovery, but don't kill yourself. Come, sit down. I'll bring you some soup. Tomato and basil, from the garden."

"I'm not one of your bloody patients, Sister Calea," he grumbled, but half-heartedly, and she kissed his cheek when he fell back into the chair.

He stared at the entry he'd found yesterday:

*March 3rd, 1980. A boy! A bouncing bonny boy, as one of the nurses described him, born to Rasheed and Afsoon Shah in Schenectady, New York. My young American – I'll play him that lovely David Bowie song I heard on the radio the other day. I'll teach him baseball and hockey, to love ice cream and hot dogs – or do they contain pork? Does it matter if they do?*

*Perhaps he will take some other faith; it will be his
choice. We will call him Pervez, after my friend from
Dubai, who helped smuggle us out when the world
was falling around our ears. A boy!!!*

Shah stared at the page, almost overcome at his father's optimism, comparing it to the remote, tired figure
he remembered. Had he got it that wrong?

*March 4th, 1980. The news is full of images of
screaming 'students' and Revolutionary Guards in
Tehran. Stories of anti-Iranian abuse here in the
Land of the Free. Can they not see that we are as
much victims as them? I should not complain. For all
that the FBI still want to see me and wring more information than I have from me, America has taken us
in. Until this passes, we must keep our heads down.*

Shah put the book down, and thought of the clip
he'd found the day before. *That was what that cop O'Riordan was remembering.* It had been the only clip Shah
had found when he'd entered his parents name into the
search parameters. It had been a burn, long after the
event, but it had been painful that the only memory of
his father he could find had been so full of sadness.

Shah levered himself out of the chair and tottered
across his room, holding his traitorous body's urge to
stagger in check. He sat in front of the console and
picked up its attached scanner, fitting it onto the shaven
patch on his temple, then pulled the hood over his
head. He'd tried to surf the web 'bareback' but found
the outside world impinged too much.

Leslyn had had to show him how to do it. When it
came to performing tasks that should be automatic his

warehouse-empty mind was unable to do things that were easy for Leslyn and Doug.

Inside the hood the world seemed very far away. It muffled sounds, blocked odors, while no light penetrated the thick lining. Sometimes, as it had earlier, the hood helped, depriving him of sensory distractions. Other times, like now, it simply created a vacuum into which an overwhelming rage – worsened by having no tangible focus – slipped like a dark fog. He had found the memory of a dementia sufferer a few days earlier, and it was both familiar and strange at the same time. Strange because of the jumble of memories shuffled into randomness, but familiar in its sense that the world had been somehow tipped on its side.

Shah tried to shut the rage out, but it refused to go away. He said "Shah, New York.", but when the list of clips scrolled down in his mind's eye, nothing jumped out. Nor did anything block the thought that he had six weeks to somehow regain his knowledge of the world. He tore off the hood and crossed to the window. Thoughts whirled like butterflies within his mind, and he suspected that some of them were the ghostly shadows of memories of the attack itself. The doctors had told him what had happened, and warned him although his memories were gone, the mental bruising of the trauma was still there, made even worse by having no perceptible cause.

He paced up and down until he shook with fatigue, and had to prop himself up against the table. Only when he felt his legs buckling did he finally concede defeat, and sit down.

This time bareback, he reattached the scanner and studied again the download of meeting Leslyn, the only thing of his that he'd been able to track down, wondering whether he had been lucky enough to track a bit of his memory that had been ripped, or whether he'd simply posted it to the web himself long before. *Wonder how I can tell the difference?* He thought, then wondered whether he'd always been so obsessive about memory, or whether the attack had made him so. He'd read stories of people made compulsive by such events.

When he'd experienced his meeting Leslyn half-dozen times, he played O'Riordan's memory of bullying his father. He realized that he was clenching and unclenching his fist. He replayed it again, squeezing it for a meaning like juice from an orange. Father was a detective in the Shah's secret police in Isfahan before the Ayatollahs took power. *They emigrated to the US,* he scribbled on a piece of paper he'd kept at hand. *He was murdered when I was eight. It was believed it was an exile's execution by an overseas supporter of the Ayatollahs but no one was ever brought to trial.*

He paused, and wrote: *Was Father's murder the reason I became a cop?*

# XXII

Dawn sunlight crept across the walls as Leslyn paused on the white-plastered mezzanine between the twenty-eighth and twenty-ninth floors. She put down the Perhaps Bag. Doug had taken the name from the string bag which Soviet housewives took with them wherever they went: "Perhaps there will be potatoes, or meat," they would say. He liked to grumble that today's erratic food supplies were as bad as the days of communist Russia.

Leslyn felt every day of her fifty-five years, but took deep breaths, ignoring the pain shooting up her calves from her varicose veins. She had just finished an eight-hour shift, and the walk home was just too much.

When she'd been a teenager early in the century people had said, "Fifty's the new thirty," and fifty-five year-old women seemed impossibly glamorous. Everyone had believed that life would keep getting ever longer, that soon sixty would be the new thirty.

Now it was the other way round: thirty year-olds looked sixty.

Leslyn took one last deep breath. "Daydreaming won't get this shopping home," she muttered, then wondered why she was being quiet. The building was half-empty, like much of Manhattan, the skyscrapers too tall to be livable for anyone but the young, the fit or the crazy.

Leslyn was out of breath again before she was halfway up, but momentum kept her going. Low blood sugar made her hand wobble, and her key only scratched at the lock.

Before she could try again, the door swung open and Doug gave her a tremulous smile. "Heard you coming." He gave her a passionate kiss on the mouth which she half-avoided. She was too tired for that now. He took the hint and extricated the bag from her fingers.

"I stopped at the morning market," she said of the erratic gathering that sprang up several times a week on the corner of Canal and Church, showing him her bargains.

"Ooh, imported luxury." Doug found a home on a cluttered shelf for the couscous, put the lamb in a fridge that was nearly as old as they were and equally given to groaning, and, switched on the kettle.

"How's he been?" Leslyn said in an undertone.

"More nightmares," Doug murmured.

"I heard at the market." Leslyn lowered her voice. "There's been another attack – this time it's a guy. Beaten and wiped."

"Should we tell him?" Doug's features took on a sudden animation. "Morning, Pete!"

"Hey, Leslyn," Shah mumbled from the doorway. "How's the worker?" Dark rings made it look as if someone had punched his eyes, although the real bruises had now faded, four weeks after the attack.

*How much did he hear?* "Tired, but give me six hours and I'll be good as new."

"That's good."

Doug was studiously concentrating on making tea. "You want some?" He poured water into a third cup.

"I found a memory of us meeting," Shah said.

"No!" Leslyn said. "In Denver?" She saw anguish flicker across Doug's face, felt for his hand and gave it a quick squeeze.

"M-hm." Shah bobbed his head. "I was there for a conference. I tried to find when it was, but couldn't."

"Lot of old records lost now." Leslyn longed to be able to take her mug to bed. "That was toward the end of when people could journey across country. If it had been just a few years later, we'd never have met, and I'd never have followed you to New York." She turned to Doug and hugged him. "I'd never have met you, either." Doug smiled, but talk of her and Pete's pre-Doug relationship always made him uneasy. Leslyn added, "Travel nowadays, that's for the rich and the powerful, isn't it?"

"I'll turn down the bed for you," Doug said, vanishing from the room.

Shah exhaled heavily. "I found the memory last week, but I thought it might upset him. I should have just kept quiet about it altogether."

"Living with us must sometimes be baffling." Leslyn added, "But Doug finds it equally hard, you know. He's bending over backwards to try not to make you feel like a stranger, to help you fit in."

"Trouble is," Shah said, "right now I feel like a stranger, even to myself."

Leslyn said, "You're learning everything again, questioning everything; it's like we're shining a big searchlight on the marriage, and all the cracks in it. When Doug joined us, he made it clear that he didn't want kids, which suited us." She sighed and yawned. "But maybe us staying together wasn't such a good idea – perhaps separating then might have been better."

Leslyn knew that she risked opening a Pandora's Box by mentioning *her*, but couldn't help it. The urge to ask was overwhelming, like a chickenpox scab and Leslyn suspected picking it would be equally messy. "Do you remember anyone from before the attack?"

"Like who?"

"A girl called Aurora," Leslyn said. "Something happened."

"Did I...?" Shah clearly realized that this was significant, but not how, and Leslyn breathed a little sigh of relief.

Shah had been discreetly bringing women home since Leslyn had invited Doug into their marriage eight years earlier, ostensibly to provide the company lacking due to Shah's long hours and their mismatched shifts. They had an open marriage so she could hardly complain, and sometimes Shah indulging his libido elsewhere was a relief. None of Shah's occasional and short-lived flings had unsettled her like that stunning young woman.

Normally Leslyn was uninterested in looks – including her own – but the girl had made her feel an old frump. She wasn't sure whether learning that Aurora was a companion had made things better or worse. *I've been a dutiful wife and mother for years, for what; so he can bring home a whore?*

Shah's next question was so unexpected that it caught her completely off-guard: "Has Doug always been so whiny?"

"What do you mean?"

"I heard him yesterday. Asking you what you see in him. How needy is that?"

Leslyn was surprised by the surge of anger she felt. She had always laughed Doug's clinginess away, but right now she was too tired, and attack seemed the best form of defense, especially since she had hoped that this blank slate might turn out to be less harsh on his co-husband. "He was distressed. How needy would you be if every breath was a struggle?"

"Is this what this place is, Leslyn, a home for lame ducks – first him, now me?"

*He's thinking out loud. He can't mean to be as tactless as he sounds.* "Since you ask Pete, most of Doug's attraction is that he isn't you. You're pretty much exact opposites. You're dogged and unrelenting as now, to Doug's quick-silver. You're unpretentious, but sometimes I *like* his little affectations, reading a passage aloud from an ob-scure novel or burbling about whatever issue or human interest story from the news snags his attention."

Shah didn't seem offended. "When I came into the kitchen yesterday, you were out on the balcony tending the plants. While he read something to you."

"Rex Stout. We both like Rex Stout." Leslyn laughed. "The compost bags!" She clapped her hands together.

"So he was reading aloud with his little finger in the air. Then he started pontificating about it." Shah adopted a clipped, prissy voice: "'My dear Leslyn, the very idea that a grown person could hide beneath com-post bags is grotesque and unlikely to fool even a child, let alone supposedly trained detectives'."

Leslyn couldn't help laughing at the accuracy with which Shah mimicked Doug's mannerisms. She'd had no idea he possessed such powers of mimicry. *What else has been buried all these years within the old Shah?*

"It seems to me that the less Doug knows about a subject, the stronger his opinions."

Leslyn goggled. "Say that again."

"What? The less Doug knows about a subject?"

"Exactly – where did that come from?"

"Dunno. Just thought of it, as far as I can tell. Why?"

"Because you've said it before, Pete. So either you're reaching the same conclusions as then... or your memories are starting to come back..."

# XXIII

Sweat, blood, amniotic fluid, and tension form a dizzying cocktail.

The power went off an hour ago, but the nurses and midwives simply switched to manual and battery-operated equipment. It's easy for them; they have no emotional investment beyond wanting to perform as professionally as always, and they have duties to distract them. You wish that you had duties beyond holding Leslyn's hand.

"Regular breaths, now, Ms Calea," the midwife says.

Outside, the corridor resembles a charnel-house. Another airborne virus has mutated, taking three thousand people this week. One of the toughest decisions was whether to come into the hospital at all for the birth, or have the baby at home. But six, even seven apartments have the crosses of tape with the skull and crossbones motifs stuck across their doorways, denoting plague victims inside, so it seems no safer to stay at home.

"On my mark, push," the midwife says, and tells you, "Wipe her forehead, please."

Leslyn shrieks, her vocal cords standing out like rope hawsers, her body straining to expel the baby. The latest shortage is anesthetics, so even if Leslyn wanted it, pain relief isn't available at the moment.

"I can see the crown!" a nurse says. "Oh! The umbilical cord's wrapped around the neck!" He reaches in beyond your sight, in between your wife's spread-eagled legs, and you hear a small snipping sound. "OK, that takes care of *that*."

"Come on," the midwife urges again, smiling as she sees you recording the scene with your cellphone in your free hand. "One more push!"

Leslyn obliges with another hoarse bawl, squeezing your hand so hard that you believe your fingers may splinter at any moment.

"You're doing fine, Hon," you add.

"The head's clearing now," the nurse says. "One more big, bi-i-i-ig push!"

*Anyone would think she was coaching at Flushing Meadow.*

Leslyn yells and pushes again, another spasm, and she squeezes again – two minutes ago you'd had have wagered your fingers couldn't hurt any more, but now you know better.

"Oh, yes, it's a beautiful baby girl!" the midwife cries. They manhandle the dark, blood-smeared little body. There's a slap, and a thin squall joins the adult voices. The nurse wraps the tiny form in towels and says, handing your baby to Leslyn, "You have a healthy baby girl, Ms Calea."

"Perveza." You utter the name you agreed several weeks ago, feeling a vast sweeping sensation of joy at this new life that you've brought into the world, and before you know it, you're wet-eyed at the sheer beauty of her.

"You old fool," Leslyn says indulgently as you wipe your eyes.

"She's every bit as beautiful as her mother," you say. It's true; Leslyn is transfigured with sheer overwhelming joy from an ordinary, perhaps even slightly plain woman into a latter-day Madonna. "This is the best day of my life," you say.

# XXIV

That afternoon, McCoy shuffled in the doorway to Shah's room. "You have visitors."

A man stood in the lounge, medium-height, solid, but from the slight double chin that appeared when he lowered his head, the muscle was turning to fat. He wore an expensively-cut dark suit that emphasized broad shoulders while minimizing the slight gut that peeked out from under the jacket. "Dad." His rumble was so low Shah thought it started in his boots. "How are you?"

Shah had got his new eyepiece earlier that day, stuffed with as many downloads as his colleagues could lay their hands on. "A get-well present for your return," the commissioner had said on her PR visit earlier that day. "Which I hope will be soon." She didn't say, "You have three weeks." She didn't need to. A big, invisible clock ticked silently in Shah's head every waking minute. Especially after she'd mentioned the old man who was the latest Ripper victim. Shah accessed Rex on his new piece: *DOB June 12th 2022. Height 1.75 meters. Lawyer. Married, one wife, two children.*

"About as well as can be expected." Shah hated that he couldn't keep the quaver out of his voice. He needed to practice speaking more, to learn to sound as confident as his visitor. "You're Rex, my... son." He almost said oldest, but the memory of the last download stopped that; he'd barely bridged the pause. *I'm pretty sure that that baby girl in the download was our first, so how come all the data's saying that Rex is our oldest child?*

"The doctors say you're making good progress." Rex's tone of voice implied that he was somehow responsible for Shah's recovery.

"Climbing the damn wall here."

"Please, Grandpapa," a petite woman whom Shah's eyepiece tagged as Angelica said. "Not in front of the children."

His puzzlement must have shown; Rex said, "Hasn't Mom mentioned George and Leonie?"

Shah wasn't absolutely sure. There had been so many conversations with Leslyn, so much to learn, that he almost drowned in the tsunami of information that accompanied every meal. And the facts were easy compared to the nuances that accompanied them. Shah vaguely remembered something that Leslyn had said, now that he thought about it: "Him and that Angelica, behaving as if they're something special with their sole relationship and their two kids and a cottage on Fire Island."

"Sorry, Angelica," Shah made himself say.

It drew the thinnest of smiles from the woman, who was all frills, on her high-necked collar, her sleeves and the breast of her white blouse. Her details said she was twenty-six, but the voice that said, "Say hello to Grandpapa, children," belonged to a little girl. *Don't be fooled by that spun-sugar coating,* Leslyn had warned him, *she's got a heart of granite.*

"'Lo, Gran'pap'." George looked about four years old. Leonie gurgled something that might have been a greeting, but Shah wasn't sure.

"Hello," Shah said. He caught Rex's frown at Angelica. *What was wrong with that?* He said to Rex, "I have to learn everything all over again. I've hired access to some memories on the web, but they're all old ones."

"But that's awful." Angelica said, as Rex laid a hand on her arm.

"I pay under an alias." He attempted a smile, but inside he was boiling. *Thanks for your words of support, bitch. What else am I supposed to do?*

"Sounds very practical, Dad," Rex said. "At least you get your memories back."

"We have an interview with the School Board," Angelica said as if Shah's amnesia was inconsequential. "To put Georgie's name down to attend Park Avenue." She added, "We wouldn't want anything unfortunate to spoil his chances, would we?" She frowned, clearly realizing how her words might be construed. "Of course Rex and I feel awful for you, but please, be discreet."

"Well, thank you for your support," Shah said.

Before Shah could answer, Doug called from the kitchen, "Can I make either of you coffee? We have concentrated recycled Columbian."

Shah caught a look of absolute horror pass between them, there and gone as quick as lightning. *Might've lost my memory, but I haven't lost my powers of observation.*

"Thank you, but we should be on our way," Rex said. "We're having dinner at the Mayoral Banquet tonight, and we need to settle the children before we go."

"We were hoping to see Grandmama," Angelica said.

"She's asleep," Shah said. "She works, you know."

"We know, Dad," Rex said.

Angelica said, "No matter. We can stop by another time. Give her our love." She held her hand out to Shah as if expecting it to be kissed. Unsure what to do, Shah stared at her. She withdrew it with a "humph."

Shah turned instead to Rex and said, "Can I call at the office sometime? It'd be nice to have a change of scenery."

"Could be a bit tricky, Dad."

"I'll put on my best suit and wear a clean shirt." It was meant as a joke.

By the flush darkening Rex's features, it fell flat. "I meant they're uptown," he said stiffly. "It'd be a long walk or subway ride for only a few minutes between meetings."

"I wanted to ask your advice." *I wonder if the bastard would charge his own father a consultation fee.*

"I'm not sure if I can help. My specialty's intellectual copyright."

"Yeah," I checked that out." Shah was making it up as he went along. "My memories include thought processes. Aren't those covered by intellectual copyright?" Rex looked as if he was going to launch into a lecture, and Angelica cleared her throat, so Shah held up his hand: "That's why I want to come and see you!" Rex nodded, mind already on precedents and case law. Shah continued, "I have the feeling that this is a legal minefield, especially if more than one person's involved, and there's any overseas connection."

"You're right, Dad," Rex said. Shah wondered at the warning look his son shot Angelica. "It does impinge on my area of expertise. Given that the US doesn't recognize the Pacifican net-haven's laws that make it perfectly legal to sell one's memories and any consequential ideas, you're right to be concerned. Where a team is involved, it's led in the past to legal disputes…"

"I sense a 'but' coming."

"But this is part of a wider case. You'd be better off talking to the NYPD lawyers."

He was right, of course, if all that Shah had wanted was legal advice. But he didn't; the pretext was the only way he felt able to bridge the wall between Rex and him, from the start of this conversation.

"Can't I call upon my own son for advice?" It hadn't meant to sound as querulous as it did, but Shah felt rage building within him at his own clumsiness. *Can't even have a damn conversation with him without screwing it up! Did Old Shah have this problem?*

"Of course, of course," Rex said. "But we must go. Good to see you up and about again." He turned to Doug, loitering in the kitchen doorway. "Tell Mom we're sorry we missed her. We'll catch up with her."

When they had gone Shah said to Doug. "Is it always that strained?"

"That was about as good as it gets."

"Really?" Shah said.

"Yeah."

"Hmm. Was it me, or was Respectable Rex embarrassed by Pa's working-class origins?"

"I certainly got that impression," McCoy said. "But you know me; the less I know about a subject, the more I hold forth on it."

Shah closed his eyes. "I guess I had that coming."

"You did." McCoy looked uneasily toward the bedroom, as if expecting Leslyn to appear at any moment.

"Come on," Shah said. "Spill."

"You used to – you adored George and Leonie."

"What do you mean?" Shah made himself unclench his fists. *Doug means well...*

"I always got the impression the grandkids were the only reason that you put up with Rex's pomposity, and Angelica's point-scoring and petty malice. But you barely spoke to them – hey! Where are you going?"

"To find my damn daughter," Shah said. "Maybe I can manage not to upset at least one member of my loving family."

Saturday evening in New York. From clips that Shah had seen, at its height NYC never slept. Now sometimes he walked alone for a block at a time, though the crowds grew thicker whenever he neared a station.

When he grew too tired to walk he boarded the subway and rode the One, climbing above ground for the last part. Shah watched the sun sink behind the skeletal remains of urban New Jersey. The train slowed to cross the ramshackle Broadway Bridge at walking pace. Forty minutes after descending the steps of the 14th Street Station he was leaving Marble Hill.

The utilitarian boxes surrounding the station were uniformly dilapidated; many had doors and windows boarded over, while the walls had fallen in on a few, leaving their tawdry interiors exposed. Perveza's address was only a few minutes' walk.

The door was open, so Shah pushed his way in. Inside, the house stank of mildew, rotting garbage and cat's piss. The stairs were falling in, so it seemed a safe bet that any residents would be on the first floor. "Hey?" Shah called

Four bodies lay outstretched in the last room at the back, side by side on sleeping bags as filthy as their clothes. Bones jutted out from scabrous skin.

"Who?" called the nearest one in a voice as androgynous as its emaciated body.

"Perveza Shah," Shah said loudly, to cover his nervousness.

From the bag at the other end of the line a hand raised and waved.

"Perveza?" Shah tiptoed over to the filthy, emaciated figure and stood over it – her, he corrected himself, glimpsing a breast. Shah studied the dark-haired figure clothed in scraps stretched out below him, trying to reconcile it with his eyepiece picture of Perveza. *DOB March 15th 2025, Manhattan. Height 1.60 meters.* He thought, *It could be – the height's about right. But look how thin she is! She can't weigh much more than 40 kilos. If that.*

His doubts were resolved when the girl said, "Daddy?" and giggled. "What are you doing in my room?"

"I've been meaning to come and see you ever since – well, for several weeks now," Shah said. "I was attacked." There was no answer, so he said "I had hoped that you might come and see me, but since you couldn't make it, I thought I'd come to you instead."

Shah wasn't sure how much the fever-eyed girl understood. He closed his eyes in despair when she said, "Is it time for school?"

He'd read about the effects of Scramble, how it distorted the sense of time and shuffled memories as a side-effect of the euphoria it induced. Leslyn had downloaded her copies of the files and correspondence, but Shah had no more idea than he had ever had why, despite having had what they'd thought was a happy childhood, his daughter should have become bulimic in adolescence, then taken drugs to control her cravings.

"Don't do this, Perveza, please." Shah crouched over her. "Come home. We'll work something out." He might as well have talked to the wall. "Goddammit, don't do this!"

Perveza began to cry, a long thin keen like an air raid siren.

Shah lifted his hands, then dropped them again – he had no idea whether to strike her or cuddle her. Instead, wondering how many times he had done it before, he turned and left.

# XXV

**Tuesday**

Shah dressed for work and shaved extra carefully. *For work, for work.* The words sang, of stimulation and excitement, but also a warning, of an overwhelming world that wouldn't be as nurturing as the womb-like existence of the apartment.

He'd long regained motor control, and the day before the doctors had pronounced him fit enough to undertake light duties. He still had a week to make a decision on whether to take a disability pension and retire, but he was getting bored with life in the womb. The thought of work carried with it an odd little thrill.

He was out on the street before he could lose his nerve.

As a compromise against Leslyn's insistence that she or McCoy accompany him, Shah took a pedicab to work. When he alighted he learned that his return was news.

"Officer Shah!" shouted one reporter.

"Officer, look this way please!"

"How does it feel to be returning to work?" It seemed a sensible question, and Shah might have answered it.

172

But before he could respond, several more questioners followed. He caught someone talking about "the heroic police officer", and realized they meant him.

He put his head down, and somehow made it through the chaos into the building.

What he didn't expect as he walked through the doors into the public area was to find every officer – both uniform and plain clothes – standing and applauding him in.

"Nice to have you back, Pete!"

"Good to see you again!"

"Catch those bastards, eh?"

It was the last that made Shah realize that he was a symbol. Any one of those officers could have been the victim of the attack, so his return was proof that there was hope that such an attack was survivable.

"Just don't expect speeches." Shah tried not to feel overwhelmed and hid it beneath gruffness.

"Oh, yeah, he's back," someone said, and they all laughed. "Charming as ever, I don't think!"

Shah blew a Bronx cheer at the heckler, and strode through the ragged honor guard they'd formed for him.

"Nice to see you back, Pete," van Doorn said, hand extended. "You're on half-days for this week; really, really light duties only. Come meet your new partner."

Shah realized with a start that he'd barely thought of Marietetski. *Does being an invalid always do that? Make you turn inwards and self-obsess?*

Van Doorn led him into the captain's office, where a young blonde girl – *no, woman* – perched on the edge of a visitor's chair. Shah sank into the other one.

"You OK?" van Doorn said.

Shah nodded, drawing deep breaths. "It's tougher than I expected."

"Sara Bailey," the woman said. Shah sneaked a peek at her profile and was shocked. *Nineteen, not quite twenty? They've partnered me with a kid!* Bailey watched him from beneath her lashes, blonde, petite, and smartly dressed, but oddly asexual.

Recruitment had been dwindling, Shah had read, but he hadn't expected the NYPD to lower its standards quite so far. *She really is a frightened little rabbit,* Shah thought.

"Bailey's just out of Police Academy," van Doorn said. "But in many ways so are you, Pete. We have no idea of how much you've retained of your skills and aptitudes."

*Born June 6th 2030* Shah read. "First posting?" he asked, trying to look reassuring.

"Yessir," Bailey said.

"Pete," Shah corrected her.

"Pete," she said with the tiniest of smiles. "And I'm Sara." As if he'd left her with any choice once he'd insisted she used his first name. "It must have been awful, the attack–" she blushed as if he'd just flashed at her, and he guessed that she was worried that talking about it might traumatize him.

*She's my nursemaid,* Shah thought with a flash of irritation. *They think I'm not going to last, and she's here to shepherd me out the door. Well, stiff that!* He hoped his face betrayed none of his inner anger as he said evenly, "I can't really remember much about it." Which was true – the nightmares that awoke him every night had nothing to do with that, as far as Shah could tell and he'd seen no shrink to tell him otherwise. "So feel free to talk about it as much as you want. Don't be embarrassed, Sara."

• • • •

Removing the hood, Shah remembered his cup of coffee – now cold – and swigged it, grimacing. He'd forgotten how strong the precinct dispenser made it.

"How are you getting on, sir?" Bailey asked.

"Told you before, Sara, it's Pete."

"Sorry. Pete."

"Sir makes me feel old. Which – right now – I feel. Who'd have thought my first half-day would be so tiring? Just found another burn of Kotian's memory." Shah tapped the pile of files. "Sheesh, this guy is *everywhere.*"

"But only as a witness, or a Person of Interest."

"Which my notes say is in itself a pattern. Someone crops up in more than one case then probability says they're involved in something." He exhaled through his nose. "This guy's posted pretty much his whole life on the web. Kotian in Bangalore. Kotian marries an American heiress. You name it, it's there."

"But they're all legal?"

"Oh, yeah. But they're revealing: ego the size of NYC. And this," he indicated the pile of outstanding cases, "is so damned daunting." Shah couldn't understand how he had once been so easily able to examine the tags, and see which files really were legit copies, and which ones bore fake ID and were really rips. And if he couldn't do it soon he ought to pack his bags, take the proffered half-pension and find a job waiting tables at the local diner.

He wanted to punch someone, anyone, but generating adrenaline in that way was just his way of staving off exhaustion. *It's probably counterproductive punching your new partner, in any event.*

He pushed back his chair. "I was determined I was going to see out the day, but that might put me into hospital. So for one of the few times in my life, I'll be sensible."

"Good idea," Bailey said. Shah wondered why she looked so relieved.

## Wednesday

When Shah removed the hood, allowing the subdued hubbub of the office to ease him out of the images he'd been immersed in for the last forty minutes, he saw that a woman had sat beside him.

She was middle-aged, with clothes that highlighted her figure in all the wrong ways: a sleeveless blouse that drew attention to the ample flesh of her upper arms. It had a deep plunging neckline, at the base of which was a bust so buttressed that it seemed to defy gravity. Shah suspected that her hairdresser – if she had one – simply placed a bowl on her head and cut around it. Below the fringe deep frown lines creased her forehead. She smiled nervously.

"You waiting for me?" Shah said. "Sorry, I can't sense anything when I'm under this damned thing."

The woman smiled, although it never reached her eyes. "That's the idea. Don't worry, Pete. Van Doorn assigned me to help you both, so there's no rush."

"Okaaay. You weren't here yesterday, were you, so we never got introduced…"

"Holy crap!" The woman studied him. "You really have been, I mean you've lost…"

She stopped at Shah's, "Yeah, I really have no idea who you are."

"Right." The woman drew the word out into several syllables. "I'm Detective Lynn Stickel. We sometimes worked together before you were attacked."

Shah thrust out his hand. "Pleased to meet you. Do I

call you Lynn, or Stickel, or…?"

"Call me what you like. You used to call me 'bitch' when you thought I wasn't listening. We didn't always work together. Your last partner was Marietetski."

At the mention of Marietetski's name, Shah felt a pang of guilt; he had barely given his partner a thought. *That's what being an invalid does to you,* he thought. *Makes you turn inward, become self-obsessed, listening to every breath, watching every sign for improvements, or – worse – for a deterioration in your condition. I'll go tomorrow and see him. Or the day after, if I'm not up to it.*

Shah watched her. While the woman was a little frosty, at least she had a personality, unlike Bailey, who Shah would have sworn jumped every time he spoke to her. *OK, I let my impatience show a few times yesterday, but I was tired.* Much of Shah's frustration with her came from the way she spoke about nothing except work, and when she did talk, it was as if Shah was made of nitroglycerine and might explode at any moment. He wondered what Bailey had been told about him – had some joker told her that he was a perv or something?

"Seen enough?" Stickel said.

"Just thinking."

"That what the burning smell was?"

Shah chortled. "Yep." He hoped it had been intended as a joke. "If we didn't get on, it must have been at least fifty per cent down to me. So I apologize sincerely and unreservedly." *Because I'm going to need every bit of help I can get here. I feel like I'm drowning.*

"Wow." Stickel raised her eyebrows. "That sounded genuine."

"It was. Why should I kiss off someone who van Doorn has set to help me? New start and all that?"

"Yeah." Stickel leaned forward and lowered her voice, "You can still call me Bitch if you want. Just don't spit after you say it, like you used to."

"OK, Bitch," Shah said, drawing a smile that mirrored his own. "Where do we start?"

"With coffee."

Shah sighed appreciatively.

When they returned, Stickel sat with Shah while he worked through the new cases. "If you take the newest ones first," she said, "you stand the most chance of getting a result. There'll be evidence, and witnesses will remember things that they've forgotten. But unlike most officers, you won't yet be following up your own cases, where you can't offload them. Our partners will work together for a few days following up."

"Offload them?"

"It's a numbers game," Stickel said. "We have to show our fund-providers we're giving value for money." She held up a placating hand. "Don't take this the wrong way, but coffee-machine gossip was that you're the best actual detective in the NYPD. What let you down was you never learned how to play the game. You got dumped on by other 'tecs looking to offload, but never sent any back."

Shah thought about it. "So police work's not just about solving crime?"

"Got it!" Stickel said. "Let's go through these: spousal violence. Send uniform off to that one. Mugging on the subway – that goes to the Transit Division. Memory rip. That's one we keep. Middle-aged man can't remember the last five weeks." Stickel grinned. "Of course, he could just have got a little honey on the side, and now she's drained his bank account he's got to make up with wifey."

"Do many people fake amnesia?"

"More than you might think," Stickel said. "Alibi of choice." She pitched her voice up: "Ah cain't remember uh thing, honey-chile. Don't be mad ut me."

"You're very cynical." Shah added quickly, "Or maybe I'm just naive."

"Maybe you are." Stickel smiled slightly at some unspoken memory. It wasn't a very happy smile, Shah decided.

They worked through the morning, offloading cases in a way that Shah found daunting, before Stickel left him alone for an hour while she took a lunch break.

Shah felt as if he was working in slow motion, the clock seeming to leap onward with every call that he made and every dive into the interweb. A headache built behind his eyes, and by the time Stickel returned, he felt as if he'd been working for days without a break rather than hours.

"You look tired," Stickel said.

"I'll be OK once I've got some air." Shah levered himself out of his chair.

"You realize that it'll take a while, you know?" Stickel said. "You've still got all the innate ability that you had before. But relearning the skills you developed to hone that ability will take much longer now that you're older – you know, Old Dog New Tricks Syndrome?"

"Gee, cheer me up why don't ya?"

"I am trying to, jackass," Stickel said. "What I'm trying to say – and obviously not doing it very well – is to be patient."

"I guess." Shah thought, *I don't have time to be patient.* "Maybe..."

"What?"

"You were saying about not following up our own cases?"

"Yeah, until you get back to speed."

"One thing I'd like to do is see this Kotian guy. He's at the heart of most of our cases."

Stickel looked dubious, but Shah ploughed on. "I'd be happy to just swing by his place on the way home, you know, just a social visit." He grinned. "I'll introduce you. Just to see what his reaction is; if he was behind the attack in some way..."

"It might force a reaction out of him," Stickel said, thinking about it. "Maybe. It's sort of against protocol, but then again, there is no protocol."

"Say again?"

"We've never had an officer attacked before, Pete. Not like this. Generally rippers are loners – they don't go attacking pairs of officers. I'll talk to van Doorn, see what he thinks."

# XXVI

The heat outside is almost as hard as the noise assailing your eardrums. You've been inside all day in the dim coolness of the call center, which, for all its subdued but relentless babble to the punters about soaps and reality shows is a haven compared to downtown Bangalore's raucousness. Every hour is rush hour here.

Great steel penises thrust up through the labial lips of the clouds into the sky, and you realize that you'd better find a whore tonight. At fifteen, everything reminds you of pussy, but when even the sky reminds you of it, it's time to scratch the itch. Not that you can ease it as much as you'd like – you need the money for the future. The sort of whore that you want costs money. Not for you a cheap musky minger from the Gaya, but a proper whore with blonde hair and white skin and expensive perfume, like you'll have as a wife when you make your first million dollars.

The Americans are the latest whites to ask your countrymen to become their servants for a fee, and your head is full of American slang. *Whatever, awesome, dude* and *ain't that the case?* rattle round your brain like dice in a cup. And dollars, and how to make them.

You stop for a cup of ice-cold lassi, chilled in the latest fashion.

"You work in there?" The lassi vendor asks you, his head waggling from side to side to emphasize the bond he'd like there to be between you.

"Ay-uh," you reply, in turn moving your own chin through fifteen degrees either way in affirmation. You work with an American, and the best way to ease the tedium of the day is watching him try to master the all-purpose wiggle – and fail miserably. Hilarious.

"Must be good." The youngster has a wall eye, which excludes him from ever getting a job there. Even though no customers would ever see his face, the people who run the call center have an almost superstitious reverence for physical perfection, as if it somehow mirrors an inner goodness. But you won't ruin his dreams

"It's a stepping stone." You watch a taxi disgorge a businessman, high-class, talking on one of the latest videophones. It looks like half of a pair of glasses. The future is in that frame, and you shiver. "It pays in real American dollars, still the best currency in the world, see? For all their troubles, America's where it's at. I'll make my fortune there."

"Need some help?"

Seeming to ignore his question you drain the lassi. Wiping the foam from your top lip, you look round for something to dry your wet fingers on. Careful not to stain your crisp white slacks – American style, of course – you rummage in your pockets for a tissue. "You need to provide these." You wave the used tissue at him. "What does your customer want?"

"Lassi?" When you shake your head, he tries again: "To wipe his top lip?"

"To feel better. You're not just selling him a drink, you're selling him satisfaction."

"Alas, while you're undoubtedly right, reality is preventing me from realizing this dream. I can pay for lassi, or I can pay for tissues, but not both – yet."

"You need investment." You recognize an opportunity. "You're undercapitalized."

"You're an entrepreneur?"

"Not for me the life of a wage slave." You grin and, winking, peel away a business holo-card with your name and cellphone in 3D. "Give me a call tonight. What's your name?"

"Aravinda," the vendor says.

"Abhijit Kotian." You offer your hand.

# XXVII

### Friday

Shah slammed one palm down onto the desk, and cradled his forehead in the other. Across the desk Bailey watched him wide-eyed. Shah restrained the impulse to snap at her.

"Problem?" Stickel said.

"This damn thing is *so* slow. I entered the next set of parameters while I was waiting. Now it's locked up."

"While you're waiting for the system to respond at busy times." Stickel's patience reminded Shah of Leslyn at her most unbearably reasonable. "You file or check your mailbox." She added, "You look tired. Maybe you're pushing too hard?"

"I'm OK."

He didn't tell her that he'd spent much of the previous evening searching the web for his memories. He was falling asleep in the chair, waking in the middle of the night to stagger to bed, then struggling to be ready for work the next morning. While dressing he'd caught the news of the latest victim, reduced to barely a vegetable after she'd been raped. *Does he think he's being kind, wiping the memories, or is it to hide his identity?* His eyepiece chimed, and he took the call wondering how he'd ever found this job easy.

"Officer Shah?" The caller was black, close-cut curly hair tinged with gray at the temples, deep-voiced. "I represent Justice for Victims." Shah could hear the capitals in the man's voice. "A clip of a lynching at Kiawah Island has been removed from the public domain. Your name appears as the certifying officer."

"Yeah?" Shah stalled as he wondered what he should do.

"We'd like this important historical document returned to where it belongs, and we're issuing a subpoena to that effect."

After several seconds, Shah managed to retrieve the appropriate procedures from the training manual and read directly from it, "You should call Internal Affairs, sir. Would you like the number?"

"This is outrageous, Officer. People have a right to know–"

"Would you like the number, sir?" Shah repeated, as the procedures advised.

"–that such crimes were committed–"

"Unless you advise otherwise sir, I'll assume that you have the number." Shah finished with, "Thank you for calling."

"What was that about?" Stickel said. When Shah told her, she scowled. "These lobbies They're not so powerful now that times are hard, but they can still be a pain in the ass. Copy the call to van Doorn, so that he can give IA a heads-up. It may be genuine, or a lone crank."

Shah glanced across at Bailey, putting on her jacket and gathering her handbag. Shah sent the list of off-site calls for follow-up onto her. Moments later, she said, "Thanks."

"Doing anything this weekend?" Stickel said as Bailey passed her.

Bailey shook her head. "Catching up on sleep," she said, walking away. "And household stuff."

"Enjoy," Shah called, but she didn't answer. He sighed. "What's her problem?"

"I'm guessing that she's always wanted to be a cop," Stickel said. "Now she's finding out you should be careful what you wish for. Ten years ago she wouldn't have been allowed into the force – now we're so desperate we'll take anyone. She's good at all the theory stuff that makes the brass cum in their pants. But she's scared of her shadow, let alone a perp."

"She'd be better off as a specialist."

"But all the jobs are frontline." Stickel added, "She needs to get used to working with a partner by Monday week, or the week after."

Clasping his hands together, Shah adopted a squeaky voice: "Please, don't leave me alone with him."

"Jackass. You're doing OK, Shah. Van Doorn said he's amazed how an old fart like you manages to clear half the workload of a star like me."

Shah snorted. "Yeah, right."

"What time you working till?"

"I'm doing a full day." Shah had worked longer and longer hours since his first day back, though he still found it exhausting – even without his nocturnal web-hopping. He had almost managed to work a full shift the day before. "Why? You asking me out?"

"Hah. 'Fraid you got the wrong chromosome for me." Stickel's tone was gentle, to soften the rejection.

"I was joking."

"Yeah."

"Believe it – or not; no odds to me."

"Actually," Stickel said, "I was thinking of us leaving together–"

"Hah! Me knew the lay-dee did protest too much!"

"–and calling on Kotian."

Shah stilled, all his attention on Stickel. "Van Doorn agreed it," she said. "He wanted to give you a few days to ease back in first. Keep shaving the caseload-mountain down, get your strength up, and you're back solo. He thought a little visit to Kotian might act like a stick poked into a wasp's nest."

"I'll get shaving that mountain now," Shah said.

"Good," Stickel said, "Because the fucker struck again last night. Teenage girl. We traced her back to out of town, but we got no leads on her. Bailey and my partner'll take this one, but the pressure's building, Pete. The commissioner's getting antsy. We got to stop this."

Shah was putting on his coat when his eyepiece chimed. He held up one finger to Stickel in a *wait* gesture. She was doing the same. The call was to both of them.

"Pete, this is Ray Eller over at the FBI. I heard what happened, so I guess you won't remember me." The man was close to Shah's age, thinning hair swept across his scalp, with the flushed face of a hypertension sufferer.

"Afraid not, Ray," Shah admitted.

"Sorry to hear about it. Bastard of a thing, these rippers." Without waiting for a reply, Eller ploughed on: "You put a request through a few weeks ago to look out for odd financial transactions. Something popped up when a data-entry supervisor gave access codes to his account for his annual audit, but gave the wrong codes – sort of stupid mistake that anyone can make.

But instead of the usual in-and-out small payments, this guy's got big money coming in irregularly, and money going out overseas."

"Oops!" Shah said.

"Indeed, oops," Eller agreed. "So this mook admits to falsifying information, including the supposed corpse of Aurora Debonis. It isn't her, nor anyone that we have on file."

"So not a US citizen?" Stickel said.

"Absolutely not," Eller said. "I know that it isn't much, especially as he won't identify who paid him to bodge entries, but we'll keep working at him, see if we can turn him."

"That's great, Ray," Shah said, though the Fed was right – it wasn't much. But he might yet turn up more. "We really appreciate the call."

"Hey, it's nothing," Eller said. "If you turn up a memory of us at the MSG with a couple of cuties, I'll deny everything." He closed the call with a smile and a wink.

Outside, wet pavements indicated that rain had swept through recently, although the sun beat down from a clear sky. Shah and Stickel rode the subway to Kotian's car showroom where a young woman greeted them at the door to the back office. Perhaps her eyes widened when she saw Shah, but the movement was so slight it could have been his imagination.

"Kotian Senior around?" Stickel said.

"Who shall I say is calling?" The woman said after the tiniest pause.

Shah decided to gamble: "Unless you're really new here, you know *exactly* who I am."

The woman shrugged. "I'll see whether he's available." She exited through at the back, leaving them standing around. Stickel crossed to the door and nudged it fractionally open, and spent the next couple of minutes craning her neck around the doorframe, until she said, "They're having a hell of an argument in there."

"About what?"

"I can't make it all out, but your name's featured heavily – oopa! Here they come." She scuttled back to Shah.

"Officer Shah!" Kotian burst through the door without seeming to notice that it wasn't properly closed. "I heard what happened – my dear fellow, I'm so pleased to see you back at work!" Kotian's British accent sounded fruitier than any of the clips, as if he'd been practicing. "Are you fully recovered?"

Shah studied him. Kotian was tall, dark, saturnine, and distinguished-looking – *very prince-like*, Shah thought. He swept back thick hair seemed unnaturally black but for the gray bangs flopping over his forehead. "Probably about ninety-eight, ninety-nine per cent of the way there," Shah said.

"What do you want?" Sunny called from the doorway. Shah caught his father's frown.

"Just a social visit," Shah said. "Let you know I'm back." Shah stared at Sunny. He had no memory of the son except what he'd read in the files, but already he felt antagonism; it was an atavistic reaction.

Kotian seemed genuinely concerned. "This must be awful for you, Officer. Our memories define who we are, how we view the world."

*Either you're a helluvan actor, or you're innocent.* Shah showed no emotion as he said, "I'm gradually getting them back." He watched their reactions. "It'll only be a matter of time before I'm back to full speed, and I'll nail the bastard who did it, however long it takes."

Again Shah couldn't be sure, but thought he saw Sunny flinch.

"You should put that little shit in a concrete casket," Sunny spat when Shah had gone.

Kotian smiled. "Always the fiery one, aren't you? He's no threat to us."

"He's a cop, for Chrissake! Of course he's a threat, Dad!"

Kotian blinked, and frowned. "There's no need for profanity, Sunil."

Sunny had that gut-clenching fear he always felt at his full name; it reminded him of a leather strap and his father's fake-regrets after the beating. "Sorry, Appa." The old man liked it when he talked that Kannada gobbledygook.

Kotian waved a dismissive acknowledgement. "We feed Shah some trivia, let him think he's onto something. Better to be dealing with a broken man than a fit one, no? They have a phrase for it around here; *better the devil you know, than the one you don't.*"

Sure, Dad," Sunny said, and the old man beamed.

# XXVIII

## Wednesday

"Do I divert this case onto Narcotics, or the River Police?" Bailey said. "The body was found in the Hudson, but drugs showed up in the tox screen."

"What do you think?" Shah kept the irritation from his voice, but it needed an effort. This was the third time she'd asked and it was hard gaining momentum with constant interruptions.

Bailey shrugged. "I'd say Narcotics, but they've bounced it back already."

"Probably because they're stretched right now, and they're focusing on the kudos cases. I'll guess, he's either a user or a low-level dealer."

Bailey checked. "Priors for possession only."

"So there's no glory. Bounce it back at them with a note saying it's clearly a Narco case, and to spend less time playing ping-pong with it, and more time working on it." Shah caught her horrified look. "OK, omit that last part, but send it back."

Bailey tossed the flimsy into the recycler, and made the call. "This is Officer Bailey of the 28th Precinct. We're reallocating the case of the John Doe fished out of the Hudson with amphetamines in his bloodstream. We, um, we believe that it's more appropriate–"

Shah screened out the rest and concentrated on devolving the morning's seven new cases. Five of them he rerouted straight away. Of the others, one was an amnesiac who suffered personality disorders from a burn that had stripped his recent memories, the other a known associate of Sunny Kotian accused of beating a girl up. Shah put both into pending, and returned to Bailey as she ended her call. "You ask a lot of questions," Shah said. "Which could be good – except they're questions you could answer yourself."

A flush spread up Bailey's neck and across her pale, freckled features. "I – I suppose I'm slightly lacking in confidence. I don't mean to cause problems."

"You're not causing me problems. It's you I worry about. You need to gain that confidence quickly. People have been telling me it's amazing how quickly I pick things up. But that's bull. I've just learned very, very quickly to look and sound confident. New York's a shark pool where criminals and other departments smell weakness like blood in the water." He made himself smile and as she flashed him a feeble attempt at one in return he added, "That case will soon come pinging back with a snotty footnote." He put his credit card on the table. "I'll bet lunch tomorrow on it."

Bailey shook her head. "No, you're probably right. Are we going to spend the next three months playing table tennis with Narcotics?"

"If we have to," Shah said. "Because it'll set a precedent. Every case that comes their way that they can fling at us, they will. That's what we'll do, the first weak link we find there." He stood up. "What are you drinking? I'm getting coffee."

"I'm OK, thanks. I'll get something later on."

"For the love of... I'm not going to drug you, you know!" Shah saw several people grow momentarily still in the way eavesdroppers do, and lowered his voice, "Would you like a glass of water? There are no calories in water, so you're not fleecing a poor old man, if that's what you're worried about."

Bailey stared at her desk. Her voice when she spoke was thin and high, and so quiet Shah had to strain to hear her. "I just believe that it's best to keep work and home separate. I know that you're floundering, and you want to build a rapport with as many people as possible, but we're colleagues not friends. Just two people who work together."

"Suit yourself." Shah shrugged and ambled over to the machine. A young woman walking past caught his eye. Shah saw a glint of recognition and said, "Hi."

"How's John?" the young woman said. "Oh, you probably don't recognize me."

Shah checked his eyepiece. *Kimi Hudson, Communications* – he cut short the data. "Kimi? Yeah, I've almost no memories from before the attack. How do we know each other?"

"Through John Marietetski," Kimi said. "We – he and I – were friends, before. You know." Kimi blinked and Shah thought for the first time in too long of his partner, who had also had a life, and friends, and people affected by the attack. Shah made a vow that he would go and see him, if only to show solidarity with Marietetski's family. *Should have done it weeks ago, you selfish toad.* Kimi added, "We were nothing but friends, but... " her glassy eyes hinted at more.

"Yeah, I know," Shah said and reached out to her, then drew his hand back. Don't want any misunderstandings.

"There's been no change to his condition since they stabilized him immediately after they took him in – still little better than a vegetable. They didn't just wipe his memories, but much of his ability to even learn – I've never heard of any attacker going so deep into the brain." Shah realized he was getting emotional himself and wiped his nose. *That could've been me lying in that bed, tubed up.*

Kimi ducked her head as she turned away, and dived into the ladies' rest room.

"Mister Tactful – as ever," Shah muttered.

The day inched by in endless downloads, images of men, women and children, a kaleidoscope of eating, sleeping, quarrelling. Trying to broaden his knowledge beyond his own private universe of pendings, Shah happened across a file containing a picture of a blonde woman. He had never seen anyone so beautiful.

*Aurora Debonis. That name sounds familiar.* He called up her details. After he had listened to the sounds of breathing, the thud of fists on flesh, he read the notes and sat slack-jawed. *I beat her up? What the hell was I doing?*

Shah sat deep in thought for the hour until shift-end, when he pulled on his coat.

As Bailey did the same, Shah said, "You don't need to nursemaid me – I can walk home unaccompanied."

"I don't mind."

"So why walk with me? Any time we talk about anything but work or the weather, you clam up. There's a reason why people make small talk, Bailey. It's called switching off."

They walked down the stairs. "I have a partner," Bailey said out on the street, breaking the silence. *A partner?* Shah thought. *Well, that's a surprise.* Somehow he couldn't imagine the delicate Bailey engaged in anything as coarse as sex. Bailey continued. "There. You know something about me. If you want to walk alone I'll give you a head start."

"Naw," Shah growled. "Don't be stupid. I'm just a little antsy." Sometimes Shah felt as if he was being watched, but when he looked around, there was no one there.

"It's your mind trying to make sense of it all," Bailey said. "Paranoia, dementia-type symptoms, there are all kinds of possible side-effects to a major rip."

The walk home was in near-silence, and Shah still couldn't work out why Bailey was nursemaiding him – unless she was following van Doorn's orders.

That night Leslyn was sleeping with Doug, so left alone, Shah was free to ride the web, looking for his or Marietetski's memories. Again and again he came up blank.

The next thing he knew an angry hornet was somewhere in the room.

"Huh?" He said, blinking at the sunlight streaming in through the window, and wincing at the pain in his back where he'd fallen asleep in the chair.

The angry hornet was his eyepiece's alarm buzzing him with an override. "Shit."

"Where are you?" Bailey said. "I've been waiting at the corner for ten minutes."

"I'll be there."

"No need. I'm outside."

Shah cut the connection, cursing, as Leslyn let Bailey in.

As Shah shaved, Bailey fussed around his part of the apartment and Shah felt his temper rising. "You go on

in," he called. "Van Doorn'll give me a verbal warning,
but he won't do more than that. No point in us both
getting warnings."

"No, it's OK," Bailey called back.

Shah heard the sound of wardrobe doors opening
and closing. "What you doing?"

"Getting your shirt out. I thought I'd help–"

"Look, you can help by waiting outside!"

"I just thought–"

"Well, don't!" Shah wiped gel from his face.

He heard voices murmuring; Leslyn and Bailey moving through the flat to the doorway. Leslyn said, "The
old Pete always had a bit of a temper, but now he's far
worse."

"It's frustration," Bailey said.

Shah shouted, "Don't you dare! You two got something to say, say it to my face!" Pulling on his shirt he
stormed into the corridor. "What you doing here, anyway? This goes way beyond partnership!"

Bailey said, "I've had enough. Find your own way
in."

The sign on the wall said Bassinet Street Mosque. It
was small, unobtrusive, like the mosque.

Shah had seen mosques on the interweb. They were
gold-plated palaces of ostentation with turrets spearing
the sky and megaphones rending the air with nasal
wails.

This one was different.

Shah's legs ached and his feet felt as if his shoes were
two sizes too small, but he'd walked the frustration and
rage out of his system. As so often happens, the lost
rage only left a vacuum. Curiosity was better than
anger Shah decided, and pushed open the door.

When Bailey called the third time, he'd not only cut her off but turned off his eyepiece as well. *Let them wait*, he thought. He'd tried playing by their rules.

Inside the building was cool, airy, the smell of coffee and almonds providing homeliness. One man read aloud while others asked questions or offered opinions.

Shah knew he had been a Muslim before. From what Doug and Leslyn said not a particularly devout one, but he had gone a few times a year, at important festivals. He'd remembered none of that, so had looked up the references.

It seemed to him that the best of churches and mosques and temples were schools that would provide guidance while allowing the individual to grow, but all too often they devolved into prisons for the mind, where people were told what to think, what to believe, how to live.

There was nothing for him here Shah decided, ignoring the Imam's call of, "Wait, friend!" He would be better working out his own problems, and deciding in his own time how he should live his life. Until then he would lose himself in the semi-familiarity of work. It wasn't *the* solution, but it was a solution, even if only a temporary one.

# XXIX

Shah slid late into an office in uproar. "What's happened?" He asked a passing uniform.

"The Ripper. Bastard's left the latest one on the steps of One Police Plaza."

"Van Doorn says Interview Room Four," Stickel called over. "Soon as you arrive. No stopping for coffee."

Shah rolled his eyes but obeyed. In the interview room he saw van Doorn and Bailey arguing, but couldn't hear through the soundproofing. Hesitantly, he entered.

Bailey stopped in mid-sentence.

Van Doorn grabbed his jacket. "You two are going to clear the air. Don't come out until you have a working relationship." The door slammed behind him.

"I... I offered to resign," Bailey said. "T-told him I couldn't work with a man who was so contemptuous of me."

"I'm not!"

"A– aren't you?"

Shah took a lungful of air, breathed out, took another breath. "I'm sorry," he said. "Can we start over?"

• • • •

Shah felt a fool standing with a flowering plant in his hand that evening at the hospital, but Leslyn had been adamant. "John can hardly eat chocolates or grapes, even if we could afford either. A bouquet will perish, so take him something that'll last. Watering it will give you an excuse to revisit."

Shah knew that he should have come before. There in the case notes, all the memories that his colleagues had burned onto an antique get-well CD: Shah and Marietetski at work, clowning in the office, at the annual Bowling Meet. He really had intended to call.

But throwing himself back into work was his way of fleeing the attack. Visiting Marietetski before would have been the opposite of what Shah needed. *So in some ways visiting is a sign of progress,* Shah told himself.

He took a deep breath and stepped into the room where Marietetski lay, tubes in his veins, another in his mouth. Beside the bed sat a small black woman, the wrinkles on her face etched deep enough to have been cut by a knife, her white curls partially hidden beneath a hat that would have been old-fashioned in Shah's childhood. Unusually, she wore no eyepiece. Her hands held a handbag with knuckles that were pale, and continually twisted the clasp; open, then closed, then open, then closed again, with the rhythmic persistence and precision of a ticking clock.

But her voice as she spoke to Marietetski was steady, and warmed by a Jamaican lilt. "Joseph should graduate next summer. You wouldn't recognize him, he's grown so much. He wants to go into the police, but I'm sure you understand your Aunt Evelyn isn't keen at the moment. Perhaps she'll change her mind when you recover." Her hands finally released the clasp of her handbag and one of them took Marietetski's left hand, stroking the knuckles. "If you can hear me John – no you can hear me, I know you can– just give me a sign."

Shah felt as if he was spying on something too intimate for his presence, and drew back, but only succeeded in attracting the woman's attention. "Who's there?"

Shah stepped out of the shadows. "John's partner, Mrs… Marietetski. Pete Shah."

"It's Mrs Trebonnet, Pete Shah."

Shah looked around for somewhere to put the plant. There was only a small table almost covered in cards, and he slid it to the back of them, knocking several of the cards off. *They must've cost a fortune*, he thought. *Some of them sound like they're made from real cardboard, rather than plastique.* He realized that the woman was talking. "Pardon me?"

"I said, you've been slow to visit my grandson."

Shah smiled. "I guess I have, Ma'am." He held his hands open in a what-can-I-say gesture. "I've been… away. And maybe not as good a friend as I should. You visit every day?"

"Every day," Mrs Trebonnet said, closing her mouth so tightly that Shah imagined he could hear the sound of jaws snapping shut. "Not like some of them, fair-weather friends. They come at the start, but they fall away. They don't think my eldest grandson he is going to come out of it. But I know he will." Her eyes glinted, her glare defying him to argue.

Instead Shah pulled up a second chair from where it sat in the corner and perched on the edge of it on the opposite side of the bed. When he leaned forward, he could barely see the little old woman over the mound of Marietetski's body. "So what's the plan, Mrs Trebonnet?"

"No plan. We just keep vigil till our love pulls him back from the edge of heaven."

Shah said nothing, but leaned forward in an attitude of prayer. Instead of praying, he tried to empty his mind of all thought. It was scarily easy.

The gloom thickened as the evening advanced.

"Why aren't you out catching that Ripper Man?"

Shah had done nothing but look at the latest victims all day, trying to find a pattern. A police-employed young woman; a mother of three; an old man. They seemed unconnected but for the fact that they lived in New York. Not quite once a week the Ripper had struck. But the only pattern was a lack of pattern. There would be months between attacks, then a whole cluster of them, as was the case now. "We're trying, Mrs Trebonnet."

She snorted. "To try is to fail. Don't try, just do. That was how my John lived. Lives." Shah saw a tear trickle down her cheek. "This was his stepping stone to the Justice Department, maybe even Congress. It wasn't supposed to get him killed. Because he might as well be dead." She blew her nose vigorously. "I shouldn't say such tings, John. I'm sorry." She cleared her throat. "Sometimes the despair creeps up on me, catches me by surprise."

"It does that," Shah agreed.


That night whatever cyber-gods ruling the Web forgave Shah, or his visit earned him the karmic equivalent of a doggie treat. Or maybe just random chance caused the inside of his eyes to flicker with the results of his search.

Streams of hits rolled down his inner eyelid, the closest matching one flashing at the 'top' of the circular list. Shah paid the fee, noting the properties of the copy for tomorrow when he would check whether those properties were faked, and dived in–

In the darkness she's in your arms, nails digging into your triceps as you kiss her. She thrusts her tongue into your mouth. You've never drunk alcohol, but you've heard about the symptoms: clumsiness, wild mood swings, a sense of vastness – you've got it all. You're drunk on her. "Intoxicated," you slur, coming up for air. She kisses your throat, down in the hollow at its base. "Thass what I am. Intoshicated." You clap your hand over your mouth.

"What?" she whispers, pulling your hand away.

"Thin walls," you whisper back, giggling. "Don't want a Noisy Neighbor summons."

"Sorry." She nibbles at your ear. You slide your hand up her thigh but she bats it away. "There's no rush. We have all night."

Now, lying together, her leg wrapped around you, she answers a question you asked in the bar. "Most men just want to fuck me. Those who do want to talk usually go on about themselves, impressing me with their alpha-male boasts. If they ask about me, it's always clichéd questions like, 'What's a nice girl like you doing in a job like this?' Like this is by implication somehow unworthy of consideration as a nice job." She adds, "You're different."

"Few sh-weeping generalizations there," you slur, echoing her earlier criticism of you.

She digs an elbow into your ribs, but ignores the interruption. "When we met, you seemed genuinely interested in me, like you'd be interested in anyone. No subliminal desire to reform me, or save me, just natural curiosity. And you're not bad looking, you know."

You laugh. "Yeah, see the pretty young girls beating down my door…"

"Lamp," she says. The bedside light's low glow is enough to show her features, but dim enough to airbrush out any distinctiveness. She studies you. "You're just that little bit too intense. It probably scares most women off."

"But not you?"

She shakes her head. "Nuh-uh. Not me. I don't scare easy, bud." She runs a talon down your chest, and kisses the curls that carpet it. "Lamp off." She carries on kissing your chest in the sudden darkness, running her nails down you, until your breathing grows ragged.

You blank your mind so you lose control too soon, but your calm shatters when she takes you in her mouth. As you slide your hand down her side, she wriggles and the dress falls away. Her nipple is hard in your hand, and as you run your hand down further, she stops what she's doing, "Pete," she whispers. Your hand reaches her waist, and suddenly you feel–

"Sharmuta!" you yell, pushing her away. "What the – you have a cock?"

"I was going to tell you!"

"You *thing*!" Rage possesses you. Gripping her hair in your left hand, you punch her with your right. She doesn't fight, but while you couldn't normally hit a defenseless woman, this is different. Only when your fist hurts so much that you release her hair does she crawl away, sobbing. You hold your sides, shivering.

Eventually she whispers, "I thought you were different."

"Get out."

The sound of rustling is followed by the click of the door, closing.

# XXX

The sand is everywhere, in your nose, ears, and whenever you breathe through the gauze mask in your mouth. Only your goggles keep out the worst of it. You wriggle forward on your belly, the stony ground pressing through your fatigues.

You think of Soudabeh, soft flesh and softer lips pressed against you in your marriage bed, and the rocks do not hurt quite as much, leaving only the pain in your heart and head.

Only three weeks ago you stood with tens of thousands of other men, the women respectfully indoors as they should be, pounding your fist against your chest in your shared condemnation of the *Great Shaitan's* latest incursion. Not content with corrupting the people of the Gulf for over fifty years, their fleets now massed off the south Yemeni coast, readying to invade that pious land. They claimed provocation, and protection for their lackeys in the House of Saud, but everyone knows that Hitler claimed provocation too.

For you the anger was a safety-valve for the grief that threatened to blow you apart.

When you reported to the *Bassidji* Office you expected you would be fighting Americans, rather than crawling on your belly through the border with Turkmenistan. But it makes sense. The infidel cadre of Hindu, Sikh, Buddhist and atheists comprising the Pan-Asian Republic are now a greater threat to Pan-Islamic security than the Great Shaitan. "The brothers in Turkmenistan need our help," the officer at the briefing told your team. "Since desertification's set in, their government's increasingly propped up by the heathens. Our fellow Muslims need our help to overthrow their oppressors."

For the Americans, it's all about oil. Their gas-guzzling lifestyle has finally caught up with them. Their oil addiction rendering their country as decrepit as one of their wizened alcoholics on the educational feeds about the perils of alcohol. Instead of broken veins and bloodshot eyes their country has a broken society and a blood-soaked history.

You see the border fence through the swirling curtain of sand, and glimpse the figures of your two colleagues. Your bowels are like ice-water, but you breathe deeply for courage. *Soudabeh would want this, were she alive.* You only hope that your martyrdom will be quick. There are stories that the Pan-Asians have found a way of jamming detonators, although others whisper that the failures are more down to faulty detonators or even faulty willpower.

You reach one of the myriad gaps in the fence – Iran's border with Turkmenistan is a thousand kilometers long – and wriggle through on your belly. "Are you all right, old man?" One youngster says.

You nod, wanting no further conversation.

You kneel, and pray towards Mecca and take the picture of you and Soudabeh from where it's secreted in your pocket. Lifting your mask for a moment, you kiss the picture and bid her farewell. "I'll see you soon, my darling."

Then you walk onwards out of the sandstorm, toward the infidels, and beyond them in heaven, Soudabeh.

# XXXI

**Friday**

As morning sunlight streamed through the window, Shah rubbed grainy eyes and stood under the shower, turning it up to full blast. What disturbed him wasn't the revelation of Aurora's gender as much as his furious reaction to it. *Why'd it bother you? Why doesn't it now?*

He parked the thought and dressed quickly. He left without waiting for Bailey, sending a message to her mailbox not to call round. He wasn't sure whether she would have after yesterday's furore.

The morning was cool, limpid, but the heat was already building, drawing out the sickly-sweet smell of uncollected refuse. Shah walked quickly, grabbing a Danish on the way. He was entering the office when his eyepiece chimed.

The avatar had the face of a blocky, heavyset man who looked like a weary bloodhound with five o'clock shadow. "You're Officer Shah?" The caller had a heavy Russian accent. "I am Pahlyuchenko, at the Russian Embassy."

"Good morning," Shah said.

"I have news for you, and apologies for taking so long. The request for identity only arrive this week, and it takes three days to get answers from my own bureau. Is same world over, nyet?"

Shah took it as an apology. "Seems that way. What's your news?"

"You have Jane Doe, you call her." An image of a bruised and battered girl on a mortuary slab appeared in Shah's vision; originally ID'd as Aurora Debonis, in error. She looked nothing like the girl he'd seen in the burn. Her hair was too short, but Shah recalled the tag about record tampering and incorrect DNA reconciliation. Pahlyuchenko continued, "We call her Natalia Sirtisova, according to her DNA. She is supposed to be in Vladivostok. Her brother Aleksandr is in US on student visa, but does not answer our calls to him."

Shah was tempted to chew his ear for calling a dead girl's brother about a US investigation, but held his temper. Turf wars could wait until later. That the Russians had already checked with Vladivostok explained why they'd taken so long to get back to him. "Thank you sir," he said. "We'll take calling the brother from here as this is a criminal case, but we'll keep you informed." Shah cut the line before the Russian could argue.

Ten minutes later Shah had a copy of Aleksandr's student visa and confirmation that Homeland had no immigration records for Natalia Sirtisova. Shah had a good idea why; Vladivostok was a gang-run war zone whose citizens would consider the US a paradise by comparison. Shah looked again at the picture of the brother, and rifled through pictures.

Then he put in a call to van Doorn. "I need a warrant, and backup."

• • • •

The police wagon disgorged a SWAT team at the back of the showroom. "Ready?" Stickel asked, at the front. Her partner Martinez nodded, as did Shah and Bailey.

As they strode through the doors Sunny Kotian yelled, "Now what?"

Shah stood at the edge of the showroom transmitting the warrant while holding a hard-copy of it aloft. "Sunil Kotian, we've a warrant to search these premises and an arrest warrant sworn out for a supposed student who just happens to be one of your grease monkeys." He paused, shooting Sunny a bleak smile. "Our boys have this moment stopped two bolts of lightning at the back door. One of them matches the description of Aleksandr Sirtisova, named on the arrest warrant. The Homeland Department will be paying you a visit later on today about your employee screening." Shah waved the CSU forward, and walking away, ignored Sunny's protests while hiding his smile from the younger man.

For the next half an hour Shah stonily ignored Sunny's long rant of protest as Bailey and the rest of the team went through every file they could access.

Kotian senior arrived in a chauffeured limousine. As he entered the showroom, Shah took another call and waved Bailey forward. Shah called to Sunny, "We rushed a DNA comparison between the dead girl and the arrested guy." His expression turned suddenly bleak. "Sunil Kotian, I'm arresting you on suspicion of human trafficking. You do not have to say anything – oh, finish it, Martinez." When they led the still-yelling Sunny away, Shah turned to Bailey. "You go with him. I'll stay here."

"We still can't tie Sunny to the dead girl's murder," Bailey said.

"Not yet." Shah turned to the CSU and the accompanying detectives and said in a loud voice, "Make sure you put it back tidily. Don't leave the place a shit hole."

One of the detectives gave Shah a hard stare, and raised his eyebrows. Shah winked at him, and the detective mouthed "OK."

"Officer Shah, this persecution cannot continue," Kotian said.

Shah said, "You seem to think that there's something personal about this."

"Isn't there?"

*Of course there is, you fuckwit. Everything says that it was your dirtbag son that damned near burned my brain out.* "I'm not the same guy you used to know, Mr Kotian. Everything that made that man who he was has gone, like you said the other day. There's nothing personal about this."

Kotian nodded, watching Shah. Even knowing who he was, Shah could feel the man's magnetic charm tugging at his emotions. *Hell, he probably is a nice guy – for a gangster.*

Shah strolled over to the gleaming limo. "You've been here a long time, Mr Kotian."

"Sunny was born here," Kotian said. "So sad, what happened to his mother."

"Accident?" Shah said, although he'd seen the file.

Kotian shook his head. "No one ever caught the burglar. I think that it was at that point that we gave up believing in law enforcement, Officer." Before Shah could reply, Kotian said, "I'm sure that you're a decent man, but the system – well, it doesn't favor us, does it?"

"Us?"

"Entrepreneurs. Men who move between social stations, those who don't know their place." Kotian paused, choosing his next words. "I'm a Millennium Baby, Officer, as you'll know from your checking of my records. Do you know how it feels – not the abstract, but the reality of being born on January 1st, 2000?"

*It means no one ever said 'no' to you until it was too late.* "I guess that it makes you sort of special."

"I was always the center of attention." Kotian might have been bragging, but his voice was matter of fact. "Even after the death of my parents when I was twelve – *especially* after."

Shah wondered. *A lot of people seem to die around you, Kotian.*

"Do you know what my given name – Abhijit – actually means?"

Shah shook his head. *Guess I'm going to find out.*

"One who is victorious." Kotian laughed, opened a packet of pistachios and offered some to Shah, who shook his head. "What sort of nonsense is that? Pressurize your children to succeed, huh?" Kotian's head waggled in the all-purpose wobble. "But in some ways it worked. I had to succeed. So you know what? I got rich doing anything and everything – I'm not scared to get my hands dirty, if need be. Though I left it all behind when I came here, except for some of my wife's family. They followed me over. But new country, new start."

"You left everything behind?"

"I left behind any disregard for law."

"With your family?" Shah smiled, to make it a joke.

Kotian didn't laugh. "Already dead. All killed in the Bhangala Massacre. As I'd have been, had I not already left for Bangalore."

Sectarian massacres weren't unknown, but to leave no survivors at all? That sounded like one of the reprisal killings he'd read about in India while reading up on

Kotian. When someone wanted to send a fugitive a message. *Life is cheap – if we can't get you, we'll get your family and friends instead.*

"You've done well," Shah said. "Two gorgeous wives."

"And a complex web of family loyalties." Kotian sighed. "Family is a wonderful thing until they want something."

"Why did you want to come over?" Shah said. "Life in Pan-Asia is supposed to be wonderful – or so I'm told."

"If you're very rich it is wonderful," Kotian said. "But parts of the subcontinent are no better off than here. They simply manage what they have better than Americans." He roused himself. "I'm not being very hospitable, am I? Would you like a glass of Chai?" Without waiting for an answer Kotian clapped his hands. "Serena!" He shouted several something in what Shah guessed was Indian, despite Shah's protestations.

A few minutes later a young woman in traditional Indian dress appeared with a tray of drinks. Kohl-eyed, her sulky mouth was heavily lipsticked, and as she bowed, placing the tray of drinks on the table she gave Shah a look that he couldn't quite interpret. When she left Shah said, "You don't seem very concerned about Sunny. We're chatting while your son languishes in a police cell."

Kotian chuckled. "Hardly languishing. He's sitting in a comfortable interview room with his lawyer present. We've been hauled in by you enough times for it to be no big deal now. My wife, Madeleine, was scandalized the first time that it happened."

"So were her family, I'd imagine." Shah had read the file. Within five years of arriving in America, Kotian's burgeoning millions had hooked him a bride from one of Boston's patrician families.

"They've gotten over it. We married as a business arrangement, pure and simple; I had cash, but no status while her family had influence but was short of money. The marriage has persisted as a political alliance, but there's little love left." He looked at his watch and clucked. "I have to be at my office soon. Let me give you a lift – it's on my way. We can carry on talking."

Shah shook his head. "I need to be somewhere else. But thanks."

"Call again, why don't you?" Shah saw something in Kotian's eyes beside amusement, but couldn't work out what it was. Loneliness? Sympathy?

"I may do that," Shah said.

"You don't need a warrant."

Shah shrugged. "It's a good excuse."

*A good excuse*, Kotian thought in his office that afternoon. *Is it just that, Shah?*

The Dying Years – when obesity had scythed through the youngsters with diabetes and strokes and cardiac arrests – had left Kotian without contemporaries. Maybe Shah felt equally alone. *My enemy's enemy is my friend*, Kotian thought. *Both Shah and I want this Ripper stopped. Even if my motives are different from his.* Rips had been going for years, and if it were controlled, surgical in its precision, a small amount of it was good for profit – wealthy connoisseurs would pay a fortune for unusual clips. But the indiscriminate butchering that had mushroomed in the last couple of years was getting out of hand. Kotian had learned over the years not to annoy the authorities too much.

"Hi, Appa," Sunny said from the doorway. "Sleeping on the job?"

"Thinking, my boy." Kotian smiled. "A vastly under-rated concept." He looked up. "They released you, then?"

"On bail. The preliminary hearing is set for tomorrow. It's all circumstantial, anyway." Sunny studied his nails. "That cop been sniffing round again?"

"Shah's been here, yes."

Sunny shook his head. "Whoever ripped him and his nigger should've finished the job properly."

"And started a murder hunt?" Sunny shrugged and Kotian said, "You don't know anything about that, do you Sunny?"

Sunny shook his head, lips pursed. "Not a thing, Appa."

"Because if it adversely impacts the business, we stop him, whoever he is." There had been too many coincidences for Kotian's liking; too many times when Sunny had been in the area. *One of his no-good friends, no doubt. He never could pick them.*

Kotian's son stared at him. "Of course. Whatever you say."

*Why don't I find that reassuring?* Kotian thought.

# XXXII

The feed of an Indian family disembarking at the border with Pakistan suddenly darkened, red staining the electric-lit glare of the arrivals hall. *Priority interruption,* a disembodied neuter voice said. *Lieutenant van Doorn calling. Take, Reject or Park?*

Shah sighed, the moment broken. "Take."

"Shah, in my office. Now." Shah severed the link without bothering to confirm.

"Want to bring me up to speed, Officer?" Van Doorn said as Shah sat opposite the captain, with Bailey to one side, studiously avoiding Shah's gaze. "You divert from home to office without clearing it with me, you play gangbusters with warrants, then stay behind for a social call on the suspect's family?"

Shah uploaded a recording of the conversation with Kotian, then said, "I didn't realize I needed to ask permission to walk a different way in."

"Spare me the sarcasm." Van Doorn put out a hand, palm down. "You're convalescing, and there's always a possibility of a follow-up attack. I make no apology for watching over my men. If you're telling me that you're fully recovered, a medical officer needs to sign you off.

Make an appointment with the Department of Health."

"What's this crap about gangbusters, Cap? You tell me which procedure I violated with that warrant? We got a court appointment set for Monday morning, and it'll hold. Unless the kid can show that he was working there entirely voluntarily – and the numbnut forgot to turn off his eyepiece at least once when someone mentioned his pay – we've got Sunny for employing illegal immigrants."

Van Doorn's head inclined fractionally. "OK, there were no procedural violations–"

"So what's the problem? I didn't convene a meeting in the office first and make some speeches, giving the Russkis time to leak and prime Kotian to squirrel them away?"

"There were no procedural violations," van Doorn repeated, loudly enough to make Shah pause. "But best practice says we go through the op in-house first to ensure that everyone knows their role. We got lucky this morning, but we might not again."

"Utter crap."

"Protocol," van Doorn repeated. "No more calling warrants on the hoof, summoning out SWAT teams from the street – unless you're in imminent danger. Clear?"

"Clear."

"Now," van Doorn glanced across at Bailey. "What was with the talk with Kotian?"

Shah took a deep breath. "If we get Sunny or Kotian, it'll be on a technicality, not for the attack on Marietetski and me. So to prove that it's Kotian selling memories, I need to get close to him. I can use my memory loss to get him talking about himself."

"Sounds dangerous." Bailey said hesitantly.

"He'll know that I'm taping everything, but he's happy to talk about himself. Hell, he's *desperate* to talk about himself. Guy has an ego the size of the old Empire State Building."

Van Doorn said, "It can't get us any less results than we've had already. We'll run it, but off the clock. You want to charm Kotian, you do it out of office hours. Got me?"

"Yep."

"Good." As they stood to go, van Doorn said, "Shah. Wait around." As Bailey left he added, "Shut the door."

Shah pushed it closed. *What now?*

"You've been accessing foreign sites." Van Doorn sent from his eyepiece a list; the Pan-Islamic Republics, Pan-Asia – almost every Asian country not in the PIR – Europe, Australasia, even what was left of Africa.

The captain was a stolid man not given to leaps of imagination. How to explain?

"Sir, tackling Kotian as the Department has done is never going to work. We need something completely unexpected. Learning what made Kotian tick is the only way we're going to do that, which means looking in areas outside the normal ones. Kotian has lawyers all over the net-havens, as well as the ones physically here in New York for when they need a warm body to keep him company in the interrogation room. One AI in the net-havens has made it clear that the case has international ramifications – the third-world footage ripped from the memories of a recent immigrant–"

"Our jurisdiction's New York, Shah – we're not Interpol. If it's really an international case we bring them in and hand it over. Do I bring them in?"

"No, sir."

Van Doorn relaxed. "Good. Stick to relevant footage. We've only got him on a chicken-feed charge, but getting one of the Kotians on a chicken-feed charge is a start."

The last part of the day passed in awkward silence, Shah and Bailey's polite conversations kept strictly to work, with no more warmth than a corpse's kiss. But at the end of it, when Bailey packed to go Shah said, "Want to visit Daddy Kotian?"

"As part of your off the clock investigation?"

"Yep. You learn more things about the job that aren't in a manual, you get free tea or coffee if he's feeling hospitable and you get to keep your eye on me."

"You implying I don't trust you?"

Irritation seemed to have given Bailey a spine, Shah decided with a smile that he kept under wraps. Perhaps he'd have to keep her irritated. "Not implying, saying."

"Why should I? You expect me to trust you, but you won't tell me what the plan is?"

"I can't tell you what it is, because I'm not really sure myself." Remembering van Doorn's orders and his own decision to work with her, not against her, Shah took a deep breath. "I'm working on instinct. Whether that instinct is from memories that are wiped from a conscious level, or whether I'm just freestyling... I dunno."

Bailey thought for a long time. "Maybe next time. When I can help, not hinder."

"I should have you thrown from the building," Kotian said, although his deadpan expression gave no clue whether he really meant it. It was an old-fashioned office, echoing the days when lights were left on in empty buildings round the clock, with furniture made from enough wood to cover a county.

It was full of people staring at screens while they muttered at the audio pick-ups on their eyepieces. Shah heard foreign languages interspersed with occasional English like 'stock-market' and 'bonds.'

"You could. It's your right." Shah held up his hands in a surrender gesture. "I want to establish if your son was careless, or deliberately hired that kid. Cause he's 'fessed up to being paid. Once he learned his sister was on a slab in the morgue he held nothing back."

"The mechanic's sister is dead?" Kotian looked aghast.

*If his innocence is an act, it's a good one.* "She is. It makes the boy's future doubly doubtful. He's working on a student visa, and she wasn't supposed to be here at all."

"That's awful," Kotian sat down heavily into a chair. It almost swallowed even his bulk. "The boy was clearly trying to provide for his family, however misguidedly."

"Sure. Look, we've all cut corners. Last time I drove I jumped a red light. I've turned blind eyes to stuff. We all do, don't we?"

"Do we?" The corner of Kotian's mouth twitched and his eyes crinkled. "I've known people who do cut corners, but I don't, Officer."

"Pete," Shah said. "Look, I'll level with you, Mr Kotian. We're not so bothered if you pay your taxes on time, or hire guys that you shouldn't, except where they affect more serious cases. Someone wanted to convince us that this girl was Aurora Debonis. Maybe they killed her *because* she looked a little like Aurora."

"Call me Abhijit, since we've cast formality into the corner with our coats." Kotian made a come-here gesture. Shah removed his coat and Kotian held it up for one of his staff to take. "What do you need from me, Pete?"

"You know a lot of people. Some – like Tosada – are perfectly legit. But some may not be. Let us go through your employee records at the garage without having to get warrants binding us to specific areas or times, and we'll look away if we glimpse anything that isn't to do with a major investigation, like the murder or the memory rips."

Kotian called for drinks, and Shah agreed to a mineral water. Shah looked at a set of pictures, one of a stunning redhead in her late twenties, holding onto Kotian's arm as she laughed into the camera. In another she looked wan but euphoric as she held a pair of babies while Kotian's hand rested on her shoulder. "Your wife?" Shah said.

"Amy, yes, and our boys," Kotian said, devotion audible in his voice.

*Trophy wife*, Shah thought. "How does Sunny feel about you extending the family?"

Kotian's hesitation was eloquent, but he said smoothly, "Sunny will always be the first born, Pete. My heir."

*You're torn in two.* "It can't be easy for either of you." As Kotian wiggled his head in an it-doesn't-matter gesture, Shah added. "Are they in Boston with – Madeleine, is it?"

"It is Madeleine," Kotian said, "but Amy and the boys live here by Central Park South."

It was a testament to Kotian's wealth and influence that he'd been able to keep family data hidden from snoops, although the Feds probably knew. *More to the point, why tell me? Is he playing games, or is he really so lonely that he wants to impress a mere flatfoot?*

They chatted for another hour about things that might yield Kotian money – classic American cars, ecological politics and the dream of the commercial exploitation of Mars, even the asteroid belt. They didn't interest Shah, but he was happy to let Kotian talk – *it might lead somewhere*. More interesting were ice hockey and Asian history. "When I retire," Kotian said, "and I don't intend to work until I'm eight-five as you do – I think that that's disgusting, Pete, I really do – I'm going to sail my boat to India."

Shah remembered a download from Leslyn, of going out on a little sailboat once, when they were newly-weds… off Coney Island, or somewhere like that. Shah freaking as the little boat threatened to capsize, Leslyn laughing at first until she realized that he wasn't ham-ming it up, then concerned.

"Calorie for them," Kotian said.

Shah thought Kotian's eyes gleamed with amuse-ment. *If he's seen my memory, he'd know about that. Is this some sort of test? What do I say to pass it?* He shuddered.

"What?" Kotian said.

"I hate the ocean," Shah said. "It's called hydropho-bia."

"As in rabies?"

Shah laughed. "That is a symptom."

"How can you be phobic about the ocean?"

"Any body of water much larger than a bath makes me feel ill. I can stand up in the swimming pool, but ask me to take my feet off the bottom – *oof!*"

Kotian nodded. "Well, when I get to India, I'm going to research my family's history." He paused. "Send your men around in the morning, Pete. They can check the records."

Shah nodded. "Thanks." He quashed an urge to punch the air.

# XXXIII

## Saturday

"You not got a home?" Hampson's soup-strainer mustache twitched.

Lifting the flap, Shah slid through from the waiting room into the almost empty office. "Thought I'd see if you work as hard as you claim."

"Funny guy. Your girlfriend's in." The desk officer jerked his thumb at Bailey, pouring herself a glass of water from the dispenser.

Shah went to get a coffee. "You can't tear yourself away from the place either?"

"My partner says I shouldn't work unpaid, but if I don't those cases will be backed up by Monday."

"I heard the Department factors that in."

"How'd your visit to Kotian go?"

"Kotian talked a lot, and I listened," Shah said. "I didn't expect much from the first meet, to be honest." Bailey played with her lower lip. "Speak your mind," Shah said.

"It's just – well, I'm worried about you getting too close to Kotian."

"I reckon Sunny will feel the same when he finds out." Shah grinned. "It may be the only time you and him ever agree on anything." For once Bailey *really* smiled. *She looks much better for it.* "Thing is, Sara, Kotian loves the challenge. He loves bragging about the things he's *heard* that criminals do – not him, of course, no, no, no – not me, Officer."

"You sound like you like him."

"Not exactly like. But he's almost an ordinary guy." Shah chuckled at Bailey's shocked look. "I said *almost*. He certainly likes to play games. He taunted me at least a half-dozen times, hints and little sly comments to see if I'd react."

"And did you?"

"I pretended I was hard of hearing." Taking their seats they began work. "He's agreed we can look through his employee lists to see if there are any names that leap out at us." He added, "I'm guessing it's only a partial list."

"Wow." Bailey looked at Shah with a sudden new respect. "Even a partial list's some sort of result." She grunted. "Your visit was probably worth it just for that. Good work!"

For the next two hours they scythed through the list of smaller, easy-to-finish jobs and those that could be delegated. For once their silence was companionable. Bailey asked fewer questions, Shah made sure he didn't snap his answers.

As the morning progressed the office gradually filled up, with uniformed and plain clothes officers on duty, plus a few like Shah and Bailey pulling an extra – un-paid — shift.

About mid-morning, having cleared the easy and minor items, Shah returned to thinking about Kotian. "You know, as well as two wives Kotian has several companions who he mixes with regularly."

"Yeah?" Bailey looked up. "What're you thinking?"

"Anyone ever pulled together a list of *their* close friends, relatives, and so on?"

"Dunno. I'll look." As the results poured down her eyepiece, she mouthed names, lips working silently. She shook her head, abstracted. "I ran a match on all the named victims with the list of family members – nothing there. Let me see where we have victim's next of kin or family members, see if anything intersects." She exhaled, still intent on the search. "No."

"What about companions?"

Bailey focused on Shah. "How do we establish who he mixes with? They're not employees."

"Bet your bottom dollar they'll be listed as contractors. If they ring any bells regarding the victims, or the victim's families, we'll have our connection."

"When did you arrange for us to, uh, drop in and check those lists?"

"Monday," Shah said.

Seized by an impulse, Shah accessed all downloads for the day before Natalia Sirtisova was found in the river, and the day before that. Then he checked her DOB, and filtered for gender, ethnicity and age, but left location open. He counted them. Nineteen hits.

Shah had cross-referenced two of them – both were busts – when Bailey checked her schedule. "We're supposed to be at the hearing in–"

"–an hour," Shah said. "Don't worry. I hadn't forgotten. Ready?"

"Will they need us?"

"I doubt it, but it's probably no bad thing to be around in case they do." Shah downloaded the other seventeen onto his eyepiece. It took so long that Bailey was fretting by the time they left.

• • • •

Bailey nudged Shah. "Here comes Grunwald."

Nancy Grunwald was smart, chipper and – to Shah – terrifyingly young as she faced the media. "We made a case for Sunny to be detained as a flight risk, the defense objected and we compromised on Mr Kotian Junior surrendering his passport and *very* reluctantly agreeing to report each evening at 17.00 hours until the trial. That's set for two months' time. Thanks for coming." She smiled, and walked away.

"So we weren't needed" Bailey stared at the ADA's back. They had sat outside the courtroom for ninety minutes, kicking their heels.

"Wasn't a complete waste," Shah said. "While we waited, I went through all seventeen downloads. The first seven were busts. I skipped the eighth, and I've eliminated another three – ah, here's Sunny."

As the Kotian legal team passed Shah and Bailey, Sunny whispered, "Don't think I'll forget this little stunt."

"That a threat?" Shah cocked his head on one side.

Shah watched the retreating group. "You know, after Kotian agreed to let us see the lists, he opened up a little. That was also when he started hinting and making those little taunts about how much he might know about this and about that."

"Why'd you think he did?" Bailey said.

"I think he thought giving us the list earned him a calorie's worth of liberty.

"But amongst all the taunts something came out. He doesn't have much faith in Sunny, despite what he says. There are problems ahead, there."

Bailey whistled. "He thinks Sunny isn't up to taking over?"

"He tried to dress it up, but yeah." Shah could see from his new perspective that both Kotian and he were a little lonely, for all their wide circle of acquaintances. Apart from Leslyn and perhaps McCoy, he knew few people outside of work, and fewer still were real friends. When he asked Leslyn, she had shrugged. "You were always a hard worker. It doesn't leave much room for anything else, and time's whittled away at those you had."

Shah checked the time. "I've got that medical this afternoon." *Then I'll study those downloads.* A face glimpsed in the eighth download was nagging at him.

Later, when the medical was over, and he'd been signed off, the face clicked and he rushed back to the office. When the search came up with what he was looking for, he sat back for a moment, running his hand through his hair.

Then he made a call. "Cap? Shah here – I need a favor. A big favor."

### Sunday

Shah was surprised that no one had revoked his driving license after the attack, but most people who were stripped of their memories were unlikely to want to drive again, so it was probably off most officials' radar. His heart fluttered as he packed the small carryall, but he had the medical permit to drive interstate and van Doorn's reluctant permission, given late the afternoon before. He hoped that it would be enough.

Leslyn stood watching him with half-folded arms, leaning against the wall. The only clue to her thoughts was one hand picking at a hang-nail on the other. "You sure this is wise?"

"Van Doorn's agreed it. And I've had enough lessons." Shah had been taking driving lessons in the lengthening evenings since he'd downloaded meeting Leslyn and driving back to New York afterwards – anything to bridge the gap with Old Shah. He smiled at her. "I'll be fine. Don't worry, honey."

Her eyes filled. "Know how long it is since you called me anything sweet?"

His only answer was a sad smile.

He took the subway up to the car hire office, picking up the keys to a little Dodge LPG-powered runabout just after eight.

Shah eased it out cautiously, heart thudding. He took the minor roads at first, before joining the I-95 in Westchester County. The countryside into Connecticut was vaguely familiar from some of his downloads, and he had little attention to spare for sightseeing. He tried to relax his grip on the wheel when his hands started to hurt, but the car wobbled with every pothole in the raddled concrete strip, so he put both hands back on the wheel.

When he reached the state line with Rhode Island he slowed for the toll-barriers, and wasn't surprised when, as soon as his card had been debited, a trooper waved him over to a lay-by. "New York plates," the cop said. "You got transit papers?"

Shah handed him the permit signed by the doctor the day before, when he'd been signed back to work full-time, just ninety minutes after the "eureka" moment on COTUS, when everything had changed.

The cop's right hand didn't leave his gun the whole time he looked left-handed through the tox screen results for Ebola, AIDS Plus, SIDS, everything that had savaged the world for the ten years of the Dieback.

There had been an outbreak of something nasty the year before in Providence, Shah had read. In New York Shah could pretend that life was unchanged, but out here in the boonies, there was no getting away from the fact that the world was a scarier, emptier place.

Finally the cop handed him back his permit. "What you travellin' for?"

Shah could have told him to mind his own, but there was no point. "Witness interview."

"Must be an important witness, send a New Yorker scurrying up here." When Shah didn't answer the cop waved him on. "You have a good day."

Toward lunchtime, as Shah's hands cramped up, he stopped at a diner in plague-haunted Providence, trying not to be spooked by the locals' sideways looks. The ghostly city made his daughter's squalid accommodation in Marble Hill look classy. Every window was boarded up, feral dogs roamed in packs on another street, and a half-eaten body lay in the road near the diner.

When Shah handed over his calorie card, the attendant squinted at it. "What's this? We don't take no New York State shit up here. You got real money?"

"Dollars?" At the attendant's contemptuous snort, Shah rummaged and pulled out what foreign currency he had and handed most of it over. *Guess that rules out staying in a hotel tonight,* he thought.

Shah drank the foul coffee which was even worse than what came out of the precinct machine as quickly as he could, wolfed down an equally overpriced and tasteless protein-burger – *whatever the hell that is* – and left as quickly as he could.

Back on the road, he finally began to relax when fifty miles later the interstate took him into Boston,

Massachusetts, down vast concrete arteries whose decay was a forlorn testament to the previous century. There was still more traffic than anywhere since New York.

Shah parked up soon after lunchtime and settled down for a long wait.

He half-dozed through the quiet Sunday afternoon in May; a few young couples passed the car, but though Shah felt the weight of their stare, he never took his eyes off the ordinary little house. As night fell, he slept uneasily, still in the driver's seat. When light finally came, his neck was stiff and he ached down his left side.

It was just after eight on the Monday morning when a woman emerged from the house. As she passed, Shah stepped out from his car and said, "Hello, Aurora."

# XXXIV

It's the early hours of the morning, but Washington is still awake. Though the Dieback has killed millions of people, the lack of gasoline has sucked people in from the suburbs – the vast sprawls of houses built on the premise of endless supplies of gasoline for automobiles to link them has proven unsustainable – and this is still the nation's capital.

Lobbyists, journalists, government employees and those dependent on the government still behave as if this was the last decade of the last century when the United States all but ruled the world in the benevolent glow of their triumph over communism. Even more than New York, this is the city most in denial that the world has changed, and not for the better.

Still, all those people mean that you can window-shop for your next victim in perfect safety, with almost unparalleled choice. All those *Oh So Important* people going about their important business around the clock because it's always high noon somewhere in the world.

Unlike Peoria, Illinois, or Arlington, Texas, or any of the other multitude of places once again tied to the rhythms of the sun and moon, here you can walk at midnight down streets still thronged with people networking, schmoozing, eating, drinking, flirting – and right on cue, you notice a pretty girl sitting in a bar on her own, sipping a cocktail. She looks bored and lonely. Good. All the better if she's an out-of-towner.

You wait outside the bar, hoping that, bored, she won't jump into a cab, although she doesn't look that prosperous – one of the reasons you selected her – and Washington cabs are eye-wateringly expensive. That no one will pick her up while you wait, though it's clearly a couples bar rather than a pick-up joint, and half of the clientele look gay anyway.

You're checking the time for the fourth time as she leaves – *01.23*. She turns right, away from you, which is good. No need for any attempts at clipping. Cutting parts of memories out is like editing primitive tapes from early television shows, nearly impossible. One day perhaps, the technology will exist, but you very much doubt that you'll see that.

Too autobiographical, you realize. Focus. Focus on the girl.

She's had a couple of drinks, and it shows in the relaxed way she's walking, although she doesn't weave or stagger as she would if she'd had too many. Good. You're not in the mood to get puked on tonight. She turns off the main concourse, and immediately your task becomes both easier and harder; easier because there's less chance of being seen by a passer-by, harder because she's more likely to see you and bolt.

You close the gap slightly, battening down the desire rising within you. Keep your distance, but don't lose sight of her. This must be how it felt for early man, stalking the mastodons across the tundra.

You're caught by surprise when she turns off again into a narrow alley, and nearly lose her. You speed up.

She's climbing the steps to a square Reichstag-style apartment block when you spray her with the relaxant and she goes down like a building that's had its foundations dynamited.

You catch her before she lands, rolling her around so she faces you. Her limbs are twitching, but this stuff is formulated to knock out everything but the respiratory system and voice box, so all she can do is flutter her eyelashes and whisper, "Please."

"Don't struggle and I won't hurt you." Your filtered voice always sounds strange, but it lengthens the odds against a voiceprint match.

You push her skirt up and tear off her panties, cheap nasty things with hearts on them, and push her legs apart. She's dry down there, but a little lube takes care of that, and you harden at the terror in her eyes. She flinches as you enter her, which is even better.

It's over all too quickly, and even as the probes enter her head to find their way to the memory of the rape, you feel yourself shriveling inside, matching your increasingly flaccid cock.

The shame eats away at you, rendering your joy ever more bitter. Guilt fills your mouth with bile. Now, all you want to do is forget what you've done.

# XXXV

Shah noted Aurora pale beneath her impeccable make-up. *Good*, he thought.

"Pete... I... Should I call you Officer? Are you on duty?"

"Get in the car, please, Aurora."

"I'm supposed to be... somewhere."

"I can drive you there. Or I can arrest you and drag you down to the local precinct. Which do you want?"

Aurora sighed but climbed into the passenger side. She gave Shah the address, which he repeated for the eyepiece to get journey instructions. She – he couldn't think of her as it – wrinkled her nose and opened the window fractionally. He started the engine.

"I didn't expect to see you again. Considering you beat the shit out of me last time."

"Supposed to be in Rikers, was I?"

Aurora looked puzzled. "Rikers seems a little extreme, but yes, appropriate."

Shah drove in silence, slowly, cautiously. After yesterday's odyssey, driving at twenty miles an hour felt almost comfortable.

Aurora licked her lips. "How well do you know Boston?"

*She looks terrified.* "I can get from here to where you want to go, with the eyepiece help." Shah drove. He toyed with the idea of putting the radio on, but decided against it. Silence might make her talk.

It didn't.

"Surprised you're up here," Shah said at last.

"As opposed to where? Poughkeepsie?"

"I meant that it doesn't seem that big a place, to be able to support you…"

"It's smaller than before the Dieback." Aurora stared straight ahead. "But it's still one of the two or three biggest cities on this coast."

"But nothing like New York."

"It's a big IT place. Twinned with Silicon Valley Urb and Bangalore."

Shah said, "One of many reasons why Kotian has interests here, I guess."

Aurora licked her lips. "What do you want, Officer – Pete?"

"To see you."

"Why? To hit me again?"

"No." Shah slowed, allowing pedestrians to cross. Gulls swooped low and he guessed that they were near the harbor. "You can relax; I'm not here to hurt you. Just to talk."

Aurora studied Shah, and then seemed to come to a decision. "There's a motel nearby. They charge by the hour, and they're discreet. You can shower, while I meet my client."

"In the same suite?"

"Ha, ha – funny guy. No, next door."

"How do I know you won't run for it?"

"You can listen at the wall. Or you can trust me, like I'm supposed to trust you."

Ten minutes later they parked outside a small two-floor motel with peeling paint and acne'd concrete walls. At least it looked clean. Shah showered and dressed again, then lay on the bed fully clothed.

An hour later a knock roused him.

Aurora brought in glasses of juice, sipping one. She sat on the bed and patted it, but Shah took the chair facing the bed. She smiled in triumph, as if she'd just won a bet with herself. "I won't talk with an eyepiece running."

"OK." Shah turned it off and put it in his pocket.

"You seem... different," Aurora said.

"Being framed for murder has that effect."

Aurora's eyes widened. "What?"

Shah said, "A SWAT team kicked in my door a few hours after you left. I had no idea how much shit I was in, so I invoked the Fifth. The only thing that saved me was that the perps underestimated just how badly NYPD needs experienced staff. Even so, one more incident woulda put me in Rikers for sure. Everyone says I just got lucky, but it didn't feel like it. Then we got an ID: Natalia Sirtisova."

Aurora gasped, but said nothing.

Shah noted it for later. "I found a Russian-speaking clip which fitted Natalia's profile. Maybe her last download," Shah added. "I glimpsed someone in the background who looked familiar. I finally realized that it was someone I'd seen on the web. When I found the clip again, I ran the facial recognition and passed it through COTUS. Surprise! It threw up a small-time Boston crook. If they had connections here, then probably so did you. Like a dummy I thought just 'cause

Kotian had a wife up here, he still had all his businesses in New York. When I finally stopped thinking locally, it fell into place. If you needed to hide, where better than another of Kotian's operations? And I found another Debonis whose registered address was here."

"My father left it to me, but I never changed the registered owner." Aurora shrugged. "And?" Despite her so-what? reaction, her eyes never left his face.

Shah didn't answer straight away, but sipped his coffee, letting silence and tension do his work for him.

At last, realizing she knew such tricks or had more self-control than most, he said as if thinking aloud, "I just realized that this may well be where our Ripper kept his gear. So why'd I never think of this before?" Aurora spread her hands in an I-dunno gesture. Shah continued, "Cause we're all used to thinking locally. That's how the world works nowadays, but maybe our crim don't. Maybe he thinks nationally, even internationally."

"It's fascinating to hear the detail of your cases, but is there a point to this?" Aurora flicked back her hair, gradually relaxing

"Natasha's DNA was identified as yours."

"WHAT? You. Are. Kidding. Me!" Aurora leaned forward. "How? Why?"

"That's what we want to know. Your lawyer knew you were alive, but wouldn't even tell us that we'd made a mistake. Why?"

"Oh, that's easy. It didn't want to bother me. It's hugely protective of my privacy." Her voice grew harder. "When you've had the shit beaten out of you a few times, or been treated like something from *Ripley's Believe It Or Not*, you learn to value privacy."

"I'm sorry about hurting you." The violence that Aurora had aroused in him had been someone else's anger, someone who wasn't him. "You shocked me. But that's no excuse."

She nodded, and her lips quivered so she pressed them together.

He realized that she'd been using her anger as fuel, and now he'd apologized, she was suddenly running on empty. And equally suddenly Shah wanted to hold her and tell her it was all right. He stamped on the feeling.

"You seem... different, somehow."

He was silent for a moment, then made his voice as gentle as possible. "Tell me about that night, Aurora. Someone hired you to sleep with me, didn't they?"

"I was hired get you back to my place and told to dope you if necessary to do it. I guessed it was to set you up for blackmail. They knew you have an anti-toxin injection at the start of every month, so knowing it's weaker at the end of the month they probably targeted you then."

*More likely they intended to rip my memory,* Shah thought. *Maybe Marietetski would be OK if I'd gone home with her.* He shook his head. There was no point thinking like that.

Aurora continued, "I tried several times to get you home, but you insisted on going to your place, so I went with you. I guess your anti-toxin was stronger than we thought – and if you had a strong sense of self – it allowed you to overcome the worst effects of the drug. But not enough to stop you beating the shit out of me." She stared at him, a trace of her former anger returning. "Unless you're just a Neanderthal creep who gets off on beating people up."

Shah wasn't going to allow her to distract him with guilt. "Who hired you, Aurora? Who paid you to take me back to your place? Who was waiting for me?"

Aurora shook her head.

Shah wasn't sure whether she didn't know, or was scared to tell him. He leaned forward. "There aren't many people who could tamper with ID files. That takes a lot of influence. You may be in more danger if you don't tell me than if you do."

# XXXVI

"No," Aurora said. "I'm in no danger, as long as I keep my mouth shut. And if you were that worried about putting me in harm's way, maybe you shouldn't have come."

Shah sensed that arguing wouldn't work, so he said nothing. Instead he studied her long thin legs, knife-sharp cheekbones, long blonde hair. He wondered whether she had to take estrogen supplements to stay so feminine. Now wasn't the time to ask.

This time his silence worked. Aurora began to fidget. "Are we done now?"

Shah shook his head.

"I really didn't know they were going to frame you."

"I should believe you, why?"

"Because it's the truth."

"Just coincidence that you fled the day the girl's body was found and I was arrested?"

"I'd been beaten up! My face is my livelihood, and you disfigured me!"

"A young girl was beaten to death for no other reason than she looked a little like you. She knew she was going to die, Aurora. Her last moments on this earth were filled with terror."

"I don't know anything about it. You have to believe me!"

"Convince me."

Aurora licked her lips. "I knew that you liked me, the first time I met you. It was mutual. I've always been attracted to powerful, older men." She laughed, a thin nervous sound. "Call it father-figure attraction if you want a cheap diagnosis. It was hardly work at all, except that they gave me a phial with a drug in. It was easy slipping it into your drink when you weren't looking."

"What was supposed to happen when you got me back to your place?"

"The other girl and I were supposed to take it in turns being filmed with you, you know, Tasha would wear a strap-on for a while, then me. Make it look like you were a real perv. It seemed plausible enough, given your age and the way it was described." Aurora chewed her lip. "I never thought – dreamed that Tasha would get hurt." She stared at Shah with haunted eyes. "I had no idea they were planning anything but blackmail."

She seemed genuine, but Shah urged himself to be sceptical. "Why Boston?"

"Kotian told me one of his local supervisors had suddenly quit. He needed someone to manage the girls for a few days. Days turned into weeks. I was planning on going back, but time passes so quickly." She added, "After you knocked me around, I was relieved to get something temporary, where looks didn't matter. My confidence took a helluva battering."

*Here comes the guilt trip.* "Not as big a battering as Natalia Sirtisova took."

Aurora's jaw clenched, but she was quiet for a while. "You realize," she said, "that that was partly down to you. When the others saw what you'd done, everyone went crazy. They went crazy, shouting and yelling..."

"The yelling didn't kill her," Shah said. "It was hands around her throat. Whose?"

"I don't know," Aurora said. "There were about twenty people there at Sunny's loft apartment. Forry, Raison, Paulie, Adonis – all of Sunny's usual pack – were there, with some other guys, and girls for all of them. Millie – another of Sunny's girls – took me into a bathroom to clean me up. When she'd finished and we came out, they'd all gone."

"You were Kotian's girl? Or Sunny's?"

"Abhijit's companion," Aurora said, then spat, "Sunny's whore, occasionally."

"You're telling me," Shah crammed his voice with skepticism, "you knew nothing about a body pulled from the East River that was identified as Aurora Debonis – her face smashed beyond recognition, fingerprints removed?"

Aurora insisted, "I didn't see anything."

"If he's convicted of a felony, you'll be charged as an accomplice."

"Why? I'm his girl – I had nothing to do with killing her."

There was a long, long silence. Aurora shifted her position on the bed.

Shah cleared his throat, said, "If the plan was to get me back to your place, why didn't you leave me where I was when I insisted on going home? Why sleep with me if it wasn't going to work out? It's not as if I'm either young, or good-looking, or rich."

"You wouldn't believe me if I told you."

"Try me."

Aurora exhaled. "I liked you. I wanted you in me." She blinked. "Part of me still does. Though judging by your reaction the last time, I can't see *that* ever happening."

Shah didn't answer. He wondered what she would say if he told her that he'd trawled the net looking for his memories of what had happened, trying to understand that other Shah, who was so revolted by the reality of her. *She'd probably use that knowledge. You been dancing round the fact that she's a companion; her affection's worth whatever you can afford.*

"No," Aurora said, then added, "I thought not."

"You ever wonder what it'd be like to be just average?"

Aurora leaned back on the bed. "You think I always looked like this? Half of it's surgery, Pete."

"You were a guy?"

Aurora shook her head. "No, I was always a girl with an extra surprise." She stared at him. "That's the problem, isn't it? You still can't get past that, though you're different." She shook her head. "I never thought I'd see you again, let alone here. What's changed?"

Shah couldn't tell her. For all he'd studied endless downloads he didn't know how to make a move. He'd lost his judgment of how to court a woman, and didn't want the humiliation of messing it up.

"Once I'd got past the 'I'm screwed' and realized that it wasn't you at all," he finally said, "all I could think of was *why*?" He stared at her. "Who sent you up here? Sunny? Or Kotian Senior? Or was it always part of the plan?"

Aurora looked down at the bed. "Abhijit knew nothing about the date. Sunny set it up, said he'd heard you were a sucker for a pretty face. When I called Abhijit to tell him I'd been smacked around, he sent me to Boston. I told my other *patrones* I had a family emergency." She looked up. "Abhijit arranges to come as often as he can."

*That explains his frequent disappearances out of town,* Shah thought. *It's to see her.*

"You're in love with him."

Aurora smiled, almost shyly. "Not quite. Though he can be very charming."

"What about Sunny?"

Aurora's face tightened. She glanced at her watch.

"You got to be somewhere?" Shah said.

"An eleven o'clock meeting." She caught his look, laughed. "It's not like that. I don't do two guys in one morning any more. I can afford to be picky. This is the girls I supervise."

"I'll drive you back."

"There's no need."

"I got no other reason to be here."

"You're kidding? You've driven two hundred and twenty miles to talk to me?"

"What else am I going to with all those days off?" Shah thought, *Now we know where you are sweetie, this is only the first of many, many such conversations.* Shah had heard it called "The Long Game". It seemed an apt description. His voice revealed none of his thoughts though. "I cleared it with my captain late on Saturday. I could hardly make it official, given that all I had to go on was a hunch, but he stumped up the calories if I took the time as leave."

Aurora's smile couldn't hide her bemusement. "Why not just send Boston PD?"

"You'd have talked to them like we just talked?" Shah smiled back. "Two old friends gossiping, no tapes, no lawyers?"

"Maybe not." Aurora gathered her things.

"Let me buy you lunch, after your meeting," Shah blurted.

Aurora stared at him. "You *are* different. Not sure how, or why, but…"

*Now would be the time to tell her,* Shah thought. He just couldn't bring himself to do it. Not yet. He still didn't know quite how she'd take the news, whether she would try to use it. *Unless Kotian's already told her. But somehow I imagine they have better things to do than talk about than a tired old cop who's just another little local problem.*

They stopped at reception.

Aurora said to the desk clerk, "It's on the Kotian account."

"No it's not," Shah said, still smiling, but steel in his voice. There would be no accusations of bribery from the Kotians when he got them to trial. Maybe they'll be more accepting of out of state calories.

They were, fortunately.

Outside, the sun was shining, so Shah clipped his eyepiece to a pair of sunshades on another half-frame, making up a whole pair of sunglasses. He wondered whether Aurora had assumed that he had a second tape on him somewhere. *Probably*, he thought, as they strolled to the car in the sunshine. *To an outsider we'd look like old friends, even lovers.* "When's Kotian visiting next?"

"Friday," Aurora said. "But Sunny will be up tomorrow." She shivered.

Shah decided to exploit that momentary revelation. "You know he's out of control, don't you?" He added, "We know he killed that girl. We've lost count of the beatings he's handed out."

"Then why haven't you put him away?" Aurora said, though Shah sensed she was defending Sunny from duty, not because she wanted to.

"The complaints are always withdrawn later on."
Shah added, "I'll leave you to work out why – you're
not stupid."

Aurora didn't answer, but got into the car. "Just
drive. Or I'll be late."

# XXXVII

"I'm not sure we should celebrate Eid this year," you tell your mother. "It feels wrong, when thousands of families are mourning their dead. And it highlights that we're Muslims."

"But Pervez, we had nothing to do with what happened to those poor people!" Madaar cries. "And the neighbors know we're Muslims."

"Knowing it and rubbing their noses in it are two different things." You button your uniform shirt and reach for your shoulder holster. "Eid's a time of joy. There seems nothing joyful at the moment in watching them dig bodies out of Ground Zero." You've been spared that, but you've seen the devastation etched into the faces of the rescue teams. That has been bad enough. You're finding it hard to sleep, but it seems an insult to the memory of the victims to request counseling. What have you suffered, compared to the victims' families?

You can't really talk to your mother about it. She's cried enough for the victims already, even though she probably never knew any of them. But she knows those who knew them, and no one in New York or New

Jersey is wholly untouched – the consequences of the bombers' actions have rippled outwards in the three months after the bombings, changing those they touch and bouncing into new directions.

"The grocer's assistant wouldn't serve me today," she'd complained the week after the bombing. She never knew that you went down there the next day after and reminded the grocer that you are perhaps more American than he, who emigrated from Vietnam thirty years before. "I was born here," you'd said, pointing to your badge. "If your assistant insults my mother, he insults me."

The next day you saw the assistant was gone. The way the owner glared at you told you that you only won that battle because you're a cop.

"We'll talk about this tonight," you say, wondering whether you can turn things around and how. Meanwhile you must become a cop first, a Muslim second, and face the wounded city once again. It's becoming easier with each passing day, as you see what's been done in the name of your religion.

# XXXVIII

While Aurora was in her meeting, Shah sat in the car outside the apartment complex and called van Doorn.

"How's the weather up there?" The captain said.

"Better than what you got. I saw snow in Times Square on the newsfeeds."

"Mostly melted within an hour, but yeah, it caught everyone by surprise." Van Doorn said cautiously, "Find your friend?"

"Jackpot. She's not given much up, but I've got a couple of ideas. One thing made me think. You might want to discreetly check bank balances."

Van Doorn didn't immediately reply, digesting the implications. "You think they have someone inside, on the take?"

"She knew about timings of anti-tox shots," Shah said. "Admitted that they doped me at a specific time. But they underestimated the strength of the shots, so it's not someone with access to the dosages, which rules out the ME's office. Maybe HR. They'd know the timing."

"I'll look into it. I'll need to narrow it down as much as I can before involving IA." He added, "When you coming back?"

"Tomorrow. And I might bring a friend."

When Aurora returned, Shah greeted her with a peck on the cheek. "Lunch?"

"That would be nice." She didn't sound enthusiastic, but then he wasn't sure he'd be keen to dine with someone who'd knocked him around the room.

He reached out to touch her chin. She flinched, but held still while he examined her jaw. "It healed up well," he said.

"Better than I feared it would." She met his gaze. He sensed the effort it cost her.

"How the hell did you intend to blackmail – oh, your eyepiece. It would've recorded everything."

Aurora nodded. "I fitted an image intensifier to it. But even without it, your voice would've been incriminating enough."

"Who spoofed my fingerprints onto the scanner?"

"I used a gelatin mould."

Shah started the engine. "And I guess you took my eyepiece?"

She grunted. "If they could've spliced memories in, rather than only cut segments, you would have been in deep, deep trouble."

"I was in enough," he said, noting she said 'they' not 'we'. He pulled out into the main road. There was more traffic this morning, so he had to concentrate. He was still painfully aware of how erratic his driving was. "Why don't you come back to New York with me? It's a good way to avoid Sunny for a few days."

"Why should I?"

"Because you're scared of him."

"Crap!" Aurora looked about to say more, but bit her lip. "Not many men repel me," she finally admitted. "I can't afford to be put off by one, however creepy, but there are certain kinds of guy who scare me." She added, "One got a little possessive before I came to Boston. It took him a while to track me, but he managed it eventually. I told him to shove off, which he *really* didn't like."

Shah smiled, a slight smile hinting at the irony of this. "But that wasn't Sunny?"

Aurora said, equally dryly, "Of course not."

"Why not tell this guy's papa?"

"You have no idea of how much Daddy spoils him, do you? No companion would ever win an argument about his son."

"So come with me," Shah repeated.

"I don't think that's a good idea." Aurora stared fixedly ahead.

"Look, I'm not happy about what I did. I can't undo it. But–" Shah stopped. *What did he want? How much of this is really about turning her?* Shah took a deep breath, and another. "You said I seem different."

"Yeah."

"Do you believe that we're born the kind of person we are?"

"What the hell kinda question's that?"

"Or do you think that we're the result of our lives?"

"I don't know! What is this? Philosophy 101 with Pete Shah?"

Shah blurted, "If you believe we're the sum of our memories, then there's a reason I'm different." This was proving harder than he'd thought. Shah swerved into a curbside parking space, provoking a blast on the horn from the car behind, which only just missed them.

"Can't be more than a dozen cars in the city," Shah muttered, "and I have to get the Tailgate Queen."

Comprehension dawned in her eyes. "You've been ripped," Aurora breathed. "Oh, Pete! I'm so sorry!" She touched his arm.

Shah had almost convinced himself that the attack had happened to someone else. But the anger and grief bubbling up threatened to overwhelm him. He put a hand over his mouth to keep them inside.

"What did they take? What did they leave you with?"

Shah shook his head and scrambled out of the car, almost into the path of the traffic. He made himself think about something else. *She seems to know about it. I suppose everyone in big cities knows someone who's been ripped. Cities draw them like planets catch passing meteors. Then again, ripping don't usually happen in small communities. It's hard to hide, and away from 'civilization' justice usually includes a rope and a lamp post or tree.*

Distraction wasn't working. Shah had thought that he couldn't mourn for what he didn't know he'd lost, but some part of him knew and he had to clamp his eyes shut and rock backwards and forwards to stop from screaming his grief aloud.

He was dimly aware that Aurora had left the car and was holding him, smoothing him down with her hands and hushing him. He was acutely aware of her warmth, and her perfume, and the softness of her as she held him. "I'll drive," she said at last. "And we'll forget about eating out. I'll make us lunch."

They parked in almost the same spot that Shah had greeted her from earlier that morning. It seemed like days ago.

Despite the distraction of their small talk Shah was agonizingly aware of his own fragility, and burned with embarrassment. He had inherited Old Shah's disdain for the kind of people like those mourners at funerals who rended their clothes, tore at their hair and beat their chests with grief. That he'd allowed his feelings to explode in the car had been almost as self-indulgent.

As they left the car Aurora said, "Keep to the left side of the path and turn your face away. You'll stay mostly out of sight of the house's surveillance cameras. But try not to be too obvious about it."

"You expect Sunny to check the tapes?"

"Wouldn't you, if I wasn't here and didn't answer my eyepiece?"

Shah stared at her. "You're coming back to New York, then?"

"Just for a day or two. With luck, I'll fly north again as he's returning to New York. Now come on, I'm hungry." She led Shah up a side path to a gate, and through there into the kitchen. "We'll just talk about generalities, the weather, baseball, yada yada yada." Aurora unlocked the back door.

The cottage seemed impossibly old to Shah, but he'd noticed the day before that it had solar panels and a windmill, and the kitchen was modern, albeit minimal. "You make the coffee, I'll do the rolls." Aurora nudged him out of the line of sight of the kitchen camera. She disappeared, leaving Shah to make both before reappearing – just as he'd finished – with a small carry-bag tucked behind her. She placed it beside the garbage dispenser, into which she dropped something as cover.

As they ate they made small talk. It seemed so stilted it would scream "suspicious" to anyone checking the footage. *Her paranoia makes sense if she's coming to New York, though.*

When they finished, Aurora said, "Thanks for coming round, Jim. If you could drop me at the Dalern Mall, that'd be good. I've got a three o'clock there."

"Sure," Shah muttered and followed her out. He waited in the shadows again while she locked the door.

The drive back was uneventful, as Shah had hoped. They made small talk, often about the idiots who still worked on local radio stations, trying not to talk too much about Kotian or Sunny. Aurora seemed genuinely shocked that he had been ripped, but Shah realized she could be playing him, just as he was trying to play her.

Playing him would involve asking about his memory loss to learn how much he knew. Shah tried to walk a tightrope of seeming to be open about it while fishing for tidbits about Aurora's employers.

"They're not strictly my employers," Aurora said when he used the term. "They're *patrones*, clients to use an old-fashioned term."

"But they still give you money."

"So do a lot of other people, many of whom even you would consider legit."

"They gave you a job." Shah looked away from the road momentarily to return her smile.

"True."

As they entered Connecticut Aurora said, "Have you got your memories back?"

"Most of them are other people's views of me," Shah said. "But what they don't tell you is that they're not the same as having your own. Even when I've got a copy of mine, from where I downloaded them onto the web for friends or family years ago, they seem to belong to someone else."

"That's horrible."

Shah shrugged. Keeping his eyes on the road made it easier to keep his emotions in neutral. "Uploading memories allows us to share other people's experiences – it doesn't make us become someone else."

"What about personal memories?"

"Mostly gone. I found burns of my children being born, plus meeting my wife – odd little things I've shared over the years."

"That's terrible." Aurora touched his shoulder, gently. "I'll burn the day we met. It's nothing very exciting, and it'll have some content removed, but it's a start."

"Thanks."

"I'll drop it round tomorrow."

The rest of the drive passed quickly, and before long Shah was parking the car at the hire firm's premises.

"I'm going to get the subway into town while you finish up here," Aurora said. "But I'll see you tomorrow?"

"Definitely," Shah said. "After work."

"Well, take it easy." She leaned across and kissed his cheek.

Shah watched her walk away, unable to identify too many of the emotions boiling away inside him.

## Tuesday

"Far as I'm concerned," Shah said, "We can connect Sunny to Tasha Sirtisova's murder."

ADA Grunwald snorted. "We got nothing."

"Not quite true," van Doorn said.

Harper was silent, but attentive.

Nancy Grunwald's office was full of recent shots of her in college and law school, islands of personality amid the sea of files that filled the office – the criminal justice system still firmly believed in hard-copy. But there was no mistaking the idealism that she radiated. It took Shah a few seconds to work out who she reminded him of, with her ruthlessness and ambition. Then the memory from a download clicked into place – Marietetski.

"I'm as desperate as you to land Kotian, Shah," she said. "But without this... Aurora's testimony, Kotian's defense lawyer will tear our case apart – all we have is a string of coincidences. Even with her testimony, she didn't see him do the deed. We need more. We need her to cough her guts up."

Van Doorn looked at Shah.

Shah stared back. "I can do that, but it'll mean taking more time out."

"You're owed enough leave, sick leave, and so on," van Doorn said. "Kotian and his equivalents in the other boroughs cost millions, and wreck lives. Do it."

# XXXIX

Instead Shah returned briefly to work to offload as many of the new cases –which had bred faster than rats – as he could.

"What are you going to do?" Bailey said.

Shah looked across, torn. He needed someone to talk to. And Bailey couldn't be the mole because she wasn't working for the Department at the time. "If anyone asks, I've taken the afternoon off to visit my daughter."

"OK." Bailey added, "Is anyone likely to ask?"

"I dunno. People like to gossip." *But not with you.* Bailey was already getting a rep as aloof, even rude. Shah said, "Don't take this the wrong way…"

"But?"

Shah grinned. Bailey smiled back, though it was clearly an effort. Shah said, "You could try making small talk at the water cooler. Not like Olivia Germain, who used the same phrases all the time, until people mimicked her. Ask them how they are, like you mean it, or what they're doing at the weekend. Tell them your plans. Unless you're having an orgy."

Bailey frowned. "We don't have orgies."

Mentally shaking his head in despair, Shah returned to work.

When he checked out at twelve, Bailey said, "Enjoy your afternoon." She even smiled.

Shah hid his surprise. "Thank you."

Outside, heat rippled the air off the sidewalk. Shah draped his jacket over his shoulder.

He had a memory from among the copies provided in his Get-Well Disk, of the guy who'd provided it and Shah walking with jackets draped over their shoulders, eyeing up the pretty girls. Whoever it was watched Shah chatting to a blonde bagel-seller, and recognized that the dirty old man had a thing for long-legged blondes.

Shah stopped dead, causing someone to barge into him and snap, "Wake up fool!"

*Whoever knew that might be the leak.*

Shah walked briskly to where Aurora waited at a cafe, midway between the office and her apartment.

"How was your morning?" Shah gave her a peck on the cheek, noting her raised eyebrow as he sat.

"Busy," she said, smiling. "You wouldn't believe how hard it is to do business on your eyepiece while dodging calls from some of your *patrones*." She added, "I'm only avoiding Sunny. I told Abhijit that I'm here, but I had things to attend to. I'd had two calls from Sunny that I diverted to mail. After I'd spoken to Abhijit I had five more, the last sounding like an angry hornet." She broke off to order two coffees. Shah noted wryly that she'd remembered his order from the day before. He'd accepted her paying for it, after he'd realized he'd have to ride the generator bike out back for a week to pay the calories.

"So what memories did they take?" Aurora said. "I know it's not easy to talk about, but it would help to know."

"Why?"

"What did they take?"

"Everything," Shah retreated into facts: "Semantic memory – general knowledge of the world, acquired through school, concepts, facts. Overlaps with procedural memory, which are skills like learning to drive. Episodic memory, which is unique experiences, the things have happened to us."

Aurora stared at him, her eyes glimmering. She closed them. "Jesus," she whispered. "How did you cope?"

"I relearned everything from scratch." Shah laughed a humor-free bark. "I was lucky."

"Lucky? *Lucky?* How exactly?"

"Let's change the subject," Shah said. "You going to see Abhijit?"

"Maybe." Aurora's eyes narrowed, "Why?" Her voice was amused. "You jealous?"

Shah smiled too, but when he said "maybe", there was an edge to his voice. "Damn. That's a surprise." Aurora's chin rested on her fist, elbow on the table. "Stop looking so smug," he grumbled.

"Now, why," she tapped his forearm with a long red nail to each word, "would you be jealous?"

Shah looked away, not sure how to answer. Had he always been so uncertain of everything? He suspected not, from the clips of him that he'd seen. That Shah had cut through life like a laser. Now the only thing that he was sure of was work. Or maybe that had always been the case, and the old Shah had been a better actor?

"Pete." Aurora used her nail to get his attention. "I was only teasing."

He forced a smile. "Sometimes I think that I should have taken a new name, show that I'm not him. Maybe

I should use Pervez?" She shook her head. He said, "Maybe not, then."

Their coffees arrived. "What did you have planned?" Shah said.

"I have things to do," Aurora said, "But not till later. We can sit here for a while, if you want, or we can go somewhere – just to talk."

"I have someone that I have to see," Shah said. "I could use some company, as well."

"Oh?"

"Moral support."

"Duty call? Rather than something you want to do?"

"A little of both. I'll explain on the way."

Aurora wrinkled her nose. "Classic hospital smell. Bleach and that institution smell – dunno what it is. Decades of dust and a base note of scrubbed puke and shit." Shah stared at her. "My grandma had cancer," she explained. "I've hated hospitals ever since."

Marietetski lay exactly as he had the last time Shah had visited, but now there was another woman beside the bed. Black-skinned, high-cheeked and pretty, she was younger than Mrs Trebonnet, although the lines were etched even deeper into her face than the older woman's, and Shah could see the resemblance to both Marietetski and Mrs Trebonnet. Unlike the old woman, she was wearing an eyepiece.

She looked up as they approached the bedside, Shah clutching another plant. He noted that the older one looked neglected. The woman returned Shah's thin smile, glanced at Aurora and looked away again.

Shah said, "Are you John's mother?"

She nodded. "You must be his partner. I've seen you in the uploads John sent."

"I'm very, very sorry for what happened to John. No one should have to suffer what you've been through."

Mrs Marietetski nodded, her gaze already back on her son. "Why him? Why did you survive and he's lying here?"

"I don't know. Pure luck, I guess."

She sighed. "Pray for him. If he doesn't recover soon... we can't pay for this forever."

Aurora nudged Shah. "I should wait outside."

"I'll be out in a few minutes," Shah whispered.

He stayed in silence, and when he left, Mrs Marietetski refused to look at him. He couldn't really blame her for reproaching him for surviving, when her son hadn't.

Outside, Aurora was talking agitatedly to someone on her eyepiece, and she walked out of range when he appeared, only returning after several minutes. "You OK?" She said before he could speak.

"What's wrong?"

She shook her head. "I'm just upset at seeing *him* in there. How come he's so bad?"

"And I'm not?" Shah could feel anger rising from deep within, fuelled by his own guilt at his inability to answer Mrs Marietetski's question. "Blind luck, maybe. Now you know what I meant, heh? Though I don't feel too lucky sometimes. Maybe I'm just too ornery to give up." Shah finger-combed his hair. "I don't know!"

Aurora nodded rhythmically, her lower lip thrust out, deep in thought. Suddenly she turned. "Do you think that I had something to do with this?"

"Did you?"

"NO!" Aurora took a breath. "I wouldn't – I mean, I'd never do anything like this." She shook her head. "You've got this obsession that Abhijit's mixed up in this."

"Or Sunny." Aurora stared at him. Shah continued, "The sheer number of people who've passed through their circle or who know someone who has, there has to be a connection." He added, muttering, "Time we got back"

Aurora said, "I'll send you the burn I promised you later on."

They walked down the street in tense silence, Aurora still visibly simmering, Shah still angry at his own survivor guilt, and for her seeing through him. Maybe he had wanted to show her, *this is what your precious patrones do to people.*

A man bumped shoulders with Aurora, muttered, "Watch where ya goin', *bitch*." He was just a stoned punk. He flipped them the bird and strolled on.

Shah started after him, but Aurora pulled him away. "No!" She held his shoulders as Shah took a deep breath. They walked on slowly. Aurora said, "Come back to my place."

They walked with an arm around the other, for support or comfort, Shah wasn't sure.

"That look in your eyes then, that was too reminiscent of one of Sunny's rages," Aurora said in a tremulous voice. "He'd been moaning about Tasha for weeks, though I don't know what about. Just before we met, I heard him say he was going to take care of her." Shah said nothing. Aurora continued, "I heard he beat the girl to death – he just lost control."

"I'm sorry about losing it," Shah said, as if she hadn't spoken. "I think it was seeing John lying there, and then that little bastard walking around mouthing off."

"Just – just don't let me see that look in your eyes again."

They reached a tall building with an actual doorman waiting under an honest-to-God awning from which a burgundy carpet led to the street. "Come up, yes? I have tea, or coffee."

Shah said at last, "Tea would be good. Please."

In the elevator Aurora took Shah's arm. "You know, if you were any more tense, you'd shatter." She ran her hand down his sleeve. "How much did you pay for this suit?"

Shah's brow wrinkled. "Can't remember. About four kilocalories, I think."

"Hmm, yes. It feels like it."

"What do you mean?"

"It's like handling barbed wire."

"Hmph. Not all of us can afford bespoke tailoring, you know."

"I know a tailor uptown. His roof-garden is given over to silkworms. He only sells to recommended clients, because if he didn't – the prices he charges – the queue for customers would be around the block. Let me give you his address, and I'll copy him, so he knows you're recommended by me. Now, tea," she said, as they left the elevator.

While she made it Aurora called, "I'm uploading a burn." Moments later his eyepiece chimed its arrival. You see again the chaos in the reception room. You recognize Hampson, the duty officer, then you hang round for twenty minutes, until Hampson signals Shah's approach. You see the hunger for you in his eyes and it warms you. For all that he's old, he's sort of cute.

That evening you journey through the rain to the bar, checking that you're showing just the right amount of cleavage. In the bar you doctor Shah's drinks, but still the stubborn bastard won't come back to your place. Your frustration's nothing compared to your fear of Sunny's rage. *Maybe I'll stay here.* You kiss, and you feel Pete's hands slide over you.

Then comes the moment; he feels the three-inch clitoris emerging from your labia like a penis from its sheath. He shrieks. His fist slams into your nose and you feel blood spurt –

Shah cut the recording, looked down at his feet. "I'm sorry."

She sat beside him, stroked his shoulder. "I'm not the first, you know?"

"First *I've* ever met."

"Maybe. Maybe not. There are more of us than you realize, perhaps fifteen thousand in the US before the Dieback." She took a deep breath, then resting her head on his shoulder indicated a small painting on the wall. "See her? Levi Suydam, a Turkish intersexual who lived in the 1840s. She had both male and female genitals, even masturbated like a man." She felt him gingerly put his arm around her. "That was two centuries ago," she said. "But things haven't changed much, for all our supposed enlightenment."

"What about Kotian?" Shah said. "He's really not bothered?"

"Indian society even has a caste for us. The hijras: The unclean." She added, "I'm sure he's not the only rich Indian guy who's queer for freaks."

"And your parents?" Shah said. "Didn't they…"

"Consider cutting me?" Aurora said. "No. Their parents'd had gender reassignment and knew how it fucks you up. I was my parents' pride and joy." She sighed. "Sometime I'll tell you about it. But right now I've got to get ready to visit a *patrone.*"

# XL

You shiver. Although you know it's late on a balmy spring evening, your senses are adamant it's winter and your breath is streaming on the night air. Scramble does that. You're aware enough to know the symptoms, but not so far gone you no longer care. When you're high all the good times you've ever had come flooding back, but better, more intense. You don't want to think about the downer and the accompanying bad memories.

Typical fucking CIA, developing something like that.

You wipe your nose, and as a car crawls toward you, adjust your tiny skirt and paste on the biggest smile you can manage. The car slows and a window winds down. You lean forward so that the john can see your tits. They're your best feature. "Hey handsome. Want some company?"

You can't see the guy's face, but he motions toward the passenger side, and you hear a clunk. *Central locking,* you think, nudging your price up. You can't charge as much as the legit whores, but they don't allow Scrambleheads in the Companions Guild, so you charge what the johns will bear. From the smell of his cologne, it'll be a lot.

You jump in, and the car pulls away.

"It'll be–" his gesture cuts you off. A hand passes you a wad of notes, enough to keep you in Scramble for weeks. You count it, and there are mega-calories there in yuan and new rupees and yen, some worthless dollars – even a prepaid debit card. You should be happy, but you're starting to get a bad feeling. Good thing the guy didn't have the sense to take off the huge ring on the little finger of his right hand. You'll remember that antique coin at its center.

It tells you that maybe you won't survive tonight.

You force a laugh, "You want me to stroke you while you drive? Let that power steering take care of the road?" You reach for him, but he slaps your hand away.

He's driving you deeper into the industrial estate running parallel to I-128, and you can see the occasional car headlight speeding north around Boston toward Canada. He parks up and reaches behind you. "Put this on." He passes you a harness with leads running from it. A neuro-probe. He wants to burn your memory of him fucking you. A lot of Johns like to know how it feels from both sides.

"When do you want me to set it from?"

"A half-hour ago."

He's fitting another probe, and while he's finishing up you scoot into the back through the gap in the front seats, and lifting your skirt pull your tights off. By the time he clambers through you're already spreading your legs to take him in, condom in your hand. He's a little soft, but the rest of him is as stiff as a board with tension. You stroke his shoulder as he slides into you, his cock hardening with each thrust, his bulk weighing on you.

It's all entirely usual, and you switch your mind into neutral, wondering how long it'll be before you can score some Scramble.

Until his hands lock around your windpipe.

You dig your nails into them, but aside from a hiss he doesn't react, so you go for his eyes, but he jerks his head away. Each breath is a fiery battle, your throat hurts and too fast, too fast the world is fading away. Unlike cliché, life doesn't flash before your eyes, there's just the feel of his hands–

He hisses, "If I time this right and rip it before–"

# XLI

Shah returned to the office and worked until late that afternoon, when he headed uptown.

He worried that he would be late for his meeting with Perveza's social worker, Helen Mendoza, but he still reached her office before her return.

"Sorry, sorry," she gasped, dropping a handbag that could have held most of New York City onto her desk. It made a loud *thud*. "Last meeting ran late – in fact, I been running late since the first one –and I missed my connection."

Shah had the distinct impression that Helen Mendoza was rarely on time for anything. But as soon as she sat down and took out a thick A5 file, she was businesslike and brisk.

"I got your call, Officer, and I appreciate your wanting to help. But to be honest, it's probably too little too late." Seeing him about to protest, she held up a heavily ringed hand. "That's not a criticism. Perveza is an addict, which means that she will suck you dry of every last drop of time, money, attention and kindness. And still want more."

"So what does this mean, Ms Mendoza?"

"Helen," Mendoza said.

"Then call me Pete."

Helen smiled. "Pete, Perveza is legally an adult. New York State is geared toward helping children before adults, who are considered to be able to look after themselves. That's debatable, but once you enter the adult system, you only get a few chances." She gazed at Shah. "I offered her the option of attending this meeting, but she declined."

Shah's eyepiece chimed. Perveza said, "Another bit of token love from Daddy Dearest. Huh. Why bother? It's just an attempt to convince himself that he cares about me."

Shah looked away. There seemed little point in saying anything.

Mendoza sighed. "I'm sorry. I can't help Perveza because she has a DNR order on her file."

"I assume that we're not talking Do Not Resuscitate?"

Mendoza seemed to understand the black humor. She smiled dutifully. "DNR is Do Not Resettle, in this instance." She placed her hand on the file. "I agree getting Perveza away from living with other addicts would be better for her. But *she's* got to make that move. I can't help. She's blown all her chances."

"There must be something you can do?"

Mendoza shook her head. "The Federal Government's tough love policies insist that any addicts who want welfare must sign a pledge to give up drug use. Perveza's broken that agreement three times, which is why she has a Do Not Resettle order on her file, putting her off-limits to any further Federal Aid." She added, "I understand your position, Pete, but this one's beyond my help."

Shah thought, *I know what Perveza will say.* Knowing

it wouldn't make it any easier when she accused him of turning his back on her – again. But at least he'd tried.

When he got home Doug and Leslyn sat out on the twilit balcony, sipping drinks amid the night-flowering lilies. Shah felt, as he often did now, that he was intruding.

"Homemade mint juleps," Doug said to Shah's unspoken question.

"Want one?" Leslyn said. "We have alcohol-free Bourbon."

"Which is as nasty as it sounds," Doug slurred slightly. He'd clearly been drinking the "proper" stuff.

"Thanks. I'll fix it."

"Let me," Leslyn said. "You've been working."

"Sort of." Following her into the kitchen, Shah told her of visiting Marietetski and the encounter with the punk.

"You should be careful," Leslyn said. "He could have been carrying a weapon. Just as well she pulled you away." She passed him a glass. "Are you going to see her again?"

Shah knew who "she" was. "I have to meet her again. It's work. We need her to testify."

Leslyn followed him back out to the balcony. "You know that's not what I meant."

"Would it be a problem if I did?" Leslyn couldn't physically stop him, of course, but if she couldn't cope with it, it could strain their already faltering marriage beyond repair.

"I don't know."

Doug spoke for the first time, "Maybe you should look for a new partner."

Shah looked up in time to see Leslyn's warning nudge. "Something you two want to tell me?"

Leslyn looked embarrassed. "It's nothing. I'd rather have waited until there's something definite to tell you."

"Tell me anyway." Shah sipped his drink, watching them carefully.

"There's a Sino-Californian research project on telepresencing." Leslyn lifted her chin defiantly. She knew Shah's opinion of the secretive, sometimes sinister Californians, who rarely emerged from behind their wall. "They're looking for volunteers to test new projects. Initially Montana, then China or even California for the successful applicants."

"And why aren't they looking for volunteers among their own people?" Shah said.

McCoy waggled his head in a gesture strangely reminiscent of Kotian. Shah wondered whether it was the latest fashion among retired academics, a new social meme – or whether the two of them knew one another, and McCoy had picked up the gesture. "Of course there's an element of risk, there is with any experiment."

"Yeah, but it's usually a risk of failure," Shah said. "This sounds to me like failure will be more risky to the volunteer than the project." Shah hadn't read much about Californian research – he hadn't had the time, and it didn't seem relevant to his own situation – but enough to know that rumors swirled around the Californians and their obsession with anything that might bring them closer to cybernetic perfection.

Leslyn talked over McCoy's snort, "I don't know that anything's going to come of this, so let's not ruin a nice evening."

Doug interrupted, "No, Leslyn, Pete should know the whole story."

"Which is?" Shah said.

Leslyn sipped at her drink, perhaps summoning courage, Shah decided. "If it happens – and it's a big if – I'll need certain augments to already be fitted."

"Which no doubt they'll pay for," Shah said sarcastically.

Leslyn shook her head. "I have to pay for the initial ones. I'll have to save up in case it does happen. If it doesn't, then obviously we can use the calories elsewhere."

"On what?" Shah said.

For the first time Leslyn looked irritated but quickly hid it. "Dunno. We'll worry when it happens. But meantime I'll need you to pay your share of the housekeeping up to date. I know things have been hard, so I've let it slide the last few weeks, but that can't go on."

"If you'd said you could've had it before." That wasn't quite true. Shah's sick pay had only been half his shift basic, and had excluded the payment for the overtime that he worked almost every day.

He thought that they'd exhausted the idea years before. Leslyn would become a prisoner in the apartment as soon as she returned from visiting one of the Westchester County clinics. Tech companies sited clinics in isolated communities desperate for old-fashioned jobs and spin-offs like imported food, despite their fear of the Other. Most people in these little towns felt the worst ayatollahs were kindred compared to the Augmented. The Augmented won't 'help' an ordinary human become like them; instead it's up to ordinary humans to make the first moves, until they reach the point of no return to ordinary humanity, at which point the post-humans will consider them committed enough that they will complete the changes.

Leslyn seemed to know what he was thinking. "Let's face it," she said, "Most of what people hear about The Augmented are scare stories put about by Fundies."

"Not all of them. There were enough instances of people going into feedback loops and autism to convince Congress to outlaw it. Half the reason California built the Wall when they seceded was over that."

"Only in the early days. When was the last time one of the stories was confirmed?"

"That's because they keep 'em all behind the wall."

Doug interrupted, "California's wall was to keep out economic migrants."

Leslyn got up and went indoors. She returned after a few minutes, wiping her temple clear of the glaze of anesthetic gel with a cloth.

Moments later Shah's eyepiece chimed, and he took a downloaded message with a time-stamp of about a minute before. It was strange staring at Leslyn in person, while her avatar said in his screen, "I guess this must be baffling to you – but trust me, we've had this discussion before. So I've burned a copy of the relevant memory. Here you are."

You know that Shah's not going to take this well, but the look on his face is still scary.

"Why?" His look of bewilderment is painful, but not so painful as the hurt look. You hadn't expected that, if you're honest. Anger, revulsion, but not hurt.

You say, "Because telepresencing is the only viable way of properly exploring the outer solar system. Robot probes aren't responsive enough once they're out past Mars. By the time the signal's gone to the asteroid belt and it's responded, we've lost at least five minutes of response time that we could get back by having someone do the job. Even basic mining needs that capability."

"I still don't get it," he says. He clenches, then opens, then re-clenches his fists. Does he know how frightening he looks when he does that? You let him work it out. You deliberately picked a moment when Doug would be out. His inability to shut up when Shah needs time to process something new is a big reason why you haven't been able to convince him before.

Shah still doesn't answer, though, so you try to explain. "Even a five-minute gain on a response time out of – say – a half-hour is a big deal. Asteroid miners are hugely expensive, even for Chinese and Californian and Japanese and Indian consortia."

"No, no." Shah waves his hand in dismissal. "I get that, telepresencing helping on the ocean floor, and exploring the mantle and stuff. I know why those countries are so interested. They want to get ahead, they don't share the results except as they need to, as and when it suits their purposes." He stares at you. "What I don't get is, why you? Why are *you* doing it?"

"Because I want to make a difference," you say, but it's a lie. The truth is that your life is empty. There has to be more to life than working long hours to earn enough to live.

Shah ended the download. He still didn't really understand, but it was up to her, however much the idea of having one of the last constants from his old life knocked from beneath him frightened him.

### Wednesday

He was equally baffled the next day, in the ADA's office, but for different reasons. Grunwald had called first thing telling him to report to the office at 10.30. Bailey had had the same call.

When they arrived, Shah saw Aurora Debonis sitting in the reception area. She was white-faced, her lips pressed together, and the look she gave Shah before she turned away would have blistered paint.

"What's going on?" Shah said as soon as the door closed on the still-waiting Aurora.

"Good morning, Officer. Yes, I'm very well, thanks," Grunwald said.

"Spare me the sarcasm. I thought we had a plan. But you seem to have other ideas."

"Not my decision." Grunwald jerked her thumb upwards, in the general direction of the DA's office. "It's not for discussion. Accept it or get off the case."

They fell silent, reviewing their notes. After several minutes, Grunwald summoned Aurora. Grunwald said, "Tell me about the night that Natalia Sirtisova went in the river."

Aurora shrugged. "Pete and I had a few drinks; I escorted him back to his place, because that's what I do. When I left he was fit and well. If he reacted to a drug that he took earlier…"

She shrugged. "Sorry, that's not my problem."

# XLII

The interview carried on for an hour, but yielding nothing new.

Aurora became increasingly defensive, until she finally said, "I'm not answering any further questions. Either arrest me or I'm going."

Shah stood but Grunwald said, "Officer Shah!"

Shah sat down again. When she had left, he said, "What was that about?"

"DA's orders. Carrot and stick. You friend her, that's the carrot. I'm the stick; talk or face the consequences." Her stare was unyielding. "It's not negotiable."

"You've just undermined five days' work in one hour."

"Bull!"

Bailey cleared her throat.

Shah and Grunwald turned, the argument hanging in the air. Bailey reddened but said, "Pete, you looked as baffled as I felt. If I could see that, she could too. Maybe you could use that – when she's calmed down a little."

"Assuming she hasn't flown straight back to Boston." Shah softened: "You may be right. But if I'm to salvage anything of this mess, I need to do it now."

Grunwald called as he left, "Van Doorn seems to rate you, Shah, but don't think you're indispensable. The DA's office doesn't need your approval."

Shah turned. "I'll accept that you just fucked up five days' work because I have to. But don't expect me to tell you how wonderful you are. You want a kiss-ass, go find one."

Aurora made Shah sweat for five minutes before she instructed the doorman to let him up. She was stone-faced when she answered her door. "What do you want?"

Shah followed her in as she walked away from the open door. "To apologize." Her laugh was a snort of derision. "You're probably right to be sceptical," he said. "But I really didn't know they were going to summon you. I was as surprised as you."

"Yeah, course you were." Aurora marched into her bedroom, where a half-packed case lay open on the bed, a pile of clothes beside it. "Doesn't matter, Pete. I was flying back to Boston for a few days anyway."

"Why didn't you bring an attorney?"

Aurora stared at him. "Because I was blindsided. I thought the missing eyepiece they said they wanted to talk to me about was the one I reported lost the day I met you. Turns out it was your missing eyepiece that turned up. I was a stunned as you – assuming you weren't just acting. Which I'm not sure about. Or anything else." She blinked, several times.

Shah studied Aurora. She continued to not meet his eye. He said, "What's happened?"

"Once I've trained my replacement in Boston, I'm returning to New York. In the meantime, I'm going to commute." That she could afford the giga-calories needed for regular air travel told Shah how wealthy, important, or both she was.

"So what's the problem?" Shah said.

"No problem at all."

"It doesn't sound like it." Shah thought, *change the subject, take the pressure off her.* "Can I make a cup of coffee?"

Aurora stopped and stared at him. "Of course you can." Her training as a companion, or inherent good breeding took over. "Grief! I'm forgetting my manners–"

Shah touched her shoulder. "It's. OK. Do. Not. Worry." He went into the kitchen. It took a few moments of rummaging to find everything, but he soon had the percolator hissing.

When Aurora reappeared, she looked as composed as she usually did.

"I think when I switch my eyepiece back on I may find I'm suspended," Shah said.

"What! Why?"

"I told the ADA what I thought of this morning's stunt."

Aurora shook her head. "Damn fool. Call her back and retract it. Tell her you were drunk or drugged or deranged – tell her anything! You can't afford to be suspended!"

Shah shook his head. "I'm not going to be her gimp."

Aurora poured them each a cup of coffee, and cradling hers as if to draw warmth from it, stared into space.

Shah stayed quiet. She would speak when ready.

"Abhijit fucked me last night," Aurora said at last. She laughed, a thin brittle sound close to shattering. "Nothing new there, I know. But he was different, rougher. Before he went, we talked. Once you strip down all the pleasantries, what he said was that if I offended his son, I offended him. And that if Sunny wants to yank my head back by my hair while taking me from behind, he can do so. Or if," she shuddered "he decides to stub lit cigarettes out on my flesh, that's his right. Whatever Sunny wants he gets. I'm to stop avoiding Sunny."

Shah exhaled. He chose his next words with care. "How do you feel?"

"Oh, Pete! I'm scared outta my head! But you give the client what they want…"

"Do you want him as a client?"

"What I want doesn't matter. It's what they want that counts."

"Do you want him as a client?" Shah repeated.

"No, not any more." Aurora seemed to finally remember to drink her coffee and was silent for a few moments, then put the cup down. "But I can't leave him."

"Can't, or won't?"

"They amount to the same thing."

"You're scared to."

"Yes."

"What about witness protection?"

Aurora smiled, but there was no warmth in it. "Ah."

"Don't give me that 'ah' like I planned this all along."

"Didn't you?"

Shah shrugged. "I'd have had to have known that he was going to turn on you eventually, I suppose, but you credit me with too much if you think I saw this coming."

"If you say so."

"I do."

"We-e-e-ll, anyway, Pete, thanks, but no thanks."
She drained her cup. "I have to go."

### Friday

"Those bloody cops are here again," Sunny said.

Kotian held up a hand. "Don't worry about it. This is just a social visit. Shah called me earlier to suggest we meet for coffee. I invited him here, instead."

The set of Sunny's jaw told Kotian what the boy thought of that. *Good. He must learn that he cannot have everything he desires, when he desires.* It was such a shame that he hadn't been firmer with Sunny when he was younger. He might have turned out less wilful. Kotian doubted it. A flaw was a flaw. Much though he loved his oldest son, he no longer *had* to indulge him as he had when the boy was younger and his only heir. Sunny realized that too...

"Why, Appa?" Sunny said with a frown he couldn't quite hide.

Kotian chuckled. "To quote Sun-Tzu, or Machiavelli – whichever you prefer, 'Keep your friends close, and your enemies closer.' Show them in, Aurora." When she had left the room Kotian said, "If they're here with us, they can't be elsewhere rootling around – can they?" Abruptly, Kotian beamed. "Pete, and – Officer Bailey, isn't it? How are you both?"

The policemen sat on the couch Kotian waved them over to, Shah heavily, Bailey more gingerly, but both oozing into the plush softness of the couch. Kotian chuckled inwardly. So puritanical, this generation, even a comfortable chair made them purse their lips as if sucking on a titty. Bailey was no exception. *It's almost as much fun teasing her as Shah and Sunny.* Sunny was green with jealousy of Shah.

Kotian allowed none of his thoughts to show, but instead listened to Shah's small talk, his compliments at the furnishings – as if a mere cop's opinion mattered – his complaints at the weather, and more interestingly a few tidbits about the NHL off-season; at least the man was relearning his hockey, if nothing else. "So how goes the hunt for the Ripper?" Kotian's duels with Shah were much more than just talking about ice hockey. Kotian liked to give him little gems under the guise of "I've heard", or "someone said." Some were true, with names, dates or places changed, some were complete rubbish that Kotian had invented, some were genuine, but the people that Kotian was giving up were in no position to do any damage, as long as he was careful; a few were even rivals, and Kotian felt an inner glow at Shah doing his dirty work for him.

Shah held up a hand palm down, waggling it from side to side. "You know how it is, one step forward, half a step backwards." Kotian saw Bailey give Shah a look and almost chuckled aloud. She didn't appreciate what her colleague was doing, and her inability to hide her suspicion that Shah was growing too close to him was as obvious as an open book. Equally obvious was Shah's knowledge of that, and his annoyance with her. *In other words, you've got nowhere.* Kotian watched Aurora out of the corner of his eye, watching Shah.

Kotian knew that she was attracted to older men – character, wit and intellect were more important to her than looks, however hard Shah might find it to believe. Kotian wondered just how attractive she found Shah, and how long he could keep her around before she became a liability.

# XLIII

It's an interesting sensation, looking at memories you've ripped from your own mind, especially when it contains its own memories. A bit like the doppler effect of a freight train passing in the night.

There are memories you look at now and feel nothing, but at the time they were almost unbearable. Bad enough the need to hurt that builds like a woman's cycle without any clear sign of any pattern, but then the self-loathing that follows... how did you survive them?

Before the memory excision technology was developed to first access, then excise the data in the hippocampus and prefrontal cortex, you wouldn't have been able to. Need, action and guilt would have built a vicious feedback loop, eventually resulting in a mistake that would lead the police to your door. Even acing your chances by working across the land to minimize detection by one of the Little League-minded PDs wouldn't have been enough.

You look back at that first botched attack on that whore in Boston, and wonder how you could have been so dumb as to let her see your ring and to talk to her, even through a vocoder. Thank the gods that you chopped the version you sold to that creep in the Azores. No one will know the truth.

You're cleverer now. Training by studying rips may not be as efficient as 'normal' learning, by experience, but it's good enough, as the attack on the girl in Washington showed.

Appa might almost be proud of you, if that perversion he uses as a sex toy hadn't blinded him. Sometimes it feels as if the whore is spying on you, but you're careful – she doesn't know about this secret room. If she does find it, she'll never get past the alarms without the combination.

And now he's going to give her to you, maybe she'll teach you a few new things before she reaches the end of her usefulness.

You feel your cock hardening at the thought of being in her. Perversions are good with their mouths, desperate to worm their way into a man's affections any way they can, eager to make up for not being able to give a man proper pleasure in the right way. To ease the need that's starting to build already, you relive that first attack again, smelling the whore's cheap perfume, her faked gasps of pleasure as she lifts her feet further up your back, the feel of her warmth below you and the contrast with the coldness of her body where it's been exposed to the open air. But the real pleasure is in watching the terror on her face as your hands fasten around her windpipe, the way she tautens in panic around your cock.

In now-time your hand strokes the bulge in your pants as she bucks and thrashes beneath you, then fights back, digging her nails in, but she's fading fast already. Caught by surprise she lost vital seconds.

In your memory you download hers and you feel, as she dies, her own terror and she's bucking and writhing beneath you and terrified of you pumping pumping pumping above her –

–and you rip out the memory even as she dies with your cum shooting into her.

# XLIV

### Friday

Aurora stared out of the guest bedroom's window over the lush grounds, filing off the nail she'd caught. She sat on the four-poster and sighed. Abhijit had been adamant that he'd wanted her so she'd come out to the country, as he'd asked. Where Sunny waited with his predatory smile.

She heard voices down the corridor, and putting the file back, went to join them. *They're talking about me!* She shrank back against the corridor wall, straining to hear. One of her grandmother's sayings popped into her head: eavesdroppers never hear good of themselves. She thought, *bad manners are less important than survival, Grandma.*

"You shouldn't toy with Shah, Appa. He's spent years trying to pin something on us. Your games only encourage him. Why take risks?"

Aurora smiled. Sunny was so jealous of Shah he'd even risk arguing with his father, something that she never thought she'd hear.

"Not like you, heh, Sunny?"

"I – What d'you mean, Appa?"

"You know. You like risk. Where do you think you get that from?" Kotian chuckled. "We'll use the hijra to keep him stupefied. She can be useful for a while longer."

"If you say so."

"I do," Kotian said, their voices fading as they went back downstairs.

That broken nail was the only reason she'd heard them talking.

She'd deliberately ignored their business dealings over the year she'd known them. The Kotians liked to bend the law, but who didn't? Who didn't steal bits of stationery from the office, break the speed limit, forget to declare some of their income? And if the Kotians were better at it than others – so what? It wasn't her problem. Until the night she'd returned to tell Sunny that she hadn't been able to bring Shah as instructed.

She'd always known that there was something wrong with Sunny, something broken. Too often Sunny was dead behind the eyes, until it came to causing pain, when the light in them was even scarier than the normal deadness masking it.

But to realize that they were both using her *for the time being* was as shocking as watching Sunny beat poor Tasha, his knuckledustered fists repeatedly slamming her head back against the wall with a dull thump.

What to do?

She still had a couple of temporary eyepieces stashed in her room. One hadn't been registered, so was effectively anonymous. She needed to get some more 'pieces and copy everything that she could find onto them, and then start hiring some safe deposit boxes scattered around the city out of harm's way. *Time to start taking out some insurance.*

She hurried back to her room.

### Saturday

"I'm going to enjoy this," Shah said. "Ruining this bastard's afternoon just feels so good." He rubbed his hands together as if it were cold, rather than thirty Celsius.

"Try not to gloat too obviously." Bailey waved at the SWAT team to take up their positions at the front and side exits to the Estate. Llewellyn Park's park-like streets weren't accustomed to black-clad men and women, and one local had walked into one of the period Victorian lamp posts, while a second had nearly crashed her Daimler. "Wouldn't want him to claim there's a vendetta. Which I guess he will."

"Was that advice?" Shah pretended to be shocked.

"Just making a suggestion," Bailey said, straight-faced. "Nice suit, by the way. And a haircut as well…"

Shah shrugged. "The barber's was next door to the tailor. Only a couple of kilocalories more than the last one I had. Feel that? That's proper natural silk, not your cheap pseudo-silk shit – oh, we're here!"

The gate to Shah's address was manned by a guard whose eyes widened at the sight of the SWAT team's helmets and insectile goggles. "Open the gate." Shah showed him the hardcopy warrant. The team was jamming eyepieces around the house to prevent any over-loyal employee raising the alarm, so he couldn't transmit it electronically.

It wasn't actually one team: since the raid was on New Jersey soil, one vehicle came from the State Police's Technical Emergency and Mission Specialist's team, one from the New York State equivalent, and one from the NYPD's Auxiliary Police Support Unit. Shah wasn't sure what strings Nancy Grunwald had had to pull to arrange such rare inter-jurisdictional brotherhood, but he was glad that she had. The convoy of three SUVs swept through and rolled up the long gravel drive while one SWATter stayed with the guard.

"Wow, that's what money can buy you," one of the team said, chin-cocking what Shah had read was an "English manor-style home" in a two-acre lot. To Shah it looked like a pink and brown block with a pointed roof from which thrust two high, thin protuberances, but what did he know?

The vehicles halted at three equidistant points around the house in a spray of gravel, marksmen spilling from the vehicles and sprinting into position. Shah and Bailey marched toward the door, which was opened by a liveried footman, whose indignant protestations the officers ignored. Instead they brushed past him into the lobby, then the house proper.

Sunny emerged from a side corridor shouting, "What's this about?"

Shah ignored the question, waving an officer forward to fit the cuffs while a second pointed her rifle at Sunny. "Sunil Kotian, I am arresting you on suspicion of murder. You do not have to say anything…" he screened out the rest of it even as he recited it on auto, instead looking around at the mahogany paneled fittings, at the separate doorways in which stood Kotian and a woman, who must have been Kotian's wife, clutching at two small children. *No sign of Aurora. Good.*

"Why, officer?" Kotian senior said.

"New evidence, Mr Kotian." Shah wondered whether he should mention the ring that he'd spotted in the last download. "That's all I can say. I'm sure that you'll have your attorney meet us at the courtroom."

"Oh, depend on it."

### Monday

Kotian steepled his fingers and sighed. "At least you're out, even if only on bail."

Sunny snarled, his voice rising and tightening with each word, "Oh, yes, Appa, there is that. I can't leave the immediate vicinity, let alone fly up to Boston or Washington, I've got to report to their bloody, *bloody* front desk every evening at six, and I've got to wear this *damned* ankle tag. But it could always be worse."

Kotian stared at his son. Sunny's skin speckled with sweat, his eyes swiveled from side to side, and the cords on his neck stood out. *My boy, what am I going to do with you?*

"We have the best defense lawyers available. They'll disallow the prosecution evidence piece by piece. Sit back and let them do their job."

Kotian wished it were as simple as that but he allowed none of his doubts to show. "All we have to do is create doubt in the jury's mind. Meanwhile, we'll start our own campaign. File harassment charges against NYPD and attack Shah's standing as an investigator." He couldn't let Sunny know that even as they were talking, the IRS, Homeland Security and the DEA were rampaging through the Kotian family's files. The bastards had clearly been biding their time, and when Shah had struck they too had pounced.

Kotian couldn't tell Sunny how stark a choice they faced. To allow the boy at least a little autonomy he'd ignored his son's sideline of running a memory-ripping operation. Selling the memories to Pacific net-havens allowing subscribers to download the victims' –and sometimes the attackers' – memories was a lucrative operation, but it was also risky.

Kotian was sure that the killings were never part of

his son's original plan, but Sunny's propensity for violence had gradually escalated with each successive attack. Worse, he had been criminally careless. *How the hell did Shah get the original of that first killing in Boston? It has to be that bitch hijra. I don't know how, but it must have been her. Why else would she refuse my calls?*

She'd personalized a voicemail response to his number: "I can't afford any scandals, Abhijit, I'm sure that you know how it is."

He was too soft, that was his trouble. He should put a contract out on her. But it would be too obvious, and if anything went wrong, there were too many ways they could trace any instruction or even hint back to him. He was sure that at least one of the agencies ransacking his houses and offices were watching him.

Worst of all no one would believe that he wasn't running Sunny's operation. It was ironic that allowing his son that little independence was probably going to cost him dearly. Unless he could find a way of putting some distance between them...

# XLV

## Tuesday

Shah sat in his chair, hooded, but playing no burns or rips. Instead he used the hood's sanctuary to think, assembling the multitude of downloads that comprised his memory. The ME had checked him over the day before, pronounced that Shah had recovered seventy-five, perhaps eighty per cent of his memory.

It didn't feel like it.

He'd relearned most of his semantic memories, and many of the procedural ones like how to drive. But his own episodic memories, the sense of who he was, were mostly missing. Some parts were almost completely reassembled, if he counted those events he'd been involved in being remembered by other people. But they weren't his.

So every little fragment was precious.

When the antique CD had arrived on Saturday morning, Shah was instantly suspicions. Physical packages were rare. Data was too easily moved electronically to need the mail. The wrapper was blank but for the name "Officer Pete Shah" in block capitals on the envelope. It had been screened, X-rayed and smelled by sniffer dogs the night before, so there was nothing to fear, but its very strangeness made Shah handle it as if it might bite off his fingers.

Inside was a single disc, unlabelled; attached to it a note, also block lettered:

## YOU HAVE TO KNOW WHERE TO LOOK

Shah swallowed, licked his lips nervously.

It took several minutes to find a machine that still had a CD drive; when he read the disk's properties, he had to find another machine, to which he attached a scanner. When he'd loaded the disk, Shah saw there no tags, no clues to where it had come from. He assumed it had been downloaded from a web address, but it was only a guess. There was one file.

Despite the clues, he'd been completely unprepared:

You're walking beside John Marietetski, snow crunching underfoot, although the sky has cleared to a glorious bright day.

Marietetski says, "You know, you haven't mentioned this Aurora once since the news broke that you were off the hook."

"Funny that, isn't it?" You squirm inside at the thought of touching that little cock. "You'd think I'd be talking about it nonstop."

"I guess as a Muslim, you disapprove," Marietetski says. "Is that right? Does the Qur'an have opinions on intersex people?"

"I think the word 'abomination' probably covers it," Shah said. "Can we change the subject?"

"Because you were fooled – or does the whole subject disgust you?" Marietetski said. "I mean, you know

I'm bi, yeah? Neil and me, it's not like you and McCoy where you just share a partner rotationally."

You open your mouth. Close it again. *Rotationally?* You try to banish the images of Leslyn that word conjures. "Yeah, I know. I got no problem with that." The thought of Marietetski and another guy kissing makes your gut clench. "So you and the girls?"

"Oh, we got a rota for that, too," Marietetski says. "Just like your laundry."

"Yeah, funny."

"I wasn't being funny when I asked you about her," Marietetski says. "I got no problem with gender, but you obviously have."

You ponder. "Back to your earlier question, I guess I'm mostly pissed because he – she, it, whatever – fooled me. But also, I really, really liked her. I let my guard down, and look what happened."

"What you going to do if we ever see her again?"

"Do?" You lie, "Nothing. Far as I know, it committed no crime. We got nothing to say to each other."

"Haw," Marietetski says. "You're so deep in denial you're up your own ass. Compromise, talk to her."

You wait on a corner for an oncoming pedicab but Marietetski dashes across the road, drawing a barrage of abuse from the cabbie. You eventually cross to where your sheepish-looking partner waits. "Thought you was with me," Marietetski says.

You wag a finger. "You are so damned impatient."

"Part of my charm." Marietetski grins.

"Maybe," you say. "But while I find opinion, impatience and ambition constantly amusing, not everyone finds a rookie with that combination so endearing."

"Uh-oh," he says. "I sense a wise sage lecture."

You shake your head. "Nope. I'm not going to waste my time, John. I know you think you already know it all."

"I know I don't," he says. "That's why they teamed me with you."

You continue as if he hasn't spoken, "You've already irritated a lot of people within the Department, and made enemies out on the streets – that isn't a promising combination for someone who wants promotion." He laughed. "And *you're* lecturing me on compromise? That's quite something."

"Yeah, well maybe seeing you beat yourself up is the reason I'm suddenly embracing the concept."

"It's a bit late for epiphany," you say.

You've been so deep in conversation that you've only just noticed the block you're passing through. It's haunted by dealers, hookers and other crims. Some sixth sense triggers.

Too late: there's a hiss, and you smell something like the old-fashioned nail varnish your mother wore when you were young. *A muscle relaxant.* You jerk your head away, in case it's something the anti-tox injections don't screen out.

A blow sends you sprawling and as you land, pain shooting up your wrist, a boot thuds into your ribs, winding you. The blow of the impact jerks your head around, scraping your eyepiece away, where there's a crunch of it being trodden on and ground to minute fragments. You try to shout for help, but blows and grunts indicate that Marietetski is busy as well.

You glimpse a masked assailant as someone grabs your ankles and drags you backwards into an alleyway. Marietetski shouts, *"Officer down!* We need help at eighty-sixth and–" A kick in the ribs guillotines his Mayday.

You wriggle and kick out, your foot connecting with something. "Bastard!" Someone grunts, but you've no time to do more than clamber to your feet before a fist crashes into your ribs with the force of a brick, driving the wind from your lungs.

A pair of clasped fists slams down onto your shoulder blades, driving you to your knees. A hand grips your hair, yanking your head back. As if from a long way away you hear a scraping sound: two hooded man hauling Marietetski into the alley.

Hands push your wrists together behind your back and handcuff you. Analgesic stings your temple, and seized by panic you jerk your head away, but the hand yanks your hair back.

Someone says, "Leave him functional. I want him to be a walking, talking reminder of what happens to people who ask awkward questions."

*That's Sunny Kotian.* But just as sensation fades from your temple, you feel the kiss of a probe. Then something's drilling into your mind, and everything goes black.

For a moment, Shah sat still, thinking. He could have been watching a film of a stranger viewed through a close viewpoint camera. *So that's what it was like,* he thought. *How much of me has it destroyed? Can I get it back?*

Then the bombshell hit him. He had eyewitness testimony of the attack.

He leapt into action, and by the afternoon, they were in Llewellyn Park.

For three days now, he'd been retreating under the hood. Bailey assumed that it was to gloat, but the truth was, he was trying to make sense of his reaction.

He felt nothing. Sunny Kotian was on borrowed time. But instead of triumph, Shah felt hollow. *That* was what he'd been battling to recover? Sighing, he removed the hood.

As if waiting for him, Shah's eyepiece chimed with the deeper tone of a secure line, supposedly proof against eavesdroppers. Shah was sure that in the never-ending race between security and counter-measures, someone had – or was about to – devise a gizmo to crack the line's countermeasures. Kotian's face appeared. The man looked tired and rumpled, and his greeting was curt. "We need to meet."

"Why?"

"I want a deal. But you come alone, no taps, no eyepieces, no surveillance."

"Nothing we discuss will be binding without witness," Shah said.

Kotian's smile was wintry. "*Those* talks are what we're going to talk about."

"Ah. Talks about talks."

"Exactly." Kotian added, "Meet me at the East 66th Street entrance, in thirty minutes. Alone." The call ended.

Shah sighed.

Bailey looked over. "Who was that?"

"Kotian," Shah smiled at her look of surprise. "Wants to talk, but only to me. And bareback."

"You're kidding."

"Nope."

"You going?"

Shah made a *dunno* gesture. "Every instinct I have says no. Could be a hit, hell, could be anything, but it might also be our chance. Guess I have to." Pushing back his chair, Shah grabbed his coat.

"Then I'll come with you. Give me a minute." Bailey scrabbled for her handbag.

"Nope." Shah kept walking.

# XLVI

The alarm radio blares into life with Rebel Cutie blasting out "Keep on Loving You". You stretch to slap the alarm down, but Mom's moved the freaking thing out of reach and you forgot to move it back last night.

"Ohhhh!" You growl as the moron jock yells out, "Monday morning Binghampton! Get yo' tushies outta the sack!"

Finally you reach it and slap him into silence. He's a jerk, but since the power's had to be rationed and most of the radio stations have gone to the wall, he's the only halfway listenable one, though even that's debatable.

You feel like crap, so everyone's a jerk today, even your Mom. Especially your Mom.

As if you've conjured her up, she bangs on your door. "You awake in there, sweetheart?"

"Hrmph," you grumble.

Your nipples are sore, and your gut hurts. The curse first struck about a year ago, but it's been irregular as fuck, so it'd be no surprise if you hadn't started a week early.

Monday morning, and your period's started early. How much worse can it get? Diving under the duvet, you will the world to go away and leave you alone.

*Think of something nice,* you tell yourself. Seth, who you let pick you up the night before, over in Johnson City. Seventeen, with his own car – even though it's a junkheap. He has wheels, and he's the hottest boy you've ever seen.

You've got big tits, and can pass for much older than thirteen, so when he gave you that big, pussy-melting grin you thought you'd die with happiness. Even when he got a bit grumpy 'cause you wouldn't let his hands go anywhere near your pussy, instead kept moving them back to your tits; you didn't mind distracting him with a blow job.

You smile. From the look in his eyes you hadn't done a bad job for a beginner, braces or not. And it hadn't tasted as gross as you'd heard the other girls say.

*The other girls.* You wish you hadn't thought of them.

Bang bang bang! "You up, missee?"

No escaping it. "OK, Mom!" You haul your but out of bed and totter over to the door, pulling your night-shirt down, past your crotch.

Pulling the door open you squint out at the world outside your room, and dash to the bathroom.

Turn the shower on, good and hot, stand under it, let it blast your thoughts away. Your gut still hurts, you feel bloated and ugly, and touching your arms feels *ugh.* You wonder whether you're coming down with something. Or is this adolescence for everyone? Probably just you – Ms Freakazoid, as the Shelly Kovack Bitch would say.

"Aurora Debonis!" Mom yells. "Are you determined to bankrupt us?"

"For – oh, Mom, it's just a shower!"

You begin to towel yourself off, and then it all gets too much for you. *When Seth learns you're a mutie, 'cause the hottest boy you know won't settle for a metal-mouthed blow job forever, think he'll want anything to do with you, cum-bag?* You can almost hear Ellie Maitliss' voice.

Suddenly it's all too much.

You sit on the john and cry.

"Sweetheart, what's wrong?" *How the hell does Mom do that? Has she got the place bugged?* "Are you ill, honey?"

"I think it's the wrong time of the month," you quaver. "Can I stay home today?"

The door rattles, and you get up to let her in before sitting down again. Then Mom's there, cradling your head to her ample bosom. "Are those girls bullying you?" Mom says. "Because I know how you feel, honey, I really do."

"Ho-o-ow?" You wail.

"Because I'm like you, too, like I've always said. You take no notice of bigots. There's nothing wrong with us."

"Yeah sure, that's why Dad's not around!"

"Honey, it was lack of money, not us, that made him go away."

*Yeah, right, Mom.*

# XLVII

"Nice afternoon." Kotian squinted up at Shah from the park bench on which he sat.

*He looks tired,* Shah thought. *But if he's feeling the pressure, he's not showing it.* "You wanted to see me." He gazed around as he hitched up his trousers and sat. *The park's probably changed less than any part of the city.* Lovers still strolled hand in hand, the horses pulled their carriages around as they had for over a century and a half, and old men sat playing chess.

Eventually Kotian cleared his throat. "This isn't easy."

Shah didn't reply.

"If I knew who the Ripper was…"

Shah had narrowed it down to one of two or three men for some time, all of them in Kotian's organization. Now he was sure, at last. "You have to give him up."

"You have children, Officer. Wouldn't you do anything to protect your junkie daughter, for all her flaws? Love is unconditional." Kotian added hastily, "Not that I'm admitting that my son has anything to do with these attacks."

"Don't insult my intelligence, Abhijit. We both know who it is. Are you protecting him by letting him put himself in harm's way? If he's not caught, sooner or later he'll attack someone who's able to protect themselves. You want the knock on the door to be someone asking you to come identify his body?"

"If I was prepared to do some sort of deal, Officer, what could we scale the charges down to? Would the DA's office be prepared to settle for a diminished responsibility plea?"

Shah was damned sure that they wouldn't; the Ripper had shattered too many lives. But he said only, "I'm sure they'd consider it. But you know I can't promise anything. Even if we were on record, it's down to the DA. You need to hand him in."

"I'll think about it."

"Don't take too long. I'm going to have to tell my people about this, which means they'll come after the boy like a pack of wolves. You think that we've been all over you up until now? In the words of the old song, Abhijit, you really, really ain't seen nothing yet."

Kotian nodded, mind half elsewhere. Then he refocused, on Shah. "You did this, with your damned persistence."

"You expect me to apologize for doing my *job*?"

"It's more than a job to you, Shah. It's like a religious calling. "

Shah stared at Kotian. "If it is like some sort of calling, ask yourself Kotian, what else do I have, since everything else has been taken from me? It's all I have left. You want someone to blame, look in the mirror."

When Kotian had gone, Shah returned to the office, taking his eyepiece from his pocket calling in on the way. As he expected, van Doorn patched in Nancy Grunwald, who was scathing that Shah had kept his end of the deal. "You think that that piece of crap wouldn't double-cross you first chance he gets?"

Shah ignored her, instead asking, "What do you want to do?"

Van Doorn thought. "We focus on junior's trail over the last two or three years. We work with the Feds – and through them – other jurisdictions to nail down every move this bag's made, and see if we can get enough circumstantial to build an overwhelming pattern, even without solid evidence. The priority now is Sunny. We throw everything at nailing him."

"Can we get his bail revoked?" Shah said.

"Unlikely," Grunwald said. "We'd need to prove both that there is significant new evidence, which we don't have, and that he's a risk, which we can't yet prove."

Shah's eyepiece cut in: *Emergency incoming, personal.* Shah flipped the line over.

"Pete," Leslyn said. "Where are you?"

"About five minutes away," Shah said. He was almost back at the office, which was near the clinic where Leslyn worked.

"Can you meet me?"

*She looks terrified,* Shah thought. "Now? Where?"

"Outside the clinic."

"I'll be there."

Shah flipped the line back. "Got to go." He ended the call.

He broke into a trot, but couldn't keep it up, so alternated between as fast a walk as he could manage and a half-trot. By the time reached Leslyn, he was panting.

She grabbed him in a fierce hug. "Some guy just stopped me as I was going into work." This was one of the weeks when his shift and Leslyn's barely overlapped.

"He knew my name. When I asked him how, he started telling me all kinds of personal stuff about me, things he shouldn't, couldn't have known. As if he knew me intimately. Then he said what a shame it was that you'd been attacked." Leslyn held Shah even tighter, squeezing him until he struggled to breathe. "It was really, really creepy." Leslyn wiped an eye. "Sorry. I freaked."

"Don't be silly." Shah put his arms around her, rocking her from side to side. "Did he physically threaten you?"

"Not an actual threat, as such," Leslyn said. "He did say how awful it was to lose one's mind, like that partner of yours. Said it could happen to anyone at any time."

"It'll do," Shah said. "Did you get him on 'piece?"

"Not fully," Leslyn said. "He tried to stay out of my line of sight, but–"

Shah's piece beeped with an incoming; Leslyn sending the man's picture. *Generic Asian-Indian*, Shah thought, looking at dark skin and darker, hyperthyroid eyes. He sent an enquiry to the COTUS Cray and hugged Leslyn again.

Minutes later his phone pinged again. He forwarded the ID to Bailey with a covering message. "This guy's just threatened Leslyn. It's too much of a coincidence. Scour *every* camera in New York. I want to find something, sometime, somewhere tying him to Sunny. And I want protection for Leslyn sent to our home address. This is witness tampering, and it isn't diminished responsibility." Shah flagged down a cab, ushering Leslyn into it over her protestations. "Call it in as a family emergency," he said, joining her in the cab. "No arguing."

Shah and Leslyn spent a nervous half-hour at home until the detail arrived led by Bailey. "You both OK?"

*Said with barely a stammer,* Shah noticed with approval. He saw Stickel in the background, and inclined his head. She forefinger-saluted.

"The guy didn't touch her," Shah said, "but it's still a threat."

"We're here aren't we?" Stickel said, joining them. "What more you want?"

"What *are* you doing here?"

"Brought your protection detail." She indicated two uniformed officers.

"Thanks," Shah said.

Bailey said, "We have footage of them meeting. Not good enough to make out what they were saying, but we have lip-readers working on it. We've already snatched the other guy off the street, but he's probably one of scores. We need to cut off the head."

"He's over in Chinatown," Stickel said. "Acting as innocent as can be. Drinking coffee, yap-yap-yapping to his buds, studying the race odds, like he's on vacation."

"We going to pick him up?" Shah said.

"*We* are," Stickel said. "*You're* going to stay out of the way. If you get involved after he threatened your family, you know what line his defense team will take."

"Still." Shah followed them out, "I want to see this piece of crap get taken down."

"No grandstanding." Stickel dived into the squad car's front passenger seat.

Shah yanked open the rear door. "As if."

The cars sped through the city streets, blue lights ablaze, but sirens silent. Their lights cleared a path, though several times they only narrowly missed jaywalkers. Shah's thoughts raced through possible outcomes. Whatever happened, Leslyn's protection needed to stay in place for the moment, however much an imposition she felt it.

The radio squawked, "Ten-Thirteen!" the code for an officer needing assistance, "Suspect escaping–"

"There!" Stickel pointed, as Sunny erupted from a colonnaded arcade. The car screeched to a halt. Sunny skidded and fled away. The cops leapt out as Sunny fired over his shoulder, shattering glass. The crowds around him scattered in a starburst of panic.

Shah, Stickel and Bailey dispersed, racing after Sunny from different angles.

Sunny fired again and Stickel dropped as if coshed.

Shah knelt and took careful aim, mouthing a prayer that no one would cross his path. But before he could fire, shots rang out – one, two, three times – from several yards to Shah's right. Sunny's hands spread-eagled as if surrendering, and he fell in an untidy sprawl. Shah turned to see Bailey also kneeling.

She turned, white-faced and gazed at him.

Shah sighed, and thought, *Old Man Kotian is going to go fucking ballistic.* Shah didn't even like to think about what was going to happen now.

# XLVIII

"You OK?" Shah said.

Bailey got to her feet and nodded. "I had to shoot him. I couldn't let you do it."

"Stickel! You alright?" Shah bellowed over the screams and shouts of the crowd who had scattered when the shooting started. They had returned and were now pressing in on Bailey, who knelt on one knee over Sunny's prone body.

"Yep. He didn't hit me," Stickel called back.

They elbowed their through the throng to join Bailey, who was checking Sunny's pulse, fingers to carotid. She shook her head. "He's gone." She leaned back, studying the corpse. "Two shots." She pointed at Sunny's shoulder, then at his heart.

Shah's eyepiece chimed. Van Doorn said, "I've just had the call. You shot Sunny."

"Nope," Shah said. "Bailey did. He was fleeing from an attack on an officer, I shouted for him to stop. He didn't, he was firing and there was a risk to the public. Before I could fire, she beat me to it."

"Good thing, too," van Doorn said. "But however righteous the shooting you're *all* reassigned to desk duty until IA have investigated it." He smiled bleakly, "Which means you'll meet Officer Harper again."

"Who?"

"Ah," van Doorn said. "You haven't met him, far as you remember. If your reports are corroborated by your eyepieces and witnesses, you've nothing to worry about."

"Why both?" Shah slapped his forehead. "Course. We might've tampered with them."

"Exactly. Now, get back here."


Aurora saw the precise moment that Kotian finally took of his protective mask of charm, or began to disintegrate, depending which version she wanted to believe, the psychiatrist for the defense, or the police.

She had agreed to meet him for a drink. She knew the barkeep, and was fairly sure that he wasn't one of Kotian's men. She sat with her back to the wall, and watched everyone coming in and going out.

"My 'piece is streaming a live-feed to a safety-deposit box," she said with a sad little smile after they had exchanged hellos and kisses. "Just in case there were any misunderstandings."

"My dear, why would you want to do that?"

"I've heard certain… rumors… that my reliability is in question," Aurora said. "Not you, of course. But some of your associates have hinted at things. So I thought it best to be sure."

"Always best to be sure of things." Kotian ordered drinks. "So I wanted to be sure that you weren't avoiding me because of any mis–" His 'piece chimed. Aurora recognized his customization of the priority incoming. "Excuse me."

Aurora just happened to be looking at him, saw his face turn ashen. "When? How? Who?" His hand went to his mouth, and she noticed him swallow, Adam's apple rise and fall once. "Keep me posted." His voice sounded as if he had a throat full of gravel.

"What's wrong?" She said when he took off his 'piece. Even now, she hated to see him distressed – and he clearly was.

He shook off her hand. "They shot Sunny."

She took his hand again, and this time he let her as he shaded his eyes with the other hand. She didn't say, *But you have another son, now. You've been saying for two years that now you have another son, you don't have to look the other way to his little peccadilloes.* "Oh, Abhijit, I'm so sorry."

"Shah did it. That bastard, double-crossing Shah."

Aurora frowned. What did he mean?

He put his 'piece back on, and sat for a moment, scanning the newsfeeds. He laughed, a single explosive bark more like a cough. "They're accusing him of being the Ripper now, now that he's not here to defend himself. The cowards."

"Abhijit, you should go to Amy and the children," Aurora said.

He took off his 'piece and gazed at her, and at the terrible look in his eyes, she fell silent. "They're saying he was the Ripper," he said in a quiet voice that nonetheless nearly made her wet herself with fear. "They will *not* besmirch our name."

Stickel rode back with Shah and Bailey in a squad wagon, leaving a uniform to drive her pool car back. "I thought you might get caught in the crossfire," Bailey said

"Change the subject," Stickel said. "They don't like us talking 'bout incidents, in case we swap stories."

"Are they going to keep us apart?" Bailey said.

"Yeah, that's the by-the-book," Stickel said, "but this be the real world. Desperate shortage of veh-i-cles, so we get to ride back together. Cozy, huh?" She winked at Shah who smiled. "You OK?" Stickel said. "You don't look too good."

Shah shook his head, decided it would be a waste of time to try and explain his odd feeling of numbness. "Is it always like this?" he said. "The whole 'Get your ass back and don't talk to anyone' thing?"

Stickel nodded, giving Shah's arm a reassuring squeeze. "We hit people a lot of the time, not like in films where everyone shoots a lot but no one ever gets hit. This all about convincing people that it's a good cause. Politics, it's called."

They arrived at the precinct, and bundled out.

Inside Shah took a few minutes to compose himself. He resumed working through the outstanding dockets, but it was difficult to focus. His thoughts kept sliding away – to the shooting, to Leslyn, to Aurora – anywhere but where he was.

Every time he closed his eyes, Shah saw Sunny's outflung hands.

He sat back and closed his eyes. There had been no revenge. Just duty, and closing off the old life. *Maybe now I can draw a line under it.*

Shah suspected though, that while he had finished with Sunny Kotian, the young man's family hadn't yet finished with him.

"You OK?" a woman's voice said.

Shah opened his eyes. Kimi stood with a sheaf of notes in her hand, looking worried. "I heard what happened."

Shah half-smiled. "News travels fast."

"Good news." She patted his shoulder. "John would approve."

"It isn't like that," Shah said.

"Glad to hear it, Officer," a man said.

"Got to go," Kimi muttered, and fled.

Shah twisted in his chair. The speaker was a tall, red-haired man with a closely trimmed beard.

Shah checked his eyepiece's log. "Harper," he said.

"You needed to check?" Red-hair said.

"Surprisingly, none of my 'Get Well' downloads included a memory of meeting you."

Red-hair thrust out a hand. "Officer Marius Harper."

"Internal Affairs Guy." Shah stood and shook. "You investigated me before, I gather."

"So it's true," Harper said. "You don't remember?"

"You must have read my dossier," Shah said. "Doesn't that tell you everything?"

"But it's the change in you. When I read about it, I assumed that they'd stick you together again, and I guess they have enough for you to function as a cop." He paused. "But it's like meeting a different person."

"How so?" Shah said, waving at Harper to pull up a chair.

Harper shook his head. "I need to get on. I'm pulling together visual evidence, so I'm going to need your eyepiece. Don't worry, I'll give you a receipt." He added, "You seem calmer, not so edgy. Like you've been reset to zero, and the job hasn't monsterfied you – yet."

"Is monsterfy even a word?" Shah grinned, handing over his eyepiece. "Regs say I can have a union rep present. He hasn't called me back yet. Soon as he does and agrees to rep me, you can start applying the thumbscrews. Joke," he added.

"We'll talk tomorrow," Harper said.

When Shah got home the two uniforms in the lounge were trying to look inconspicuous. Leslyn jerked her thumb at them as she dutifully submitted to a peck on the cheek. "How long will Cheech and Chong be here?"

"Until the Department's sure there's no one else roaming around with a gun." Shah still felt dislocated, but more and more on the way home that image had stabbed into his brain, of Sunny flinging out his arms as the bullets hit.

Shah's eyepiece chimed. *Unknown caller.*

"Are you OK? " Aurora said.

"What's with the 'unknown caller' ID?"

"Different 'piece. I got some prepaids. If Abhijit should check and sees I've been talking to you…"

"Are you OK? Has he hurt you?"

She shook her head. As with most cheap prepaids, the icon was grainy and occluded much of her beauty. "He's called me from home – where he's with the family – seven times in the last three hours, each time a little less coherent. But he's not threatened *me*."

"He's struggling to cope."

"He's ranting about the NYPD, and you in particular."

"I could come over, if you wanted?"

"I wish you would," Aurora said. "Funny, you'd think I'd be relieved at the death of a monster, but – oh, I dunno what I feel." She added, "But it's not a good idea right now. Abhijit might turn up at any moment."

"What about somewhere else? I just wanna talk," he added hastily.

"I don't need you to talk." Aurora laughed. "Doesn't that sound awful? I meant if you want to just sit and sip coffee, that's fine. Just you being there helps."

"Give me twenty minutes to get changed and fix something to eat."

"I'll get something," Aurora said. "It's your fee for babysitting me."

"OK." He cut the line.

"Was that *her*?" Leslyn said.

Shah stared at Leslyn. "It was Aurora, yes." He held up a hand to forestall whatever Leslyn was going to say. "It's probably safer for us to legally separate at the moment," Shah said, "although I want to stay in the apartment." *Judging by the look on Leslyn's face*, Shah thought as he left the room to shower, *she's more relieved than upset.*

# XLIX

"Why was she relieved?" Aurora said when Shah told her at her apartment. They'd ended up there despite her anxiety that Kotian might learn they were meeting. "It's just as likely his people'd see us out and about," she admitted as she joined him on the couch.

She had sensed something was troubling Shah, chipped away at his diffidence until he gave it up. She leaned on his shoulder, then nudged him. "Why relieved?"

"We been drifting apart," Shah said. "Long as things rolled along on a day-to-day basis, we could gloss it over. But thugs threatening her changes things."

"Surely that goon wasn't the first?"

"Yep. Over thirty years and Leslyn's never been threatened."

"That's quite an achievement."

"Is it?" Shah deliberated. "I guess it is. The downside is, far as she's concerned, my job's no more dangerous than any other." He added, "Until now."

Aurora stretched out a leg. Lately he seemed to have been thinking far too much about those legs... She nudged him again. "Penny for your thoughts, as my grandma used to say."

"A penny?"

"Like a cent, only probably worth more."

"Most things would be," Shah grumbled. As she rested her head on his shoulder in a blaze of blonde hair, he closed his eyes and swallowed. He was acutely aware of her perfume, and – when he opened his eyes – her cleavage. She wore a black dress barely bigger than a postage stamp. When she moved, he glimpsed midriff. "Are you wearing anything under this?" He flicked her thin shoulder strap.

"No," she said, gazing into his eyes.

He suddenly found it very hard to breathe.

She stretched and her lips touched his. When she pulled back, he followed her lips with his own, and they parted. Her tongue touched his, momentarily at first, then the kiss grew deeper, more passionate.

They peeled apart, slowly.

"You're shaking." Aurora looked puzzled, frowned. "Am I repulsive, Pete?"

Shah shook his head. He wanted to say, "You're the most beautiful woman I've ever seen."

"Give me time to get used to this. It's all a bit new to me. *Everything's* new to me, but this is especially so."

She shifted, faced him eye to eye. "You can ask me anything you want, Pete, anything at all. Questions phrased, how shall I say… respectfully… are no problem. It's the 'what kind of weirdo freak are you' comments that bother me."

Shah scratched his head. "I dunno where to begin."

Aurora put on her eyepiece and sent something. Moments later his chimed, and he downloaded the clip she'd sent him.

The alarm radio blares into life with Rebel Cutie blasting out "Keep on Loving You". You stretch to slap the alarm down–

The clip ended and Shah removed his 'piece. "So that's you," he said. "That still how you feel? A freaka-zoid?"

"Sometimes," Aurora said with a faint smile. "Let me give you the technical stuff. No, I don't have a penis, I have a giant clitoris. Engorged, it's about three inches long. I don't pee out of the end of it like men, and I don't produce semen. Genetically, I'm a woman."

"It all sounds a bit clinical," Shah said. Aurora swung a leg over him so that she was sat on his knees, facing him. "Were you born like it… I mean, I read about guys being operated on at the start of the century to become women…."

"Those were transexuals," Aurora said. "I'm an inter-sexual. They chose to change gender. I often wonder why their *patrones* paid the money that enabled them to change; paid to buy a girl with a cock when they could get a woman. Which brings me to another question."

"Go on," Shah said.

"Why are you here? Why aren't you trawling bars with the other guys from the precinct, chasing ordinary pussy?"

Shah thought. "I hardly ever go into bars. I used to during hockey season, 'cause it's nice to sit with fans. But during the closed season – well, Muslims and bars. Not exactly a winning combination, if you see what I mean."

"OK, so dancing classes. Or is that against Muslim tenets?"

"Islam isn't against people enjoying themselves!"

"Never said it was. Stop dodging the question."

"I don't get time."

"Oh, bull!" Aurora said. "You got time to meet me, but not to hunt a girlfriend?"

"I could ask you the same sort of 'what's going on' question, Aurora. You tell me you just wanna talk, but you're wearing – everywhere I look, I see skin. It turns me on but I'm *so* scared of how I feel. My only memories of romancing are thirty years outta date. I got almost no idea how be around a woman 'cept for work, what to talk about–" He ran out of words.

Aurora slid off him and pulling her skirt down, stood up. "Didn't mean to overload that poor old man's brain." Her half-smile said otherwise.

"Please don't–"

She hushed him. "I'll be back in a second." She ducked into her bedroom.

Shah wished that he'd had the guts to blurt out the truth; that he'd started to fantasize about her at night, that she haunted his dreams nowadays. The truth was, dreams were safer than reality.

She emerged from her room wearing trousers and what looked like about eight layers of clothing, most red or black, although one dark blue sleeve peeked out through a gap. She then ostentatiously draped the *chador* over all of them, leaving only her eyes visible. Shah sensed barely suppressed laughter. "Better?"

Shah sighed. "Clown." He patted the seat beside him, and she sat. "You didn't need to go that far," he grumbled.

"Never happy, some people."

"Maybe somewhere between the two extremes," he took her hand. "Can I still ask you anything, in a respectful manner?"

"Of course." She rested her head on his shoulder.

With his free hand, he slid the chador off and stroked her hair. "What do your parents think of you?"

"They're dead now." She put a finger to his lips to forestall his sympathy. "Grandma decided when she had Mom not to cut her, as always used to happen."

"It's common – the mega whatever-you-call-it?"

"Clitoromegaly," she said, smiling. "I'm genetically female. Used to be about one in fifteen thousand need what they called gender reassignment, supposedly for the *kids'* benefit. I think it was more for the parents, to make their kids normal – whatever the hell normal is."

"Oh, my," Shah breathed.

"Oh, my," Aurora agreed.

"Your mom was intersexual?"

"So was Dad," Aurora said. "But he was genetically male. He left when I was a baby. Mom always insisted it was nothing to do with me." She added quickly, "No cheap psychology about me looking for father-substitutes, please."

"I wouldn't dream of it," Shah lied. "Nor nuclear families. But you had your Mom."

"Till I was seventeen," Aurora said. "Lost Mom the year after the cancer took Grandma. In Mom's case it was a head-on." She stroked his hand with her thumb. "I ran off to Washington, where I met a guy who wanted to look after me – at least at first."

"What happened to him?" Shah wondered whether the guy had been Kotian. "I met Kotian," Aurora said. "He helped me set up – genuinely set up – on my own. I owe him, Shah. That's what makes this so hard. He's a complex man."

*Who's just lost his son,* Shah thought, squashing any sympathy he might have felt.

Do you want to stay the night?" Aurora said. "I can make up the bed in the spare room. Or..." she smiled lazily.

"Not tonight," Shah said. To ease the disappointed look he said, "Maybe next time. Sometime soon, anyway."

They kissed goodnight at her apartment door.

It seemed to Shah as he left the complex, that the streets of New York had never looked so beautiful.

# L

The evening was still early. Shah could go home and make uneasy small-talk with Leslyn and Doug, with all the attendant risks of stepping on an emotional mine, or ride the web. But trawling the past was less attractive than earlier.

Instead he strolled the streets and watched people: late shift employees hurrying from work with faces drained by the day, or to work with the set expressions of those who had to be somewhere whether or not they wished it; shoppers headed home from the delis and grocery stores that had sprung up, as small mammals replaced the dinosaurs, to replace the hypermarkets, carrying paper bags full of the groceries they couldn't grow or barter for themselves; couples, wandering past hand in hand.

He ran through the events from meeting Aurora to Sunny's death, wondered whether it was as inevitable as it seemed now. Maybe if he and Marietetski had taken another route, or if he'd ignored Aurora's pleas for help? But they would almost certainly have been ambushed at another time, or Sunny would have found another way to incriminate him. Whichever way he looked at it, the chain of events that led to Sunny's shooting seemed foreordained.

Part of Shah's re-induction had been training to pay greater attention to his surroundings, to minimize the chances of another attack. For the first time since then, he was walking a block on which a sign advertising *Manny's Sports Bar* was mounted on one wall.

Shah stopped. Talking to the guys at the station, he'd learned that it was baseball season now. The old Shah had been a sports nut – perhaps, Shah sensed, as a way of getting along with guys with whom he had little else in common – but had liked to watch the matches alone and talk about them next morning in the squad room.

For a moment or two, Shah stood, undecided. Then shrugged. He could always drink water. Or beer, for that matter. Old Shah had rarely thought about his religion it seemed, and New Shah had no idea why or whether that was significant. New Shah hadn't abstained from alcohol because it was forbidden, but whenever he'd been in a social situation it was with people like Leslyn who knew he didn't drink, and therefore didn't offer it him.

But tonight he was alone.

Shah pushed through the doors.

The noise inside almost stopped him in his tracks – it was like walking into a solid wall. The drinkers were six deep around the bar. It was an interval, judging by the ads for local shops and services on the screens.

Shah took a deep breath, pushed his way through the throng. Several people moved out of his way anyway. One beefy guy grinned. "You given up holding up that stupid badge to clear your way, then Pete?"

*Ah*, Shah thought. *That was how he used to do it.* He took it out and held it up, "You mean this?" To roars of laughter. Someone said, "Like you needs to with that eyepiece shrieking, 'I'm a cop, get outta my way!'"

Shah thought, *yeah, it is cheesy,* and put the badge away again.

A third man turned and said, "Hey, not see you in here a while. Wifey been lockin' you in of a night?"

"Something like that." Shah forced cheerfulness. *No reason he should know what happened, if he only sees me here.*

One of the barmen turned as he said, "What'll it be–" He broke off when he saw Shah. He turned white and muttered, "Got to go. Sorry." He called to a colleague, "Pat, serve this guy!" and fled.

The man who had spoken before said, "Does Karl owe you money, or sump'n?"

A second man said, "You musta caught him bangin' your wife, way he ran fer it."

Both roared with laughter, and Shah – making an effort – joined in, although his main reaction was curiosity. *No barman flees a returning regular – quite the opposite.*

"What'll it be?" Pat said. From the voice Shah gathered that Pat was a woman, although with the tattoos, cropped blonde hair and bodybuilder physique it was hard to tell.

"Beer," Shah said. *Maybe she's intersexual, as well. If there's a one in fifteen thousand chance, like Aurora said, there must be close to five thousand in the country. Most would come to a city like New York, than stay in the 'burbs.*

A large tankard banged onto the bar. "On the house," Pat said. "Stevie's compliments." She chin-cocked one of the other barmen, who was halfway through serving a customer. Shah returned Stevie's wave.

"You must be in his good books. You covering as the weekend doorman?" Shah's second new acquaintance said.

"Maybe." Shah smiled, and sipped his beer, which was sweet and gassy and bland. *Maybe it's an acquired taste,* he thought, unsure whether he could be bothered to acquire it.

The interval ended. Most of the drinkers jostled for position near the screens, while a few laggards frantically finished ordering their drinks.

Shah leaned against the bar and watched men throwing balls at other men, who were armed with sticks with which they sometimes hit the ball. It was as incomprehensible as one of the Inca sacrifices he had watched on a history feed.

Someone tapped his shoulder.

"Stevie," Shah said to the barman/doorman looming over him.

"Nice to see you, Pete," Stevie said. Shah suspected he was cleverer than his slow, deep voice made him out to be. "Sorry to hear about your trouble. You better now?"

Shah nodded.

"That why you drinkin' beer, now?" Stevie said. "You forgotten what it tastes like?" He nudged Shah, and smiled. Shah smiled back. The humor here was different from the station, harder to fathom. But Shah instinctively liked Stevie. "What *did* you hear?" Shah said.

"Youse got worked over. Memories ripped. How 'bout your partner?"

"That why Karl took off?" Shah said, ignoring the previous question.

Stevie didn't seem to mind. "Said he had an urgent call to make. Yeah, he's taking a long time, isn't he?"

Stevie grinned, clearly relishing the idea of Karl discomfited.

"Why don't you go look for him?" Something about Karl's reaction had been too extreme, and Shah wanted to know why.

Minutes later Stevie returned through the 'Staff Only' door he'd left through, and catching Shah's eye, shook his head.

Shah made an "oh well" gesture, and saluting in farewell, pushed his way to the doors.

Where he came face to face with Kotian.

# LI

"Celebrating, *Officer*?" Kotian sneered. His eyes were red-rimmed, though Shah guessed from their glaze that tears weren't the only reason for that. Minders stood just behind each shoulder. South Asians like Kotian, they stared at Shah, their expressions unreadable.

Shah knew nothing would ease Kotian's pain. But if he said nothing, he'd look callous. "I'm sorry, Abhijit. I tried–"

"Spare me the phony sympathy, Shah. And save your excuses for the hearing. "

All around them conversation had stopped and people stood, staring *too* intently at anywhere other than Shah and Kotian.

"Good night, Abhijit." Shah had to brush past them, and as he did so he felt the bodyguard tense. Shah braced himself for a punch or even a knife thrust, but the bodyguard relaxed and Shah emerged into the open air.

He breathed a huge sigh and checked his hands. They were shaking. His head felt woozy. *I only had one drink. How can people put so much away? And what's the attraction?*

Slowly, he weaved his way home.

### Wednesday

Even on only one beer Shah felt groggy the next morning, but managed to reach the office only five minutes later than usual.

Just after nine-thirty his eyepiece chimed.

Harper said, "Let's talk about Sunny Kotian."

"When?"

"Now."

"But–" Shah held up his hands. "OK. I'll talk to my union rep."

"No need. He's already here."

Shah grabbed his jacket, frustrated at having no time to farm out any of his outstandings, and fuming at the peremptory nature of the summons – including the fact that Harper had already talked to his union rep. Shah felt that he'd been played.

His mood got no better when he passed Bailey in the corridor. She looked away.

*What was that about?* Shah wondered. He lowered his head like a bull about to charge. By the time he had marched the eight blocks to One Police Plaza, he'd psyched himself into an unusually aggressive mood. The truth was that he was scared, and anger seemed a better response than fear. He'd heard bad things about IA from every cop he'd spoken to. His stress levels climbed further when Office Security dragged him off to a side room and gave him a full body search, refusing to tell him why.

So by the time he was allowed through to meet his rep, Lafferty, Shah was breathing heavily, and a bad headache had settled between his eyes.

"Easy, easy," Lafferty said. The guy was even older than Shah, and chewed gum incessantly, something Shah hadn't seen for years. Lafferty led him into the interview room, where Harper was talking on his eyepiece. "Got to go," Harper said.

"Don't rush on my account."

Harper stared at Shah. "Problem?"

"Dragging me out of work with no notice, so I have no time to reassign cases. So you're a Big Important Guy and you want to show me who's boss. How does interfering with ongoing work help? And I don't like that you order me direct, rather than through my rep."

"Ah, that was my fault," Lafferty said. "I've had three different officers to rep this morning and I thought it'd be OK. Sorry."

"Then let's get on," Shah said, pulling out a chair and dropping onto it. "Ask your questions. I'll answer what I can."

Harper said, "If Kotian is making accusations, I'm duty-bound to investigate them. You see that, don't you?"

Shah grunted, nodded reluctantly. "I guess."

"This feud of yours with Sunny…"

"No feud," Shah said.

"Oh come on, this persecution's been going on for years. You're supposed to have no memory of anything from before losing your memory, yet the first thing that you do is slip back into the old routine and go after Sunny, like a dog after a rat. You just wouldn't let it go."

Shah took a deep breath. How to explain that slipping back into work was an easier option than confronting the emptiness of his life?

"Well?" Harper said.

"Didn't know if the pause was just you drawing breath before the next barrage of crap. OK, so it's like this: I have no memory of what's gone before. I read the case notes. Kotian and Junior are acquainted with a huge number of people who've disappeared, or their employees are. You can say it's because they know lots of people, but some of those who disappeared only vanished *after* it looked like they might embarrass the Kotians. As for going after them, I was following the directions of my superior officer. So when you've finished playing defense counsel for the Clan Kotian, you want to get to what this is all about?"

"I agree," Lafferty interjected. "Let's not spend any longer here than we all have to. You've got Shah's eyepiece; you've had Bailey's and Stickel's."

"All of them point to Bailey shooting a man in the back when the man was fleeing–"

"While firing shots…"

"–while firing shots," Harper agreed. "But you shouldn't even have been there. *You* were specifically told to butt out because of your emotional involvement with someone Kotian allegedly threatened. How much was Bailey influenced by you, I wonder?"

"Why don't you ask her?" *So that was why she looked so pissed.* "Listen Harper, you got a rep as a good cop. What the hell is this crap about conspiracy theories? You really think we're that desperate? We had the guy already. We didn't need to shoot him–"

"Exactly!"

"*Except for the fact that people were in danger.* No two ways about it. We had a hundredth of a second to make a call, and there looked a good chance of civilians getting killed." Shah banged his palm on the table to each word: "*It was a good call.*"

Lafferty said, "At least one policeman had been shot. I know you have to play Devil's Advocate, Harper, I know Kotian's lawyers are all over the Department like poison ivy, and their pressure's getting transmitted down the line, but you have nothing but claim and counterclaim." He added. "What do the shop cameras nearby show?"

Harper's exhalation signaled deep frustration. "Most of the shops didn't even have working cameras."

"Were any of them working?" Shah said.

Harper was silent. Instead he shook his head as if trying to clear it.

"So all you have is 'he said, she said' testimony," Lafferty said. "And the eyepieces."

"Which are inconclusive," Harper said. "So until I feel that we can make a call one way or another, you're still on desk duty."

Shah left, shaking his head, wondering whether Harper would ever make a decision – based on what he had seen, it seemed unlikely.

*Oh joy,* Shah thought. *An eternity of desk work, my ass slowly spreading across the chair.*

# LII

You call the others in on the intercept once you're sure which way the target's headed.

When the diner providing the cover for the off-track betting shop called, you listened silently to them interrogating Forry. You'd know those smartass voices anywhere. They've drilled their way into your dreams...

For a horrible few minutes as you weaved the T-Bird through the clumps of shoppers, workers and gawpers that it seems to suck off the sidewalk and into the road, you didn't think that you'd get to the shop in time. Sliding the car to a halt a block away, you ran for it. Raison will park it up. That's what you have a driver for.

Forry's such a windbag he kept them talking long enough, so you just rounded the corner before they vanished at the far end of the block. Your lungs were burning, but that didn't matter; you took a deep, fiery breath and set after them. "Keep 'em in sight!" you'd gasped. Paulie, longer-legged, younger and faster than you, ran ahead.

Luckily, the targets are so deep in conversation that they're just ambling, so you've already caught them and Paulie up by now. You could detonate a bomb beside them and they wouldn't notice it. It's harder keeping out of the nearest camera's line of sight without drawing attention from those on the far side pointing your way. Very few of them work anyway, but it would be better when the police operatives go through the data that you leave no clear view for facial recognition software to match, and do nothing to attract their enhancement gizmos.

Your eyepiece was stolen to order a few days before. You call up a map on it showing that there's only one alleyway they can go down when they cross the next intersection. This near Joan of Arc Park and its lowlifes, crowds have already thinned out. "Move in," you say.

For a moment you fear the opportunity's missed as Marietetski dashes across the street, catching Mike and Wilkowski out of position, and is quickly followed by Shah.

"We'll take 'em from behind," you tell the others, and Mike gives you thumbs-up to acknowledge, which is risky, but he's disposable.

Just as Wilkowski's cosh descends, Shah stiffens and whirls, but too late, and the blow sends him sprawling, and as he lands your boot thuds into his ribs, drawing a satisfying "ugh!" from him. It jerks his head around, scraping his eyepiece away. You stomp on it, grinding it to pieces. Then you grab the old man's ankles and drag him backwards into an alleyway. Marietetski shouts, "*Officer down!* Track our eyepieces, we need help at eighty-sixth and–" Mike thumps him into silence.

Shah wriggles and kicks out, his foot connecting with Paulie who grunts, "Bastard!" As Shah clambers to his feet you slam a fist into his ribs, driving the wind from his lungs.

You bang your clasped fists into his shoulder blades, forcing him to his knees, and gripping his hair, yank his head back. Paulie pushes his wrists together behind his back and handcuffs him as you swab analgesic on his temple. He tries to jerk his head away, but you keep a tight grip on his hair.

You say, "Leave him functional. I want him to be a walking, talking reminder of what happens to people who ask awkward questions."

You enjoy seeing Shah's eyes widen in recognition.

# LIII

For the rest of the day Shah worked in near silence. He tried to convince himself that he wasn't being treated like a pariah – a cop under investigation was nothing unusual, as Bailey and Stickel could testify – but it certainly felt like it.

Only when he glimpsed his reflection in a shop window did he understand why the others might have stayed quiet. The set-jawed stranger who glared back at him looked capable of ripping his colleague's heads from their shoulders and chewing on them.

As Shah approached the subway he consciously made an effort to relax, breathing out, rotating his head. Then he saw nearby commuters giving him sideways looks and stopped. The old New York where street crazies were tolerated was long gone, and he had no desire to explain himself to a transit cop.

The ride out to Marble Hill on the One was as bleak and depressing as before, a symbolic descent from a Manhattan still recognizable as the old Big Apple – albeit fly-blown fruit – to the skeletal burnt-out remains of the suburbs, a concrete indictment of their dreams of oil-mortgaged utopia.

The journey seemed to pass faster than before and Shah stood outside Perveza's slum before he'd had time to properly marshal his thoughts. This time the door was shut, so he pounded on it until a weary voice that could have been male or female called from inside, "Who's there?"

"My name's Shah, I'm looking for my daughter, Perveza."

An emaciated woman who looked nearer fifty than twenty-five opened the door

"Hello Perveza," Shah said.

She didn't answer but turned inside, leaving the door open, Taking it as an invitation Shah followed her in, into the kitchen where some sort of cooked meat lay on a plate, beside a solitary grilled tomato, halved. It was such a pitiful attempt at a meal that for a moment Shah wanted to hug her. It passed when Perveza said, "Whaddya want? Come tell me what a disappointment I am?"

Shah thought, *at least she's remembering to eat.* "No, I came to see how you were."

"How am I?" Perveza said. "Well, I know who you are, so I guess I must be outta stash. Gonna give me a little cash for some stash, flash?" She giggled, but her eyes teared up.

"I'd sooner take you out, feed you up, and buy you some new clothes."

Perveza flushed. "What use are they?"

"Finish your dinner, before it goes cold."

"It *is* cold," Perveza said. "Gus cooked it for me sometime. Someone gave it him. Said it was pork," she added defiantly.

Shah said more to himself than her, "Probably a feral pig they caught."

"You're not angry?"

"Why should I be? It's your life, if you want to eat pork."

Perveza began to cry, but Shah felt nothing except a mild irritation that her attempt at manipulation was so blatant.

"At least when you were angry, it showed you cared!" Perveza yelled.

"Can I ask you something?" Shah said. He'd sensed the subject was off-limits with Leslyn. He'd raised it once, and she'd said, "Don't ask," so finally that he hadn't dared.

Perveza smiled slyly. "Will you pay me?"

"Maybe."

"Then maybe I'll answer."

Shah handed her two nearly worthless thousand dollar bills. "You're younger than Rex…"

"So?" She stuffed the money down her blouse.

"Why do I have a memory of your mother having our first born? Calling her Perveza?"

Perveza stared at him. Her face seemed to slowly crumple inwards. "You bastard! For years I had to listen to that shit! If it wasn't your little fucking shrine in your wardrobe, it was Rex telling me you never wanted me. You only had me to replace her when she died! I hate you, you bastard! Get out get out GET OUT!"

Shah was almost home before he stopped shaking. Even with limited memories he'd felt anger, but never been on the receiving end of anything so raw and full of pain.

Should he have told Perveza that he'd lost his memory? He wasn't sure it would have made any difference. Most people who knew him from before noticed the difference when they met him, but Perveza was completely absorbed in her addiction.

Shah saw a sign saying 'Cathedral Parkway.' On an impulse he jumped out of the subway car and climbed the steps. He was shocked to note that he was a little out of breath. Age creeping up on you, old man.

Directly opposite the station were the offices of Bannerman, Douglas and Shah. He got lucky – as he was crossing the street, Rex emerged from the glass doors. He stopped when he saw Shah. "This is a surprise." His tone gave no hint whether the surprise was a pleasant one.

"I wondered…" Shah stopped.

Clearly fearing an ulterior motive, Rex held up a hand. "Dad, I've heard about what happened with Sunny Kotian. I've dealt with the Kotian family in the past, so I can't answer questions about them."

"No, that's not it," Shah said. "I've been piecing memories together, from years ago."

"Oh, good." Rex ostentatiously checked his watch.

"I wondered why you told Perveza that we only had her to replace her dead sister."

Rex's face went blank. "I think it's a little late for questions like that, don't you?" He marched away.

"Not if we're playing into damage time!" Shah shouted at Rex's retreating back.

Shah was halfway home when he rounded a corner and nearly walked into someone talking to his eyepiece. "Got to go!" The man snapped. He beamed. "Pervez, old man! How are you?"

Shah needed a moment. "Erokij Tosada?"

"Exactly!" Tosada thrust out a hand. "I heard about your unfortunate mishap. This place is one big village, down to the gossip. How are you adjusting?"

"Slowly, I'm afraid," Shah said with a rueful smile. "Well, this is a surprise." It seemed the sort of small-talk that he ought to make in the circumstances.

Tosada took it literally, though. "Not really. It's still relatively well-populated but Manhattan's much more geographically discrete than thirty years ago." Snapping out of his reverie, he grimaced. "Sorry; lecturing's my default conversational-mode nowadays."

Shah made an "it doesn't matter" gesture.

Tosada said, "I'm missing our chats, you know – do you have time for coffee? Come on, say yes! There's a deli here!"

Inside the deli, Shah's head spun as he tried to keep up with Tosada's conversational shifts, from politics to baseball to his web appearances. Tosada seemed to have strong opinions on everything. When they touched on Tosada's research, Shah said "It seems to me that immortality's fundamentally unnatural."

"Nonsense," Tosada said. "Luddites have said that about every scientific development from powered flight to genetic engineering! Define natural, for that matter?"

"Surely mankind's finite lifespan is an integral part of its humanity," Shah insisted.

"You could say the same about the appendix. Does taking death away make us less human than taking away our appendix?"

"Yes," Shah insisted. "If we're immortal, we perceive the world differently, just as I perceive it differently from before the attack. Everything is new to me you see, even when I have downloaded memories."

Tosada nodded. "I see your point but–"

"Why are you so vehement about immortality?" Shah said.

"Check my profile," Tosada said. "See how old I am?"

Shah used his eyepiece. "Sixty-five."

"And my father was how old when he died?"

Shah checked. "Sixty-seven."

"My grandfather?"

"Sixty-four. So?"

"I'm living on borrowed time. In damage time, to use your hockey language."

"Nonsense!"

"It's true," Tosada insisted. "Both were researchers, neither cracked the mystery." He turned suddenly gloomy. "Sometimes I think that we're all doomed to echo our fathers' lives."

Shah started to object, then thought of his own father. *Was that why I joined the force?*

Then he thought of how different everyone said he was now, and Rex, and wondered. "Maybe," he agreed. "But at other times we seem to live trying to *avoid* being our fathers."

# LIV

**Thursday**

Shah received a call from Building Management. "Package for ya here."

"Who from?"

"No return address." The operative had to be genetically obese – no blue-collar could afford the calories to get that fat – with sweat-beaded forehead and a squeaky, exasperated voice: "Building policy is you come down, open it in the containment cage. Then only one person's hurt if all the sniffers and scanners missed anything." The call cut off before Shah could ask whether the guy had bio-scanned it, although Shah guessed the guy had, and ruled that threat out. Opening it in the cage was covering all bases.

It took Shah two minutes to walk down to the first floor, five times as long to track down the containment cage and its grumpy operative, who were out the back of the building facing a walled yard.

"Those walls would be nasty falling on you." Shah nodded in their direction.

"Ten feet thick," the fat man said. "Need a nuke to blow *them* down, and it'd be rerouted 'fore it ever got here." He opened the cage. "Here ya go." He ducked behind a low protective wall.

The package was an A5 padded packet. Shah put on latex gloves. "How come I get the treat?" He called. "Some crazy sends something and I get put in harm's way?"

"What'd ya expect? That I should?"

"Suppose the commissioner gets one? She come down herself?"

The operative laughed contemptuously. "She'd send a flunky like you to take the hit."

Shah muttered, "Yeah, fuck you too." He tore open the packet with trembling fingers, and felt inside.

It was another CD. Shah's eyebrows lifted. He shook the envelope but nothing else fell out. "It's safe to come out now."

Upstairs, Shah waited impatiently for the CD player to finish scanning the files. He was sorely tempted to press override, but if it did have an electronic virus, he'd be in deep shit.

Finally it came up all-clear. Checking the properties, Shah saw it was voice-only.

Shah hit play.

A voice said, "If you're in the public eye in any way, even if or you're just doing an everyday job, the hardest thing about it is that it makes vulnerable those you love."

"That's your voice," van Doorn said.

Shah frowned. "No, that's not me."

"That's you," van Doorn insisted, tapping his finger in a vain attempt to jog his memory. "I've heard it before. Get it over to CSU. It's unlikely the sender's dumb enough to leave any trace, but we ought to check."

Shah did so, putting a priority flag on the seal, which meant that he'd probably get it back in about two weeks rather than three, but it was the best he was going to get.

But van Doorn must have lit a firecracker under someone, for that afternoon CSU called Shah. That it was negative was unsurprising but still faintly disappointing, for all that Shah had expected no more. But the caller confirmed that the lab tests had confirmed the voice as Shah's.

"I'd guess it was from when you were in your early twenties," the tech said, adding, "It's probably a compilation of two or more recordings stitched together."

Shah poked his head around van Doorn's door. "The voice *is* mine."

Van Doorn waved him in. "Found this."

Two clips arrived on Shah's eyepiece, and he felt again his concern about his mother, and the guilt at being a Muslim in post 9/11 New York. On the second one he talked about reprisals, but played it down. "It's the same for anyone in the public eye–"

Shah blew his cheeks out. Whoever sent it pieced it together from them."

"I got the records library looking at archaic media," van Doorn said. "I found a couple of old radio interviews you did, after a bit of a ruckus with some vigilantes that got picked up by the media."

"It's obvious who sent it: Kotian." Shah sighed. "It's a thinly-veiled threat."

"Against who?" van Doorn said. "It don't sound very threatening."

"It does if you factor in Leslyn and Doug," Shah said. "Or Aurora."

"The tranny hooker?" van Doorn said. He frowned, and drilled Shah with a look.

"Nothing to it, Cap," Shah said. "Just professional."

"Hey," Shah said, when Aurora finally opened her door to him. She had a new hairdo, swept forward much more than the old one. Shah wasn't sure that he liked it.

She smiled thinly and stepped back to allow him in.

Shah stared. "That a bruise?" He reached out to touch the cheekbone beneath the hair, but she shied away. "Hold still." Shah eased the hair away and hissed. "Kotian?"

Aurora's head inclined a centimeter. "He was half-mad with grief. I thought better me than his wife or children. He pays me…"

"Not enough," Shah said. "You could go into witness protection?"

"He can't help himself at the moment," Aurora said. "Until Sunny died, I thought that he was nothing like his father. Now I realize that Abhijit's learned how to act around civilized people, but it's only a veneer." Her laugh was brittle. "Anyway, it's irrelevant. I was just preparing to visit a client, so I have to get ready."

Shah watched her walk into her bedroom. Half-tempted to follow her, instead he sat on a couch, leaning forward with his hands clasped as if praying, elbows on his knees. He was still in the same position when Aurora emerged from her bedroom a few minutes later.

He tracked her as she moved across the room, fixing her earrings, patiently, unwavering, as if trying to see her properly for the first time.

She wore a short backless skirt, and slipped into high

heels, still fiddling with the second earring, so her head was tilted.

"Can I kiss you?" he blurted.

For the first time since he'd arrived, she smiled. "I don't know if that's wise." Her smile slipped when he didn't return it. "I was joking."

He nodded, tried to smile.

"Come here," she said.

Shah crossed to where Aurora stood, left hand holding her ear, right elbow out in front of her. He looked up, and laughed. "It's weird, looking up to kiss someone."

Without speaking, Aurora stepped off her shoes. She smiled. "But I'm not kneeling."

They kissed until Aurora pushed him away. "I have to go."

"Kotian?"

Aurora shook her head. "Is that what this is about? Are you competing?" She frowned. "Are you just using me, to score against Kotian?"

Shah thought, *she's as uncertain as me, even if it is for different reasons.* He said, "If anyone's using you, it's Kotian. And he'll happily sacrifice you, if necessary."

"I don't know," Aurora said. "I don't know anything any more, Pete. Not even how much longer I have in this game." She sighed. "I shouldn't have kissed you."

"Tonight?"

"Or last night," Aurora said. "I don't usually get involved…"

"You want out?"

"I don't know. It's a young girl's game. I earn a lot of money, but I pay high taxes. Kotian takes a management fee, and I spend fortunes on clothes and beauty treatments."

Shah realized she'd misunderstood him, so switched to her topic. "Sex may be a lucrative profession but it's not a lifetime career."

"What is?" Aurora grinned. "Apart from being a cop."

"What would you do? If you could choose anything?"

"I've always wanted to help people."

"Couldn't you study part-time?"

Aurora shook her head. "He's so demanding. And he's gotten more possessive since you shot Sunny." She shivered.

"Cold?"

She shook her head. "Afraid. I'm attracted to you. But am I just substituting one older protector for another?" Before he could answer, she shooed him out, saying, "I have to go."

Shah knew they'd left the conversation unfinished. *Sooner or later it needs finishing.*

# LV

## Monday

"You *bastard* creature!" Kotian lunged for the poodle. It bared its teeth, snarled and ducked under the bed.

"Abhijit!" Madeleine called from the doorway. "*Why* are you chasing Mitzi like that?" Out of respect to Sunny, she wore a black knee-length dress. It was unadorned and at least ten years out of date, but despite that, and being more pear than hourglass-shaped nowadays, his wife was as self-confident as ever; she could stare anyone down – sometimes even Kotian.

But not now. Kotian held up his slipper. "That bloody *thing* has pissed in my shoe!"

Madeleine's hand went to fetch the dog's collar, but she gave no other sign of emotion. "That's awful. I'm sorry. But *I* will discipline her. Mitzi, come here!" The little dog ran to her and as Madeleine bent, leapt into her arms. "Mitzi is a naughty little dog. Bad girl." It was obviously meant to be a stern voice.

Kotian didn't realize he was baring his teeth until Madeleine said, "Heavens, Abhijit, you look positively feral." She motioned with her head to the lounge. "Come, have a drink."

He'd been in Washington a week, and all he done was sit on his ass in meetings, or drink at social occasions in which nonentities expressed wholly insincere condolences at the loss of a young man few of them knew, and fewer liked. But according to them the sun had all but shone out of Sunny's ass and the boy had been a cross between a saint and superhero. He wanted to spit at them "Where the bloody hell were you while he was alive?"

But that would be poor form and one didn't show poor form among the Georgetown cocktail set. So he nodded, and boiled inside. Until now.

It was all he could do not scream. He took a deep breath, and let it out. And again. Again. Deep breaths, his doctor had told him. "I'm going to go for a walk." He kicked off his remaining slipper so hard it flew through the air and thudded against the wall. He slid his feet into slip-on pumps. "I need some air."

"Was it the call?" Madeleine murmured; "The one just now?" Madeleine made no effort to move out of the doorway, so he would have to push past her. He didn't want to look her in the eyes, didn't want to see sympathy. His brain was boiling. "It was Harcourt," Kotian said. "He called to tell me that the police's precious Internal Affairs have decided that my son's murder was a legitimate shooting."

"Oh, Abhijit," Madeleine breathed. "My dear." She reached toward him, but didn't quite make contact. It summed up their marriage.

Kotian shook his head. "Their findings were that he was fleeing arrest and presented an unacceptable danger to the public. I might as well have not bothered complaining. Shah is off desk duty and back out on the streets, while I've buried my eldest boy."

Grief threatened to overwhelm him, and Kotian would not – could not – stand that. He would be strong. He was the Lion of Bangalore. Better to be angry at the whole rotten world than he should give way to tears. It wasn't Kotian's fault that the man he'd tried to deal with was as corrupt and rotten as everyone else. He'd thought that because Shah came from an Asian background he would understand. He'd forgotten that the man was a Muslim, and therefore as devious as any other Pan-Islamist. "It's not right!" Kotian bellowed. "Land of the free – hah! Justice in America is still a matter what race you are!"

"Abhijit," Madeleine said. "Come now. You're upset, but there's no call for such talk."

"Isn't there?" Kotian snarled. "God, you stand there all superior with your *breeding* and your *manners* and you lecture me about decorum even as my son rots in the ground?"

"Abhijit, stop it!" Even Madeleine backed away a little in the face in of his rage, not far, but into the hallway, allowing him access to the corridor. "It's nothing to do with race. Not all of those witnesses could have been biased. Perhaps justice has been done."

It was too much. She'd only married him for his money. Even their occasional coupling had been as bloodless as everything else about her, and now behind that stoic exterior she was laughing at his grief, like all the others were. She'd never liked Sunny.

He wasn't even aware of raising his hand. Madeleine's head jerked back, her eyepiece flew across the room, and blood from her nose spattered the wall and his light gray suit.

If it had been anyone but Madeleine, he would have taken her in his arms and consoled her, but she only

flicked her hair back into place and stared at him, refusing to wipe the blood which trickled down across
and around her mouth, down to her chin.

"Abhijit. In our twenty-four years of marriage I have
accepted your boorishness, your infidelities, and your
volatile temper because that is what our kind of people
do. We endure." Taking a white handkerchief from her
sleeve, she finally dabbed at the blood, and when she
had staunched it, said in the same voice to tell the gar-
dener where she wanted her flowers planting, "But if
you ever do that again, I will very publicly divorce you.
I hope that is clear."

"Oh yes," Kotian said. His eyes were wide and his
voice shook with rage, but he had a measure of self-
control back. "It's absolutely clear. It's probably
pointless me apologizing–"

"Quite."

"–but I do, in any event. Not just for striking you
which was inexcusable, but also for directing my anger
at you at all. That was wrong." Kotian stalked past her
and down the corridor, toward the lounge and beyond
that, the door to the outside world.

"Abhijit!" Madeleine called, voice quavering ever so
slightly for the first time he could ever remember. "Abhijit, you won't do anything foolish, will you? Please!
Abhijit!"

Kotian rounded the corner in the corridor, and
stopped to adjust his jacket before leaving the house. A
cold front had settled over Washington, so he couldn't
venture outside without it. His jaw clenched so tightly
that it hurt. *That CD was just a taster of what's to come, my
friend Shah.* He bared his teeth in a cold smile.

# LVI

You disembark from the Hindustan Aeronautics HA-777 with your shirt sticking to your back. Your teeth are furry, when you sniff your pits they stink, and the miniatures of champagne courtesy of the pretty stewardess stuffed into your pockets distend your jacket. You stop briefly in Arrivals to shunt them into your carrier bag, so you don't clink at the body searches, and resume. Gulbar told you, "Don't stop too long in the arrivals hall: they have cameras everywhere, looking for anything different." *Welcome to LAX 9* the signs say. While you rubber-neck them you check for the micro-cams.

The long lines of people of Middle-Eastern and South American origin snaking around the block from passport control are in stark contrast to those of Caucasian, Chinese and Japanese. The Pacific Nations pump too much money into the Californian economy to risk offending them, whereas the lunatic remnants of Shining Path Onward still fighting their obsolete guerilla war have recently bombed *Yanqui* installations in Peru and added themselves to the Axis of Terror lists.

You're somewhere in between. India has too much at stake in the country to risk offending its citizens, but there's no hiding the fact that you're brown-skinned, even if it is a very light brown. So the numbers of customs people processing your flight are greater than the one security man processing the six hundred arrivals from Lima, or Buenos Aires, or whatever dump it is.

As you near the next available kiosk, you feel your gut clench. *Not now*, you think. It should be at least twenty-four hours before you need to use the washroom.

A Latino woman, so very similar to the shuffling zombies in the Lima/Buenos Aires/Wherever queue holds out her hand. "What's the purpose of your visit... sir?"

You show her your visa and work permits. "I am joining my Uncle Vinod in his business in Baltimore," you burble. There is a Vinod in Baltimore, but he's no more your uncle than the President. You'll be a free man when this job is done, and what's more a free man in what is still – just – the richest country on earth. You wonder what she would say if you told her, "The purpose of my visit is to shit a kilo of heroin in a sealed bag into one of your American toilets tomorrow morning." You decide it's better not to find out.

Nonetheless you smile at the thought, and it seems to offend her, but of course your papers are in order. She stamps the papers with furious purpose. "Welcome to the United States of America, Mr Kotian. Good luck in your new career."

# LVII

## Tuesday

Things moved quickly. At eleven o'clock, van Doorn called Shah and Bailey. "You're both back in the field."

"What about Stickel, sir?" Bailey said. She seemed to have hardened since the shooting, as if the event had burned away her uncertainty. Shah wasn't sure that she hadn't lost something else with it. Her innocence. He felt sad for a moment.

But as soon as the lieutenant hung up, they both did a little jig around the desk.

"Thanks," Shah said. *For saving me, from a bullet, or a disciplinary hearing, depending how things had panned out.*

"De nada," Bailey said, suddenly shy again. Then she added, with a hint of defiance. "I couldn't afford to lose a partner so early in my career."

Shah nodded, smiling inside.

Twenty minutes later, he was dancing again. He put through a call to van Doorn and the others. "Sunny's first murder victim – the Boston hooker – was called Sharon Wilmette."

"How'd you find that out?" van Doorn said.

"When I checked the Boston death rip against that old Oregon clip I found some weeks ago, I realized it was the same girl. They *felt* the same. Trouble is, she was born just before The Burning Time. When the secessionist guerillas unleashed a virus into the Census Bureau database they trashed most of it, but not everything."

Van Doorn ran one rip after the other, again and again. "I'd say you're back to full speed." A smile eased the tension from his face *"Damned* if I'd have made a connection."

"See the way in both clips she hugged herself when she was nervous?" Shah couldn't resist a little grandstanding. "And she liked the same flavored gum. Inconclusive, but enough to be worth following up."

"So what do we have on this... Sharon Wilmette?"

Shah uploaded the details: born April 17th 2025, Sharon had been a few months short of her twenty-second birthday when she was murdered. "He dumped her body into a vat of acid," Shah said. "Damaged it so badly there was no way of identifying any seminal fluid or other contact residue. The DNA was broken down into pieces almost too small to identify."

At the time only the teeth had matched any local records, to a 'Sharon Portland' registered to a Boston practice. *No one seemed too broken up about her,* Shah thought. *I guess that should've given someone the idea she was from out of state. But there are so many of these people. We can't find them all.*

Shah said, "That earlier rip, from the Oregon-California state border. She'd have been about sixteen at the time, ran away to the Silicon State, but probably got picked up by a slaver gang instead. For what it's worth, Ma and Pa Wilmette posted a Missing Persons on her

nine years ago, but they're both dead. There's no next
of kin for Boston PD to notify."

"She ended up in Boston, how?"

Shah said, "Dunno. How important is it?"

Van Doorn considered. "Reasonably. If we can trace
her back to Oregon, maybe we can nail the traffickers.
Less important to us than other forces but it gives us a
few points should we need to call in favors in the future." He added, "We already earned ourselves a few
with Boston by clearing up this case."

"I'll keep on it."

"Until something critical crops up."

Shah's eyepiece pinged. It was building management,
even more irritated than the last time. "Another package for ya."

Shah spread his hands wide and explained.

"I'll send a uniform," van Doorn said. "We haven't
got time to dick around."

Shah settled down to search the web for tags to girls
of the right age at the right dates. Then screened the
tens of thousands of hits by possible geography and ethnicity where it was listed, and settled down wade
through the results. Even watching only the first few
seconds with Bailey's help meant brain-draining hours
of tedium.

Shah surfaced for a break an hour later with an
aching head.

In the meantime the uniformed officer had collected
the package, opened it, screened the CD that was in it,
and uploaded the message on it to Shah's eyepiece.
Shah's voice said, "You can't protect them all, you
know."

Shah shivered.

• • • •

Stickel fired the clip across to CSU with a priority flag, but it yielded nothing, as Shah expected, other than it came from the same set of interviews as the previous one. Bailey said, "Presumably there isn't much out there, so the perp's used whatever's come to hand."

"I guess so." It didn't make Shah feel any better. He didn't like the thought that there was someone spending time putting bits of old conversation together and sending them to him. Getting a conviction for harassment was almost impossible even if they caught the perp, but Shah didn't think it was going to stop at voice clips.

The clip rattled Shah's concentration badly, his already leaden progress through the mass of clips slowing to a standstill. When he finished for the day, his headache had become an almost unbearable vice squeezing his forehead.

He stayed alert all the way home, trying to see if anyone was following him, but no one showed. Any potential stalker could track him easily enough. Shah considered varying his route to and from work, and cursed. Life was already complicated enough without playing such games.

Things weren't much better indoors – Leslyn jumped when he walked into the kitchen.

"You OK?" Shah said.

Leslyn nodded and gave him a watery smile. It had started to rain, and McCoy was bringing in the cushions and newspaper from the balcony.

*Only Doug would demand an actual paper copy,* Shah thought, smiling inwardly.

His inner smile vanished when he glanced at Leslyn. He knew that the encounter with Sunny had scared her badly. For years Leslyn had been slightly dismissive of his work, for which he had been partly to blame. Shah had been too good at protecting her from the world that he sometimes had to walk through, and his occasional scare stories she had treated as exaggerations.

When she had met Sunny she learned the dismal truth about how vital his work was and how dangerous the world could be. That the threat had barely spoken was irrelevant. Like the CD, it was the mere fact of the intrusion that did the damage, not its appearance.

"I think…" Leslyn said. "That is, that incident with – what's his name? Sunny?"

"That's the one," Shah said.

"It's clarified my thoughts. I've felt for some time now that New York's changed too much since I came here. Not for the better."

"Hasn't everywhere?"

"Maybe. But New York's gotten much *too* dark lately. The children are grown up. Rex has his own life. I suppose you could say Perveza has, though what kind of life she has…"

"You're moving out of town. Going to one of those clinics."

Leslyn nodded. "For years I've been a wife and mother first. But now it's my time."

Shah said, "You sure that you're not using the situation as an excuse to do what you've always wanted to do?"

"You bastard!" Leslyn cried. "I've been sitting here worrying about how I can afford it, and arguing with Doug about what it does to you, and that's what you come back with?"

Doug interrupted with, "I'd have just told you when it was time, instead of worrying sick about whether you'd have enough time to find another co-tenant."

*That's because you're a jackass.* Instead Shah said, "I'm sorry. When do you go?"

"Three weeks," Leslyn said. "I can come back after the first treatment, but...."

"I know," Shah said. "Not a good idea to go anywhere with augments, least of all round here, right now."

He poured himself a coffee, and raised the cup to Leslyn in a toast. "Good luck," he said. *You're going to need it.*

# LVIII

**Thursday**

Aurora's doorman gave Shah a thin smile. He and his colleagues were starting to recognize Shah, which wasn't necessarily a good thing. The ambiguity of the last tape worried Shah.

He'd discussed it with Aurora the evening as she sat on the other side of Marietetski's bed in the hospital. "We're all bugged," she had said. "Get used to it. And that's my greatest protection at the moment. If Abhijit's people are listening, they'll know I'm no threat."

*She sounds more hopeful than optimistic.* While Aurora hadn't told Shah where any of the bodies – actual or otherwise – were buried, he wasn't sure that Kotian would care. Any hint of supposed disloyalty might arouse the man's anger.

Shah entered the elevator, keeping a watchful eye on the man who leapt in at the last moment, but the weasel-looking guy with gray bushy hair and stubble left on the twenty-fifth floor, whereas Shah was headed for the thirty-second.

Aurora opened the door before he could knock, and drawing him in by the tie, kissed him on the lips. He tried not to notice how short her dressing gown was.

"I see the door guy's doing his job," he said, smiling.

She smiled back. "I've got him well trained." She pushed the door shut.

She bustled into the kitchen and he hung his coat up. Again he looked away from the glimpse of thigh as she walked. He wasn't sure that she wasn't simply teasing him, and she was still technically a person of interest, however peripheral her involvement. But for that he would have bedded her in a heartbeat. He wondered why she hadn't pushed the issue. *Perhaps*, he thought, *she doesn't realize how much I've changed.* He hadn't told her that he couldn't understand why Shah had been so scared of her sex.

"There's something you ought to know." Following her into the kitchen, Shah told her about Leslyn's leaving New York.

Aurora frowned. "When was this?"

"Tuesday," Shah said. "I should've told you last night, but I needed time to think about it." Unlike most days Shah hadn't called Aurora that evening because he'd felt it wrong to run to her for comfort, even though that had been his instinctive reaction. That he'd needed comfort proved there'd been more left in the relationship than he'd thought. *Or the severing of one of your last few ties to the old Shah is what hurts,* a cynical inner voice said.

"I thought you were a little… distracted last night," she said. "What will you do now?"

"I don't know. Probably advertise for someone to share the rent." A co-op maintained the building. "Part of me wouldn't mind moving out altogether."

"Move in here," Aurora said. Her eyes widened as if she'd spoken a thought aloud, and only realized it afterward.

"Yeah, I'm guessing that you hadn't really thought that through when you said it – and then you did." Shah grinned. "I'd cramp your style."

She said half-defiantly, "I'd just make outcalls, not have any *patrones* calling here."

Shah cocked his head to one side, as he took the proffered coffee. "You don't think that that could make things... messy?"

"Why? Am I under suspicion?"

She was, though not by Shah. But she was too close to Kotian, at least while the investigation was live, and while they'd done nothing wrong, it could look bad if someone in the media wanted it to. Shah frowned, wondering why Kotian hadn't leaked it already. *Or was he waiting until he had something really juicy, like shots of them in bed together?*

"Not under suspicion," Shah admitted.

Aurora stepped closer, fiddling with the tie of her dressing gown, allowing it to fall open and drawing his gaze to the shaven junction of her thighs. He'd expected to see a penis, but she was like any other woman. "You could stay the night."

"No I couldn't. However much I might want to." Shah gulped his coffee. "Things are still too chaotic, too – oh, I dunno!"

"Things aren't chaotic," Aurora said, watching him. It was easier to meet her gaze than to look down again. "It's your mind that's chaotic, I think. Leslyn moving out's rattled you more than you want to admit."

"Maybe.But that's why it'd be wrong to stay the night, now."

She smiled, and retied her gown. "It's straightforward for me," she said. "I want you in me. I think you want me."

"So why do you want me?" Shah said. "Look at me – I'm ten pounds too heavy and twenty years too old for this."

"Has it ever occurred to you that I might not want anything? That I might just want to be with a man who treats me kindly and doesn't want me to dress up in leather or tie him to a rack and whip him?"

"I guess." Shah moved reluctantly to get his coat. He'd been looking forward to an uncomplicated evening of making small talk.

He left wishing he didn't have to and feeling like a fool, albeit a virtuous one.

### Friday

Shah spent the next day studying rips that might be Sharon Wilmette, but which all turned out not to be. He and Bailey left the office together at shift-end. "See you tomorrow," Shah called as they headed in opposite directions.

"Nah, I got a day off," Bailey said.

Shah stopped. "Going anywhere nice?" It was a question from when people went out of town, to the beach, on vacation. He wished they still could: New York was like a furnace already, and July and August promised to be unbearable.

Bailey shook her head. "Not having to get up tomorrow works for me. See ya next week."

"Yeah." Shah wished too for that easy familiarity that Old Shah had with Marietetski. Every conversation with Bailey that wasn't about work was like walking through a minefield. Bailey never got angry. She just clammed up, which made it harder to understand what he'd said to make her clam up.

Shah varied his route, as he had for the last few nights,

and passed by the institute. He wondered whether Tosada was working, and on impulse called in, passing by a couple of big men standing in the doorway. They looked familiar, but Shah couldn't quite place them.

If he had called ten minutes later, he thought afterwards.

Instead as he entered the building, he passed Kotian. *Damn, they're his bodyguards.*

Kotian curled his lip. "Murdered any more young men lately?"

Shah still owed Kotian a slap for the way the guy had treated Aurora, and damned if he would let a gangster smear him with comments like that, however upset he was. "You want to know about murder?" Shah leaned into Kotian's face. "I got a clip for you of your scumbag son strangling a girl as he fucked her, together with the clip of her dying. You want me to send them to you? Or did you know about them already?"

From the way Kotian paled the old man hadn't known, although he must have guessed. "Lies!" Kotian snarled. "You could've had him alive if you'd worked with me, but you wanted him dead!"

"Yeah," Shah breathed, staring into the old man's eyes. "You were going to give him up, 'cause you knew deep down what he was like, and either it scared you, or you didn't care.

All you cared about was it might make you look bad."

"Bull!"

"And now it's all gone wrong, the guilt's eating you alive. You can't bear the thought that he'd still be alive if you'd done it differently."

"You bastard!" Kotian swung a fist.

Shah saw it coming and grabbed Kotian's lapel. "You want me to arrest you for assaulting a police officer?"

"Arrest a grieving father, why don't you?"

Weeks, months of bottled resentment came pouring out. "You've never grieved for a damned thing in your life, you cold-blooded snake."

The moment he said it, Shah knew he'd made a mistake.

# LIX

### Monday

"Shah." Van Doorn stood in reception. "In my office. Five minutes."

Shah had been about to trawl the web, but the look on van Doorn's face said refusing wasn't a good idea.

He carried his coffee into the captain's office.

"Shut the door," van Doorn said.

Shah pushed it closed with his foot. It closed with a *clunk*.

Shah's voice echoed around the office: "You've never grieved for a damned thing in your life, you cold-blooded snake."

Shah winced.

Van Doorn said, "Want me to play it again?"

Shah shook his head. "Not my finest moment."

"I could say lots of things, Shah. Like what the hell possessed you?"

Shah held his hands palm up, in a "what-can-I-say" gesture.

"I was going to come in especially on Saturday to tell you your fortune. Lucky for you my wife warned me last week that if I even thought about leaving the apartment before we'd finished decorating she'd make herself a widow. That's about all that that saved you. I've had forty-eight hours to calm down, but give me one good reason why I still shouldn't fire you?"

Shah could've argued that the captain couldn't dismiss him without going through the disciplinary process, but now didn't seem a good time for that. He stayed silent.

Van Doorn sighed.

"Would it help if I apologized?"

"Probably not," van Doorn said, confirming Shah's suspicion. Kotian wanted Shah's blood. The captain continued, "I told the commissioner that you'd been receiving death threats – I played them up – and it was starting to take its toll. Even so, it was all I could do to stop her from chewing you a new windpipe personally." He jabbed a sausage-like finger at Shah. "You can take this as a final warning about your future conduct, *Officer*. If you give me any reason to, I'll remove you from the case and fire your ass."

Shah lowered his chin. "Cap–"

"Not a word, Shah. You'll walk on eggshells. Got it?"

"Got it."

"Then close the door when you leave."

Shah left the office as Bailey arrived. She raised her eyebrow in a silent question.

"I got a promotion. Been made chairman of the Kotian Fan Club." He added, "Keep your coat on, hon, you just got lucky."

Bailey turned without stopping and followed him out. "That line ever work for you?"

"Feisty," Shah called without slowing. "Been on the vitamin supplements, or are you always so sharp on a Monday morning?"

He motioned Bailey to switch off her eyepiece. "Just for a moment," he added.

"Where are we going?" Bailey said.

They walked down to the street. Shah waited until they'd left the building and plunged into the rush-hour commuters before he answered. "We're going to see a personnel agency. One of these exclusive headhuntery type of places that saves you having to find a new job yourself if you're an executive or you got something an employer wants."

"Let me guess. It's run by Indians, for Indians?"

"You're sort of half-right. This one is fronted by old school-types, blazers, ties, Massachewsets nasal accents. But they're not proud, they'll take anybody's money." He switched his eyepiece back on, and Bailey followed suit.

Regency Placements' offices were only a short walk uptown. Shah pushed open the door barely two minutes after they opened. One of the young women was still taking off her jacket, which Shah noted was reassuringly expensive. *Like the decor.* He noted the prints and furniture which were either genuine antique, or aged fakes. His feet sank into a thick carpet.

"Good morning sir, madam." The man who met them had the obligatory Ivy League manner, even down to a fraternity ring on his little finger. Almost two meters tall, he was fashionably thin, almost skeletal. Shah wouldn't have believed such stereotypes existed until now – he wasn't sure the guy's mannerisms weren't overacting. "How may we assist you?"

Shah uploaded his ID, watched the man's face become even more impassive if that were possible. Shah followed it with five mug-shots. "Any of these people on file?" He knew that two of them were, since he had pulled genuine placements from the agency's own on-line brochure on Saturday morning. Two others were career criminals who shouldn't be agency clients, while the fifth was the reason they were here.

"May I ask why you're enquiring?"

"You may," Shah said. "But I may not answer. Now, you want me to call up Homeland and the IRS, anyone else I can think of, get a warrant, or..."

Skeleton-Man said, "The fourth man. And the first and third." Shah had thought it unlikely that the career guys would be on file but they were suspected associates of Kotian's, so it didn't hurt to ask.

"I need their details. Or I can get a warrant."

"I'll... ah, need a few minutes."

"You got five."

While Shah and Bailey waited, the bell above the door rang to indicate another arrival, a bulky looking man in a sharp suit. When Shah's eyepiece chimed with Skeleton-Man's upload, they turned to leave. The new arrival blocked the doorway. "Officer Shah."

Shah had an idea who the man was but frowned in mock innocence. "Do I know you?"

"Partington," the man snapped. "I represent Abhijit Kotian. What are you doing here?"

"If it's any of your business...?"

"You're annoying Mr Kotian. It stops now."

"I'm here because of a call from Boston PD. Guy stopped on a traffic violation was found to have false papers. He was green-carded by this place." Shah straightened, in obvious realization. "Wait a minute, this is *Kotian's* business?"

"As if you didn't know."

"No idea at all." It was true – up until the call to Shah's friend in the FBI on Saturday afternoon. Shah cocked his head. "So this place is a front?"

"It's a genuine employment agency!" Skeleton-Man sputtered. "We had no idea—"

"Charles," Partington said

Skeleton-Man fell silent.

Shah wondered at the power that could silence a man with a lifted hand. "But it's owned by Mr Kotian?"

"You know that already. I said, this stops now. The arrested man is being processed by Boston PD. While you'd doubtless like to go fishing, we'll assert vigorously in court that not only were my clients duped, but that this has nothing to do with you. It's all part of your war of nerves against Mr Kotian, a man grieving for the son you shot. Need I say more?"

"I guess not," Shah said. "Sorry to bother you and Mr Kotian." He put his hand on Bailey's arm to keep her quiet.

Out on the sidewalk Shah said, "My, didn't he come a-running quick? We got Kotian rattled, partner."

Inevitably on his return, Shah had his metaphorical new windpipe ripped for him, but he took it without complaint since van Doorn stopped short of suspension.

When the captain had finally finished, Shah said, "One question, sir?"

"Go on."

"Tosada. Do we eliminate him as a person of interest?"

Van Doorn stared. "Why?"

"Only that my running into Kotian on Friday night came because of a social call to Tosada. We got mutual acquaintances, see, and I'd hate a social visit to be mis-con-strued."

Van Doorn looked as if he were sucking on a lemon. "Is there any obvious connection between our investigations and his projects?"

Shah shook his head. "Don't think so. One big problem with investigating a social gadfly like Kotian is that everyone the guy meets automatically becomes a person of interest."

"But?"

Shah pulled a face. "I think we was sidetracked by a potential connection between them that probably isn't anything more than one of Kotian's token legitimate projects."

"So…" van Doorn said, thinking furiously. "You can visit Tosada and when you do, you make sure that you let him know that it's a *social* visit." The captain glared at Shah. "No more games, no more stratagems, got it?"

"Sir."


That afternoon they held an impromptu meeting around Shah's desk. "How many people are sending these clips?" Bailey stood looking down at the antique CDs, forming the apex of a triangle with van Doorn and Shah. "Kotian wouldn't send you rips incriminating his own son. And who *was* ripping Sunny?"

Van Doorn fanned himself with a piece of paper. At eight-thirty in the morning the air in the office was already stifling, despite the fans blowing it around. "ME's report indicates trauma to Sunny's brain consistent with ripping activity over a period of many years. Either Papa was the culprit, or he was self-ripping."

"You can't rip your own memories – the extraction causes the trauma!" Bailey protested. "You'd just shut off the machine!"

Shah said, "In theory. But you can override the safeties if you know how, and you're prepared to endure the agony. From the ME's report, and the rips and burns we've been able to piece together, Sunny fits that psych-profile to perfection."

"Still doesn't answer who sent the Sunny rips. No CD, but sent from different eyepieces. All stolen."

"We've got Sunny's accomplices," Shah said. "Uniform are bringing them in. Maybe they can shed some light on who our mystery informant is."

"Maybe," Bailey said. "Can we make a case for attempted murder on Marietetski?"

Shah looked at her. *You got a mind like a grasshopper, girl.* If he were honest, she was simply faster than him. His joints had ached for several mornings, and when he'd finally got to see the medic, the young woman had smiled sadly, "Rheumatism, Pete. You're getting old." This morning he seemed to be suffering from mental rheumatism, as well.

Van Doorn shook his head. "I'll talk to Grunwald, but I doubt it. Aggravated assault's probably the most we can hang on them, and as friends of Sunny – and therefore Papa – they'll walk free in a year, maybe less."

"Like Sunny thought, they're expendable," Shah said.

Van Doorn shrugged. "Still a result. Anyway, I have a meeting to go to. Performance figures. Oh, joy." He blew out his cheeks.

"You sound down," Bailey said when van Doorn had gone. "Thought you'd be walking on air getting confirmation it was Sunny and ID on his accomplices turning up outta the blue."

"Not sure an unsupported memory of a dead man is admissible," Shah said. "And unless we get separate corroboration, if the defense get the clip thrown out, any evidence that arises from it also gets thrown out." He blew out his cheeks. "It's that 'out of the blue' part that bothers me. Ever heard of the phrase 'beware Greeks bearing gifts'?"

"Nope," Bailey said. "What Greeks are those?"

At first Shah thought she was joking, then shook his head in despair. *Kids,* he thought. *What are they teaching 'em nowadays?*

Shah finished late that evening; they'd palmed off the getaway driver onto another precinct, but kept the three accomplices. The three – career villains all – had clammed up while they waited in the interview rooms, kicking the table leg in one case, tapping the table in another.

"Let 'em sweat," Shah said to his relief, Itandje, a middle-aged plodder of Nigerian parentage. Only when it was clear that he'd miss visiting hours did Shah hand over to another shift. "Take 'em right to the time limit, then charge them."

"Based on the rip?" Itandje said around a mouthful of appetite-suppressant gum.

"We'll have got corroboration by then," Shah said, more confidently than he felt.

"We'll take our time with the paperwork," Itandje said. "Drag it out enough to miss the morning deadline for non-urgent cases."

"Their lawyers'll argue they should be expedited."

"Then we'll argue that one first, which'll delay 'em still further." Itandje grinned, showing white teeth yellowing. "We'll bury *them* in red tape for a change. Buy time to find more evidence. I'll have the guys hunt down more camera footage, and accidentally stumble across anything we find – we wasn't looking for Paulie and the others yer honner, no, no no."

"Good man." Shah clapped him on the shoulder.

Outside the evening sky was dark indigo, verging on nightfall, but the heat still rose off the pavements, assailing Shah with dust and bird droppings and decaying food spillage.

Shah jumped into a pedicab, but even so the straining Thai driver only just got him to the hospital before closing time for visitors. The ward was unusually busy with people milling around like an ant nest poked with a stick. Many were strangers, but Shah recognized Marietetski's mother and grandmother. Neither looked particularly pleased to see Shah.

"Who're you?" said an ebony-skinned old man Shah hadn't seen before.

"Shah. I'm John's work partner. Where is he?"

"Gone," the old man said, staring at the wall rather than meet Shah's gaze.

"Where? I don't under–" He added, realization dawning, "Oh."

"They turned off the life support machine," Marietetski's grandmother's voice buzz-sawed into the conversation: cold, harsh, her accent thickened with emotion. "They turned it off when we couldn't afford to pay, because the in-sewer-ance people said that there was no brain function, so they wasn't for going to pay no more."

"Oh, shit," Shah mumbled. "I'm sorry, Mrs Trebonnet."

The old woman nodded, but Shah's condolences seemed to act as a lightning conductor for the other man's grief, which turned to rage, his breathing growing ragged as he shouted, "What for you doing here, anyway? You some sorta ghoul, gets pleasure going to wakes, or are you hopin' to sell us more in-sewer-ance that's no good when we need it?" The old man had clearly forgotten who Shah was. "G'wan now! Away wit' you!"

"John!" Mrs Trebonnet said. "There's no need for that. It's not his fault."

"He was the best, the brightest of any nephew a man could have," the old man gasped. "Never mind that no-good Polack father of his, he was *our* boy."

Shah couldn't sort out the tangled stew of emotions within him – sympathy for Mrs Trebonnet, a muted grief at losing a friend he'd never really known, sadness at another prop from the old days being kicked away.

Mrs Trebonnet steered Shah to the door. "Don't mind Uncle John," she whispered. "He always was a crybaby. And he feeling guilty 'cause – well, with his feelings about the police and how much he hated John joining the force, it hardly be surprising he's a little upset. Calling the boy Uncle Tom and Race Judas isn't how he want to remember young John."

Shah pulled it open, pausing in the doorway. "I wish I could do something." For a moment he was tempted to ask about any memories John had sent her, but it was too soon. *Maybe later.*

"Catch the killers," Mrs Trebonnet said, her lower lip quivering, but otherwise in control. "Catch them, make them pay."

"One of them's dead already. My colleague shot him as he was running away."

"Good." Mrs Trebonnet snapped, hard enough to bury the word in the wall.

"In custody. We've charged them with token offences to keep them in, and we have a team working on it

COLIN HARVEY                    371

through the night." He dared not admit that the team was a Nigerian too fond of doughnuts, even if he did know all the old dog tricks.

"Anything you need, anything at all, you call us." Mrs Trebonnet's voice diamond hard. "You pay your respects to my boy by catching his killers."

Out in the main corridor Shah tottered into the washroom. He splashed water on his face. In the mirror a gaunt, hollow-eyed old man stared back. *I'm adrift*, he thought. *One by one the ropes that hold me in place are being cut. First Leslyn, now John.*

His eyepiece chimed, counterpointing the angry buzz marking a 911 call: "All units 10-18 to corner of West 13th and 9th. Shots fired – all units 10-18 to corner of West 13th and 9th. Shots fired – all units 10-18 to corner of West 13th and 9th. Shots fired – all units 10-18–"

It took Shah until the fourth iteration to register that the address was his.

Then he was off and running down the stairs.

# LX

It's been a quiet evening, like every evening is recently. Johns are an endangered species this far from Manhattan. Maybe you'll have to admit defeat and move back into town.

Unless you score soon, there'll be no more Scramble-dreams of childhood, those glorious few months between Rex starting school, and you following him into kindergarten. Make the most of what you have.

Instead of a muggy summer's evening with its furnace breeze carrying the raw-sewage stink, you're the center of your parent's attention again. It's one of the days leading up to Christmas, when even Granny Afsoon's disapproval of infidel customs can't dispel the joy.

A hand on your arm recalls you to the present, and Granny to the grave she's occupied these last twelve years. He's about thirty, thirty-five, well-dressed, superficially Caucasian. But like your father, skin tones and dark eyes hint at Asian ancestry. "For someone who's showing so much flesh," he says, "you don't seem very interested in working."

You sketch a smile. "Hi, Honey. You caught me daydreaming. Looking for fun?"

"You know I am. I'm parked over there."

'There' is a big old planet-raping gas-guzzler with darkened windows. The sight of the thing arouses an embarrassed flush no sexual proposition could, and you slow to a stop. "You think I'm getting in *that*? No way!"

He keeps walking. "You will if you want the kilo of pure Scramble in my pocket."

That much Scramble can set you up for a year, with some left over to deal as well. But though your brain's got more holes than a Swiss cheese, the size of the fee is alarming. "What do you want?"

"Six guys," he says. "Uncle Pablo and our cousins are visiting with gifts, and we thought we'd show them a good time as a thank you." His hand rests on the passenger door.

He's no more South American than you, although the Columbians still have some say in what comes in and goes out. Maybe they're the high-ups, and he's a glorified errand-boy. *Nah, something's not right.* You lick your lips, calculating. "Six guys at once?"

He shrugs, opens the passenger door up front. "We'll find a girl who's more obliging. There'll be one on the next street."

"Wait!" You think, *three orifices, two hands.* "I can do five." You force a laugh, though this is spiraling out of control. With a pang, you unexpectedly think of Daddy, and his last visit, and wonder what he would think. Then you remember that even in the good days, there was that ghost of an unseen sister, haunting them, haunting you. "Yeah, I can do five. The last guy can jack off on me."

He opens the door behind him for you. "Good enough. The loser can give you a facial. We'll burn copies later."

As you climb in, you force another laugh. "Porn, huh? Do I get royalties?"

You look around. The others are more clearly Indian, Pakistani or Bangladeshi than the front man – the older handsome movie dude apart. Their faces are flint-hard and cold.

You swallow.

Older handsome movie dude has a look in his eye that makes you want to be anywhere else as he says, "Don't worry, Perveza, you're going to be the star of the show."

You grab the door handle, but it doesn't move.

He chuckles. "Feel free to scream, darling. Daddy will appreciate it even more." He pulls out a wad of Scramble, enough to blow your brains out. "Come, have some of this."

# LXI

Shah had to run half a block before he could commandeer a rare LPG cab. Forwarding the APB to the driver's eyepiece as authorization, and his ID to the protesting passenger, he hauled the man out. "Sorry sir. Make a claim for the inconvenience quoting my ID, the date and 'officer responding to urgent call for assistance' and please accept my apologies and have a nice day thank you." Pulling the door shut on the still-complaining passenger he took a lung-filling haul of air, then exhaled.

He'd just about got his breath back when the cab arrived. He pushed through to where a uniformed officer was guarding the building entrance. Shah knew the guy by sight if not by name, and when the guard waved him through raised an acknowledging palm.

Shah couldn't take the stairs because they were blocked by a pair of overalled CSIs scrutinizing them step by step, but the elevators were free, and the five-minute wait for the protesting antique gave him time to chat to the second cop, guarding the lobby and CSIs.

"I dunno much," she said, chewing a wad of gum. "All I heard was that shots were fired on the penthouse floor–" *Oh shit, Leslyn!* Shah thought "–but there are no fatalities."

Shah exhaled heavily, and tapping his foot pressed the call elevator button a third time.

"Won't come no quicker," the cop said with a friendly flash of teeth.

"Makes me feel better, though."

"Always so impatient, you oldsters." She added hastily, "Didn't mean–"

Shah waved her half-apology away. "Don't worry 'bout it. At last!" He jumped into the square box and rode it alone, listening to every screech, every clank, every groan, sure that at any moment it would judder to a halt between floors, leaving him even more in limbo.

It seemed like hours later that he leapt out, but it was probably less than five minutes.

The steel-paneled door he and Doug had reinforced during the last food riots five years earlier hung off its hinges. The thugs hadn't bothered going through it, but simply blown its weak spot – the hinges – with explosive bullets. *If you'd gone to a proper outfit who fit covered hinges 'stead of letting that tightwad talk you into corner-cutting this wouldn't have happened.*

"Doug," Shah said to a crumpled figure on the lounge floor, who was being treated by a pair of paramedics. Stickel stood watching a pair of CSIs tagging debris. "Where's Leslyn?"

"He can't talk now," one paramedic said. "The other vic's outside. She–"

Shah was already running to the balcony.

The rooftop patio ran around the penthouse, a lip about six feet wide on each side. Chairs and tables were smashed, and Shah followed the smashed windows and bullet-riddled walls until he found Leslyn, who like Doug was also lying prone between two paramedics. CSIs photographed beyond her.

"Leslyn!" Shah called out. In answer, she held up her hand.

One of the paramedics stood up. "Give us a few minutes," she said. "She has multiple splinters from the wooden frames the Gro-bags were resting on, but aside from that and being severely shocked, she's un-harmed. That's a miracle, given how bad they shot the place up."

Shah went inside. Doug lay groaning on the ground while one of the CSIs took a memory copy, and Shah hovered impatiently. "You wait your turn," Stickel called. "Give Bailey a hand hunting the clowns that did this. Your friend," she indicated McCoy, "wasn't the main target, at least when they shot their way in. He bought her time to hide."

"Bailey can take care of it," Shah said. "We know who's behind this, and it isn't a couple of hop-heads." He stared at McCoy in disbelief. "*He* stood up to armed intruders?"

Stickel held up a hand as she downloaded from the scanner. "Here you go." Shah's eyepiece chimed the an-nouncement of an upload. She laughed, "You didn't get it from me."

"Of course." Shah hit PLAY:

The door crashes in. You gawp at the motley gang of villains spilling through it.

"Where is she?" a tall black kid yells.

"What?" *This isn't happening. It can't be happening.*

"Where's the bitch, grandpa?" the youth yells. He waves a gun in your face. You almost pissed yourself with terror, but damned if you'll let this little punk see it. "I gotta ask again, I'm gonna blow your balls off."

"In which case, young man, I'm even less likely to answer your questions. My co-husband is a policeman–"

"Oh, he's a policeman," sneers a second youth, this one white. There's an Indian, and a Hispanic one as well. *It's like the old United Nations.* Then your reverie is shattered by the backhander that snaps your head back.

"I said, grandpa, where's your bitch?"

"Calea," you say before you can stop yourself. There's blood or snot or *something* running from your nose, and you're close to crying. Shah has always said that your pedantry will get you into trouble one day. "Her name is Leslyn Ca-l-ea, you little thug, and she isn't here." *Please God, whatever they do to me, don't let them find her, rape her, whatever they intend to do to her.*

"Where." Slap! "Is." *Slap!* "She?" This last accompanied by a punch that slams the air out of you, as if someone's pushed a Hoover down your gullet and switched it on. You can't tell them anything now, even if you wanted to.

Another punch tears your cheek. Lights flash across your field of vision, and you try to play possum against the punches raining down on your head and body–

Shah cut the feed. "My God, they're dumb," Shah said.

Stickel shook her head. "I get the impression that these aren't Kotian's regular goons. Someone's subcontracted a stage too far. While you were vicariously enjoying your buddy getting the crap beaten out of them" – she grinned as he mouthed "enjoy?" at her – "I stomped all over your good lady's civil rights by demanding a copy before she could forget anything or get counseling. Here you go."

"How is she?" Shah said.

"Shaken up. But hiding under them man-sized Gro-bags was a masterstroke. Damned clever woman. Makes me wonder why she'd marry a donut like you."

"It's my hidden charms," Shah said as he opened the clip, and the last thing he heard was Stickel's snort.

–you look around, your heart rattling like an out-of-control piledriver. *Behind the chairs? No, too obvious. There's no way down from here, and no way back in, so it has to be* – and you remember Doug's scorn at the Nero Wolfe story where they hide her under the orchids – *under the Gro-bags!* There's a bathtub-shaped depression beneath the bags barely big enough to squeeze into, and for the first time in your life you're grateful you're so small.

The sacking is cold and damp against your flesh, but you lie very, very still, barely even daring to breathe.

"Where the bitch gone?" You hear one of them say. Sounds of movement, something being dragged.

"She under these bag things?"

*Please God, no, don't let them look under here.*

"Naw, nowhere to hide there, dumbo."

More scraping sounds, a crash. A shattering sound, that of a pot dropped on the ground. Another crash.

"The bitch ain't here!"

"Jimbo was sure she was here."

"Ain't gonna do no rip today."

"Fuck it, let's trash the place!"

The last comment is followed by a staccato rattle. Fear feels like a large stone lodged in your throat. Something stings and you bite into the sacking to stop yourself crying out. A couple of seconds of quiet is followed by another two-second burst of fire. Quiet again, and you lick your lips. There's another rattle, and something burns your arm; you whimper, but luckily they don't hear you.

Then there is silence until someone calls, "Pigs coming!"

You lie there for what seems like an eternity, biting your lip against the need to piss.

Only when you hear someone call, "Hello!" do you dare push back the sacking.

# LXII

"They caught the Hispanic one," Stickel said.

Shah surveyed the devastation that was his bedroom. "Anyone we know?" The gang had circled right round the balcony, spraying the walls with explosive bullets and they had smashed through the walls as if they were made of paper. Pictures had been blown off, Shah's comp and music system were pockmarked with through-and-throughs and were unusable, while his clothes had been shredded. Shah sighed.

"You can't stay here," Stickel said. "Book into a hotel."

Shah wondered whether Aurora was working, and called her. "No answer," he muttered and was about to hang up when she finally answered.

Before he could speak, Aurora whispered, "It's not a good time. I'll call you back."

Shah raised his eyebrows and turned to Stickel, who was studying the bullet-riddled walls. "Who's the perp?"

Stickel was silent. Finally she said, "Rico Calvatoni. His rap sheet includes serious assaults, so this is third strike for the little weasel. He lawyered up before we even read him his rights. Hasn't said a word since."

"Let me guess. One of Kotian's lawyers."

"Surprisingly, no. Which makes me think it's a sub-contract gone bad."

"Guess if he's not Indian and was subbed, there'd be no reason for one of Kotian's tame Rottweilers to counsel for him. Where's the kid now?"

Stickel shook her head. "Oh no, no. You cohabit with the victims. You set foot in the same room as him you compromise the case."

Shah held up his hands in surrender. "Just asking."

"Just saying. Go visit your girlfriend or a bar or something – anything, but you stay away from that little bastard. Leave it to us, Pete."

"Sure," Shah said. "Guess I ought to buy some things from an all-nighter. Can I take any of my stuff that's undamaged?"

"You already know, so why ask?"

Shah shrugged. "Making conversation, is all."

"Make it somewhere else. Scram."


Shah was buying an overpriced shirt, toothpaste and toothbrush, soap and deodorant in the convenience store when Aurora called back. "Where are you?" She sounded slightly out of breath, as if she was walking as she talked.

Shah told her.

"Wait outside," she said. "I'll be there in ten minutes."

She took barely five. When she came close, Shah noticed her lower lip was cut.

"Kotian?"

She nodded. "He tried to get me to set you up. When I was less than enthusiastic…" she gestured at her lip.

Shah gazed at her, but she looked away. Gently, he reached out and touched the cut on her lip. She hissed an indrawn breath, but stayed still. "At least it's stopped bleeding." Shah stroked it as gently as he could. "If he hurts you again, I'll kill him myself."

Her eyes glinted. "Don't go all white knight on me. Remember what I said before – about not being sure I want to exchange one protector for another?"

"You can't expect me to stand by while he beats the crap out of you – I don't do it for strangers, so why would I for someone I care about?"

"Do you?" Aurora said. "Care?"

"You know I do."

"I guess." Aurora paused, as if thinking. "When Kotian had gone, I called Grunwald to ask for Witness Protection. She agreed."

Moving his hand up Shah touched her cheekbone. "If you go into Witness Protection…"

"We'll never see each other again. If we'd been a couple already, we'd have been OK, but they won't let someone else into the program."

"I couldn't anyway," Shah said. "Old Shah used to believe it was my father's murder that triggered my becoming a cop. Now, I'm not so sure. I've only a few memories of my childhood, but I can barely imagine never wanting to be a cop. Pursuing the truth sounds glib, like the sort of thing a hack speechwriter would write, but what if it is just that? Maybe my old idea of why I became a cop's wrong. Instead of my father's death, there was no trigger, and being a cop is simply hardwired into me?"

Aurora kissed his hand. "I'm guessing you're staying put?" She winked to make a joke of the question, but Shah caught the quaver in her voice and kissed her cheek. "Where are you sleeping tonight?" she said. "Kotian told me about the attack on Doug and Leslyn."

"When?" Shah said. *If it was before the attack…*

"Before he turned off his 'piece to ask me to set you up. Just before you called."

Shah checked timings on his eyepiece, and his shoulders slumped. The news release had been two minutes before his call.

As if reading his mind, Aurora said. "I had to turn my eyepiece off after, so there's no evidence he asked me. He's too careful." She shook her head. "He's getting nasty. I've always known he was ruthless, but it was easy to shut my eyes to it, especially when he was so nice to me." She shook her head, and now it was Shah's turn to keep quiet, to let just her talk it out. "He's been getting more and more erratic, but I never thought he'd hurt innocent people – he was going to have Leslyn ripped, I'm sure of it."

"Got any evidence?"

Aurora shook her head. "Nothing you could use."

"So it always was Sunny, doing the ripping?"

Aurora nodded. "Sunny beat him to that money-spinner."

"Not Papa's sort of thing." Shah thought of his mother's scorn for Twitter and blogging and iPods when he was young.

Aurora nodded.

"Leslyn and Doug are being kept in hospital overnight." Shah laughed bitterly. "Would you believe it – my apartment's a crime scene. I'm going to the nearest hotel."

"I don't want to go home, either, till Grunwald's set up a new identity. Said they'd need a day or three."

Shah snorted. "Budget cuts, no doubt. Next they'll

tell us we can only turn so many witnesses a year."

"I know somewhere." Aurora looked suddenly shy. "That is, if you want."

In answer Shah kissed her. When they broke, he felt suddenly awkward. "I've always dated shorter women, like Leslyn." He laughed ruefully.

"Does me being tall bother you?"

"Not exactly," Shah said. "It's just sometimes, it feels odd. I musta dated others before, but I can't remember…"

"It's your inner caveman coming out." Aurora put on a deep voice. "Me man, must be big; you woman, must be carry-able."

They started walking, Shah's hand on her hip feeling the movement. "You realize," Aurora said, "They'll be short of rooms. May only have one."

"As long as they have a bed."

"Just the one? You won't insist on twin beds?"

"Nope, one's fine."

"Want a bolster, or other protection?" She grinned.

"Nope."

Shah and Aurora both checked every few hundred yards they weren't being followed, but saw no sign of it. Almost fifteen minutes later, they reached the hotel. It was small and sparsely furnished but it had four walls and a bed, which was all Shah wanted.

He unpacked his shirt and hung it up, and turned around to find Aurora already in bed. She smiled and pushing back the sheet on his side, patted the mattress. Shah felt awkward undressing in front of her, and as soon as he could turned off the light. He slid into the bed, wincing at the cold sheets, and tried to remember to keep breathing as they fused together.

"Are you sure?" Aurora whispered, perhaps sensing his last minute nerves.

"I'm sure."

In the end it was like any of the other women he remembered making love to, if he disregarded the lump pressing against his cock as he slid into her. As he approached climax, he ceased to even notice it.

Later they fell asleep, in each other's arms.

# LXIII

The next morning Shah rose in the pre-dawn half-light, eyes gritty from lack of sleep and dressed without showering. He glanced at the clock: four-oh-five.

"Hmm?" Aurora murmured from the bed.

"Back soon," he whispered, kissing her head.

He pulled the door closed.

As he walked down the street, he called the hospital. Once he'd gone through the routine of identifying himself, the ward clerk confirmed that both patients were OK. "Unless their status changes we'll discharge them at nine o'clock."

Then he called Itandje. "Yeah, we booked in a Ms Calea and a Mr McCoy for a ten o'clock interview," the other officer said. "You need to be in on it? I can leave a voicemail."

"Nah, it's OK. I just wanted to check the state of the game."

"We've scheduled a hearing for twelve o'clock tomorrow on four specimen charges against your boy Rico. The top of his lawyer's head nearly blew off when he heard, and the guy threatened to call all kinds of shit down on us via IA, but hey. We made sure we filmed the chaos in here last night; we'll plead pressure of work, and take the slap on the wrist."

"Thanks. Appreciate it."

Itandje grinned. "Let me borrow your Rangers season ticket a few times next year, and we'll call it quits." He added, "Where are you now?"

"Getting breakfast." Shah ended the call.

As he walked to the nearest diner, Shah wondered whether he was wise to use his regular eyepiece. It had all his personalized features and short-cuts, but unlike the Department, Kotian had seemingly unlimited time, manpower and money to track him via the signal. *He might just be bloody-minded enough to do it.*

Shah stopped at the next shop, and bought a dozen prepaids. All had only minimal features, but the cost still nearly drained his account, leaving him barely enough for breakfast for two. *Maybe I can get the calories back from van Doorn.* He wasn't hopeful. *But being broke and alive's better than the alternative.* Shah switched off his regular piece, and replaced it with one of the pre-paids. It was a typical cheap set; rough against his temple where a tiny lump of plastic hadn't been filed down to complete smoothness, while the bridge pinched his nose. And he would have to download numbers from his own piece, which would mean activating it for a few minutes later on. *Better that than it being on all the time.*

He bought breakfast for two and telling himself he was being paranoid, returned to the hotel by a different route. *Must remember to bill the hotel to the Department,* he thought. *They can slug it out with the Crime Victims Board over who finally pays the invoice.*

Upstairs, Aurora was still asleep, but stirred again as he pushed the door closed. It was still not five o'clock yet. "Hmm?" Aurora murmured, then grabbed at the cheap bedside clock. "What?" Releasing it, she fell back. "It's the middle of the night! What is *wrong* with you?"

"Couldn't sleep."

Turning over she draped an arm across his lap. "Got a cure for that," she murmured.

"I need breakfast first. Didn't get to eat last night."

He unpacked coffee and waffles. Aurora heaved herself upright, and switched on the feeble bedside light. Leaning on his shoulder, she unpacked her half.

"This is two days' food for me," she grumbled as she wolfed it down. Shah liked that she ate with gusto.

"You still ate it." Shah gazed at her. "You serious?"

"Half-serious. I take stimulants and appetite suppressants and exercise hard." She laughed at his expression. "You think staying this thin is easy?"

"I thought… oh, I dunno," Shah said. "I just bought what I wanted, and doubled it."

Aurora cut the conversation short by forcing the rest of her waffle into his mouth. Her laughter at his attempts to chew it died, and her face grew serious. "You realize that when we check out, that's it? We should stay as late as possible. I assume Grunwald will be looking to slot me into the program at any time, and once that happens…" she cupped his cheek in her hand. "Mr Stubble."

"I have to be in work by eight," Shah said, trying not to let his feelings show. *We wasted so much time. No, I wasted so much time.* "So I should shave now," he said, "So that when Mr Stubble comes back to bed, he doesn't burn your lovely face."

When he returned to bed they made love again, then fell asleep.

He awoke at nine-fifteen, and scrambled out of bed, cursing.

Itandje had already handed over to Bailey, who said, "I tried calling you, but you switched your piece off."

"Yeah." Shah ignored her accusatory tone. "I'm using this prepaid one." He called her 'piece, and hung up when she answered. "I'll use it until the prepay runs out. Then switch to another one."

Bailey raised her eyebrows. "Bit, uh, spy-tech, isn't it?"

"We didn't have a leak in the Department, then?" Shah said. "And Kotian hasn't got country-fulls of money, and a grudge against me?"

"OK." Bailey nodded slowly, mulling it over. "You'll let the cap know?"

"OK," Shah said. "But only him. I'd appreciate it if you handle any other calls for me. Can we do that?"

"We can."

Shah switched on his regular eyepiece, and put a divert instruction on it to Bailey's number, then switched it off again. "Done."

He spent much of the next hour waiting anxiously, first for a chance to brief van Doorn, who nodded. "Yeah, that makes sense. We still got nothing formally tying Kotian to the threats and attempts on your partners, we can't assume he's unconnected, and – on a personal level – I'd be mightily pissed if anything happened to Marietetski *and* you."

Van Doorn looked up. "You know they turned him off."

Shah nodded. "That's where I was when the ten-eighteen came through."

"Funeral's next week, day to be confirmed. We're all

attending it. And don't worry about the hotel and phones. I'll sort them out."

"Thanks," Shah said, keeping an eye on the nearest interview room in which two familiar figures sat with Stickel.

"You got somewhere to be?"

"I wanted to speak to Leslyn and Doug, Cap. I've had no chance to check they're all right, let alone..." He sighed, wishing he knew what to say to them when the time came.

Van Doorn said gently, "They'll get counseling Pete. They should recover." He added, "Without wanting to downplay what happened, they were pretty lucky. Doug took a beating, and Leslyn got scratched up and cuts. But no bones were broken, and no one was killed."

"Not for want of trying." Shah shook his head. "Maybe we *have* been lucky. In forty-plus years, my job has never brought grief like this down on them – until now. Maybe they're right to want to get out."

"And ever since I can remember, people have said *it never used to be this bad*."

When Doug and Leslyn finally emerged from the interview room, Doug moved more like a man of ninety than sixty, while Leslyn stared round with darting eyes, jumping when someone dropped a box of files.

"Hey," Shah said. "Come and sit for a few minutes."

Leslyn looked at the legal counsel who'd accompanied them. Shah recognized her as one of the regular pool used by the city. The counselor said, "I assume you're asking as a spouse, not a policeman?"

Shah nodded, and the woman waved them to seats that she gathered from other desks.

"I'm sorry that this happened." Shah reached out for Leslyn, but she shied away.

"I've had enough, Pete." Leslyn blinked, her voice unsteady. She grabbed Doug, who drew a sharp intake of breath. Shah felt a pang. Once she would have reached for him, "Doug and I are leaving New York. Immediately. We – we're going upstate. I can't bear to be here any longer than we have to be."

Shah glanced at Doug, who sat stiffly in his chair. His face was already a patchwork of livid red welts, and even a purple one. "You know that you'll lose touch with her when she becomes post-human, don't you?"

Doug nodded, even though it was clearly an effort. His jaw was wired up, so that it was hard for him to speak. "I know," he still managed to say. "But we have until then."

They made to leave. "Doug," Shah said. The other man turned back to face him. "Just wanted to say thanks... for protecting her. For everything."

Doug blinked, his eyes misting up. "Thanks," he ground out. "Good luck."

# LXIV

The call came through as Shah was wolfing a Danish down at his desk for lunch. "Help me," a woman said. For a heart-lurching moment, Shah thought it was Aurora. Then he glimpsed lowlights in the blonde hair. Before he could answer, his own voice came down the line: "You won't stop me." It went dead. Before they could lock onto the eyepiece's signal, that too died.

Bailey said, "He or she's switched it off."

"He," Shah said. Bailey said nothing.

They spent an anguished forty minutes rousing every available unit on the Upper East Side – which was as much as they could narrow the signal – to look for the woman.

"He knows what he's doing," Valentine said. An earnest man who wore old-fashioned spectacles into which his eyepiece had been set, he was the head of the NYPD's under-funded, under-strength, under-manned Surveillance Department. "That area has fewer cameras than any other part of New York."

Shah snorted. "Cameras wouldn't stop him, anyway. All they'd do is finger the perp when we had time to go through the footage properly."

Valentine stared at Shah. "You're right," he said at last. "But if the facial recognition software throws up a match, we could get officers to the spot. Maybe even in time."

When the call came through, it took Shah a second to react. "Her ID's back online!"

Valentine was already on the line to Comms. "We're still triangulating. Keep her talking as long as you can, Pete."

Shah swallowed, licked his parched lips, and connected.

"Shah," the woman mumbled, as if she had something in her mouth, but her avatar gave no clues as to whether she was hurt.

"Yes? Who–"

"Your bitch is next. Aurora." Her voice broke; "Please–" the line went dead again.

"Damn, damn, damn!" Valentine yelled, then said, "How near did you get the trace? *Not* the Upper East Side? Then where, dammit?" Shah couldn't ever remember hearing the little man swear before. "OK, OK," Valentine fumed. "Move everyone toward the lower end."

They spent the next forty minutes swinging all units southward, even managing to borrow a Federal helicopter, something that normally took days to arrange.

The phone rang again.

It was a voice-only line. Shah shivered as he heard himself say, "You got the wrong man. Did you think when you killed him, that you ended it?"

Shah said. "Don't hang up–" He grimaced. "Hello? Hello? Dammit!"

"He's left it on!" Valentine said.

A few minutes later a passing patrol found the eye-piece, dumped in a trashcan back near where the original call had come from. "The fucker doubled back," Shah said. "You sure that that second call came from the lower end?"

"Positive as we can be. We didn't have enough time to zero in on it completely, but we narrowed it down to a ten-block radius around Battery Park."

Shah called up the map on his eyepiece. "So if he doubled back, he probably went along Roosevelt Drive?"

"That, or he took a short-cut. Should we assume he's in a private vehicle?"

"Have to. No cabbie would haul a kidnap victim round Lower Manhattan."

"Unless he *is* a cabbie," Bailey said.

"Nope, it's Kotian." Shah ticked off fingers: "Aurora; Leslyn; someone who looks like Aurora... what do they have in common? *Me*."

Van Doorn called Grunwald on a group line. "Do we have enough to take Kotian in?"

Grunwald pulled a face. "No. It's a house of cards. Kotian's lawyer will shred us in seconds. Get me *something* solid, and I'll get you a warrant faster than you can say killer."

"What about Aurora?" Shah said.

"She's under observation," van Doorn said.

Grunwald said, "She came to my office this morning. She'll be OK as long as she does nothing stupid."

Thirty minutes later, another call came in, this time from the river police. "We got a body in the water. Looks like your missing woman, though it's hard to tell, she's been beaten up so bad." The officer cut in the feed of the missing woman being pulled from the water, and turned over so that she was face up.

Bailey said, "Is it my imagination? Or is she beaten the same way that the other girl – that was meant to be Aurora – was?"

They gathered in the squad room: Shah, Bailey, van Doorn, Grunwald, Valentine and Lee the profiler. "The victim is Lindsay Wayne," van Doorn said, sending them her details.

*Any age's too young*, Shah thought, *but thirty-five?* He was glad that he didn't have to tell her partner and children that she wouldn't be coming home from lunch with a group of ex-colleagues. Someone else had that unenviable task.

"No record, no questionable activities," van Doorn continued. "She seems to have just been in the wrong place at the wrong time."

Grunwald asked Valentine, "What do we have on the kidnap trail?"

"Far as we can tell she was abducted in Yorkville. Traffic analyzed the footage. See the kidnapper's car appear here, and here. The perp's wearing a hood, so plenty of people noticed, simply because it was incongruous enough to draw attention."

"He *wanted* to be noticed," Shah said. "In his mind if he can convince enough people the Ripper's still out there, then he's exonerated Sunny."

"Conjecture," Grunwald said.

"But logical," Lee said. "His interviews have indicated that he sees his son as an extension of himself. So in exonerating Sunny, he exonerates himself."

Grunwald shrugged, told Valentine, "Go on."

"He drove down the old Long Island Expressway at eleven oh six to dump the body in Battery Park. We got people coming forward to provide info, but it's lacking in quality."

Van Doorn interrupted the lament. "We found her car?"

Valentine said, "Dumped by the Queensboro Bridge. CSU are going through it, but the perp knew what he was doing. Unless we get luckier than we have so far we'll find nothing."

"But surely..." Bailey began. She stopped, lapsing into thought.

"Finish it any time you like," van Doorn said.

Bailey sighed and looked at Shah. "You said she looked enough like Aurora that you thought it was her."

"Only for a moment."

"But you thought it was her," Bailey insisted.

"Sure."

"So she wasn't picked at random."

The others nodded. Grunwald said, "So?"

"So she's going to be on all the surveillance cameras – and so will the person who was following her? We work backwards, rather than forwards."

Grunwald gazed at van Doorn, who sat with eyes narrowed. "You know what you're asking?" He said. "CSU alone take nine or ten days for inquiries, so everyone makes *all* requests urgent, to speed things up – now even genuinely urgent ones take five or six days."

"Uh-huh."

"Even with a population way down on the city's peak of eight and a half to only three million, we still had over two hundred murders last year."

"Stop it or I'm going to cry," Grunwald said. "You know what'll happen if the newsfeeds get hold of the fact that a woman was snatched and killed because she looked like someone else? They'll slaughter us. You have to get people in numbers onto this."

"I didn't say we *wouldn't* do it, but we can't leave the rest of the city uncovered. I've been talking to the precinct heads to get them to put what people they can onto cam-analysis as back up to the facial recognition programs."

"OK," Grunwald said. "If you get any problems let me know, and I'll put my biggest boots on and kick the crap out of any precinct head who's less than completely co-operative."

Shah tried to put the thought of Grunwald in boots out of his head. "What do you want me to do?"

"We'll set the facial recognition programs to Lindsay Wayne," van Doorn said. "Go through the shit-loads of footage that they'll throw up. Bailey, you manage the current cases."

"How sure are we that this isn't the real Ripper?" Grunwald said. "Could we be wrong in assuming that it was Sunny Kotian, or Sunny Kotian ripping alone, as we have done?"

Lee coughed. "I'd agree with Shah's assessment; this is a different operation from the Ripper," he said. "He worked anonymously. The assaults escalated, but there was no contact with the police." He added, "I know this assault mirrors a woman being beaten to death, but those were specific circumstances."

"So how is this different from that one?" Grunwald said, looking skeptical.

"As far as we can tell, the earlier victim's trigger was as much proximity as resemblance. She looked like Aurora Debonis, but more importantly, she was where she was. This one looks much more like her, and has clearly been stalked. The original killing was done with minimum fuss. This is loud, self-publicizing. The killer is incredibly conflicted. He's superficially confident, even taunting us, but I suspect that in some ways he wants to be caught – or at least identified. He's saying 'come and catch me if you can.' "

"So what does all that mean?" Grunwald said.

Lee said slowly, weighing every word, "I get the impression... that if you confront him and put him in a situation where... the evidence is overwhelming, he'll admit to it. Almost welcome admitting to it." He added quickly, "But you need the physical evidence – as long as he has wiggle room, he'll deny it."

"Are we done?" Grunwald said.

Van Doorn said, "I think so. Let's get to it, everyone. Let's nail this bastard."

Shah sent messages off to the other precincts, requesting every feed they had, giving Lindsay Wayne's details for them to marry up in the vain hope that it would reduce the tidal wave of dross coming his way. He had no illusions of the likelihood of that. He knew that he would just send everything, unfiltered. At the end of the regulation forty-five minutes the timer interrupted him. For once he was glad to come up for a breather from the cumulative erosion to his self of other people's thoughts and cares.

Bailey and van Doorn stood watching him. Shah guessed that he'd interrupted a conversation. "What?" he said.

"Just had a call," van Doorn said. "Marble Hill pulled a young woman from the river."

For an awful moment Shah wondered what Aurora was doing all the way up there. Then realization clicked. "Perveza?"

Van Doorn nodded. "Sorry."

Shah put his hand to his mouth. The worst part was the guilt. *You thought it was Aurora, didn't even think of Perveza. What kind of father forgets his own daughter?* "How?"

"Drowned," van Doorn said. "She was so loaded with Scramble she wouldn't have known a thing. We think that she fell in while she was bombed."

"Could she have been pushed?"

Van Doorn looked pensive. "We can't rule Kotian out. But there are no clear signs of a fatal wound or injury, no witnesses – hell, no clear idea of where she went in. Sorry, bud."

Shah said, "Thanks for telling me," and donning the hood at once to signal that the conversation was over – working time regulations or no regulations – fled back to work, where the problems were someone else's, and maybe had a solution.

# LXV

You're normally a heavy sleeper, but something's woken you. Beside you, Angelica lies on her back, mouth open, snoring gently. *There – it sounded like glass breaking.*

You pull on your eyepiece and see straight away that something's very, very wrong; the stand-by light is off, which means there's no network. *Or,* you remember what your father once told you, *someone's jamming it.* You check the alarm console in the bedside cabinet. Unsurprisingly, it's dead. *Someone's cut the alarm.*

You're not a brave man, but the thought of anything happening to Angelica and the children lends you courage. Fumbling your feet into slippers and shrugging on a dressing gown, you reach into a bedside drawer to pull out a gun you've never really expected to have to use.

In theory, the private security firm will send men to investigate why your alarm's gone offline. But you've heard urban legends about ghost circuits that echo the alarm's "all's well" transponder, and you're not going to chance that those legends might not be true.

Angelica's still sleeping. You pause, debating whether to wake her, decide against it. You ease open the bedroom door and step into the corridor, gently lit by a night-light because Leonie won't sleep without it.

Without warning a volcano of pain erupts in your eyes. You double over, clawing at them, wanting to gouge out what feels like red-hot needles being plunged into your eyeballs, and then the pepper spray hits your sinuses and your head feels as if it's suddenly too small for your expanding brain. Then the knock-out undertone hits, and oblivion welcomes you.

You awake what could be hours or only minutes later, face down on your dining room carpet, hands tied behind your back. Everything is confusing – the world keeps spinning in and out of focus. You hear sobbing and screaming. *The children!* You look up. George and Leonie are each held by a pair of burly giants wearing masks. Angelica – similarly bound – is trying not to cry. She's white-faced, wide-eyed and shivering, naked, another masked man kneeling over her back, running a gloved hand up and down her spine.

Another man stands with an automatic pistol held horizontally across his chest.

You clutch at hope. *They're masked. If they don't want us to see their faces, maybe they're going to let us live.*

"Mr Shah," the man kneeling over Angelica says. "Rex, I'm sorry to have to do this. I was a civilized man once, before your father robbed me of joy and hope." His voice is strangely rough, mechanical; there's a vox in his mask, distorting his voice.

"I don't–" a man's boot kicks you in the side, driving the air from your lungs.

"Hush now, Mr Shah," the man says. "I do apologize for the crudity, but getting good help is so hard these days. My subcontractors are not always up to spec. Why, tonight, due to the labor shortage your father's

caused, I've had to bring along a pedophile to help out."
He nods at the man holding Leonie's shoulders. "He
doesn't want money, as long as he gets to play with the
children."

You feel an icy block form in your bowels. "Please,
pl-please don't hurt them."

"Well, that's a little tricky. But we'll wipe their minds
after he's raped them. Of course, there's no guarantee
that we'll actually carry out our threat. If you beg nicely
enough, maybe we'll kill you quickly – an eye for an
eye, as the Christian Old Testament says – a son for a
son. Or maybe we'll take it in turns to gang-rape and
sodomize your wife while they watch. Well, Mr Shah,
how eloquently can you beg us to spare your children's
lives?"

# LXVI

Shah spent so long looking for his quarry that when he finally stumbled across him, he almost missed him. He'd spent a fruitless morning studying footage of Lindsay Wayne, from the last recorded moments before Kotian vanished her from the patchwork network of surveillance cameras, working backwards through the previous two weeks, in the rare instances where the camera had enough memory not to over-record every day. Each time Shah had to isolate one person in the immediate vicinity, enter their face into the match bank, then set the system to scan for matching images.

In theory if the face matched one in the bank it would trigger an alarm, but in practice only the slightest distortion was needed – someone else walking in between the person and the camera, a shadow, even the wrong angle – to stop the software registering a match.

Even so, there were enough possibles that Shah had to study them all visually, then check them off with the near-endless list of all Kotian's known associates. Even only a week's worth of surveillance produced so many permutations, which each had to be logged and checked, that by mid-morning Shah's brain felt as if it was melting. Only the thought that while Lindsay Wayne's killer was free, others were in danger kept Shah at his desk.

It was long, dour, heartbreaking work that was the perfect answer to the paranoid fantasies of state surveillance that eddied around in the wake of 9/11. Almost fifty years later, society still had neither the technology nor the manpower to make the libertarian's nightmares true.

The software's alarm chimed: match found. With jackbooted butterflies stomping in his stomach, Shah called up the result, while he scrabbled for the eyepiece he'd removed to rub the bridge of his nose. He saw van Doorn crossing the room. "We got a match!"

Van Doorn turned and saw Shah's grin. "If you're kidding me, Shah, you're dogmeat…"

"Nope," Shah said, still beaming. "Kotian. Six days before her murder. He must've seen her, had the idea, put a tail on her." Van Doorn stood beside Shah, staring at the screen. Shah ran the footage. "See him watching her? Then making a call. I'd bet you if we could isolate that call – and what a goddamn shame it is we can't – we'd get him telling someone to put a tail on her."

"We can't isolate it from this," van Doorn said, already on his eyepiece, "but if we can sequester *all* his records, we can probably find that call." He turned and slapped Shah's bicep hard enough to make the older man wince. "Fantastic work!" He added, "Now take a break; you've earned it."

Shah walked around the block to stretch his legs, but outside was even hotter and stickier than in the office, for all that the building's air conditioning seemed to be on the fritz much of the time. As soon as he'd bought a bottle of water and a sandwich from the nearest deli,

Shah plodded back up the stairs to the office, where Bailey looked bemused. "Exercise," he said between panting. When he'd recovered his breath, Shah stuck his head around van Doorn's door. "What news?"

"Got a warrant to sequester Shah's eyepiece records. And more. Grunwald's used the Lindsay Wayne killing as evidence that this Nico, Rico, whatever the hell the kid's name is, has vital information. Got the judge to grant us a warrant to access the kid's memories."

"Lindsay Wayne?" Shah said. "You and I know there's a connection, but how did she convince a judge of it?"

Van Doorn shrugged. "Judges keep an eye on the news as much as the rest of us. And they're only human; they worry that we might ever leak that we had a case and it was baulked. Besides, it helps if you're talking to a hanging judge." At Shah's blank look van Doorn said, "Judge Warren's the duty judge for applications today. Soon as she saw his name on the roster, Grunwald lined up her arguments like it was a duck shoot."

"Poor kid never had a chance, then – Warren's a bloodthirsty bastard."

"Yeah." Van Doorn beamed. "But he's our bloodthirsty bastard. Unlike some that'd shove a stick up their ass in the name of civil liberties." He rubbed his hands vigorously as if to stay warm, although it was at least ninety-five and sticky in the room. "Maybe things are finally swinging our way."

"Be about time," Shah said.

Van Doorn's eyepiece chimed, and he stiffened. "Morning, Grunwald." He nodded, once, twice, three times. "I'll get on it straight away." He said. "Pete, you know this guy?"

Shah's eyepiece took the download from van Doorn and–

You're stood on a street corner, a guy handing you a scanner. Dilip says, "So we just rip the bitch, yeah?" He's stoned, his eyes dilated. You know the guy handing you the scanner from somewhere. *Rudi, that's it.* Not the brightest light bulb in the hallways. He nods in time to every other word: "Yeah, Mr K., he's saying he don't want her hurt, just wants a message sending to the Lady Leslyn's man-friend in the force. He axed me to do it, but I gotta 'nother job, so you guys take care of it, maybe there be some more work for youse in the future, heh?" He hands you each a pill. "That an am-nes-i-ac," he says. "You get caught, it wipes the last six hours, so we got no problem."

*Fuck that,* you think; you'll drop the pill down the nearest drain first chance you get. *Who knows what's in it. Probably a freaking suicide pill, or something. No sir, I ain't taking no tab from no stranger.*

Rudi hands you each a card. "Two hunnerd kilocals on each card, plus the same on another card when the job done. We meet here this time tomorrow, you bring the scanner with the rip, you get the rest of the payment."

Shah ended the clip. "I'm guessing Grunwald's already presenting to Warren for an arrest warrant?"

Van Doorn nodded, his mind clearly elsewhere, and smiled ruefully. "She already had when she sent that. She, ah, thought you might get a notion to Dirty Harry the job if she didn't build in a time lag."

Shah stiffened. "She thought that I might play vigilante?"

"No," van Doorn said. "But she and I both thought you might tag along to offer assistance like you did with

Sunny. Even your presence in the vicinity allows the defense a chance to distract the jury, by suggesting that you were participating in a vendetta."

Van Doorn held up a hand, listening to an incoming on his eyepiece. "OK, keep me advised." He looked at Shah and raised an eyebrow. "You're an office lawyer. You'll 'accidentally' stroll through a crime scene on your way to somewhere, or talk to someone you've been told to stay away from – look at what's happened with Kotian in the past."

Shah made a conciliatory gesture. "That was then. I'm not going to screw this up."

"Anyway, it's done. The bad news is Kotian wasn't at home or in his office." His eyepiece chimed again. As he listened, Shah saw him swallow, and lick his lips. "Problems?" Shah said, but van Doorn held up his hand again. "You're sure? OK. Keep looking, and I'll notify Grunwald." Even as he cut the line, another call came in, and then a third. When he had finished taking them, van Doorn sat, staring into infinity.

"Why do I get the feeling," Shah said, "that that wasn't good news?"

Van Doorn exhaled a long, slow sigh, but didn't answer Shah directly. Instead he made another call. "Nancy. One unit after another has reported in. They're unable to find Kotian." Shah could hear Grunwald's shriek of "What?" from ten feet away. Van Doorn said, "Looks like our friend Mr Kotian has gone underground."

# LXVII

Shah spent the day a frustrated spectator, tapping his foot while police teams swept around New York. When van Doorn summoned the rest of the precinct to a briefing Shah said, "What do you want me to do?"

"Everything that isn't Kotian," van Doorn replied, confirming Shah's worst fears. He gave Shah a long, hard stare. "If you dare go within a mile of this, I swear to God I'll throw you out of a window myself. Got that?"

"Got it."

By lunchtime, Shah had managed to offload a vagrant back to the Albany PD where his last registered address was. Suddenly lonely, he called Doug and Leslyn, but went straight to voicemail. He guessed they had already started their journey upstate. Passing van Doorn's office to get a sandwich, Shah heard shouting. Shah waited until the captain had finished and leaned around the doorframe. "You OK?"

"Damn fools," van Doorn muttered. He seemed to see Shah for the first time. "Did you know Kotian had a private plane?" Seeing Shah's surprised look, van Doorn added, "I guess that's a no, then. But it's listed. And no one thought to put a guard on it."

"That must cost... Jesus, a private plane?" Shah said. "How much is this guy worth?"

Van Doorn held up a hand as his 'piece chimed again. "OK." Raising his eyes to the heavens, he blew out his cheeks. "Good." To Shah he said, "Thank God for that. A combined Homeland and Police squad have just got there."

"No sign of Kotian, I guess?" Shah said.

Van Doorn shook his head. "No sign it was even being prepared. Just a bunch of guys sitting around playing cards."

"Just goes to show," Shah said, "the guy's got money to burn."

After lunch Shah found it difficult to concentrate, instead spending the afternoon watching the frenetic activity. As instructions went out and confirmations came back of watches mounted on ports and airports, of bank accounts frozen, Shah imagined that he could hear one by one, the sound of locks being slammed on Kotian's freedom.

But still no sign of him.

Shah gradually forced himself back to running footage from the surveillance cameras – by the time he finished the day Shah had logged nine different scenes in which both Lindsay Wayne and Kotian had appeared in within the space of two minutes. "Good work," van Doorn said as the captain passed his desk.

"Doesn't *prove* he did it."

"You're playing Devil's Advocate?"

"Someone has to."

It builds up a pattern," van Doorn said. "Juries have convicted on patterns before."

Shah had his doubts, but kept quiet. When he pulled on his jacket, van Doorn beckoned him over. The captain waved at two nondescript young men who leaned in his doorway. One was stubbled, chewing on a toothpick; he nodded a greeting. "That's Kennedy," van Doorn said. The other man was older, hair receding from a high forehead, but equally unmemorable. He raised a hand. "That's Levinson," van Doorn said. "They're your shadows from now on."

"Say again?" Shah said.

"Don't worry," Levinson said. His voice had the faintest twang of a southern accent. "We won't get in your face."

"Going to check my bathroom for bombs?"

"We already have," Kennedy said, "when we moved you into a hotel." He grinned. "Don't worry, we're good at this. After a few days, you'll barely notice us."

"That so?" Shah doubted he'd ever get used to having two men watching his every move. Then he thought of cameras. *OK,* he thought. *Maybe you can get used to anything.* "You guys cops? Feds?"

Levinson shook his head. "Contractors."

"So what do I do now?" Shah said.

"Ignore us," Kennedy said. "Just do whatever you were planning on doing."

But for the first ten minutes after he left the office, Shah found it impossible to ignore the two men. Running for a subway car he thought he might make it, but that they probably wouldn't. So held back and deliberately missed the closing doors. *I'll get the next one,* he thought, frowning at the idea. He looked around but couldn't see them at first, and had to fight a sudden flash of panic. *Have they been attacked?*

He caught sight of a stubbled face that looked vaguely familiar. Shah squinted; it was Kennedy. The other man

made an angry gesture, urging Shah to ignore him.
Shah did, breathing out in relief a breath that he hadn't
been aware he'd been holding. The rest of the journey
'home' to the hotel that the Department had moved
Shah to was uneventful.

Shah guessed that every local, state and Federal
agency in New York City booked their people into the
ironically named Hotel Splendide. Reading the guest-
book in his dingy room, the little box-like building that
cowered in the shadows of the surrounding skyscrapers
had once catered for tourists – *those on a tight budget,*
Shah thought – but now the thin-walled rooms where
the paper peeled away were haunted by transients like
Shah, individuals or the occasional woman with children, but all people who stared into space or who
jumped at sudden sounds.

Whatever was for dinner smelled equally unappeal-
ing, so Shah wandered into the darkening evening. A
breeze had gathered, bringing with it hints of tropical
scents and the promise of a storm. New York had begun
to experience a hurricane season of sorts over the last
decade, a pale shadow of the brutal monsters that had
almost wiped Miami, Daytona and New Orleans off the
face of the earth, but still shocking to people more used
to snow.

Shah spent a lonely evening nursing dinner and a
succession of still waters, before retiring early to bed.
At home he sometimes surfed news or drama channels
on his eyepiece while lying in bed, but cheap prepaids
didn't support such complex functionality, and switching on his own eyepiece risked alerting anyone looking
for him. While Shah felt marginally safer among those
he'd privately named The Unwanteds, he didn't feel
*that* safe.

Instead he lay in bed, staring at the ceiling, thinking.

Shah had no doubt that compared to the old media, video, audio and abortive ventures into virtual realities – the failure of which had led to burns as the Big New Experience – memory burns were absolutely real. Nonetheless they weren't the same as one's own memories.

So Shah mentally rifled through the downloads he'd been given, or bought off the web. The man who had been so proud of being a Muslim and a cop before 9/11, that wasn't him. Nor was the divorcee meeting Leslyn in Denver; nor even the man so proud of his daughter's birth. They were strangers walled off by time and something else, something intangible.

Shah guessed that the root cause was that part of memory was retained in the nervous system scattered throughout the body – there every thought was 'felt.' Without those receptors nothing he experienced was quite as real as the memories he now had of being with Aurora; the taste of his first ice-cream since the attack; the touch of Leslyn's hand on his face as he awoke; the smell of Doug's vile cigarettes. *How does it feel to be a stranger, even to yourself?*

Shah thought of the night before, lying in the darkness with Aurora after making love. "Why don't you leave this job?" Her voice was barely a whisper. "It's eating you alive. And you've done it for one lifetime – don't you think that's long enough?"

Shah sighed. "I've no idea what else to do."

*Aurora.* Shah hadn't wanted to admit even to himself how much he would miss her. *Has she just been a rebound fuck because of ending with Leslyn?* It hadn't felt like it. Rather that his meeting Aurora had pushed Leslyn away, for all their supposedly open relationship.

*It feels like you're mourning something.* The thought came unbidden. *Is this grief for the loss of the old memories, for the attack, or for Marietetski's death?*

He tried to think of something else. Aurora. But he'd lost her as well.

His grief came from deeper than he would have thought possible, great heaving sobs that threatened to break him apart. Even burying his face in his pillow couldn't completely muffle them.

When he had finished Shah staggered to the bathroom to splash water on his face. The eyes that stared back at him had the same haunted look as he'd seen on almost every other guest's face. He took a glass of water and, putting on the bedside light, sat and stared at his own eyepiece – the proper one. He drained the glass and returned to the bathroom again, drew another glassful of water. Stared in the mirror. "You bloody fool." He wasn't sure which was more foolish – calling her or not calling her. *She'll probably have turned hers off as well, if she has any sense.*

Shah sat on his bed again, picked up the eyepiece and twirled it between finger and thumb. He got up and moved to the little couch which by its presence was supposed to make this charmless little cubicle a suite. Moving position changed nothing.

He switched on the piece and called Aurora.

Astonishingly, it rang.

Shah hung up, heart pounding. *Has this what it's all been about? Is she a lure?* He shook his head. Kotian might be clever, powerful, well-informed, but he couldn't predict that accurately what Shah would do. *Could he?*

Shah wiped his mouth, although it felt desert dry. He mouthed the numbers again.

"H– hello?" Aurora sounded as if she'd just been awoken from a deep sleep.

Shah almost hung up at that moment, and often wondered afterward what might have happened if he had. Instead, at the second, even more hesitant "Hello", he said, "It's me. Pete." Of course, his caller ID would have displayed that already, but she might have thought that someone else was calling on his piece.

"I was dreaming about you," Aurora murmured. "Am I still dreaming?"

"If you are then I am as well. I must be frigging crazy. Though you're no better. What are you doing, leaving the phone on?"

"Hoping you might call. How are you?"

"Lonely. You?"

"The same. I– uh, oh God, Pete – am I doing the right thing? If I stayed–"

"I want to see you. I need one more–"

"Where?"

"Same place as last night. If you're sure?" Shah rested the cold glass against his head, as if it might cool his thoughts.

"I'm sure. When?"

"In thirty minutes. I'll get us a room."

"OK," she said, adding quickly, "I love you," and cut the line.

Telling himself that he was a fool over and over again, Shah dressed quickly. He felt ten years younger. His heart beat a little drum-roll as he grabbed a pair of disposable pieces, thinking, *too late now.*

For a moment he considered calling Kennedy and Levinson and telling them where he was going, but they might try to stop him – worse, they might call Aurora's detail and warn them so that they might stop her.

Instead Shah pulled the door shut quietly. *If they hear me, they can follow me all they want,* he thought, and set off down the corridor. He took the stairs. It was only three floors down, and walking would be faster than waiting for the single creaking elevator.

Outside it had started to rain, and the temperature had dropped slightly; the first spattering of raindrops was only blood-warm.

Shah set off into the night.

# LXVIII

Shah ducked from doorway to doorway to dodge the raindrops, but as the rain grew no heavier quickly gave it up as futile. He took barely ten minutes to reach the hotel he and Aurora had stayed in the night before.

Compared to the Splendide it was palatial, but Shah barely noticed his surroundings, instead concentrating on movement and things that looked out of place. While he checked in he kept looking around, to see if she had arrived, whether he had been followed, or for signs of an ambush. Every shadow, every movement was a potential threat. Shah glared at the night manager who gazed at him with a little too much interest for Shah's liking as he passed Shah the room key.

"Am I wearing something of yours?" Shah growled. The guy looked away.

Shah's room was on the eighth floor. He walked down the corridor with an eyepiece in each pocket, one a disposable prepaid, the other his usual one, which rang as he let himself into the room. Aurora's avatar appeared. "I'm down in the lobby."

"Room eight-eleven." Shah wanted to say more but he needed to end the call before anyone could trace him. Besides, she was only two minutes from his arms.

After the slightest of pauses Aurora said, "I'll be right up."

Shah paced the carpet until the tap on the door sent him racing to open it.

Aurora threw her arms around him. Her eyes were tearful as she kissed him, then said, "I know it's stupid, but I kept thinking of you–"

A familiar man's voice said, "You're right, it is stupid."

Shah and Aurora froze.

Kotian emerged from the doorway to what Shah could see now was a connecting door so, with minimal effort, the hotel could turn two singles into a suite. "Nice work Aurora," Kotian said, gun in hand.

Shah cursed himself for not checking what he had assumed was a bathroom.

While Kotian kept his gun trained on them, another man with a high-powered rifle followed Kotian through and took up station by the door to the corridor. Two others eased past Kotian. They grabbed Aurora, dragging her away.

Shah mouthed, "One one two," to activate his eyepiece. He gazed at her, wondering whether he could see anything that would make him certain one way or the other.

"It's not true!" Aurora cried.

Kotian made a little "it doesn't matter" gesture with his head, never taking his eyes from Shah, who in turn gazed on Kotian. Now that the worst had happened, Shah felt curiously calm, almost zen-like.

"He's messing with you!" Aurora cried. "He has a man in the Department!"

"He probably does," Shah said, wanting to believe her, but unable to be certain.

"I'm sorry it's so crowded in here," Kotian said. "Shirani only had one set of adjoining rooms, so we took one, hoping you might return. But that left you only with this pokey box."

*Shirani?* Shah thought. *That's a Persian name. Damn. I'd have been a little friendlier if I'd known – not that it'd probably have done much good.* "Is this where the villain explains everything?" Shah said. Anything that delayed the climax to this little scene was a good thing.

"Sadly for you, no." Kotian told one of his men, "Take his gun."

As the goon – carefully staying out of the rifleman's line of fire – undid Shah's holster, Shah said, "So the question is – what now?"

"Isn't it just?" Kotian said. "Would you believe me if I told you that at the moment I'm not completely sure? So many contingency plans had to be put into effect, with so many variables that there are an almost endless number of ways that this can be played out. Even as we speak, my Communications Director next door is recalling some, sending others out to run interference – do you like how I've mastered some of these sporting analogies?" Kotian leaned forward, no longer smiling. "I'll tell you this much. I'm not going to kill you, Shah. There are worse things than being dead, believe me. Although one never likes to think so while one can draw breath. But once you stop breathing, you stop caring, and that's entirely too little suffering for you. Being alive but bereft of those you love is one of them." He turned to the two men holding Aurora. "Take her away."

Shah's mouth went suddenly dry. Whatever her part

in this, he didn't want Aurora hurt. "What'll you do with her?"

"I'll tell you what I'm not going to do, which is to leave her as she is, to testify against me. No, I don't think so. She'll be just as useful as she is now but with her memories wiped and a near-zombie – perhaps more so. I have clientele who like gang-fucks and they like their women pliant." Kotian winked. "Never waste an asset." He lowered his voice. "Maybe I'll send you clips of her every month being asked who you are and having no idea. Or of her happily crawling around on all fours in nothing but a dog collar and lead while giving bukkake parties, all in blissful ignorance of her failed knight in shining armor."

Shah said, "I never realized before what a deeply misogynistic bastard you are."

"You forget I'm a businessman, I like women. But I have lots of clients who don't. The customer is always right." Kotian's eyes glittered. "Don't be fooled by her demure little act. She's an animal in the bedroom – likes to kneel on all fours with her head pulled back by her hair while she takes it up the ass. Don't you, lover?"

Aurora didn't answer, so Shah did. "That's just giving the customer what they want." He added, "You seem to think you can carry on as before." *Keep talking, bozo. Your type never know when to shut up.* "Aren't you forgetting the warrant for your arrest?"

Kotian's smile never reached his eyes. "Oh, that. The Americans still think they're a superpower. That they only have to snap their fingers and the rest of the world jumps. There's a warrant here, for sure, but do you think their piddling little requests for extradition cut much ice nowadays? Although that's another reason I won't kill you. Add the words 'of a police officer' to murder charges, and some countries suddenly take a very Old Testament view of things. So we'll avoid that." He took a breath. "Anyway, we've wasted a few minutes here, which is more than you're worth."

At his nod, the two men marched Aurora through the connecting door. She cried out, but then her voice grew muffled and Shah guessed that they'd clapped a hand over her mouth. He hoped she'd bite the guy's hand to the bone.

*Come on, come on, where are you guys?* Shah thought. Police response times at this time of night should be less than five minutes – unless Kotian had arranged a diversion.

"I'm going to leave you with Aresh here," Kotian said. "I have some other scores to settle before leaving New York, so I must bid you good night, Officer." Kotian added, "Oh, we've been jamming your piece, so don't expect the cavalry any time soon."

Shah sighed. He hadn't really expected help.

Keeping clear of the line of fire, Kotian removed Shah's eyepiece. "Turn out your pockets." From them Kotian took both eyepieces and ground them underfoot. "There," he said. "Good night!" Kotian called to Aresh, "Remember – don't kill him."

Shah suddenly realized that *that* didn't preclude Aresh maiming him. Especially as Kotian had repeatedly told the gunman not to kill him in front of witnesses with eyepieces. Shah threw himself across the bed as Aresh fired. A bullet flew past Shah's face, scorching one cheek. He scrabbled for the far side of the bed. Aresh shouted, "Keep still, mo'fucker! How'm I s'posed to wing ya, if ya keep movin'?"

He fired again. Shah screamed, and clutched his leg.

# LXIX

Shah tried to crawl under the bed, but Aresh dragged him back by his heels. Shah screamed again. Adrenaline had blocked off much of the pain, until now. It felt as if someone had put a blowtorch to his leg. "It burns," Shah gasped.

"Guess that does it," Aresh said, handing Shah a rough hand-towel. "Pack that on it. Don't move till the am'blance gets here. You comprendez?"

"Yeah," Shah gasped.

Aresh picked up the antique bedside phone. "Shirani. Call an amb'lance in sixty seconds. Don't want this fucker bleeding out."

Moments later the door slammed.

Shah grimaced with the effort of looking up. The room was empty. *Good.*

Luckily it was a flesh wound; the bullet hadn't nicked an artery or bone – Aresh probably thought he'd done more damage than he had. But it was still bad enough. Shah had once got badly sunburned; another time he'd put his hand on a stove. This was far, far worse. The wound burned as if someone had dipped a tennis ball in the hottest chili sauce imaginable, then shoved it through his leg at high speed. Shah tried to stay calm. The harder he breathed, the more he moved, the faster the wound would bleed. But his eyelids flickered closed, and Shah knew he had to move, or lose consciousness. He dragged himself upright. The towel Aresh had given him was soaked crimson.

The door flew open; two uniformed policemen stood in the doorway, guns trained on Shah. The younger one was shaking badly.

Shah called out his ID number. "I'm alone," he added.

The patrolmen, both young and scared looking waved a paramedic into the room. They kept their guns trained on Shah while the medic examined him, though Shah doubted they could miss the paramedic if they shot at Shah. He mentally tutted the sloppiness of their training – it distracted him from the awful burning.

"It's a through and through." The medic cut away Shah's trouser leg and bandaged the wound. "No arteries or bones hit. I'll give you a shot to ease the pain before these guys take you down to the station."

"I'm not going," Shah said. "I've given you my number, check it"

"No sir," the nearest cop said. "I have to take you in as a witness."

"I'll vouch for him," a glassy-eyed Bailey said from the doorway. She wiped her nose and asked Shah, "What *have* you been doing?"

Shah started laughing; he couldn't help it. When the laughter ratcheted toward hysteria, the paramedic gripped the skin on Shah's forearm. "Yow!" Shah yelped.

"Don't want you getting hysterical," the paramedic said.

Shah tried to lever himself up right. "I need adrenaline."

The medic shook his head. "No way."

"I *need* adrenaline," Shah said.

"In your current state it might kill you."

"I'll risk it."

"It's not your decision–"

"It absolutely *is* my decision, sonny. The last time I looked it was my body. Gimme the friggin' shot."

"If you insist," the medic said. "Remember, I warned you."

Bailey said from the doorway, where she still leaned, arms folded. "I've recorded it as well. Do it."

The medic grunted acknowledgement and fiddled with a hypo. "This is a combination stimulant and painkiller. You'll feel fine for several hours, then crash and burn. The danger is you'll feel so fine you may do something stupid, and fall flat on your face or do yourself big damage. Maybe both."

Shah looked away from the injection. After a few seconds he started to feel marginally better. He took several deep breaths, then pushed himself up the side of the bed. Sitting on the edge, he looked down, first at his remaining trouser leg, then at the bare wounded leg wrapped in bandages. He grinned at Bailey. "Don't I look a sight?"

Bailey didn't answer Shah but said to the uniforms, "You guys can go now. We have your testimony. We're going after the guy who did this."

The older cop said, "Night, officers."

"Night," Shah said, and looking at Bailey, took the hypo. He signaled the medic to refill it. Sighing, the medic looked at Bailey, back at Shah, then refilled the hypo.

Bailey said to the medic, "D'you have any kind of prosthesis that'll take the weight off my wilful partner's leg?"

"I've got a brace down in the ambulance," the medic said. "If he don't kill hisself by pumping up, it might just help. Get it for you now."

"Thanks."

When the medic had gone Shah said to Bailey, "How'd you get here?"

"Drove," Bailey said. "My partner has a runabout. It's parked illegally downstairs. Better hope I don't get towed away."

"Not at this time of night." Shah staggered past Bailey. His legs were unsteady, but by leaning against the wall, he could still move crabwise surprisingly quickly.

As Bailey was learning. "Where are you going?" she called down the corridor.

Shah half-turned, the effort nearly sending him toppling over. "Your car got a portable memory copier?" They were standard for most cops in case they needed testimony from eyepiece-less witnesses. Such Luddites were as rare as unicorn shit, so they mostly gathered dust in corners.

"In the trunk," Bailey said. Why d'you want it?"

"Witness statement," Shah said, baring his teeth in what he hoped was a grin. Judging by the anxious look on Bailey's face, it was unconvincing.

"I'll get it," Bailey said.

"Meet you downstairs."

Bailey said, "Take the elevator. I'll take the stairs."

Bailey was waiting for Shah in the lobby when the wheezing elevator disgorged him. The medic was waiting too, and fitted the brace to Shah's leg, clicking the circular clamp around his thigh, and a second, smaller one connected by a length of flexible plastic to his ankle. "I'm going to spray this." He ran the spray up the length of the plastic connector. The moment it made contact, the plastic hardened until Shah's leg was fully supported.

"Thanks," Shah said.

"De nada."

When the medic had gone, Bailey handed Shah the scanner.

"Thanks," Shah said. "And for coming out, as well."

Bailey smiled. "De nada, as well."

Shah approached the check-in desk. Shirani looked up, and seeing Shah his eyes widened and his dark skin paled. Shah fancied he could hear the sound of Shirani swallowing. "Shirani – that's a Persian name. From Shiraz."

"Iranian," Shirani said. "So I'm told."

There was something naggingly familiar about Shirani. "Told?" Shah said. "Where you from, then?"

Shirani shook his head. "No idea."

"Green card." Shah snapped his fingers. Moments later his 'piece chimed with the requested data. Shah took a breath. "This isn't right – the validation codes are wrong."

Shirani paled still further.

"What d'you mean, you dunno where you're from?" Shah repeated.

Shirani licked his lips. "I have very few memories before America. People talking in a language I don't understand, a woman's face…"

"Soudabeh?" Shah recited the few words of Farsi he could scrape up.

Shirani's eyes widened.

Shah gripped the other man's arm. "Tell me where they've gone, my friend. I will get your memories of Soudabeh back."

"What if I don't want them back?" Shirani said. "I must have lost them for a reason."

Shah urged, "Tell me where the men have gone, and we will get them back."

Shirani shook his head. "Dunno."

Shah slid through the gap at the end of the desk.

"I call the police!" Shirani screeched.

"I *am* the police." Shah kept his voice low. "I'm arresting you for attempted murder of a police officer, conspiracy to kidnap and not washing enough. Bailey, finish his rights while I scan this little shit."

"Wanna lawyer!" Shirani gabbled.

"After we've talked," Shah said, slamming Shirani down into a chair. Bailey droned on, ostentatiously looking away. Shah fitted the scanner over Shirani's head. The night manager tried to wriggle, but the clamps were locked tight.

"You can't do this," Shirani said. "I not want share my memories, you can't have 'em."

"Partly true," Shah said. "An ordinary memory retrieval probe can't access memories without your co-operation." He laughed as nastily as he could. "But this is adapted; the safetys are off. So basically it'll rip out your memories if you fight it." Shah hoped Shirani wouldn't realize Shah was bluffing. Shah silently flipped switches, choosing the hippocampus from among the list of pre-set location codes, taking his time over each one to drag it out.

"OK," Shirani said. "I tell you—"

"No, you share with me," Shah said. "That way I know what's truth, and what isn't, like in the old days."

"Like Guantanamo?" The name had passed into Middle Eastern legend, and grown with each generation.

Shirani looked petrified, so Shah took a moment he didn't have to explain, holding up the scanner, "That's what this was designed for, to replace Guantanamo. To read a man's mind, or at least his memories."

Shirani looked panic-stricken, then relaxed as Shah burned the other man's memories:

You watch as the gang half-drag, half-carry the lolling girl past. You duck back into the alcove. Kotian's voice carries; "Don't get any speeding tickets on the way to the boat."

He adds, "Where's Shirani?" Your heart stops for a second and you swallow the boulder that's suddenly appeared in your throat. *He might not want to leave witnesses.*

"Probably in the john. Seems to spend most of his time there."

"OK," Kotian says. "He won't be a problem – the guy don't trust police any more than us. But I'll mail him some extra money tomorrow though, just to make sure he keeps his mouth shut."

Doors slam and very slowly, just to be extra sure – because talk of money could be a ploy to lure you into the open where a silenced Beretta awaits you – you emerge from the alcove to check stairs and corridors.

Kotian's men have been gone only minutes when two uniformed policemen run through the door, closely followed by a paramedic.

Shah removed the scanner. "Kotian has a boat," he told Bailey. "It'll be registered to one of his companies, if I know our tax-savvy friend."

"I'll check the State Register of Businesses," Bailey said. "There'll be a list of assets."

Shah sat with the handcuffed Shirani while they waited for backup and while Bailey hunted the boat through the databases. After several minutes of issuing search instructions to her eyepiece in a low voice, waiting, sighing, and issuing further instructions, she looked up. "It's called *The Lion of Bangalore*. Parks and Recreation are checking the mooring registers."

"Did anyone actually think to check whether he had a boat before?" Shah said. "It may be where he's been hiding."

"I don't know," Bailey said.

The doors opened on two more uniforms, coming to take Shirani down to the station. "Let's wait in my car," Bailey said. She stilled, and listening to her eyepiece caught Shah's eye and nodded. "West 79th Boat Street Basin," she said.

Shah pushed himself upright. "Let's go. Unless you want to stay here?"

"Don't be stupid," Bailey said.

"You've developed a smart mouth over the last week or two."

Bailey blushed. "Sorry. But how are you going to get there if I don't drive you? I assume that you want to be there?"

"Let's go, then," Shah said.

Bailey was already calling in the boat's location and requesting a SWAT team.

# LXX

The wind outside had strengthened while Shah was inside. He staggered in one ferocious gust. Bailey shouted, "Lean on me."

It took them almost five minutes to walk the block to where Bailey's tiny Japanese Urban LPG was parked sideways between two occupied bays. "Nice parking," Shah said.

Bailey grinned. "Amazing where you can put one of these. I reckon I could park it inside an envelope." She propped him against a meter. "Wait here while I back it out." Bailey squeezed into the wider gap on the driver's side. Even though she was pole-thin she still only just managed to get in – luckily the door scrolled upwards into the roof for just this purpose. There was barely an inch spare on the passenger's side, but she still managed to back the car out without scraping it, and had the door open by the time Shah hobbled across to it.

"You should change your pants." Bailey indicated Shah's goose-fleshed bare leg.

"No time," Shah said. "Come on, let's go."

Bailey set off.

At the second turning Shah said, "You should've turned right." To their right the old Madison Square Gardens rose through the night, lit up by the spotlights in lasting memory of the four thousand killed by a bomb. *Before Bailey was born,* Shah reflected.

"To get to West 79th Street," Bailey said, "But we're going to the precinct. Van Doorn wants you."

"Why?" Shah turned to stare at Bailey. She kept her gaze ahead, when checking the dash to ensure she wasn't speeding. Shah said, "Do you have a spare eyepiece?"

Bailey chin-cocked the glove compartment, "In there's a prepaid."

Shah fumbled it out, activated it. While she was distracted, Shah's right hand plucked Bailey's gun from its holster. Bailey stamped on the brake and lunged for the gun, but Shah juggled it and pointed it at her. Shah said, "Lesson Primero, Newbie. Never leave your gun unsecured and on the passenger's side."

"Don't be stupid, Pete," Bailey said.

"What are you?" Shah said. "IA? Another of Kotian's moles?" He knew, deep down inside how unlikely that was – *she hasn't been around long enough to bribe, but still…*

"I'm your partner!"

"And you just happened to pitch up tonight?"

Bailey nodded. "I was in the area when Shirani called 911. I was worried about you, anyway so when it came in, I responded. But I called van Doorn while I was waiting for you to come down. He's concerned about your mental state, and the implications on an arrest."

Shah chuckled mirthlessly. "*That* I can believe."

"One of the other precincts found a hit on the web, Perveza getting picked up. And… No, van Doorn can tell you."

"Tell me what?" Shah waved the gun at her. "Sara?"

"Perveza…"

"What about her?"

"There were signs of multiple sexual encounters."

"Stop being so soft-mouthed. You mean she was raped?"

Bailey pulled a face. "Could have been rape, or just rough sex. Her brain showed the bruising you taught me was a sign of a rip. Van Doorn's not convinced it was an accident."

"Suicide?" Shah said.

"Maybe even murder. We may never know."

"I'll mourn her later," Shah said. *You should feel it more*, an inner voice said. *You callous S.O.B.*

Bailey said, "But van Doorn's right. Your presence compromises any case against Kotian. So he told me to take you in."

Shah shook his head. "Isn't going to happen. Drive."

"But–"

Shah clicked the safety off. "While we sit here arguing, Kotian could be liquidizing Aurora's brain. I'll worry 'bout the case after we've sprung her." He added, "You don't want to get in my way. You don't know what he's going to do to her. Killing her would be a mercy."

Bailey switched off her piece, motioned for Shah to do the same. "Put the gun away and I'll drive. But not at gunpoint."

Shah thought: "I keep the gun, but I'll put it away. Don't try to take it back. Deal?"

"Deal." Bailey restarted the engine, and they switched their pieces back on.

Shah called Aurora's number. It diverted straight to her mailbox. "Aurora, honey," Shah said. "I just want you to know that whatever happens tonight, I love you – at least you'll have this." He paused, sighed, then made up his mind: "I don't know if I can give this job up for good, but I *can* take a sabbatical. We'll work something out."

Shah called Leslyn, and again got her mailbox. "It's Shah. I just wanted to say thanks for everything, and Godspeed." To Bailey's questioning look he said, "Most people going to be asleep this time of night."

"Last will and testament?" Bailey said. She grinned, but couldn't hide her worry.

"Don't go thinking I'm suicidal," Shah said. "I learned a long time ago it helps not to have loose ends before you go into an op. You can always time-delay the transmission. That way you can wipe it if you do survive, and no one's embarrassed.

Bailey swallowed. "I don't have one of them, either."

Shah smiled grimly. "Then you might want to. Since your eyepiece is fully functional, I suggest you sort out a will for this partner of yours."

"Her name's Cynthia," Bailey said. "We're…" Shah waited. She said, "I'm seeing someone else. It's complicated."

"How complicated can it be?"

Bailey opened her mouth. Finally said, "van Doorn. He asked me out. Several times before I said yes. We've been, um, seeing each other for almost a week. We never talk about work. We barely talk at all, for that matter."

Shah laughed. "Well, I'm damned. You dark horses."

Bailey slowed the car. "We're here." She stiffened, held up her hand. "Repeat that – oh." She turned to Shah. "They found Professor Tosada at his apartment – dead. He was your friend, wasn't he? I'm sorry."

"He's taking everyone that's important to me, or was important," Shah said. "I'd better call Rex."

Bailey looked stricken.

Shah said, "Kotian's done him as well, hasn't he?" He took out Bailey's gun, checked that it was loaded.

"Pete, don't do it," Bailey said.

Shah said, "I'm only checking it, Sara." His eyes belied his reasonable tone. "If I have to defend myself, making sure beforehand that it works seems a sensible precaution. And that's another reason that you should stay here. One gun between two of us would be suicide."

"In which case I should go, Pete. You're unfit for duty."

"Turn your eyepiece off," Shah murmured in Bailey's ear.

When she had, Shah took a breath. "If I can take Kotian alive, I will, but let's not kid ourselves, Sara. Kotian has killed over and over again. Chances are his lawyer will get his sentence reduced to a few years, or – adding insult to injury – place him in the same witness protection as Aurora. If the bastard's prepared to testify where other ganglords have buried the bodies, so to speak."

"You think you should dispense justice, Pete?" Bailey said. She was so close Shah could smell mint on her breath.

"If he comes quietly, so be it," Shah said. "But somehow, I suspect he won't."

"What happens then?"

"We'll see." Shah leaned across and kissed her cheek as the car rocked in a gust of wind. "Good luck with van Doorn; or your current partner. Or both."

"Thank you," Bailey said.

Opening the door, Shah stepped into a howling wall of wind and rain.

# LXXI

The wind drove the rain horizontally so it slammed into Shah with the force of wet shrapnel, stinging his skin, and sending tiny electrical shivers of pain radiating out from his gunshot wound, despite the painkilling injection. He wasn't surprised to hear the slam of Bailey's door – he'd never expected her to wait for him.

Lightning flashed, illuminating a cityscape superficially unchanged since the turn of the century. In the lightning's flash, he saw the Hudson's waters almost boiling in the storm surge. Beyond the tidal barrage running across to the Jersey shore from the near side of the Staten Island Ferry Terminal – near Manhattan's southern tip – the sea churned in vast waves dwarfing those in the harbor.

Shah had glimpsed something in the lightning's glare. He set the piece to maximum zoom, and waited. When the second flash came, he was ready. This one was much closer and much brighter, and in its light Shah saw water running down the fifty-meter high harbor-side wall in streams, where the sea beyond threatened to overwhelm the barrage.

As the lightning faded, with it went most of the remaining lights.

"Damn!" Bailey shouted.

"What's the matter?"

"Lightning strike. It's obviously hit a mast somewhere and taken out the network, 'cause my piece is offline."

"Mine too," Shah said. "Like an EM pulse."

"A what?"

"Electromagnetic pulse, like – oh, never mind! Get back in the car."

"Don't be stupid!" Bailey yelled. "You can barely stand!" She staggered around the car. "Lean on me!"

When Shah did, she almost buckled beneath his weight. "You sure?" He yelled. His back was soaked through to the skin, as if someone had turned a high pressure hose on him.

*What am I doing here,* he thought. *There are people you could leave this to, Shah.* The answer of course, was simple. He loved Aurora, even if he could never be with her again. Shah had lost his little faith with his memories and hadn't regained it when he got them back. But now, however hypocritical it was, he would use any advantage to keep her alive, however improbable. *In the name of Allah the Merciful and the Compassionate,* he prayed, *in Your wisdom keep her safe.*

Bailey straightened. "Better you lean on me than really wreck your leg." She added, "Reckon he'll take the boat out, even in this?"

"Maybe," Shah said, straightening to relieve her of a little of his weight.

"Is he crazy?"

"Or desperate."

"How's he going to convince them to open the locks?"

"Dunno," Shah said. "Maybe he's got a man in the Harbormaster's office. Or he's got a way to activate the locks remotely. Nothing surprises me about this bastard."

As they neared the three meter-high chain-link fence around the marina, Shah's eyes gradually grew accustomed to the gloom. A few lamps still cast a patchwork of lights among the darkness, and Shah heard the chugging of a diesel. He guessed that that was how they had stayed on when newer, more vulnerable systems had been knocked offline.

A uniform loomed out of the shadows. "Sorry, sir, ma'am," he said. "No entry to–"

"We're the team pursuing them," Shah interrupted. He had a hunch; if both his and Bailey's pieces were offline, so might be the rest of the network. He squeezed Bailey's shoulder to tell her to keep quiet and waved his badge. "My eyepiece was smashed back at the Caspian Street Hotel."

The uniformed tapped his piece. "Hello? HQ? Nikolides calling."

"Are you picking up the transponder in my piece?" Bailey said.

"Yes, Ma'am," Nikolides said.

"Then you'll have the archived data saying where we called in from," Shah said. "I'm Shah," he added, in case his guess was correct. The instructions would have had his name attached as the wounded officer.

Nikolides nodded, and Shah breathed again. "We can probably rustle you up a change of clothes, if you want. We got enough spare pairs in the wagon," Nikolides said, signaling his colleague to let them through the gate.

"Thanks," Bailey said.

The marina was quiet, with the few lights coming from the boats bobbing on the water. Two ten meter trucks were parked just inside the empty perimeter. Shah and Bailey ducked into the nearest one, which had seats all down one side, and was filled with equipment but empty of people. *Probably still on their way here*, Shah thought. Among the dozens of pairs of clothes, they found some that fitted, along with heavy-duty waterproof jackets. Shah took his into a cubicle to change alone.

His leg could take his weight without giving way now he was out of the wind, though he dared not think what he was doing to the injury. Some blood had started to ooze and stain the dressing, which was soaked – whether from blood or rain was hard to tell.

Bailey had coffee waiting for him. "It'll probably be too sweet for you." She handed him a player. "Here," she said. "I archived the rips, plural – he got to Rex as well. I'm sorry."

Shah didn't answer, but sipped the coffee and gagged. "How many calories in this?"

"About eight spoonfuls," she said with a grin. "You need the energy. I bet you normally take it unsweetened." At his nod, she urged, "Drink."

Shah shrugged and did as he was told. He watched the first rip:

It's been a quiet evening, like every evening is lately. Johns are an endangered species this far from Manhattan. Maybe you'll have to admit defeat–

When it was done, Shah stared into space. "Are the others on record?"

"Some are," Bailey said. "We'll get them."

Shah didn't answer, instead watched the second:

• • • •

Beside you, Angelica lies on her back, mouth open, snoring gently.

As was the case with Perveza, he only abstractly felt Rex's terror. *Perhaps if I had been able to reach them, I might have felt more.* He wondered when Old Shah had lost his son so completely that Rex hadn't wanted anything to do with new Shah.

Shah swallowed, undocked the player. "What happened to them?"

Bailey licked her lips.

"Don't piss around!"

"Kotian had them ripped," Bailey said. "They're not quite as bad as Marietetski was. Not quite. They can still walk and have basic functions. But the people you knew are gone, Pete. I'm sorry."

Shah bowed his head for a moment in silent respect and emitted a juddering sigh. *Five lives wasted. How many more, Kotian?* Then he lifted his head. "Which one's *The Lion of Bangalore*?" He took a pair of binocs from a shelf that ran almost the length of the cluttered truck and surveyed the ranks of boats.

"Third from the end. See it?" Bailey too had grabbed a pair of binocs. She stared at him, unasked questions in her eyes.

"The thing that's the size of an ocean liner?"

Bailey said, "Never seen an ocean liner, but I suspect you're exaggerating."

Nikolides came into the truck. "Coffee?" he said hopefully.

Bailey poured some for him.

"What we waiting for?" Shah said, tapping his foot.

Nikolides gazed at him. "It's a little wet out there," he said in a too-patient voice. "We're waiting for the

Command Team. Before comms went down, things got pretty busy out there. They might be delayed."

Shah and Bailey exchanged glances. "Back at the hotel, Kotian talked about tying up loose ends," Shah said. "Sounds like this might be a few of them."

"Might just be coincidence," Bailey said.

"No," Shah said. "This is all prearranged. He knew we'd be watching ports. He had the boat registered under a shell company. He's known what he was doing all along."

"Where are you going?" Bailey said.

Shah turned to the uniformed officer. "Nikolides, isn't it?"

"Yessir. We met before, but I guess you've forgotten."

"I've forgotten a lot of things, my friend."

"Yeah, I heard that, sir."

"What time's high tide?"

Nikolides checked. "Three am, sir."

"Call me Pete." Shah looked at the wall clock. "Just under two hours. He's going to make a move soon, I reckon, sail on high tide."

"How's he going to get out? Those locks are controlled from the Port Authority's office."

"You spoken to them lately?"

Nikolides shook his head.

"Are the observation teams in place?"

Nikolides looked offended, as if Shah had questioned his professionalism. "The area's sealed off, but comms are down, so we have to use runners. It stretches us still thinner."

Shah nodded. "So you've no real idea what's happening on the boat right now?"

Nikolides said, "My orders were to secure the area and observe the boat. We'll only know if something changes. But as far as I can tell, no one's been on or off in the ninety minutes I been here."

"But there are people on board?"

"Oh, yeah," Nikolides said. "Thermal imaging's a struggle, 'cause they got countermeasures on board, but we counted at least four different heat-signatures."

"Then let's update the situation." Shah pulled up his collar as far as it would go.

"Where you going?" Bailey said.

"To take a look." Shah patted the pocket to which he'd transferred the gun. "Come with me." Nikolides followed them outside. "I need you to vouch for me to any trigger-happy guys you got on duty," Shah told him, "while Bailey keeps trying to raise HQ."

Bailey looked mutinous, then shrugged. "I'll walk with you part of the way."

"Sure."

They battled through the howling wind toward the moored boat, past the club house from which the police watched the boats. A couple of watchers hugged the shadows, but their challenge melted away at Nikolides' authority. They had reached the water's edge when Nikolides paused. "Here's the observation team," Nikolides said. "Any change, guys?" he shouted into the wind.

"Nothing," one of the others called back.

Nikolides said to Shah and Bailey, "I'm going to see if they have a landline up in the club house. Find out what's holding up reinforcements."

When Nikolides had gone, Shah told Bailey, "Wait here." Bailey looked ready to argue so Shah said, "Just do as I ask for once, dammit!"

Shah left her and walked past the boats to the very end, and the last boat. He hoped fervently that anyone watching from the boat would think that he was just a passing nightwatchman, though he doubted it.

Staggering with the effort, he climbed onto the end boat. Each boat was separated only by a padded bolster, to stop them knocking against one another. By taking things very, very slowly, Shah was able to step across, though he still nearly ended up in the water.

It took Shah nearly five minutes before he was able to climb over again, onto *The Lion of Bangalore*. As he was getting his breath back, an explosion at the other end of the marina split the night sky. At the same moment, the boat's engines rumbled into life.

# LXXII

Shah felt a thud behind him and wheeled, gun in hand. "Sara?"

Bailey's teeth chattered, but she managed to stammer, "Think I'm going to miss all the fun?" She stiffened as a patch of light appeared, and they dropped to the deck.

The light came from an opened cabin door. Kotian's bellow pierced even the gale, "Shut that door, fool!"

"I thought you had ropes–"

"You *thought*, crap-head! I turned off the power to the vacuum pads to float free. No need to untie ropes!" The door slammed shut.

"Not a regular deck hand, I'm guessing, or he'd have known that." Shah added, as the boat inched away from the quay. "Notice anything?"

Bailey looked mystified for a moment, then: "We're pointed the opposite way from all the other boats?"

"Yep. He planned for the getaway. Pointing out, he don't need to turn it round, which is hard with a monster like this; it's got to be two hundred feet long at least."

Bailey said. "What's the plan?"

"First thing's find out who's aboard."

"They've tried. Nikolides said they fired tunneling spy-eyes and audio pickups onto the boat, but nothing's getting through. They must be jamming the signals."

Shah nodded. "There's still the old-fashioned way." As the boat emerged from the shelter provided by the other boats, spray from the sloshing water added to the constant driving rain. Shah crawled to a porthole – that way he didn't have to put all his weight on the wound – across a deck that pitched and rolled more by the second.

Shah peered around the edge. "Where's Kotian? He's not there."

"He's on the bridge!" Bailey yelled back. Seeing his eyes widen she added, "Don't worry. It's enclosed, so there's no chance he can hear us from there!"

The engines deepened from an idling purr to a growl, and the boat accelerated. In any other circumstances Shah would have admired *The Lion of Bangalore* – she was big and lean and muscular, entirely fitting her name.

Shah braced himself against the wall and peered through the porthole again. "One goon covering Aurora – Holy Shit!"

"What?"

"Oh, does he just have a mole!" Shah lurched back to where Bailey had nested in a large alcove. From the hooks and ropes Shah guessed it was a berth for a small inflatable, but at the moment it was empty. He fell into it, almost landing on Bailey.

"You OK?" Bailey said.

"Leg's starting to hurt." Shah told Bailey what he'd seen.

"Hampson?" She said. The desk officer?"

"Took me a moment to place him," Shah said. "Never seen him out of uniform before." Hampson was notoriously reclusive. Now Shah knew why. "Too busy mixing with ganglords to bother with us."

"I thought they'd checked everyone's bank accounts when the mole allegations first surfaced," Bailey said. "How come no big money ever showed in his?"

"Dunno." Shah felt exhausted, and as the boat picked up speed he held onto Bailey – or she held him, it was hard to tell which – and fell into an uneasy doze, made fitful by the pounding and crashing of the deck.

Kotian heard footsteps clomping up the ladder to the bridge. "Take the wheel," He told da Silva.

Hampson's face was white and pinched. "I'm still having problems raising the Port Authority. Without access to their system, I can't override the protocols to open the locks remotely, and we're sitting ducks."

"Then we go to Plan B." Kotian was careful to keep his emotions in check. *Don't let the hired help know how twitchy you are.* "And we'll blow the wall."

Hampson's stare showed the man had only just realized just how determined Kotian was. "But that'll sweep through the city! You'll kill millions–"

"Then it'll be millions less to suck the planet dry," Kotian said. "And your wife won't be among them. Danielle is safe on high ground."

Hampson nodded, relaxing slightly.

Kotian wanted to laugh aloud. Hampson had learned the hard way that having a wife with expensive tastes wasn't good. Bribery could so easily lead to blackmail.

Da Silva took the boat up from the harbor limit of ten knots, past twenty. *The Lion* was good for sixty knots, but not into a gale-force headwind. It took another ten minutes for them to reach the point at which – if they didn't get the signal from the Port Authority to enter the lock – Hampson would blow the wall. Kotian frowned. If they did get the signal, how would he know that it wasn't a trap?

The question became moot when Hampson clambered up again. "The gates are locked down," he said. "Safety protocols, the Authority says."

"Blow the wall then!" Kotian snarled. "Where's the detonator?"

Hampson showed him the box in his hand. He shook his head. "No–"

Kotian shot him.

"So much for no cop-killing." Da Silva hadn't moved from the wheel.

"Circumstances change," Kotian said. "And his wife's dead anyway, so maybe it was for the best." He pressed the detonator.

Nothing happened.

He cursed, pressed again.

Nothing.

"Shit!" He hurled the detonator against the wall.

"Boats coming from the Joisey side," Da Silva said. "I'm gedding hailed."

"Balls!" Kotian roared.


"We're turning!" Shah shouted.

The engines thundered, and no longer fighting a headwind, the boat sprang forward. Only lying in the alcove saved Shah and Bailey from being flipped overboard. If Shah had thought the ride wild before, this was a whole new level of insanity: the boat surged across the harbor, driven on by the storm behind. It bounced and skipped from wave to churning wave.

With each impact the deck slammed into their backs, driving the air from their lungs. Shah guessed their speed must be almost sixty miles an hour.

The next landing almost catapulted Shah over the edge – only his grabbing the ship's rail and hanging on for dear life saved him. He edged back into the alcove. He yelled, "How long since we turned, d'you reckon?"

"Four minutes," Bailey yelled back. "Network coverage is back on!"

"Can you get a signal?"

"Nothing clear! Calls to emergency services are coming up with 'all lines are busy!' But I've got time and auto-location – he's headed back to Manhattan!"

Shah levered himself upright. "He's not only headed for it, he's headed *at* it! Jeez, he's going to ram the ground!"

"Brace!" Bailey screamed, grabbing one of the clamps on the wall.

A hideous roaring screech like the death-cries of a dinosaur filled the air as *The Lion* grounded, almost deafening them and tearing the keel clean off the boat. The shaking was so violent Shah nearly let go. Their momentum kept them hurtling across the low-lying ground, mud and an occasional spark from metal on a rock fountaining into an arc behind.

Then they slowed to a stop and but for the ringing in Shah's ears, the world was silent.

Shah levered himself upright. He headed aft, to where Kotian had to emerge. Shah was on the port side; there was a fifty-fifty chance that Kotian would walk right into them.

Kotian didn't. He emerged onto the flat aft section before Shah could reach it, dragging a clearly still-groggy Aurora, followed by two large men.

*No Hampson*, Shah thought. *What happened to him?*

The group moved so slowly, even Shah could catch them. He thrust Bailey's gun into the base of the last man's spine. The man stiffened. "Keep *very* still," Shah said into his ear, took the man's gun, and passed it to Bailey.

And their luck ran out.

Kotian looked back and saw them. He fired but luckily the shot went wide. In one movement Kotian grabbed Aurora, spinning her around to make a shield and backed away. Meanwhile the first goon drew his gun, so Shah fired and dropped him, prompting the second to lift his hands into the air. By the time he had refocused on Kotian, Shah's quarry had gone.

Bailey scuttled away to the bow of the grounded *Lion*.

Using Kotian's man as a shield, Shah edged around to where Kotian had gone.

Kotian had already dropped to the ground off the broken boat, still holding Aurora as a shield. He yelled, "Keep back!"

"Move!" Shah prodded Kotian's man, and they followed, slowly.

"I *said*, keep back!" Kotian fired into the air.

"I'm not Shah," Bailey shouted back. "She doesn't mean anything to me, except that she's a hostage that you're going to release. And we're keeping your man in between–" Shah heard two shots, and the man in front of him slumped.

Bailey screamed, "There was no need for that!"

"He was expendable!" Kotian released his choke-hold on Aurora, grabbed her hand and ran, dragging her along in his wake.

Bailey jumped off the boat and ran after them.

• • • •

"If you want to live, you won't drag too much, my dear!" Kotian panted.

Except for the last few days when he'd been holed up in various tenements Kotian trained every day but already running into the wind was taking its toll. It was harder than running up a steep hill, and his legs felt leaden and his lungs couldn't draw breath far enough in to prevent light-headedness. But he needed to speak; "Shah thinks you're my accomplice – he isn't coming to rescue you, just take you in with me."

Aurora's long strides matched his, and since she was more than twenty years younger, she didn't look as if she was finding it as hard as him. But she didn't waste breath answering.

"Stop!" A woman cried behind them, and Kotian heard the crack of a gunshot.

Bailey might have been firing into the air, but Kotian couldn't be sure. He turned, took aim, and fired. Bailey dropped as if coshed.

"Gotcha!" *Not want to kill a cop? Why ever not? It's wonderful!*

He dragged Aurora off again, the exaltation giving him a little more speed, another minute's endurance. Then Kotian saw lights and barriers ahead, and as he reached the *FDR Levee* circling Manhattan's southern tip, turned at bay, hand still clamped over Aurora's wrist.

When he reached her prone body, Shah felt Bailey's neck, found a faint pulse. Praying her piece wasn't voice-locked, he said "One one two, ambulance and police home in on this signal. Officer down."

Then he stood, his wound radiating throbbing pulses of agony. He jabbed the syringe with the second stimulant cocktail into his leg, and started walking again – even with the drugs, he couldn't manage to run.

Incredibly, they were waiting for him, twenty yards beyond the beginning of the levee, standing on the very wall, water from the breaking waves soaking them, Kotian with his arm around Aurora's throat, holding her as a shield again.

Shah shouted into the wind, hoping that his voice would carry, "There really isn't nowhere to go, Abhijit."

"Do you love her?" Kotian yelled back, gun jerking at Aurora's throat..

Shah pondered. *If I say yes, he'll kill her. What to do, what do I do?*

"No." Shah stepped forward, hoping he'd guessed right. "She means nothing to me. Just shoot the bitch."

# LXXIII

Van Doorn bit his lip, but managed not to urge the driver to go faster. The rain was finally slackening, but was still heavy enough to make driving dangerous.

He was sure Kotian had planned his escape – holed up for several days until the weather played into his hands – to coincide with a near-miss from a hurricane. Any closer, and movement around New York would have been impossible, but a Class Four Hurricane sweeping across Maryland caused just enough chaos to give Kotian cover, without stopping him moving.

And Kotian *had* planned it, van Doorn was sure. New Yorkers knew how paper-thin the city's resources were, how badly they were stretched. They could barely cope with the storm, let alone dozens of robberies and homicides, to that last diversionary explosion in the marina while *The Lion of Bangalore* slipped away. Even the lightning strikes had briefly played into Kotian's hands by knocking out the communications networks.

But once Shah had found out that Kotian had a boat (and van Doorn really, really didn't want to think how Kotian's defense team would portray Shah's interrogating the hotel's night manager) it was only a matter of time before they got him. Still, the comms network had come back online just in time.

"There," the driver said, rousing van Doorn from his thoughts and swerving close to the body. Van Doorn jumped out and ran through the rain to where she lay.

He had almost reached the makeshift command center at the 79th Street Boat Basin's Marina when the call had come through. He had prayed ever since then that it wasn't another diversion, but equally that it wasn't Sara. The heat-tracking camera's footage of the boat grounding implied an answer to the first possibility–

"Don't move her!" An arriving paramedic shouted, as van Doorn lifted a lank strand of hair to see the face. The medic barged him out of the way and went to work. "It's a gunshot wound to the upper abdomen," she shouted to her colleague. "Get her onto a stretcher and into the ambulance."

"Still a pulse?" Van Doorn yelled back as the paramedics gently shifted the woman onto it and into the ambulance. He didn't know whether to laugh or cry when he saw that it was Sara Bailey. He'd hoped, however ludicrous it was that someone else had taken her eyepiece. That rush of emotion told him how hard he'd fallen for the young woman.

"Still a pulse," the paramedic said. "But it's faint and irregular. She's lost blood, and we won't know whether it's hit a vital organ. We can work on her now."

He was dismissed, van Doorn realized.

Suddenly adrift, then refocusing on the job, he returned to looking for Kotian and Shah, who wouldn't be far away. *They might as well be joined at the hip*, van Doorn thought. If he were honest, that suited him. He could have pulled Shah in, but the man was van Doorn's best chance of nailing Kotian, although he'd never admit it publicly. Van Doorn wondered whether the visibility was good enough for SWAT snipers to be able to tell them apart, if they did a line on them. Assuming they hadn't lost them again.

*There.*

Van Doorn used the zoom facility on his eyepiece. It wasn't very good, but good enough to show two – no, three – figures on the levee wall.

It's like watching a snail-race, Aurora thought.

Kotian had backed away, slowly. The levee was almost eight feet thick in parts to keep the rising waters at bay, but even so the footing was treacherous, especially with the storm lashing the harbor, and flood water spilling over the wall and pooling on the road. So Kotian had to keep looking down, which slowed him up.

Had Shah been fully fit, he could probably have overhauled Kotian in seconds. But even with the curtain of rain reducing visibility to fifty meters or less, it was obvious from the way Shah's leg dragged and he regularly stumbled – once nearly falling into the water – that he was hurt. And had Shah been overhauled by Kotian, her captor would probably have shot him.

Aurora barely wanted to live since she had heard Shah urge Kotian to shoot her. That Kotian hadn't was little consolation. She wanted to live just enough to stop her from trying anything foolish, so instead she let the man she once thought she might learn to love drag her away from the man she *had* learned to love, and waited her time.

The gap was narrowing – down to five meters now. Kotian yelled, "Stay back, dammit!"

Still that bloody remorseless man kept coming. Beyond him, Kotian saw the flashing lights indicating reinforcements, and that the NYPD were busy setting up roadblocks.

Kotian felt like an animal in a trap. There was no way out. But he was torn between shooting Aurora, shooting Shah, or killing himself. For sure, there was no way that they were going to take him alive and scoop *his* brains out.

Now they were barely three meters apart, and still Shah tottered like some low-budget cyborg whose batteries were running down. Toward Kotian, slowly, purposefully.

Finally Kotian crumbled. He shouted "Final warning, Shah!"

Still the bastard kept coming. "Stop, dammit!" Kotian screamed into the wind. *Maybe he can't even hear me.*

Shah staggered, nearly fell into the harbor. Kotian willed gravity to help, but of course it didn't. Nothing worked for him in the end. Even that phobia of water that Shah had admitted to, weeks before, hadn't helped.

"I'll shoot!" Kotian screamed, and then as Shah closed on them to the point where he couldn't miss, Kotian fired.

Even with the wind, the gun was so close to her ear that Aurora heard the click of Kotian slipping the safety off.

*I could be inside in the warm,* she thought, *living the life: champagne. Caviar. Sex.* If she had only turned down that innocuous request from Kotian to seduce a cop. It had seemed like fun.

She felt Kotian take aim, and as he squeezed the

trigger she jerked her shoulder up and bit his other hand, the one around her throat, as hard as she could.

Shah guessed that if Sunny hadn't ripped his memories the waves soaking through his boots would have stopped him in his tracks, reducing him to gibbering paralysis. If he wasn't so tired, and the pain from the gunshot wound didn't throb through his body in waves, he might have smiled at the irony of some good coming out of the attack.

Instead he walked on. Another step. And another.

He was so focused on just being able to reach Kotian that, although he saw his quarry taking aim, the message still didn't reach his feet.

The shot flying harmlessly into the air broke his trance. A microsecond later Kotian's yell had him lunging for them. Kotian's gun flew through the air and caught Shah a glancing blow on the side of the head that sent lights dancing across his vision. Then he held a sobbing Aurora in his arms.

Shah just had time to shout in her ear, "I lied to him. Of course I love you," and kissing her – briefly, tenderly – before lowering her off the wall to the ground.

Breaking into a Frankenstein-ish lope, Shah set off after Kotian again.

# LXXIV

Kotian should have been away and gone. But when Shah looked up, teeth gritted against the waves of pain that accompanied each step, he saw that Kotian had stopped, his head lowered like a bull ready to charge.

Shah looked around.

Barriers blocked the road ahead and the side streets, lights cascading across Battery Park, even bouncing off the Jersey shore on the far side of the sound. Lights were starting to come on there, even at Ranger Place. The hockey stadium had never looked so forlorn.

*Wonder if the SWAT teams're in place,* Shah thought. *Do they want Kotian alive?* Shah wondered whether he could keep going for just a few feet more.

Kotian turned, an animal at bay.

To buy the SWAT teams a few more seconds Shah shouted, "You killed my children!"

For a moment Shah was unsure whether Kotian had heard, so strong was the howling gale. Kotian shouted, "An eye for an eye."

"You admit it then?"

Kotian's laughter carried top notes of despair. "Why not? But I didn't kill the girl. Nor your grandchildren and their mother."

"You might as well have!" With each sentence, Shah stepped a pace closer.

"I did them a favor!" Kotian yelled. "They won't re-member what they saw. I regret that but it was necessary. You had to see what you caused, Shah."

Shah yelled, "You know what? You wasted your time!"

"What do you mean?"

"It was like watching something happening to strangers, or an old flat screen horror movie. Awful, yes, but not relevant to me."

"You're lying!" Kotian screamed.

"Don't you understand?" Shah yelled. "To be truly horrifying, I needed an emotional connection to the victims, but I don't have any. They're strangers to me, no matter how much I tried to connect with them. No one's ever survived an attack like the one I did. I amassed so many of my old memories again, but I couldn't get any emotional connection. There was no context to them. In stripping my memories down to bedrock, Sunny robbed you of your greatest weapon." He laughed scornfully. "*You* shouldn't feel bad – it was your useless son who fucked up, even from beyond the grave!"

"Nooooo!" Kotian screamed.

He ran at Shah, who reached for the gun that should have been in his pocket. His hand closed on emptiness, and he cursed.

Kotian's hands reached his face, fingers splayed to gouge his eyes.

Shah tried to bring his knee up into Kotian's groin, but it was his wounded leg and it didn't even connect before a scream erupted from somewhere deep inside him.

Then Kotian's hands moved to his throat. They grappled on the wall, waves breaking around their legs. The fight lasted barely a half-second before Shah's legs gave way. He felt the tug of the wash like a giant child's fingers, poking, grasping, tugging. Before he could grasp what was happening, they were sucked into the water, Kotian's hand still around Shah's windpipe.

Something thudded into Shah's back: a ladder. He grabbed it one-handed. Kotian's hands squeezed tighter, but couldn't get a purchase through Shah's coat-collar. Shah swung right-handed, his fist thudding into Kotian's temple.

Kotian released his grip on Shah's throat, but before Shah could react, Kotian's hands formed a lattice of fingers and thumbs pressing down on the top of Shah's head, his head butting the hand with which Shah held onto the ladder.

Shah was already soaked, frozen and exhausted before they'd fallen into the water and the sucking wash was draining his last reserves faster than a vampire. His fingers slipped from the ladder.

Kotian got on top, pushing down while Shah's own boots pulled him down.

The pressure eased, just for a second and with his last strength, Shah shrugged off Kotian and gasping, sucking the air into his lungs, grabbed for the ladder.

He felt a hand.

"Come on!" Aurora screamed into the wind.

Shah took it, and with free hand grabbed for Kotian's collar where he lay limp in the water. He looked up, at Aurora holding onto the ladder one-handed (*is that Kotian's gun in her hand against the ladder?*) while frantically scrabbling for greater purchase on his coat with her free hand.

"He's only stunned!" Aurora screamed. "I hit him with his gun! Just let him go!"

"NO!" Shah roared. "He. Is. MINE!"

Shah felt his grip weakening, and that giant child had him by the legs and was pulling him under. It was all too much, and Shah just wanted to let go... of everything.

He heard a chugging sound, and a bright light played along the levee wall.

"The River Police!" Aurora screamed, but it was too late.

Shah let go. The water closed over his head, and all the memories, of his mother, his father, meeting Leslyn, Perveza's birth, even his nights with Aurora, they all played through his mind, but it was too much effort; so much easier to look back through his life and treat it as a book that he'd finished, savoring the good passages.

Hands grabbed him from above and below, hauled and pushed him up into the air. He thudded onto something that he dimly realized was a boat, then flopped across its deck.

Someone rolled him over on his face, and hands on his back pumped the water out of him. They turned him over; someone else grabbed his nose and blew air into his mouth.

Eventually the indignation of the assault on his body was too much, and he writhed away. He stared into the barrel of a rifle. Beyond the gun, others were working on a body: Kotian.

"I'm a cop," Shah tried to croak, but when he reached for his badge, his pocket was empty. It didn't matter, he decided, and started to laugh at the symbolism.

"Relax guys," Stickel said. "He's one of ours."

Strong but cold arms wrapped around Shah. "Aurora," he croaked happily.

She kissed him.

He kissed her back and wrapped his arms around her.

# LXXV

## Three Months Later

Shah knew when Aurora was returning from the washroom. A guy three rows down hadn't taken his eyes off her all evening; his head swiveled as soon as she came down the steps from the washroom exit.

*I suppose I should feel jealous, or proprietorial, or something,* he thought. *But if she wants to run off with a zit-faced dweeb she will, whether I'm jealous or not.* Not being jealous needed less energy. Since the storm he'd needed every calorie.

The people along the row all stood to allow her to squeeze through. "Thanks." She repeating it – with variations – about every four seconds. She slumped into the seat. "Whew. That's better."

Shah gazed at her. Since the night of the storm she had dressed down more often as she gradually shed her *patrones*, divesting herself of her old life. When she did wear the chador and the full make-up as she did tonight, she took his breath away more than ever.

"Earth to Shah," she said, smiling at him. "Have I missed anything?"

Shah shook his head free of his thoughts like a dog ridding itself of water. "Not much," he said. "They've called a time-out. They're cleaning the ice."

Below them, fifteen thousand New Yorkers watched the opening match of the season – against Detroit. Horns blared, while someone further around the arena hammered out a beat on their drum. Those nearest the ice pounded in time to it on the Perspex, which Shah ruefully thought was probably the most expensive item in the Ranger Stadium, or the New MSG, to give it its official title. *Rarer than rocking horse shit, Perspex is,* a notable wise-ass had said of it when the new rink was built. *And whadda they do with it? Put it around a frickin' ice rink for the hockey-moops to play the bongos on.*

*It's saying something,* Shah thought, *when watching the crowd's more interesting than watching the game.*

"You promised me goals," Aurora whispered, as if reading his mind. "Blood, spills, goals; that's how you sold me this. I could be at home washing my hair, filling in my tax return, something equally exciting."

"You got blood and spills," Shah said. "Two out of three. And I'm told by the expert next to me," he pointed away from Aurora, "that zero-zero games are both statistically rare and," he paused, "*tactically fascinating.* Two defensive teams cancelling each other out."

"You sound unconvinced."

"I can't get as enthusiastic for hockey as Old Shah," he admitted. "Though I think even he woulda struggled to enjoy this."

"Shall we?" Aurora motioned with her head toward the exit.

"There's only," Shah looked at the clock, "forty-eight seconds left, plus any damage time the referees add."

"Which is?"

Shah waggled his hand. "A minute. Maybe two."

"Why don't they just go straight to extra time?" Aurora said. "Why damage time as well?"

Shah shrugged. "Someone said it comes from brownouts knocking the official clocks off-kilter, so they added a little on. Or that some official toured Europe, got the idea from some other sports. Thought a little unpredictability would spice things up."

Aurora pulled a face. "But they're going to play till they score, aren't they?"

"Depend on it."

"So we could still be here when my flight goes tomorrow morning."

"Told ya." Shah said mock-sympathetically. "Nine's too early to fly."

"And I," she leaned in, kissed him to shut him up, "told you that course registration starts at midday."

"Remind me" Shah said, "Why you couldn't study Trauma Counseling in New York?"

"Because." She kissed him again. "DCU has the best course in the country. I'll be back at weekends, like I said." They had talked about little else for a month. Aurora had admitted that she'd never expected to be admitted, when she'd applied before Kotian's death. She'd struggled to remember why DCU would be messaging her. "Long as you don't start working weekends again we'll be fine."

That had been their other major topic of conversation; Shah's future. His sick leave had run out two weeks before, and he was finally back at work. It was already draining him.

"That isn't going to happen," Shah said. "Actually, I've got a surprise for you as well." He pulled a paper from his pocket.

"What's that?" Aurora said.

"Hard copy of my flight ticket for tomorrow morning," Shah said. "You would not believe how many calories I had to spend to get it a last minute seat."

Delight shone from her face. "You're – coming with me?"

"Got news of my own yesterday morning." Shah kept his face straight with difficulty. He'd been keeping the secret for thirty six hours, and now the moment was here, he was terrified. *What if she's angry I didn't tell her before? What if she don't want me around all the time? Maybe three months of being together almost twenty-four seven is enough?*

"I got a new job." He stressed each syllable almost spelling it out: "The Federal Amnesia Support Unit." He grinned. "In Washington. A nine-to-five job. They figure I'm... uniquely qualified... to understand their issues. And stuff."

Aurora shrieked and flung her arms around him.

"Hey, lady, keep it down!" Someone called. "They're coming back onto the ice!"

"You're not angry?" Shah whispered.

"Why would I be?" Aurora drew back and gazed at him, eyes bright. "I'm proud of you."

Shah half-laughed; "I may even be assigned to Kotian. He's changed his plea to guilty, so he'll escape the death penalty. He'll get legally ripped instead, and therapy to cope with it."

She nodded at the exit. "Come on. Let's go celebrate."

They stood as the teams faced off, ignoring the mutterings of those they squeezed past on the way out.

They climbed the steps as the crowd counted down the clock: "Three! Two! One! Damage Time!"

They were half way up the steps when a few ragged cheers on the far side split the stunned hush that suddenly shrouded the arena. "I think Detroit just scored," Aurora muttered out of the side of her mouth.

All around them Rangers fans stood, shaking their heads.

"Always happens," Shah said. "You got to play to the hooter, not stop 'cause you think time's up."

As they reached the last step he slid his arm around her. They walked out into the hallway and onward to the warm night.

# Acknowledgments

A number of sources provided inspiration for early drafts of this novel: Kenneth S. Deffeyes' *Beyond Peak Oil*, James Howard Kunstler's *The Geography of Nowhere* and *The Long Emergency* all gave me tracts to kick against, while the Worldcon panels of 2005 about "Life in the Next Fifty Years" chaired by Kim Stanley Robinson were equally thought-provoking. Luc Reid provided links to articles on memory.

Rob Rowntree, Sharon Reamer, Kay Theodotora and Josh Peterson provided feedback on the early draft, while Michael Lucas hunted clichés relentlessly, and Aliette de Bodard and Stephen Blount gave useful commentary on the second draft. If you like this book, thank them. However, any errors or weaknesses are due to me.

## About the Author

Colin Harvey lives near Bristol, in the south-west of England, with wife Kate and spaniel Alice. His first fiction was published in 2001, since when he has written novels, short stories and reviews, edited anthologies and judged the Speculative Literature Foundation's annual Gulliver Travel Research Grant for five years. Colin's reviews appear regularly at *Strange Horizons* and he is the feature writer for speculative fiction at *Suite101*.

**www.colin-harvey.com**

# Twenty minutes into the future with Colin Harvey

As part of getting to truly know our authors, we sometimes like to throw a bunch of quickfire questions their way, to see if we can get a glimpse of what they really think. Welcome to the mind of Colin Harvey…

**One film?**
*Once Upon a Time in the West.*

**One book?**
How can I pick only one? Oh, all right, then… Kim Stanley Robinson's *Pacific Edge.*

**One film to burn?**
*Home Alone.* Ugh.

**One song or record?**
*Dark Side of the Moon.*

**One record to smash?**
Joe Dolce's "Shut Up A Your Face". Who bought that pile of crap and kept "Vienna" off the top of the UK pop charts?

*One creative person you've always wanted to be?*
The Edge. All I ever needed to do was learn to play
the guitar and I could do his job.

*One book you wish you'd written?*
Vernor Vinge's *A Fire Upon the Deep*,

*One book/author who has been unjustly neglected?*
Alfred Bester – he was hugely influential when I was
a kid, but since his death he's been almost forgotten.

*Your hero?*
I've bcome more sensitized to the subject since my
stepfather developed multiple myelomas, so anyone
who battles serious or terminal illness without complaint is heroic to me.

*Ideal dinner party guests?*
Harlan Ellison and Christopher Priest on the same
table might prove interesting, especially if Ursula K.
Le Guin was the referee. Richie Benaud and Rory
Bremner. And Su Perkins, 'cause she's brilliant...

*The biggest influence on your writing?*
Style-wise, Roger Zelazny, although I've tried to make
it less obvious with the passage of time.

*What do you sing in the shower?*
I don't! Ever heard my voice?

*The biggest influence on your life?*
I suppose my parents would have to be top of the list.
Professionally, Bruce Boston and Bruce Holland
Rogers have both been major influences on my career

in very different ways.

**One influence you wish didn't keep showing through?**
I can't think of any I wouldn't want to appear. Influences are influences.

**Tell us a joke.**
Q: Why did the duck cross the road?
A: To prove he wasn't a chicken!
(It was the only clean joke I could think of...)

**Any notable pets?**
Our Springer Spaniel, Chloe, who died a couple of years ago. I still miss her.

**Earliest memory?**
We'd moved from a bungalow to a big house, and I'm sat at the top of a flight of stairs that look as big the hill on the ski jump, wondering how I'm going to get down.

**First story you sold?**
"Dreamstalker" for an FTL (non-paying) webzine called *Fragmented Infinity*

**What do you say when people ask "Where do you get your ideas from?"**
A small shop in Fishguard. Three ideas for a pound. Or if I'm feeling serious, I'll say that ideas are easy, but making them into stories – especially good stories – is much harder.

**Do you have an unusual talent or skill?**
Apparently I can add, subtract, divide and multiply

with astonishing speed; I don't think it's anything
special, but other people seem to.

### Best place you ever visited?
Cairns in Australia; with the Great Barrier Reef
nearby, semi-tropical mountains just inland, and a
hotel with a tropical atrium running up the core of
the building.

### What keeps you awake at night?
Insomnia...

### Favourite item of clothing?
I have a pair of Bermuda shorts. They only come out
in summer, so if I'm wearing them, it definitely
means it's sunny!

### Got an irritating/bad habit?
I don't think so, but according to some of my friends I
whistle tunelessly.

### Who plays you in the movie?
George Clooney.

### And what's the pivotal scene?
I wander into the bar at the convention and there's
this bunch of people sitting there. One of them is a
bloke that I get chatting to about my next book.
   I say, "What do you do?"
   He replies, "I'm a publisher..."

### Talking of bars, we're buying... what'll you have?
Beer. Real Ale. Something with a weird name – like
Evil Natterjack Toad, or something equally strange.

*Favourite possession?*
My watch, which was an anniversary present from my wife.

*When & where were you happiest?*
This is a really tough question but I guess it would be Crete in May 2005, on a writer's workshop called, naturally, Write in Crete, run by Bruce Holland Rogers and Eric Witchey. Kate came with me and we made it into a family holiday. She stayed on the beach while I spent the morning writing, before joining her in the afternoon, or vice versa – morning on the beach, then into the cool for the afternoon. We made some good friends, had a look around the island, and then Liverpool won the European Cup after being 3-0 down at half-time!

*Complete this sentence: Rewriting is...*
Almost the nicest part of writing.

*Complete this sentence: Blogging is...*
A chance to mouth off!

*Complete this sentence: I owe it all to...*
Mum, Dad, Auntie Daisy, Kate, the Bruces, Rob, Sharon, Lucas, Penny the Pole-Dancing Poet, and anyone else who knows me...

*Tell us a secret.*
I hate doing interviews. Anything I have to say that's genuinely interesting goes in the books.

*What are you going to do right now when you've finished this ordeal?*

I'm going to watch Ghana play Australia in the (football/soccer) World Cup.

**Thanks!**

'Harsh, sometimes grotesque, strongly compelling – a classical journey told in a new, uncompromising voice.' — JOHN MEANEY

# WINTER SONG

# COLIN HARVEY

"A believably harsh tale of survival in bleak and unforgiving environments. This is a yarn with brawn and brains." — *SFX*